THE DAWN STAR

Catherine Asaro

LUNA™
www.LUNA-Books.com

LUNA™

THE DAWN STAR

ISBN-13: 978-0-373-80238-8
ISBN-10:   0-373-80238-2

Copyright © 2006 by Catherine Asaro

This edition published by arrangement with Harlequin Books S.A.

® and TM are trademarks of Harlequin Books S.A., used under license.
Trademarks indicated with ® are registered in the United States Patent
and Trademark Office, the Canadian Trade Marks Office and in other
countries.

www.LUNA-Books.com

Printed in U.S.A.

Acknowledgments

I would like to thank the following readers for their much-appreciated input. Their comments have made this a better book. Any mistakes that remain are mine alone.

To Aly Parsons and Jeri Smith-Ready for their excellent comments on the full manuscript; and to Aly's Writing Group for insightful critiques of scenes: Aly Parsons, Simcha Kuritzky, Connie Warner, Al Carroll, J. G. Huckenpöhler, John Hemry, Bud Sparhawk, Mike La Violette, and Robert Chase.

Special thanks to my much-appreciated editor, Stacy Boyd, and also to Mary-Theresa Hussey, Kathleen Oudit, Amy Jones, Julie Messore, Laura Morris, Adam Wilson, Dee Tenorio, and all the other fine people at LUNA who helped make this book possible; to Stephanie Pui-Mun Law, the artist who did my gorgeous covers; to my wonderful agent, Eleanor Wood, of Spectrum Literary Agency; and to Binnie Braunstein for her enthusiasm and hard work on my behalf.

A heartfelt thanks to the shining lights in my life: my husband, John Cannizzo, and my daughter, Cathy, for their love and support.

To the Math Club Moms
With appreciation, delight and friendship

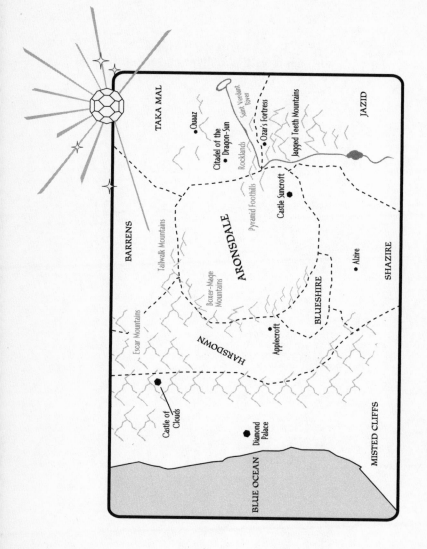

Table of Contents

The Sapphire Heir

Drummer was in trouble. Again.

He had strolled into town earlier today, his clothes covered with dust and his frayed pouch slung over his shoulder. His glittar was packed in his good travel bag, carefully protected by layers of soft cloth.

He soon found the town's inn. In many towns, such inns also served as gathering halls where townspeople could enjoy shows by traveling theater groups, acrobats, dance troupes—and minstrels.

Drummer smiled. *Especially* minstrels.

That night, he played in the inn's common hall, on a platform at one end of the room. As he warmed up with his glittar, a few patrons glanced his way, but no one showed much interest. When he launched into a medley of Aronsdale folk songs, some people moved closer to the stage. Several fellows asked him to sing love songs for their ladies, which he obliged.

Within an hour, people had filled the room. Drummer could feel their moods. Glancing at a wooden cube that adorned a post by the door, he concentrated on its shape. It allowed him to create a mood spell that gave his love of his music to his listeners. It was a minor spell, of course; he had never done any of consequence. But it heightened his joy in singing to offer his pleasure to his audience.

The customers seemed to enjoy his singing and his music. The longer they stayed in the common room, buying food and drink, the more the innkeeper beamed. He kept Drummer supplied with ale. The townspeople didn't have many hexa-coins, but they left Drummer other things—breads and beads and a fine leather pouch. All in all, it was a good night.

He was singing the "Crystal Maker's Lament" when a fiery-haired girl arrived with some other young people. As she glided to a table with her friends, Drummer glided over the high notes of his song:

My heart shatters as easily,
As these vases drawn of crystal,
Don't leave me even teasingly,
I live only as your minstrel.

He sang the last line to the fiery girl. One of the young men in her group frowned, a big fellow in the homespun garb of a farmer.

Drummer waited until the farmer got his dinner and was focused on wolfing it down. Then Drummer sang a ballad to the girl. He drew out the dulcet notes for her, until her pretty cheeks turned the same color as her tousled curls. The big fellow noticed, though, and started looking irritated again, so Drummer switched his attentions to three matrons, who clucked and chuckled at his song. When they left, they set a hefty meat pie on the stage for him. He grinned and they laughed, waving as they made their way out of the inn.

It was growing late, and Drummer didn't want to strain his voice. He rarely had trouble hitting even the highest notes, but they were the first to go when he tired. He finished his song and bade his audience a pleasant night amid calls of appreciation. As he left the stage, he winked at the fiery girl.

Drummer was upstairs, headed for his room, when a sweet voice called from a recessed doorway. "Gentle sir, you do surely sing like an angel."

He peered at the girl in the shadows, wondering if this was a trick to rob him. He was carrying his glittar, his most expensive possession, and he had his take for the night slung over his shoulder in his new pouch.

"And who might you be," he asked, "so shy and sugar-voiced?"

The fiery girl stepped forward, her blush as becoming now as it had been downstairs. "My name is Skybell, handsome sir."

Handsome, eh? His thoughts softened as he ambled over

to her. "Dear Skybell," he murmured. "Why are you hiding up here?" He couldn't resist teasing her. "Do you plan to knock me over the head and steal my possessions?" It wouldn't be the first time it had happened to him. However, he had learned to judge such matters, and he suspected the only thing on her mind was far sweeter than thievery. Smiling lazily, he added, "Or perhaps your nefarious cohorts lurk nearby, waiting to do me in."

"Oh! Never." She was aghast. "I would never do such."

Drummer ran his fingers over the strings of his harp, evoking a sensuous ripple of notes. "How can I be sure?"

Her shy smile dimpled her face. "You play with me, sir."

He quit strumming and traced the tip of his finger down her cheek. "Such a vision, with cheeks like blossoms and lips that surely men sing of everywhere. Are you playing with my poor, helpless heart, only to break it tomorrow?"

Her eyes widened. "I would never hurt you, truly." She touched a curl of hair that had fallen into his eyes. "You have nice hair. The color is like corn kernels."

"It's to match your skybell eyes." He wasn't much more than her height, so he didn't have to bend his head far to brush his lips across hers.

"Oh." Her mouth opened like a small O.

He smiled, charmed. "Has no man kissed you before? Surely every fellow in town must be wooing you."

"Only you have been so bold." Tentative, she touched his cheek. "You looked so beautiful singing tonight."

He thought of the glowering farmer. "Your young man didn't think so."

"My who?"

"The big farmer with the straw hat."

"Plowman?" Her laugh rippled. "He's not my young man."

"No?" Drummer slid his arm around her waist and pulled her well-curved body against his. "You aren't spoken for?"

"Never." She sounded breathless.

"Then I am a lucky man." He held her close as he kissed her again. A thought in the back of his mind warned that such a pretty girl would be this inexperienced only if she was barely out of childhood, which would make her too young for him. But she was warm and sweet, her body supple against his. Surely it was no harm if he dallied just a little—

Someone yanked Drummer away from the girl and slammed him against the wall. He found himself staring up, and up, at the man Skybell had called Plowman. The farmer swung a gnarled fist, and Drummer barely ducked in time.

"Hey!" Drummer slipped out of the man's grip and backed down the hallway, raising his hands to placate the giant.

"Stop it!" Skybell cried from beyond Plowman.

The farmhand lumbered after Drummer. Muscles rippled under his worn shirt, and his footsteps thudded on the wooden floor.

Drummer kept backing up. "Listen, I'm sorry. But she can choose who she wants."

Plowman lunged at him, and Drummer dodged out of the way. He held tight to his glittar, more concerned about protecting it than himself.

"Stay put!" Plowman roared. "Fight like a man."

"Why?" Drummer frowned at him. "She doesn't want you. What good will fighting do?"

"*Want* me?" For some reason, that enraged Plowman even more. He strode forward, and Drummer backed right into a wall.

"Stop this right now!" Skybell had somehow got herself in front of Plowman. "Honestly, Plow, behave yourself."

"I saw him kissing you," he snarled. "You don't even know him at all. No one dishonors my little sister."

Drummer groaned. Irate brothers were worse than rejected suitors. In earlier days, he might have reacted the same way on his sister's behalf, except she was eight years older and had bedeviled him no end in their childhood—until the day she had wed a prince. He wondered what Plowman would say if Drummer announced that his sister was queen of the country Harsdown and that her daughter had married the notorious despot, Cobalt the Dark. Probably Plowman would pound him into the ground for telling tales.

Drummer spoke in a conciliatory voice. "I have the greatest respect for your sister. I would never dishonor her fine name." He wanted to add, *She has a right to choose her men.* Women did all the time here in the country of Aronsdale. Staring up at the massive Plowman, though, he kept his mouth shut.

Skybell gently grasped her brother's arm. "We should get home before father starts to worry."

"I'm not done with this puny songster," Plowman grumbled.

"You can finish tomorrow," she offered.

"I can?" He seemed confused.

"You can," she assured him. Drummer wished she didn't sound so earnest. But she was buying him time to get out of town.

Plowman glowered and rumbled a bit more, but Skybell soon had him on his way. Unfortunately, that meant she went, too. She glanced at Drummer with a look of apology so sincere he wanted to embrace her. He wanted to live even more, though, so he stayed put. He offered Skybell his most regretful look until Plowman shot him another hard, angry glare.

Within moments, brother and sister were gone. Drummer exhaled, relieved he hadn't been pummeled. He wasn't safe yet, though.

It didn't take long to pack his belongings and settle his bill at the inn. He hated to leave so soon; the audience here had been generous. But he couldn't sing if Plowman flattened him.

Drummer was soon on his way, sneaking out of town in the middle of the night.

Cobalt Escar stood alone. He had sought refuge on a walkway of an onion tower in the Alzire Palace. His palace. It had become his when he conquered this country of Shazire. He had done it for his father, Varqelle Escar. But Varqelle lay in his grave, killed a year ago in battle. The conqueror had been conquered, and he had left his son to rule in his stead.

Cobalt's hair blew across his face and shadowed him from

the streaming sunlight. Far below, succulent grasses carpeted the hills and waterways sparkled. Wildflowers grew everywhere, swirls of color in blurs of pink, gold and blue. Spring filled the world with a profusion of life, and it was too much. He had spent most of his life in the spare, utilitarian Castle of Clouds high in the cliffs of his home, where just growing enough crops to feed the staff and animals was a challenge. The wealth of life here mocked his lingering grief. Today, on the anniversary of his father's death, the memories were poignant.

A door opened behind him. He turned as a woman came through the archway. She was a lovely vision with yellow hair, blue eyes and an angelic face. Cobalt wasn't fooled. As a sword fighter, she trained with his best men; as a woman, she could be dulcet one moment and tart the next. People called him Cobalt the Dark, the Midnight Prince, but she was the one he found formidable.

"Greetings of the morning," Mel said.

Cobalt grunted. Then he pulled her over and kissed her. He had to bend down. Although Mel was a tall woman, she didn't reach his shoulders. Her body had slender curves, ample in the right places and narrow at the waist. He tightened his embrace. She was pushing his shoulders, though, and he thought she was laughing. Laughing! Irate, he glared at her.

Her lips curved in the smile that could turn his hardened warriors into clay of the type found on the riverbank after a heavy rain. He was immune to it, of course.

"I'm glad to see you, too," Mel said.

"Which is why you laugh at my kiss?"

"I love your kisses, my handsome husband."

He never knew what to do when she talked like that. He wasn't handsome. His countenance frightened people. He and Mel had married as part of a treaty less than two years ago, and they had met as strangers on their wedding day. She continually exasperated him, but for some reason he wanted her to keep doing it. So he kissed her again. The darkness in his heart receded, and the sun's warmth heated his back.

After a while, they paused. Her eyes had that sensual glossy look he loved so well. But she was also studying his face.

"Are you all right?" she asked.

"Of course." He needed to hide his moods better. No one could read him like Mel, and no matter how hard he tried to remedy that, he never fooled her. He had learned as a child to protect his emotions, lest they spur the violence of his grandfather, King Stonebreaker of the Misted Cliffs. His grandfather had raised him. The queen had died and Stonebreaker had never remarried, so he never sired a male heir. That left Cobalt, the grandson he despised and often beat— until the day Cobalt fought back. Stonebreaker never touched him again, for Cobalt had grown larger and stronger, and could have killed him.

As a child, Cobalt would have given anything to live with his father. But he had been thirty-three when he met Varqelle, and they had known each other only a few months.

"You are quiet," Mel said.

"I was thinking of my father." He gazed at the countryside. Perhaps if he had grown up here, taking this verdant wealth for granted, he could have enjoyed its richness without feeling as if he had to escape. "I was wondering what it would have been like if he had raised me."

Mel was quiet. Why should she answer? Nineteen years ago his father, the king of Harsdown, had invaded the country of Aronsdale with no provocation, intending to take the throne and murder the royal family. Mel's family. But Varqelle had lost the war, and so he lost his own throne, in Harsdown. The Aronsdale king gave it to Mel's father. It was why Mel was heir to the Harsdown throne instead of Cobalt.

"Varqelle was a hard man," Cobalt allowed.

"He loved you," Mel said.

He had no words for that miracle. Cobalt the Dark, hated by so many, especially his grandfather, had been loved by his father.

He held Mel close and looked over her head at Shazire. He had hoped that, like his new realms, his wife would be lush and fertile and give him a son. Or daughter. But still she carried no child.

"Cobalt," Mel said, her voice muffled. She no longer sounded pleased with him.

"What?" he asked, distracted. In the distance, a group of riders were galloping across the countryside.

"You're suffocating me."

Startled, he let her go. "I don't mean to do that."

Her lips quirked upward. "You spoke."

"I speak all the time."

With a soft laugh, she said, "You grunt."

Cobalt almost grunted in response, but he caught himself in time. He squinted against the sunshine. Riders were definitely approaching the Alzire Palace. He wished he had his spectacles, so he could see better. He didn't like wearing glasses, though. Whoever heard of a warrior king in spectacles?

Mel watched the riders. "They've traveled a long way."

"Can you see the pennant?"

"It's the Chamberlight sphere, blue on a white background."

The sphere. Saints almighty! They came from his grandfather, Stonebreaker Chamberlight, king of the Misted Cliffs.

He dreaded to learn what new malice the king had for his despised grandson.

Mel waited with Cobalt in the Hall of Oceans, and her thoughts roiled with her unease. Saints willing, the envoy from the Misted Cliffs wouldn't bring unwelcome news. Cobalt had healed so much here in Shazire, away from his grandfather. But they were never completely free of Stonebreaker.

She and Cobalt stood on a dais of sea-green stone next to the Alzire Throne, a chair embedded with abalone. She couldn't deny the imposing figure her husband cut, long legged and broad shouldered, menacing with his extraordinary height, his muscled build, and that scar on his cheek. He wore a dark tunic, and his trousers came down over heavy boots. His black hair, straight and thick, fell to his shoulders. Beneath his dark brows, his gaze smoldered.

The Hall of Oceans stretched before them, with its vaulted

ceiling and geometric mosaics. Prince Zerod, the emir of Shazire, had held audiences here—before Cobalt deposed him. Cobalt had sent the prince into exile; had he killed Zerod, it would have set the countries of Jazid and Taka Mal against him even more than they were already. Mel had also entreated him to spare Zerod.

Down the hall, men in the aquamarine livery of Alzire heaved open the doors. The visitors from the Misted Cliffs entered with a swirl of motion, ten riders in leather armor and metal breastplates, each carrying a plumed helmet under his arm. Cobalt's men accompanied the envoy, as did Tadi-maja Pickaxe, who was one of the few aides Cobalt had kept from Prince Zerod's staff.

The warriors strode down the hall. Mel recognized the man in front: General Agate Cragland. He had stood with Cobalt at the wedding, when the Midnight Prince took Mel as his wife. Agate had iron-gray hair and a hearty physique unmatched by warriors half his age. He stopped before the dais with his men and they each went down on one knee, bowing their heads. Mel knew they knelt to her husband, Stonebreaker's heir and now king of Shazire and Blueshire. They tolerated her only because she was his wife.

"Please stand," Cobalt said.

Agate got back to his feet, his motions stiff. "I bring greetings from the Misted Cliffs, Your Majesty."

"Is my grandfather well?" Cobalt asked.

When Agate paused, Mel's unease grew. Then the general said, "I have a message from him."

Cobalt regarded him with a look Mel would have found

hard to read a year ago. Agate's phrasing disturbed him. She understood. What could Stonebreaker want that required a party of ten men, including the highest-ranked commander in his army?

"I look forward to hearing it," Cobalt said. Mel didn't believe him and she doubted Agate did, either, but for once Cobalt was trying to be diplomatic. He invited Agate to share wine with him after the general had a chance to change his riding clothes. It was an accepted protocol for receiving messengers, to offer succor before requesting the message, and Agate expressed appreciation. Mel wasn't fooled. None of them wanted to be here.

As Cobalt and Agate spoke, Mel concentrated on the mosaics in the ceiling. The geometric shapes were too far away and too small to give much power, but she managed a faint green spell. Anything more could create a problem; her spells manifested as light, which tended to upset people. Only the barest green shimmer gathered in the air, faint enough to blend into the sunshine slanting through the emerald-glass skylights in the ceiling.

Agate's dread snapped against her mood spell like a hard blow on a drum skin.

Cobalt watched Mel pace in front of a tall window in the Hexacomb Alcove. It troubled him; he rarely saw her so tense.

"What did you pick up from Agate?" he asked.

"He's afraid," Mel said.

He shook his head. "Agate isn't afraid of anything. Except my grandfather."

She glanced at him. "He fears you."

Surely not. But Cobalt could never be certain. Although he had known Agate all his life, he had little idea what the general thought of him. When Cobalt had been small, Agate had stood by while Stonebreaker whipped his grandson. Yet sometimes after the king locked Cobalt in a closet, Agate brought him food or water. The general had risked repercussions even with that; if Stonebreaker had found out, he could have broken Agate, imprisoned him, even executed him. Stonebreaker commanded the loyalty of his army because he was an intelligent leader and savvy in politics, but his top people knew his cruelty. Most had chosen to protect themselves rather than intercede on behalf of a crying boy. Cobalt gritted his teeth. They had stood by and watched a hardened warrior batter a helpless child. He wondered if they had really understood that someday that beaten, angry boy would be their king.

"Why does Agate fear me?" he asked.

Mel kept pacing, agitated and unsettled. "His emotions aren't simple. More than anything, he is cautious."

"About me?"

"Yes. He has bad news, I think." She came over to him. "But his wariness of you goes deeper than that."

Cobalt grimaced. "Everyone feels that way about me."

She took his hand and pressed her lips against his knuckles. "You condemn yourself for the sins others committed against you."

He watched her, as bewildered today as on the first day he had met her. She married him to stop a war. After Cobalt freed his father from prison, Varqelle began to raise an army so he could invade Harsdown and reclaim his throne. Desperate to stop the invasion, Mel had agreed to wed Cobalt and bring the throne back into his line. She ought to hate him. Yet she treated him with a softness no one had ever given him before, and she never broke, never splintered, never shrank away. He didn't understand why she loved him, but he never wanted her to stop.

"I will remember your warning," he said.

"Are you all right?" she asked.

"Yes." *Idiot,* he told himself. *You can do better for her.* He tried to smile. It pulled the muscles of his face in ways that felt strange but had become more natural this year. He could think of nothing to say, though, that wouldn't sound foolish. After a moment of trying to smile, he gave up.

Mel laughed tenderly and touched his cheek. "You have a dimple, you know."

He stared at her, aghast. "Warriors do not have dimples."

"I'm sure not." She took his arm. "We should go meet our guest. He must be done freshening up."

In Cobalt's experience, men didn't "freshen up." Still, Agate was probably making himself more presentable.

"Very well," he said. "Let us see what he has to say."

Braces covered in gold leaf supported the arched ceiling in the Ivory Room, and mother-of-pearl filigree gleamed on the walls. The pale furniture was upholstered in ivory and gold. Cobalt, Mel and Agate sat in armchairs by graceful tables where they could place their goblets. The beauty of the room only increased Mel's disquiet, for none of this belonged to them. They had stolen it from Prince Zerod. She had never wanted to conquer Shazire. Even though she knew this land had once been part of the Misted Cliffs, the war lay heavily on her conscience. She dealt with it by being the best leader she knew how to be, but it didn't lighten the weight.

Mel spoke to Agate with courtesy. "Is the vintage to your liking, General?"

He sipped his wine. "It speaks well of your wineries."

Cobalt downed his wine in one swallow and clunked the goblet on the table. "So." His deep voice jarred with the genteel room. "How is my grandfather?"

Agate spoke carefully. "I bring you news, sire."

"What?" Cobalt asked.

Mel inwardly groaned. If Cobalt couldn't learn more tact, he would antagonize even his allies.

"I have news of your grandfather," Agate said. "He is ill, Your Majesty."

Cobalt visibly stiffened. "What happened?"

"His doctors say a blood vessel burst in his brain."

Cobalt stared at him in shock, an emotion he almost never revealed. His lapse lasted only a moment; then his mask of impassivity snapped back into place.

"Is he alive?" Cobalt asked.

Agate took a deep breath. "He survived. But his left side is paralyzed. We don't know if he will recover."

Cobalt fell silent. Mel knew he hated his grandfather, and yet, he had also craved Stonebreaker's approval his entire life.

The conflicts of his tormented relationship with the king had left deep wounds. He was recovering here, but she had no idea what it would do to him if Stonebreaker died. Would he grieve or rejoice—or hate himself for doing both?

Mel spoke to Agate. "We are sorry to hear of His Majesty's illness and pray for a full recovery."

Relief flickered in Agate's eyes. "The people of the Misted Cliffs share your prayers." To Cobalt, he said, "We honor the House of Chamberlight."

Cobalt's voice went cold. "The way you honored the Chamberlight Heir while you watched him being beaten senseless?"

Agate looked as if he felt ill. "It was no honor, sire." In a low voice, he added, "It was a nightmare."

Mel froze, afraid of what Cobalt might do. Agate was the only one of Stonebreaker's officers she had ever heard admit the truth. Of all the adults in Cobalt's life, only two had regularly sheltered him: his mother, Dancer, and a stable hand named Matthew Quietland. Dancer had taken Stonebreaker's violence on herself by interceding when Stonebreaker abused the boy; Matthew had hidden Cobalt in the stables or even his home and borne the vicious brunt of the king's rage when Stonebreaker couldn't find his grandson.

Mel spoke into the strained silence. "You have done well to bring us the news with such speed, General Cragland."

"I am sorry it isn't better news," Agate said, his face pale.

"Yes." Cobalt stood abruptly. "Good night."

Both Mel and Agate jumped to their feet, and Agate bowed deeply. Cobalt glanced at Mel, and she could tell he wanted her to come with him. Then he strode from the room.

She spoke quietly to Agate. "Thank you, General."

"I deserve no thanks, Your Majesty."

The title disquieted Mel; she was the reluctant queen of Shazire and Blueshire. Would Cobalt soon rule the Misted Cliffs as well? It would make him the most powerful sovereign in the settled lands, similar to the legendary Dragon-Sun Queen in Taka Mal who had lived two centuries ago. She had allied with Jazid, and they had descended on Cobalt's ancestors with their wild, fierce armies, severing Blueshire and Shazire from the Misted Cliffs.

After Mel and Agate parted, she walked to the suite she shared with Cobalt, preoccupied with her thoughts. She knew the lure of the desert lands for Cobalt. Jazid and Taka Mal. It was more than righting the wrongs of an ancient war. Taka Mal and Jazid were prosperous countries. Taka Mal caravans were famous for precious silks, spices, pottery, and jewels, and its architects spread their exquisite works across the settled lands. Jazid had mines rich with ores and gems. How long before Cobalt turned his conqueror's eye to those rich lands? When he spoke of his dreams of empire, it stirred a ferocity deep within Mel, the wildness of her ancestors. She didn't want the temptations he offered, but she couldn't deny the lure of that seductive power.

Cobalt had once told her: *If ever I go too far, pull me back.* She didn't know if she was capable of being the conscience of a tyrant. At his core, he was a profoundly decent man. But for all that he had controlled his darkness, it simmered within him.

Waiting for a rebirth.

2

Topaz Queen

Vizarana Jade, the queen of Taka Mal, felt great pride in her country. The sun beat down on a starkly beautiful land softened by green oases. Quaaz, its capital, was the oldest city in the settled lands, a place of spires, arches, and onion domes. Ancient lanes curved through its center, crowded with oxen-drawn carts, running children, and people on errands. Mosaics shimmered in stained-glass windows, around keyhole-shaped archways, and in columns that supported even the most modest houses.

As her father's only child, Jade had inherited the Topaz Throne. She intended to keep it, even in this country where most women had few rights. Her Topaz Palace rose above Quaaz, golden in the sunlight, a wonder of yellow stone surrounded by a great wall and protected by the Queen's Guard, warriors unmatched in skill or aggression. Today, Jade sat at a long table in the Dragon-Sun hall with her top generals: Spearcaster, her senior advisor, a mentor she had known her entire life; Slate, the least emotional of her advisors; Firaz from the tempetuous Southern lands; and her hot-tempered cousin, Baz Quaazera, General of the Queen's Army.

"What I don't understand," Jade said, "is how the Atajazid D'az Ozar could sign a pact with Cobalt Escar and we didn't know about it." Although the atajazid was a king, his title translated into Ozar, Shadow Dragon Prince of Jazid. Either way, he ruled Jazid.

"Prince Zerod took the message from Shazire to Jazid," Baz told her. A large man with black hair, he was thirty-three, a year younger than Jade. Everyone expected her to marry him, but she kept delaying. Baz was like a brother, not a husband.

"I thought Zerod was dead," Jade said. "And why would he carry messages for Cobalt Escar?"

Baz gave her one of his inimitable scowls. "Escar is holding Zerod's wife and son prisoner."

"So Jazid signed a pact with Escar," Jade mused.

General Slate spoke. "It is more an agreement than a formal pact, Your Majesty." He looked tired today. The decades hadn't been easy on Slate; as he entered his sixty-fifth year, she worried that he might soon wish to leave the military. She would regret his loss, for she greatly valued his advice, his wisdom, and his even temperament.

"What does the agreement entail?" Jade asked.

"Jazid sent four hundred spearmen to support the Shazire

army," Slate said. "Three hundred forty-two survived the war. The message Zerod took to Jazid concerned them."

Jade didn't know what to make of this news, which Jazid had tried to keep secret. Fortunately, her spies had discovered it, though it had taken them too long. She spoke wryly. "According to rumors I've heard, Cobalt Escar beheaded Zerod, raped and murdered the queen and hung Zerod's son." Tales of Cobalt the Dark were rife with such lurid details.

"Well, hell," Firaz said. "Maybe he tore down the Jagged Teeth Mountains, too."

Jade smiled. "The last I looked, they were still there."

Spearcaster, eldest of her generals and the one she trusted most, spoke in his gravelly voice. "Apparently Cobalt has done nothing worse than put Zerod's family under guard in their summer palace. In return for their safety, Zerod carried the message to Jazid."

"What was in the message?" Jade asked.

Baz leaned forward, his fiery gaze intent. "Escar gave the Jazid spearmen a choice—swear allegiance to him or go to prison."

Bah. Cobalt obviously had ulterior motives. Making Zerod a courier sent another message to Jazid: Cobalt had effectively stripped the deposed ruler of his power. Allowing the spearmen to live implied Cobalt offered conciliation to Jazid, less than if he returned the soldiers to their country but enough to suggest he would consider neutral relations rather than conquest.

Jade didn't like it. Within one generation, Cobalt would

rule the Misted Cliffs, Harsdown, Blueshire and Shazire. Jazid and Taka Mal had tried to achieve a similar outcome two hundred years ago, when they attacked the Misted Cliffs, but they had failed.

"Cobalt and Zerod signed a pact," General Spearcaster said. "Zerod swore not to seek military help from Jazid or Taka Mal. If he abided by the pact, then in two years he could go into exile with his wife and son."

Jade doubted Cobalt the Dark had suddenly developed great compassion. "Cobalt must have a motive."

"He probably assumed his business with Jazid and Taka Mal will be settled by then," Slate said.

Baz thumped the table with his palm. "If he expects to conquer us, he is a fool!"

Jade frowned. "He would be mad to seek retribution for a war our ancestors waged over two hundred years ago."

"He's mad all right," Firaz drawled. "With ambition."

Slate's voice was grim. "He will come after Jazid and Taka Mal, don't doubt it."

"The hell with him," Firaz said. "We'll thrash his arrogant ass."

"General Firaz," Jade said, smiling. "You are ever the soul of poetic converse." He raised a curmudgeonly eyebrow at her.

"Cobalt's agreement not to attack Jazid was only valid for a year," Spearcaster said. "That year was done six days ago."

"Did the spearmen swear allegiance to him?" Jade asked.

"Over three hundred of them," Slate said.

Jade had hoped Escar was ignoring her country because

he didn't seek more lands. Her spies had so far found no indications that he planned on going to war again. But if he had held back only because of a temporary pact with Jazid, that could mean trouble.

"How large is Escar's army?" she asked.

Baz nodded to Spearcaster, deferring to him for an answer. It didn't surprise Jade. Spearcaster had studied the militaries in the settled lands for decades. Baz was in charge of the army, and Jade considered him an excellent leader. But if the position had been determined solely by merit, without royal heredity as a factor, Spearcaster would be General of the Army. He had twice Baz's age and experience.

"Including the Shazire forces he has gained," Spearcaster said, "I'd say Cobalt Escar has more than eight thousand men."

Damn. She had only three thousand. Perhaps Cobalt expected Taka Mal to roll over for him. If so, his expectations were in for a battering. "And Jazid's army?" she asked. "Four thousand?"

"At least," Spearcaster said.

"Perhaps," Jade murmured, "I should invite the Atajazid D'az Ozar here for a visit." The time might have come to end their chill in relations. Ozar loathed having to deal with a woman on the throne, but a mutual and bellicose enemy might give them cause to unite.

"It's a good idea," Baz said. "But even if we combine forces with Jazid, we still wouldn't match Cobalt Escar's forces."

"He may wish to avoid war," Slate said.

"He damn well hasn't so far," Firaz told him.

"He did, actually," Slate said. "He married the heir to the throne of Harsdown rather than attack her country for it."

"If we must fight this Escar king," Jade said, "then we will. But we should bargain first."

"Bargain with *what?*" Baz demanded.

"We need leverage," Jade said. "Someone in his family."

Spearcaster went very still. "You are talking about a hostage pact."

"Of course." It was a time-honored form of negotiation. In centuries past, sovereigns had regularly taken hostages from their enemies and negotiated peace for their release. Jazid and Taka Mal had avoided several wars that way.

"We probably can't reach his mother or his wife," Slate said.

"His wife's a witch, anyway," Firaz muttered.

"Oh, Firaz." Jade had also heard tales of the woman forced to marry Cobalt the Dark. Rumors spread like fire about how she stopped the war in Shazire with a sword of flame that reached into the sky. Jade found it hard to credit. Why would the queen stop her husband from wiping out their enemies? It seemed more likely she knew tricks with light. She would be a difficult target, yes, but because Cobalt would keep her well guarded, not because she wielded fire magic.

Jade looked around at her generals. "We need to find someone we have a realistic chance of stealing."

Baz's eyes glinted. "I have an idea."

Drummer slunk to the window of Magistrate Sput's house. Tardy Town was quiet now, in this hour after midnight. He had played at the inn tonight to earn his supper. Unfortunately that meant he had been "graced" with hours of hearing Sput boast about his sexual conquests. Drummer sincerely hoped the stories were no more than Sput's fantasies; if the women really existed, he hated to think how they would feel to have their most intimate secrets bared in public. The magistrate had also denigrated a whole slew of people, including Tardy Town's visiting minstrel. Sput claimed to have a better voice than Drummer, and after a few pitchers of ale, he had demonstrated it to anyone ill-fated enough to be within earshot.

Drummer winced at the memory. Then he clambered over the windowsill into Sput's house. He found himself in a den lit only by moonlight flowing through the open window. He padded into the hallway and started his search. Sput turned out to be fast asleep upstairs, sprawled facedown in bed, snoring loud enough to shake down the sky. The drunk magistrate had tossed his garments on the floor, presenting an opportunity of just the type Drummer had hoped for. Drawing on the square shape of a mirror across the room, he made a little orange spell. He used it to send soothing thoughts to Sput and sink the magistrate deeper into sleep. Then he snuck into the room and filched every item of clothing he could see.

Drummer skulked out of the house as silently as he had entered and stashed Sput's clothes in some bushes outside. Then he took off, headed out of town. As pranks went, hiding the magistrate's clothes was more extreme than his usual mischief, but it was fitting given the way Sput so crudely claimed to have removed the garments of the women he called "milk cows."

Drummer cut across the plaza beyond Sput's house and jogged past the large bell the townspeople used to warn of fires. An idea stirred, and he grinned. No, he couldn't do that. Really. He couldn't. Then he thought, *Why not?* He paused by the bell and looked around the plaza. No one. So he grabbed the bell's rope—and pulled.

A deep clang cracked open the night. Drummer pulled hard and fast on the rope, filling the plaza with ringing until lights appeared in buildings all around it. Then he let go of the rope and darted off. He climbed the stairs on the side of a butcher shop with no lights inside. Then he sat on the top step with his pouch over one shoulder and his glittar on his back, and watched.

People ran into the plaza, calling in confused voices. Sput's door slammed open, and he dashed out—as naked as the day he had come into the world. He ran to the bell, the rolls of his large stomach shaking. "I demand to know who rang that thing," he bellowed. "How dare you disturb my sleep? I insist someone put out this fire."

"Magistrate Sput!" The gray-haired City Elderwoman stood by the bell stand in a robe and stared at him, her mouth open. "Sir!"

"Why aren't you doing anything about this?" Sput demanded.

"Good sir," the elderly woman stuttered. "I do believe— I mean, that is—"

"You believe what?" Sput asked. "Get it out, woman."

"You're unclothed, sir."

"What?" He looked down at himself. Then he jerked up

his head and stared at the people gathering around. "What is *going on* here?"

"No fire," a man said, joining them. "Apparently the alarm was a mistake."

"Mistake!" True to his name, Sput sputtered obscenities. Then, darkly, he added, "I'll bury whoever has done this." With that, he whirled around and tried to sprint home. He waddled more than he ran, but it was the fastest Drummer had seen him move.

Softly Drummer said, "That's for all the people you hurt with your words, Sput-man." Then he slipped down the stairs and set off in the dark, headed out of Tardy Town.

Within moments he had left the town behind. Under a waning moon, he jogged across the low hills. His glittar plinged a note every now and then until he repacked the instrument. He laughed and spread his arms as he ran for the sheer joy of his life. At twenty-eight, he had never held a steady job. During the harvest, he worked in his father's orchard and the rest of the year he wandered as a minstrel. He rarely had to remember that he was the youngest brother of the queen of Harsdown or that his niece had married Cobalt the Dark.

Soon he was alone under the stars, away from any homestead. He could shout as loud as he wanted and no one would hear. He felt gloriously free.

That was when the strangers grabbed him.

The wagon bumped along the rutted road. The cords that bound Drummer's wrists behind his back dug into his skin.

He could barely make out his jailors; the canopied wagon cut out what little light came from the moon. This wasn't the first time he had been caught by someone irate over his mischief, but something was different this time, darker in a way he hadn't yet figured out.

They had grabbed him fast and efficient, more like soldiers than the itinerant merchant family they appeared to be. The men dressed the part of merchants, with billowy shirts and trousers. But where were the women and children? And they all had dark hair. Most people in the settled lands did, but those native to this part of Aronsdale tended toward lighter coloring. These merchants were taller and huskier than Drummer, too—but, well, that wasn't unusual. Most men were. His slender build had once allowed him to escape a lady's boudoir by disguising himself as her maid. It had amused him at the time, but right now he would have given a great deal to have the musculature and power to hold his own against his captors.

Drummer twisted his hands in the hopes of loosening his bonds, but it only made the cords bite into his skin. He was sitting on a bench with his back to the swaying canvas wall of the wagon. Five of the six men who had captured him were also in the back—two sharpening daggers the lengths of their forearms, one sleeping, and two watching him. The sixth was driving.

"Well, this is boring," Drummer said. When no one answered, he added, "I could sing for you if I wasn't tied up."

"Be quiet," one man told him, which was pretty much all they had said since they nabbed him several hours ago. He wasn't certain about their accent, but he thought it was from Jazid or Taka Mal.

"You know," he said in a conversational voice, "kidnapping the brother of the queen of Harsdown can get you into trouble." Maybe he could scare some information out of them.

One of the men sharpening his dagger glanced up. "Being the brother of the Queen of Harsdown can get you into trouble."

"I'm a commoner," Drummer said. "If you think you can ransom me for riches, you're wrong." His family did fine with their thriving orchards, but they were by no means wealthy.

The closest guard lifted his dagger and touched the tip to Drummer's neck. "You are going to be quiet, yes?"

Drummer tried not to swallow. Sweat gathered on his forehead. "Uh, yes."

"Good." The guard withdrew his blade.

They bounced along in the night, going saints only knew where.

Sunrise Suite

Mel rode Smoke, her gray stallion, just as she always did, no matter how many earnest stable hands urged her to take a mare. She and Cobalt were traveling through eastern Harsdown with his honor guard of thirty men, two of her spheremaids, and the Chamberlight warriors. Up ahead, her husband galloped on Admiral, his black warhorse. Admiral wasn't fast, nothing like a charger, but he was a glorious animal, massive and strong, able to carry even a man of Cobalt's size for long distances. Cobalt had left Leo Tumbler, one of his most trusted officers, back in Alzire, to govern Shazire while they traveled.

Smoke raced across the hills, and Mel savored the ride. She had grown up in Harsdown, but in the past year, she had hardly been home at all. She longed to see her family at their estate, Applecroft. She missed her parents, and the visits of her grandparents and uncles. Drummer always made her laugh with his pranks and cry for the beauty of his voice. But with Stonebreaker so ill, they had no time to stop.

Matthew Quietland had ridden out from Applecroft to join them, however. Mel was glad to see him. He served as stable master at one of the Chamberlight castles and had been Cobalt's right-hand man during the campaign against Shazire. This last year he had remained with Cobalt's mother Dancer, officially as her bodyguard, though Mel suspected they just liked spending time together. The two of them had been staying at Applecroft as guests of Mel's family. Another Chamberlight envoy had informed Dancer of her father's illness. While she rushed to his side, Matthew had come to let Cobalt know what she was doing.

Right now, Matthew was riding with Cobalt. A mane of silver hair blew back from Matthew's face. Both he and Cobalt were looking northward, their profiles etched against the blue sky, the same straight nose, sculpted cheekbones, and strong chin.

At sixty-five, Matthew was a year older than Cobalt's father, Varqelle. Mel wondered how anyone could have seen Matthew and Varqelle together without suspecting they shared the same father. Cobalt's mother, Dancer, had fled Varqelle only a year after their marriage, and Matthew had been among the servants who helped her return to the Misted Cliffs. Perhaps that was why few people had seen his resemblance to Varqelle; the two men had lived in different lands for over three decades. Mel's spells had given her insights into Matthew's emotions toward Cobalt, feelings

Matthew hid from most people. When she asked him about it, he made her swear never to tell Cobalt. As far as she knew, Cobalt never suspected his kinship to his stable master.

It was afternoon when their party reached the cliffs that rose up from the borderlands. They stood tall against a pale blue sky, their tops wreathed in clouds, the daunting namesakes of the country they separated from Harsdown. The Misted Cliffs.

Their party followed a path that wound into the great wall. The higher they went, the thinner the air became. It was hard for Mel to believe only a year and a half had passed since the first time Cobalt had taken her to this country, or that this was only her second trip. The few months she had spent here had been in the Castle of Clouds in the cliffs rather than at the Diamond Palace much farther west, where they were headed now. In only a few days, she would see King Stonebreaker—if he still lived.

Cobalt wanted to turn Admiral around and ride hard in the opposite direction. They had spent a full day crossing the cliffs, and another two days traveling through the pretty dales and hills of his country. Their destination had been a blur during their ride today, but he could finally see it clearly even without his glasses. The Diamond Palace. It was only a short ride away now, high on a hill known as The King's Spring. Cobalt suspected that name had been the wishful thinking of some long-ago sovereign, for the Misted Cliffs had the coolest climate in the settled lands. Today, though, mild weather reigned, and the green meadows swirled with wildflowers.

He looked eastward, back the way they had come. The distant cliffs loomed against the sky. In the north, the Escar Mountains rose even higher. South and west, the land rolled in meadows and low hills. If he could have stood on a balcony in the Diamond Palace and looked farther west, he would have seen sand dunes and the Blue Ocean.

Cobalt dreaded going home. The Diamond Palace mocked him with its beauty. Influenced by Taka Mal architecture, it cut a graceful form against the sky, with its onion towers and scalloped crenellations. But where Taka Mal was a land of fire and sunsets, here he saw only ice. Prismatic windows sparkled, and bridges arched between white towers. The palace was like frozen lace, a glittering fantasy. He wondered how such a dark place could look so light. But it was fitting that it took its name from the hardest-known substance, diamond, cold and unforgiving.

Mel came alongside of him on her smoky horse. He tried to smile at her, but it didn't work.

She indicated the palace. "It's spectacular."

"Yes." Hated, too, but he couldn't speak of those memories. In his childhood, he and his mother had spent part of each year at the Castle of Clouds back in the cliffs. For a few months, they would be free of Stonebreaker's violence. But if they stayed too long, the king sent soldiers to "escort" them home. After Cobalt became an adult, however, he and Dancer refused to go. Even Stonebreaker realized it would be going too far to have his soldiers drag his family out of his border castle and back to his palace. Instead, he set up conditions intended to make life unbearable for Dancer at the Castle of Clouds. He knew if she came home to the Diamond Palace, Cobalt would as well, to protect her, and Stonebreaker would again have them in his sphere of control. So he refused to allow Dancer any female companions and forbade any man there to speak to her, except her son. She would live in loneliness. With no female servants, she would have to care for herself. He expected her home within a month.

She never went back.

Last year, when Cobalt had ridden to Shazire, Dancer had gone with him as far as Applecroft. Mel's home. And there she had stayed, in that place of warmth and affection. He had hoped she would never have to leave. But Stonebreaker's illness called her home. Just as he was driven to see his grandfather despite—or perhaps because of—the demons that haunted his heart, so too had his mother returned to this chilly universe of ice and cold stone.

Mel fell in love with the Misted Cliffs. Before this visit, she had known this country only by the imposing cliffs on its border with Harsdown. This was her first trip to the interior. The glens, meadows, and small valleys charmed her. She could tell, though, that Cobalt didn't share her enthusiasm. He rode alone and barely spoke to anyone.

They were almost at the Diamond Palace, already passing the sentries who patrolled the area on horseback. She hoped she didn't cause a chill in their reception. Rumors about her mage powers had probably preceded them. She wished she could show Cobalt's people the beauty of the spells without alienating them. Her mother Chime, the mage queen of Harsdown, had once showed her how a prism split light into colors. The order of those colors matched the order of spells, from least to greatest: red, orange, yellow, green, blue, indigo, and a violet so dark she almost couldn't see it. Red spells brought warmth and light, orange eased pain, yellow soothed emotions, green read emotions, blue healed physical injuries, and indigo healed emotions.

A mage could do spells for any level up to a maximum color, which varied from person to person. Red and orange mages were the most common; Mel knew of roughly twenty-five. Yellow was rarer. The only known greens were Chime and the mage mistress at Castle Suncroft in Aronsdale. The mage mistress at Applecroft in Harsdown was the only pure blue. Iris, the Aronsdale queen, could blend spells of more than one hue, but blue was her strongest color.

Mel's father was an indigo. However, he could only use flawed shapes, which distorted his spells. Instead of warming a room, he could set it on fire; instead of healing, he might cause injury. He had used his abilities during the war eighteen years ago, but he no longer called on his power for fear he would harm those he loved.

Legend claimed that Mel's cousin, King Jarid in Aronsdale, was a violet mage—the color that granted the power of life—but Mel suspected the tales were embellished because of his royal heritage. He was far more likely an indigo. Violet mages were possible, in theory, but she doubted any person could actually wield such a force and survive.

Mel wasn't certain how to define her abilities. Before her

marriage, she had never done any spells above green, and she had drawn power only from two-dimensional shapes, which gave a spell less strength than those with three dimensions. But last year, she had called forth a blue spell, and done it with a sphere, the highest shape. She struggled to control her power, though. High-level spells burned her out, and it took days to recover.

Now that Mel no longer lived with her parents, she had no one to train her. Cobalt's people considered her a witch, an object of suspicion. It bothered her more than she wanted to admit, and she hid her spells, wrestling alone with powers she didn't know how to wield. So often she felt inadequate. Sometimes she wanted to write her parents or Queen Iris and entreat them for help. But she always recovered her sense before she sent such a letter. They and their mages had more important matters to attend than the floundering of a confused young woman. If she failed or succeeded, it was her responsibility, not theirs.

Mel's breath caught as their party clattered into a courtyard of the Diamond Palace. Cobalt seemed to crackle with a dark energy, as if he were calling up defenses against this heartlessly beautiful place. Its towers rose above them, white against the sky, and stable boys ran to meet them across the crescent-shaped yard.

After they dismounted and handed their reins to a groom, Cobalt took her through a doorway framed by pillars the size of tree trunks. The tip of its arch was twenty feet above the ground. Her power stirred, nudged by carvings that bordered the arch, circles and hexagons stained Chamberlight blue.

Mel had a sudden memory of her first blue spell. Cobalt had hurt his hands from striking a wall over and over, until the ragged bricks shredded his skin. It happened after he found Stonebreaker hurting Mel. He couldn't strike the king of the Misted Cliffs—so he vented his fury on a wall. Although Mel had mended his physical injuries, no blue spell could heal the wounds in his heart.

Today they were entering Stonebreaker's realm, the icy center of his kingdom where Cobalt would face his dying tormentor.

Drummer jolted awake as the wagon bumped to a stop. After fourteen days in the tedious silence of his guards, any change was welcome. He opened his eyes into the dim sunlight that diffused through the cloth sides of the wagon. His captors had left his wrists tied too long, and his arms ached. Three of the fake merchants were in the wagon, one peering out the back and the other two guarding him. Some cretin had taken off his boots while he slept and bound his ankles as well.

Drummer scowled at the man who sat on a bench across from him. "You must all find me fearsome indeed, that you need so many warriors to guard an unarmed man whose hands and feet are tied."

"You talk too much," the man said, his voice drawn out in the accent of Taka Mal.

"Where are we?" Drummer asked.

"Here," the man said.

"That was helpful," Drummer grumbled. When the guard

dropped his hand to his sheathed dagger, Drummer closed his mouth.

The man at the back of the wagon moved aside as someone opened the flaps. A man was standing outside. "You can go in," he said.

Drummer squinted out and glimpsed a wedge of sky. Onion towers and stone walls the color of amber gleamed in the rich sunlight. He swore under his breath. He knew of only one structure built from stone that color, with such magnificent architecture: the Topaz Palace of Quaaz.

Drummer had a sudden memory from another time he had ended up in serious trouble when he had been fourteen. He snuck out one night to the mill. He just wanted to climb on the wheel. It was fun. But he had fallen onto a stack of grain sacks, which toppled into another, and that into another, until many sacks had spilled. Mortified, he had spent hours trying to clean it up. But one boy could only do so much. In the end, he had confessed and asked for help. It had taken his and the millers' families all day to put the mess right, and Drummer had spent several days in jail, eating gruel and feeling stupid. When they let him go home, his father had dourly informed him that if he didn't quit misbehaving, he would end up with a life of doom. His father had been big on overly dramatic proclamations, but now Drummer wished he had paid more attention, for he had apparently landed in even worse trouble. Surely this couldn't be just because of Tardy Town. But he had no idea what else he had done.

The wagon rolled forward, its back flaps open enough that

he caught glimpses of their surroundings. They were rolling through a yard full of people in exotic silks or colorful robes. The wagon stopped so its back faced two doors with black metal braces. The doors creaked loudly as men heaved them open. The driver brought the wagon around and drove into the dim place beyond the door. Cool air seeped into the back, along with the faint scent of wine. Drummer couldn't see much, but he would have bet his glittar they were riding past kegs of fine, aged wines.

Come to think of it, where was his glittar? The soldiers had left the instrument lying on a pile of rugs in the wagon, but now it was gone. Alarm surged in Drummer. His glittar was the one possession he truly valued. His sister Chime had given it to him years ago, after he wrote a song for her praising her daughter Mel.

He turned to the man on the bench. "Where is my glittar?"

No answer. It was the same every time he asked questions.

"You can't take it," Drummer said.

"Your little harp is fine," the guard growled.

"Can I have it back?" Drummer asked.

"Flaming hell if I know."

Drummer thought of the stories his mother had told him about hell. It had no colors. Demons lived there. It contrasted with the Land of the Spirits where saints, angels, and deities lived, and especially the spirits of the departed. Spirits only landed in hell if they had committed truly evil misdeeds in their life. Right now, Drummer felt like nominating his guards as prime candidates.

"How about you untie my feet?" he said. "My ankles hurt."

The man gave a snort. "Think you can run, eh? Think again."

Oh, well. He hadn't expected it to work. He wondered how they planned to get him out of the wagon. They had probably tied his feet because the wagon was going slowly within a city, making it easier to escape. However, he couldn't walk wherever they wanted him to go, either. He hoped they didn't intend to carry him. It would be mortifying.

The wagon jerked to a stop. Voices rumbled outside, too low to understand, especially with that Taka Mal drawl. Then someone whipped aside the cloth at the back of the wagon. More soldiers waited in the dim cellar.

A hand grasped Drummer's arm.

"Hai!" Startled nearly out of his skin, Drummer jumped up. He couldn't stand on his bound ankles, so he immediately fell over. Pain stabbed his ankles. The guard who had grasped his arm held him upright with a strong grip.

Drummer glared up at the husky behemoth. "It would be a lot easier if you untied me."

"Sit down," the man said.

The warrior looked vexed enough to flatten him. He was also a head taller than Drummer and probably twice his weight, with all those muscles. Drummer sat.

The guard said nothing more. He did, however, crouch down and untie Drummer's ankles. With an exhale of relief, Drummer stretched his legs. They prickled with returning sensation, but at least they were free. His arms didn't hurt much, mainly because they had gone numb.

"How about my wrists?" Drummer asked as the guard stood up.

"No." The man indicated the back of the wagon. "Go."

Drummer stood more slowly this time. His legs throbbed, but he managed a tentative walk. Although he felt clumsy with his arms behind his back, he had a good sense of balance. When he couldn't earn his way as a minstrel, he did acrobatics. He sang better than he tumbled, but he wasn't bad at either, if he did say so himself. Right now he wasn't saying anything, though, given how much it annoyed his guards.

Three large warriors waited outside the wagon. One had a ring of keys hanging on his metal-studded belt. Drummer couldn't climb out with his wrists bound, so the guards lifted him down. Drummer wished they didn't loom so much. Why bother tying him? He was no match for even one of them. Then again, he could duck, dart and run faster than anyone. Just let them untie him! They would see how fast he vanished into the city.

His three new guards, however, showed no more inclination to untie him then had his kidnappers. One prodded his back with the hilt of a knife. Gritting his teeth, Drummer limped forward in his bare feet. They took him past rows of barrels, all redolent with the fragrance of wine, lovely wine. He inhaled deeply and thought he could get drunk just from the fumes. Eventually, though, they reached a large door with iron braces. One guard unlocked the door and heaved it open, and another nudged Drummer forward. At least these three weren't as rough as the ones who had kidnapped him.

The alcove beyond startled Drummer. It had six walls, like a hexagon. Mosaics tiled every surface in sea-green colors, as if he were underwater. The shapes fascinated him—

The mood spell came without warning. Suddenly he *knew* what his guards felt. The man with the ring of keys was angry and impatient. Drummer had a sense the fellow wanted to go gamble, though the spell wasn't specific enough for him to be certain. The burly guard felt thirsty and the third guard missed his wife.

Drummer blinked. He mostly ignored his spells, for everyone knew men couldn't be real mages, except for the royal Dawnfields, of course. Centuries of marrying the strongest mages in the land had concentrated the talents until they manifested in the Dawnfield men, too. Drummer had experienced hints of ability since adolescence, but nothing significant, just minor spells like this green one he had made. As the impatient man prodded him forward, he pondered the information the spell had given him about his guards. He wasn't sure what use it had, but one never knew.

After they went through the sea chamber, his spell faded. They came out into a corridor framed by arches. He loved the mosaics on the walls. They started with the indigo of the predawn sky. As he walked down the hall, the colors shaded into the blush of dawn, then into a sunrise, and finally the pale blue of morning.

"This is beautiful," Drummer said.

The guard who liked to gamble grunted at him. "They told me you talk too much. Don't start babbling or I'll gag you."

And you can rot in a crap house. Drummer kept the thought to himself, though. These guards were also a lot bigger than him.

Unexpectedly, the lonely-husband guard said, "We aren't going to gag anyone, Kaj." He glanced at Drummer. With a smile. "And yes, it is beautiful. The whole palace is like this."

Drummer was so amazed by the courtesy, he was momentarily without words. When he recovered, he said, "Do you mind if I ask your name?"

"Javelin," the guard said. "And you are Drummer?"

"That's right." He hesitated. "Why am I here?"

"Even if I knew, I couldn't discuss it." Javelin motioned him into an alcove, this one tiled in desert hues with a sun on the ceiling. No clouds. No shade. He felt hot just passing through. They went up tiled stairs and followed more tiled halls. Before this, he had only experienced such opulence on his visits to Castle Suncroft, home to King Jarid of Aronsdale. Drummer's sister Chime had married Jarid's cousin.

Finally they opened up a locked suite of rooms. The entrance foyer was gorgeous, with aqua mosaics on its walls. A lamp shaped like a butterfly hung from the domed ceiling and glowed with sunrise colors.

Javelin and the other guard checked the suite while Drummer waited with Kaj, the gambler. Still annoyed with the crack about gagging him, Drummer said, "I'll bet you've never guarded an Aronsdale minstrel before. Aren't you lucky?"

"Shut up," Kaj told him.

"Don't you like to talk?" Drummer asked innocently. "Good conversation is like ambrosia to the human intellect."

Kaj squinted at him. "What?"

The other two guards came back into the foyer. "Everything is in order," Javelin said, with a sharp glance at Kaj. He escorted Drummer into a parlor and indicated a divan upholstered in sunrise colors. "Have a seat."

Drummer had no objection. He was exhausted. As he sat down, Kaj spoke curtly. "Sideways."

Drummer turned to the side, and Kaj sat behind him. When Kaj untied his wrists, Drummer barely restrained his groan of relief. His shoulders ached, and his limbs felt like dead slabs, but he had no doubt sensation would return with a vengeance. He would have winced, except he didn't want Kaj to see his discomfort.

Kaj stood up and looked down at him with his arms crossed. "Don't make trouble. These rooms have no windows and only one exit, which is locked and guarded."

Javelin frowned at Kaj, then spoke to Drummer with courtesy. "You may rest. This suite and everything in it is for your use."

"What will happen to me?" Drummer asked.

Javelin hesitated. "I don't think you will be harmed."

That statement hardly rang with confidence. "Does that mean I might be?"

"Enough!" Kaj said. He spoke to Javelin. "Havej and I can stand guard here while you attend Her Majesty."

So Havej was the third guard, the one who wanted a

drink. Drummer sympathized. He could use a good strong one himself.

"Can I get my glittar back?" Drummer asked.

Kaj's face flushed with anger, but Javelin spoke quickly, before the other guard could respond. "I'll check."

After the guards left, Drummer lay on the divan. Closing his eyes, he silently cursed his fate. After a few minutes of dramatic brooding, he decided his time would be better spent exploring his sumptuous prison.

The rooms were gorgeous, with golden furniture and sunrise mosaics. For a prison, he could have done worse. He had, in fact, many times. At least in those cases, he had known he would be released soon. He had no idea why he was here, though he would lay odds it had to do with his sister being queen of Harsdown. He couldn't imagine any other reason for Taka Mal to bother with him. It scared him, despite his facade of nonchalance with his guards.

He found a bowl of fruit and feasted on bananas, grapes, and oranges. He supposed he should have worried about poison. If they had wanted to kill him, though, they could have already done it plenty of times. In the bathing room, he washed up in the pool, which was tiled with designs of blue roses. His guards apparently didn't consider him dangerous, for they had left the razor on a stand in the bathing room. He shaved the stubble on his chin. Then he wandered naked into the bedroom.

Drummer didn't know whether to be flattered or worried that the clothes in the closets fit him perfectly. Someone had planned his abduction in detail. The garments were far more elegant than his usual attire, they were similar in quality to what he wore when he visited Castle Suncroft in Aronsdale, where he tried not to embarrass his relatives by dressing like a scrubby minstrel. These trousers were deep blue and tucked into boots tooled with vine designs. The silk shirt was white. It fastened at the neck, but he didn't like tying it, so he left it open halfway down his chest. The vest he tried felt constraining, and he put it back in the closet. When he finished dressing, he felt better.

Noises came from the foyer. He went to investigate and found his three guards.

"Greetings," Drummer said.

They regarded him with impassive expressions.

"The queen will see you now," Javelin said.

Heart of Ice

Mel and Cobalt entered Stonebreaker's huge bedroom together. The room was full of people. Mel recognized none of them, neither the guards posted around the dais nor the servants seeing to the king's every need. Stonebreaker was sitting up in bed, discussing a scroll with his scribe. The king's silvered hair swept back from a face of noble lines with a strong nose and chin. He was a handsome man, proud and aristocratic, and even in his sickbed, he had a presence that commanded.

She could see a resemblance between Stonebreaker and Cobalt. But everything about Cobalt was *more*. It wasn't only that he was taller and more powerfully built than his grandfather. He had a vibrancy that the king lacked. More intelligence. A stronger sense of self. More strength of character, from what Mel had seen. Cobalt simply surpassed the king.

The aides and guards bowed to Cobalt. They darted glances at Mel, but averted their gazes when she caught them watching her. She knew the staff bowed to the royal family, but she was almost certain that when a member of the Chamberlight family arrived at the palace after an absence, people were supposed to kneel.

Cobalt's expression tightened. The older servants had seen him beaten and whipped by the king in his childhood, and she knew he brooded on their lack of intervention. He didn't care if they knelt, but it *mattered* to him that they gave respect. She had no doubt they feared Stonebreaker, especially now, when the king could misinterpret any honor they showed his heir. If they knelt to Cobalt, his grandfather could take it as a deliberate slight, a wish to see him dead and Cobalt on the throne.

The king, however, looked fine. Mel didn't know whether to feel relieved for his health or angry that he had pulled Cobalt across four countries to attend him. She saw no sign of paralysis. His face seemed normal and he was using both arms as he held the scroll. He looked up as Cobalt and Mel came forward, and he registered neither surprise nor pleasure at the sight of his heir. He just set down his quill. He waved his hand and the men attending him left immediately, pausing only to bow to Cobalt.

When everyone was gone except for the guards posted around the walls, the king beckoned to his grandson.

He didn't acknowledge Mel with even a glance, so she stayed back.

Cobalt went to the bed and bowed, as expected of the heir to the king. "I am pleased to see you looking so well, Grandfather."

"Are you?" Stonebreaker's voice was almost as resonant as his heir's. Almost. He motioned to a dark wing chair by the bed. "Sit. Tell me about your trip."

Cobalt glanced at Mel. She shook her head slightly and hoped he wouldn't press the issue of Stonebreaker's discourtesy to her.

The king spoke dourly. "I see you brought your wife."

"Yes." Cobalt held out his hand to Mel.

Her face was growing hot. She came over and bowed to the king. "It is an honor to attend you, Your Majesty."

Stonebreaker narrowed his gaze at her. But then he indicated another chair. "Bring that one over."

Relieved he hadn't found reason to take offense, Mel moved her chair next to Cobalt's. Then they sat, stiff and formal.

"You look improved," Cobalt told his grandfather.

"How would you know?" Stonebreaker asked. "You weren't here."

Cobalt's jaw tensed. "General Cragland told me of your illness. I am glad the paralysis wasn't permanent."

"Well, then, it wasn't paralysis, was it?" Stonebreaker studied him as if Cobalt were a bug under a magnifying glass. "I hope that doesn't disappoint you."

A muscle twitched in Cobalt's jaw. "Of course not."

Mel spoke. "May we do anything for Your Majesty?"

"Like what?" Stonebreaker asked. "Take over my duties? I'm not dead yet, girl."

Mel stared at him. In the same moment that she said, "I would never—" Cobalt said, "Don't talk to her that way."

Stonebreaker turned a hard gaze on his grandson. "You should have left her in Shazire. You only had to marry that rube. You didn't have to inflict her on us."

Cobalt clenched the arms of his chair. "You will not speak of my wife in that manner."

Stonebreaker leaned forward. "And you will not speak to me in that manner, boy."

"I haven't been a boy for twenty years." Cobalt's voice grated.

"You consider yourself a man?" Stonebreaker asked. "Why? Because you have a pretty wife?" He gave Mel an appraising glance that lasted too long for courtesy, and she sat under his scrutiny with her face burning. To Cobalt, he said, "So where is your heir, hmm? You've been wed over a year and I see no sign of any success on your part to father one."

Cobalt started to stand, his face darkening with a familiar rage. Mel grabbed his arm and held him in his chair. He could have easily thrown her off, but instead he took a slow breath and settled back down.

With stiff control, Cobalt asked, "Has Mother arrived?"

The king considered him. "She is here."

Relief washed over Mel. At least one person here would properly welcome Cobalt.

"That's good," Cobalt said. His posture relaxed a bit.

"Yes, I imagine so," Stonebreaker said.

Mel's tension began to ease. Perhaps this would be all right if they kept to neutral subjects.

"How is Mother?" Cobalt asked.

"As well as can be imagined," Stonebreaker said, "given that you killed her husband."

Cobalt stared at him, unable to hide his shock. Mel had no love of Varqelle, but she knew Cobalt's grief. Watching his father die from wounds taken in battle had nearly destroyed him. Her anger brought out her words before her caution could stop them.

"You go too far," she told the king.

"Perhaps it is you who goes too far, wife of my grandson."

Cobalt rose to his feet, drawing Mel up with him. "We will attend you later, Grandfather." The iron control in his voice tore Mel apart. With one sentence, Stonebreaker may have undone months of healing.

"I didn't give you leave to go," the king said.

"Nevertheless, we are going." Cobalt bowed, stiff in his anger. Stonebreaker could have imprisoned him for that defiance. He let it go—for now. Mel had no doubt he would retaliate in ways that made him look noble and Cobalt appear vicious.

After they left the suite, Mel sagged against the wall of the corridor. She said nothing, aware of Stonebreaker's guards at the entrance. Cobalt urged her forward. They followed an icy hall, so white and brilliant and beautiful, with blue mosaics along the vaulted ceiling. So lovely. So cold.

Mel was upset enough that several minutes passed before

she realized they weren't alone. Four bodyguards in white and blue accompanied them, a few steps to either side or behind. Distracted, she looked up at Cobalt. He seemed as far away as the mountains.

"Cobalt?" she asked.

His voice matched their cold surroundings. "What?"

"Where are we going?"

"My rooms." His face was unreadable. The husband she had come to love was gone and a stranger had taken his place.

Mel held back her questions. This wasn't the time. She felt the loss of her former life like a physical pain. Applecroft glowed in her memory, an unattainable dream of warmth. The humble name referred to her parents' orchards and estate in Harsdown. Her mother Chime had been a farm girl who married a prince, for a Dawnfield heir had to wed the most powerful mage he could find among Aronsdale's eligible women. Chime had grown up taking her personal freedom for granted, and she raised her daughter the same way. Somehow Mel had to adapt to the icy formality of the Diamond Palace without losing herself.

In pastoral, warm Shazire, she and Cobalt had grown close. Here in the place of his emotionally impoverished childhood, he had withdrawn. He had spent his life both hating Stonebreaker and struggling to prove his worth to his grandfather. She doubted he would ever understand that jealousy drove Stonebreaker to crush his sprit. The king would never forgive Cobalt for being more than him. He would never grant his heir the validation Cobalt sought. Mel feared this visit would tear open Cobalt's wounds and destroy his hard-earned peace of mind.

What that meant for the two of them, she couldn't yet see, but she felt as if she were grieving the loss of the man she had known in Shazire. If this visit shattered Cobalt—if it let free the tyrant within him—the citizens of three countries would suffer the consequences of his despair.

Jade met her hostage in a place that gave her advantage. It was an instinctive choice, but she knew her instincts well enough to trust them. She sat on her throne in the Audience Hall, with its golden walls and columns of rose marble. The ceiling was so high, birds flew beneath the skylights. A Kazlatarian carpet extended from the doors to the dais where Jade sat. Her cousin Baz stood by her side, impressive in his gold-and-crimson general's regalia. She wore a gold silk tunic and pants, and a dagger on her belt.

Three guards brought in her prisoner. Drummer Headwind was less imposing than she expected. His shaggy gold curls needed trimming and had no business being so appealing. He was dressed too informally to meet a queen. He hadn't even fastened his shirt, for saints' sake; she could see his leanly muscled chest halfway to his navel. He had a sensual walk, lithe and supple. Her pulse surged, but she tried to ignore it. His large blue eyes gave him an innocent look. Bah. She wouldn't trust that angelic face as far as a thirsty soldier could spit.

His guards—Javelin, Havej, and sullen Kaj—brought him to the dais and bowed. Drummer stood gaping at Jade until

Kaj shoved his shoulder. Drummer went down clumsily on one knee, finally bending his head in the expected deference.

She let him kneel for a while. Then she said, "You may rise."

He looked up, his face flushed. Then he got stiffly back up to his feet. Sweat had beaded on his brow. Either he wasn't used to kneeling, which seemed unlikely given his relatives, or else his trip here had drained him more than it should have. That troubled Jade. A great difference existed between keeping a hostage a bit off balance and mistreating him. The soldiers who fetched him had better not have abused him. He was a tool to use against Cobalt Escar, and his freedom would depend on how well his family negotiated, but she had no wish to hurt the fellow. She hoped eventually to release him, and she didn't want him taking home tales of inhumane treatment.

Jade knew he was trouble, though, with that face of his and his reputation for mischief. She should be done with him as soon as possible. And yet, it pleased her to know he was hers for a time.

"Welcome to Taka Mal, Goodsir Drummer," she said.

"Thank you, Your Majesty." He didn't look at all grateful. "I'm afraid I don't merit the title Goodsir, however. I'm not gentry."

"You are the youngest brother of Chime Headwind Dawnfield, are you not?"

His face paled. "Yes."

Good. He didn't deny the obvious. She got up and went down the stairs. Baz came with her, the jeweled hilts of his swords glinting on his belt. She stopped in front of Drummer. She was average height for a woman of Taka Mal, but the heels on her boots put her eyes level with his. She smiled and he looked alarmed.

"You will be my guest for a while," she said.

"How long?" he asked.

"You needn't trouble yourself with that."

"I'm a hostage for Cobalt's good behavior, is that it?" A bead of sweat ran down his temple. "If he doesn't attack Taka Mal, I get to live."

"You are one of several strategies," Jade allowed.

An audacious glint came into his eyes. "I've heard the queen of Taka Mal is a great strategist. No one ever told me she was also a great beauty." He made his words a challenge rather than a compliment.

She gave him an unimpressed look. "Don't bother trying to soften me up with flattery. I've heard it from the best of them."

His grin flashed, an expression so dazzling Jade wondered her hair didn't sizzle. "It's not flattery. Just truth." His smile vanished. "Your men took my glittar. I would like it back."

"Your what?" She was still recovering from that brilliant smile.

"My glittar. It's an Aronsdale harp."

"Why should they give it back?"

He considered that. She thought he would get angry, but then he tried a different tack. His honeyed voice poured over her. "I will compose a ballad in honor of your beauty."

Jade knew his words were calculated to unsettle her, flattery yes, but also a challenge to her authority. He wielded them like a velvet-coated mallet. But when his lashes lowered halfway over his eyes, she didn't think he knew he was doing it or how sensual he looked. She could see why he had a reputation for inspiring women to seek his kisses.

Bah. Foolish women. "Why ever would I want to hear you sing?" she asked.

"Because," he murmured, "my voice is ambrosia."

"You certainly have a high opinion of yourself."

"Only when I'm inspired."

Baz spoke tightly. "Take your blighted inspiration elsewhere."

Jade knew *that* tone. If Drummer didn't watch out, he would end up with a knife between his ribs. She motioned to his guards. "You can take him back to his suite." Inclining her head to Drummer, she added, "It has pleased me to meet you."

"The pleasure is mutual," he said. "It would please me even more if you would let me go."

Ha. Now he told the truth. "Why? I thought I inspired you to create great music."

His voice softened. "More than you know."

Jade blinked. *That* sounded more genuine than calculated. Flustered, she spoke formally, distancing herself from him. "Goodman Headwind, I hope you enjoy the hospitality of my court. You may go now."

Before Drummer could say anything more, the guards swept him off down the hall. At the doors, he paused to look back at her. Then Kaj grabbed his arm and pushed him out the doorway.

"That one is trouble," Jade said. She had never met anyone like him. Men in Taka Mal glowered and strode boldly and menaced with their dark ferocity. Drummer's differences fascinated her.

"If he doesn't take care," Baz said, "he will never see home again."

Jade could almost feel him seething. She turned to her cousin. "Baz, he is my guest."

He scowled at her. "He's not a toy. If you dishonor a queen's brother, her family could consider it an act of war."

"Dishonor him?" She had to laugh, though it hurt. "An odd proposition, given how most men view women in this country." Like property, though she wouldn't say it aloud. She didn't want to encourage such thoughts. "But I've no such intention."

"Well, you can't marry him. He's a commoner."

"Oh, for saints' sake. I just met the man. Stop worrying."

He scowled at her. "Admit it, Jade. You liked him."

She didn't know which irked her more, Baz's assumptions or the idea that he might be right. He and Jade had grown up together, he the son of her paternal aunt. He knew her better than anyone.

"Baz, listen," she said. "I'm no naive girl to be swayed by a minstrel's flattery. I think we should stop worrying about Queen Chime's brother and work on our plans for Jazid."

He looked as if he wanted to keep arguing. After a pause, though, he said, "All right."

But as they headed to her study, where they plotted strategy, he fell silent. It made Jade uneasy. Drummer she could handle.

Baz was the one who worried her.

A pounding roused Mel from a fitful sleep. She peered groggily at the unfamiliar canopy overhead. Someone was knocking. As she sat up, a door opened in another room somewhere, followed by an urgent murmur of voices.

Cobalt rolled toward Mel, restless even in his sleep. When she touched his shoulder, he sat up fast, knocking away her hand. She was used to his abrupt awakenings. His men thought it came from battle readiness, and perhaps that was part of it. But Mel knew the full truth; it was the legacy of a child who knew he could be dragged from his sleep and thrashed if he transgressed in the slightest against an endless and impossible set of rules.

Cobalt pulled her into his arms and held her hard. Gradually the fast beat of his heart slowed. Finally he drew back, calmer now, though he never said a word. He rarely spoke of his nightmares or fevered wakings.

"Someone was knocking," Mel said.

He nodded and left their bed, pulling on a robe he had tossed across the footboard. As he strode from the room, Mel dressed more carefully in a silk sleep tunic and pants, conscious of the rigid customs here for women. Then she went into the Silver Room of their suite. The moment she saw their visitor, her pulse stuttered. It was Quill, Stonebreaker's scribe. He was speaking to Cobalt in a low voice while one of Mel's sphere-maids hovered nearby. Cobalt had a strange look, as if he were ill.

Mel went over to them. "Is it the king?"

Cobalt turned to her. He seemed to have trouble breathing. "Another stroke."

Mel couldn't imagine worse timing. Cobalt's last words with his grandfather had been spoken in anger. If Stonebreaker didn't recover, Cobalt would torment himself with guilt. Mel wanted to tell Cobalt that it wasn't his fault, it had never been his fault; Stonebreaker was a monster who never deserved a child to raise. But Cobalt would resent her for speaking such words in front of others.

So instead she asked, "May I come with you?"

Something gathered in his eyes, moisture, from Cobalt the Dark who supposedly never wept. But Mel had seen him holding his dead father with tears pouring down his face.

"Yes," he said softly. "Come." Then he turned to Quill. "Wait here, please, while we dress."

Quill bowed. "Yes, Your Majesty."

A chill went through Mel. It was true Cobalt had that title, for he ruled Shazire. But it was a less powerful country than the Misted Cliffs. The heir to the Sapphire Throne outranked the king of Shazire. But as the Chamberlight heir, Cobalt was a Highness; only a king and his consort carried the title of Majesty. Mel remembered how Stonebreaker's staff had responded when Cobalt first arrived at the palace, as if they feared to acknowledge his status. That Quill used the title now spoke volumes about Stonebreaker's condition. Mel wondered if Quill even thought the king would survive the night.

Mel didn't know which she feared more—that Stone-breaker would live and continue to destroy his grandson, or that he would die and make Cobalt king of the Misted Cliffs.

Dancer Chamberlight Escar had hair the color of a raven's wing. Streaked with silver, it framed her alabaster face and fell to her waist. Faint lines creased the corners of her eyes, and her delicate cheekbones gave her an ethereal aspect. Tonight, a pale silk tunic and trousers draped her graceful build. The intelligence of her expression made it hard to look away from her face. As a girl, Dancer had been pretty; at fifty-one years of age, she was a great beauty.

In the dark time of morning, three hours before sunrise, Mel and Cobalt joined Dancer. She had already arrived in the foyer outside Stonebreaker's suite. Cobalt embraced his mother with awkward gentleness. She was small and frag-ile next to his massive form, and her head came only halfway up his chest. Tears leaked down her face. Then she pulled away, restrained again, and wiped away her tears with the heel of her hand.

It was only the second time Mel had seen Cobalt and Dancer hug each other; the first had been when he returned from the war in Shazire. Now they stood together, the only kin of the man dying in the next room. Mel didn't intrude on the complex waves of their grief. She folded her hand around the sphere that hung from her neck on a gold chain. It was as perfectly round as metalworkers could make the shape. Dancer and Cobalt had to decide if they wanted the nebulous aid she could offer as a mage.

They spoke quietly for a while and then came to her. Cobalt stood behind Dancer, a wall at her back, and the former Harsdown queen regarded her daughter-in-law with dark eyes. She spoke in her moonlight voice. "My son says you are a mage. A healer."

"A little," Mel said.

"Can you cure my father?"

"I cannot give him life if his illness is fatal," Mel said. Only a violet adept had the power to heal mortal wounds. Only such a mage could use spells to give life—or take it.

The queen spoke quietly. "I understand you helped my husband after the Alzire battle."

"I tried." Mel's voice caught. "I failed."

"Cobalt says you eased Varqelle's pain as he died." Her gaze never wavered. "And that the attempt nearly killed you."

Mel just nodded, unable to speak. She had poured her last resources into the dying king, but his wounds had been too severe. Her best spells hadn't been enough.

"You had every reason to hate my husband," Dancer said. "Yet you offered your life in an effort to save his."

"It is my oath as a mage," Mel said. "To bring light. To heal." No matter how much she abhorred the person.

Cobalt spoke raggedly. "If you help Grandfather—" He either couldn't or wouldn't continue. But Mel knew his question; would she live?

"I was too drained then," Mel said. "I am rested now." It was true. She didn't say she had no more training in using her mage powers now than she had that night, for she couldn't assure him it wouldn't hurt her to use her ability.

"I have heard other tales of your deeds that day." Dancer's voice had a distant quality, as if her words came across a field. "They say you walked through the battle wielding a sword of flame that touched the sky."

The stories had grown until Mel hardly recognized herself. She had done no more than create a simple red spell. She made light. But she powered it with a catapult ball. A sphere.

The Chamberlight army had already won the battle—but then a Shazire warrior broke through to Varqelle and struck him down. In his enraged grief, Cobalt would have massacred every Shazire soldier on the field. To stop him, Mel had made her desperate spell. She held her sword high, and a pillar of light stretched from it into the sky. In the dusk, it lit the entire battlefield, throwing fighters into sharp relief. She walked among them and no one touched her. It stopped the fighting. Cobalt knew the truth, that she had created no more than light, but the tales of her "sorcery" burned far brighter than her actual spell.

"I don't know how much I can help His Majesty," Mel said. "But I can promise I will do no harm."

"No harm?" Bitterness saturated Dancer's voice. "He would live. What greater harm could you do?"

Mel froze. Whatever Dancer thought of the king, she had never spoken of him in such a manner.

Cobalt laid his large hand on his mother's shoulder. "If we don't try, we will regret it."

The former queen's posture sagged. To Mel she said, simply, "Please try."

* * *

A solitary light burned in Stonebreaker's suite, a lamp on the nightstand by his canopied bed. He lay on his back among voluminous covers, his eyes closed, his breathing shallow, his body seeming to have collapsed in on itself.

The elderly physician was in a chair by the bed, dozing, his bag open in his lap. With his white hair and wrinkled face, he seemed as frail as his patient. Quill touched his shoulder, and the doctor opened bleary eyes. "Eh?"

"His Majesty's family is here," Quill said.

The doctor squinted past him to where Cobalt stood with Mel. He rose to his feet, awkward with sleep and age, and his bag fell to the floor. Grabbing for it, the doctor lost his balance. Quill put out a steadying hand to catch him, then retrieved the bag.

"How is my grandfather?" Cobalt asked.

The doctor spoke heavily. "He barely lives."

The dim light gave Cobalt an even darker aspect than usual. "Do you know why he had another attack?"

The elderly man blanched, and sweat beaded his forehead. "Your Majesty, please believe I have done my absolute best for him."

Mel knew Cobalt wasn't blaming him. But Stonebreaker's staff lived in fear of censure. Nothing could always go perfectly, and when mistakes occurred, Stonebreaker always assigned blame regardless of whether or not it was deserved. In his reality, he never erred; he only meted out punishment, anything from dismissal of his staff to the whippings Cobalt had endured as a child.

Mel spoke gently to the doctor. "I can tend His Majesty."

The physician's gaze flicked to Mel and back to Cobalt. He stumbled over his words. "Your grandfather—I...I have done what I can. But he—please give him his last hours."

Then Mel understood. The doctor feared she meant to speed Stonebreaker's death. She held her medallion, concentrating on a spell to soothe emotions, and yellow light surrounded her hand. The doctor stepped back, his gaze panicked. Then the spell began to affect him, and some of the fear left his eyes.

"It's all right," Mel murmured. The light remained around her hand, but the spell enveloped the doctor, Cobalt and Dancer, Quill, and the bodyguards. "I can help him," she said. "Ease his pain. Give him more time."

The doctor stared at her, his eyes like silver coins, flat and hard. Then he took a breath and his shoulders came down from their hunched position. Dancer stood with Cobalt, her face drawn and pale. Aware of them watching, Mel went to the bed. No one stopped her. Stonebreaker was near this side, and she sat down by his still figure. She imagined a luminous sky, wildflowers scattered across a meadow, her mother's blue eyes, and the deep, deep lakes of her home. Blue light spilled over Stonebreaker as Mel gave her spell to him. His body glowed in the radiance.

Slowly, so slowly, his lashes lifted. He stared at the canopy, his gray eyes pale in the blue light. His whisper rattled. "Dancer?"

"I am here." Dancer stepped forward, her silks rustling. Mel moved away from the bed to give her privacy. As Dancer sat by her father and gently brushed the hair back from his forehead, blue light flowed around them.

Stonebreaker took her hand. "Farewell, daughter." His voice sounded like parchment crinkling. "Remember me…"

A tear ran down her porcelain face. "I will."

He patted her hand. "You have been a good daughter to me."

Her voice broke. "Thank you."

"Is Cobalt here?"

Cobalt stepped forward into the blue light. His face had a clenched look, as if everything within him, every emotion and memory, had tightened into a fist. "Here, Grandfather."

"Closer," Stonebreaker whispered. "Just you."

Dancer hesitated, her forehead furrowed, her gaze going from her father to her son. Cobalt stood like a statue.

"I must speak to my heir," Stonebreaker said.

No, Mel thought. She knew Dancer didn't want to leave Cobalt with him, either. But who could deny the king his dying request to speak with the man who would follow him on the throne? And maybe, just maybe, Stonebreaker would offer some words of peace, as he had done with Dancer.

Dancer twisted her hands in her sleeves as she stepped away from the bed. A deep fatigue was spreading through Mel. If she held this spell much longer, she would slip into a death trance like the one she had suffered when she tried to heal King Varqelle.

Cobalt sat on the bed and leaned into his grandfather. Stonebreaker's lips moved as he whispered to his heir, and Mel saw the bewildered anguish on Cobalt's face. No! she thought. *Don't hurt him.* Desperate, she tried to reach them with a mood spell, but she had stretched her power too far, and she had nothing left. She was a blue flame, flickering, losing its essence. The room rippled in a haze.

As Mel collapsed, Dancer tried to catch her. The doctor hesitated, confusion and suspicion warring on his face, and Mel slipped out of Dancer's grip, crumpling to the floor. She could no longer see Stonebreaker, the doctor, even Dancer—only Cobalt. He left the bed and came to her in slow motion, his face contorted with fear.

Come back. Cobalt knelt down and gathered her into his arms. He held her head against his chest. His voice seemed to echo in her mind though she was certain he was speaking aloud. *Stay with me, Mel.*

Suddenly the world jolted back to normal, and with a gasp, she sagged against him.

A rustle of robes came from nearby, and the doctor spoke. His voice trembled. "Your grandfather—"

Cobalt rose to his full height, drawing Mel to her feet as well. The doctor stared up at him, fear in his gaze. Dancer was sitting on the bed next to her father, her head bent, one of his hands in hers.

Her shoulders shook as she wept.

Standing behind Mel, Cobalt gripped her shoulders, his fingers digging into the layers of her tunic. She was too stunned to react. It couldn't have happened. Not yet. Incense permeated the air, though earlier she had smelled nothing. She knew that smell. It was the scent of passing, the scent of endings.

The scent of death.

In the Misted Cliffs, along the sea, across the valleys and hills, people burned a certain incense to mourn a passing from life into the realms beyond. Tonight, in these vaulted rooms of wealth and power and bitterness, a king had taken his final breath and entered the long path walked by spirits.

Quill stepped back from the brazier where he had lit the incense. No one else moved, not Cobalt nor Dancer nor the doctor nor the guards. Mel didn't know what Stonebreaker had told Cobalt, but she had seen her husband's anguish. He had never come to terms with his agonized memories. If Stonebreaker had exacerbated that pain on his deathbed, all the settled lands might pay the price of Cobalt's torment.

Dancer slowly lifted her head. She stood up, her face streaked with tears. Her dark eyes blazed, though whether in anguish or triumph, Mel didn't know.

Then the queen knelt to her son.

Cobalt's voice rasped. "What are you doing? Get up."

She rose to her feet in a graceful motion. "Hail, Your Majesty, King of Chamberlight and Alzire."

The doctor jerked as if someone had yanked him out of ice. Then he, too, knelt, stiffly, slowly. In her side vision, Mel saw Quill and the guards going down as well. Cobalt froze, clenching her shoulders, and her fear increased.

It's too late to show him honor, Mel thought. *The damage has already been done.* She had no illusions about her husband. He burned with the fire of a conqueror. If he never vanquished his inner demons, he would pour his anguish into the crucible of war and blaze through the settled lands.

What cruelty had Stonebreaker bequeathed him from his deathbed? Nothing could ever appease Cobalt's torment now, for from this moment on, nothing could ever force Stonebreaker to acknowledge his grandson's worth.

Mel feared Cobalt would drive himself until no place and no country would be safe from the Midnight King—no matter what price they paid in blood.

5

The Midnight Throne

After two days with nothing to do except make futile escape attempts, Drummer wanted to climb the walls. His guards ignored his attempts to talk to them, so he had another desultory lunch by himself. The food was excellent, if unfamiliar, meat with curry, but as with every meal here, he ate alone. He was ready to shout with frustration at the loss of his coveted freedom.

With no warning, Kaj strode into the parlor and dropped a cloth bundle on the divan. As he turned around, a flap of cloth fell off the bundle, revealing a gleam of golden wood.

Drummer jumped to his feet. "My glittar!"

Kaj grunted.

Drummer grinned at the bad-tempered gambler. "I shall compose a song of gratitude for you."

"Try it," Kaj growled, "and your harp will be in little pieces all around you on the floor. That's what happens when you break something over someone's head."

Drummer regarded him innocently. "Do people break things over your head so often that you know the pattern?"

Kaj's face purpled. "You are fortunate the queen wants you alive and happy." He stalked from the room.

"Nice to see you, too," Drummer said, but he waited until Kaj was gone.

He sat on the divan and picked up his glittar. Its curving frame fit perfectly in his hand. He tuned the harp and was gratified to hear its mellow sound. They had even polished the wood and cleaned the strings. Apparently someone here appreciated fine instruments.

Carrying the harp, he wandered through his suite, searching for a place to practice. None of the rooms felt right. Too confining. Finally he went to where he could feel fresh air on his face, a balcony he had missed his first day because it was behind a door that resembled a wall panel. The balcony was high up a tower, with a four-story drop to the ground. Drummer had thought for all of two seconds about trying to climb down and realized he valued his life too much. The wall had no handholds, fingerholds, or fingernail holds, and a fall from up here would splatter him all over the royal courtyard.

He loved the balcony, though. He could look out over the palace and city. Quaaz teemed with life—vendors in the streets, carts rolling, children running, news criers shouting and palace guards tromping along the alleys.

Drummer sat on the retaining wall of the balcony. He wouldn't fall; the brass railing on the wall was high enough to lean against. He sat in a corner, his arm resting on the rail, and settled the glittar against his body. When he plucked the strings, notes rippled through the air. It pleased him to have the means of his livelihood back, even if he had no one to play for.

After warming up his voice and his fingers, he eased into a country song that many a fellow had asked him to play for his girl:

On the slide of sweet night,
In the time of drowsing,
In the silvery light,
And the stars carousing,
Beneath a wistful moon,
On the mosses sighing,
O kiss me softly soon,
Love is never dying.

"Such lovely words," a woman said. "False, but pretty."

Drummer nearly jumped off the balcony. Only the rail kept him from plunging to his untimely death. He hopped down from the wall and held his glittar like a shield while he faced the invader who menaced him from the doorway.

The queen of Taka Mal had come to visit.

She wore a silk tunic and trousers the color of topaz. The outfit did nothing to hide her voluptuous curves. Her dark eyes tilted upward, and their lush fringe of lashes made her large eyes look even bigger. Black curls framed her face and tumbled to her shoulders. His jailor had arrived without her scowling generals—in breathtaking form.

Drummer finally remembered himself and bowed. "Your Majesty."

"You play well," she said.

He strummed an impromptu melody and sang. "She glides into the night, or actually my noon/She's really quite a sight, I think I've met my doom."

Laughing, she winced. "That's terrible poetry."

"Thank you. I wrote it while you were standing there."

"I don't know whether to be insulted or complimented."

He answered slow and lazy. "Take your pick."

Her lips curved upward. "I'll take it as a compliment."

"When are you going to let me go?"

"I don't know. It depends on your relatives."

At least she was honest about it. He held his glittar in one hand and stepped forward. Her subtle perfume distracted him. Lifting his hand, he *almost* touched her dark hair.

"If I have to be hostage," he murmured, "I couldn't ask for a more fascinating captor." He was as incensed now as the day her men had abducted him, but when she came near him like this, his ire stirred him to do foolish things. He wasn't sure how much was anger and how much came from a different passion altogether. With the audacity that had so often landed him in trouble, he said, "I'd die for one kiss from those wine-plum lips."

Her eyes closed slightly, giving her a sensually dangerous look. In a low voice, she said, "You most certainly would."

He lifted a curl of her silky hair and brushed his knuckles on her cheek. "Are you going to call the guards?"

"To protect who? Me?" She moved his hand away from her face, but she held on to it for several moments before she released him. "Or you?"

"Do I need protection from you?"

"I think you need it from yourself."

"I always have." It was true.

"You could be locked in a cell for touching the queen."

"I'm already in a cell."

"A dungeon," she said in a voice that was somehow sultry and menacing at the same time. "With chains."

He answered in a low voice. "Your chains are as sweet as they are brutal, desert queen."

"Never brutal. Not for you." Her voice poured over him like thick, dark honey, and her eyes had a glossy look, though whether it was a challenge or an invitation, he was afraid to guess. He wondered if she even realized how she appeared to him.

Softly, he said, "You chained me the moment you took my freedom." He knew he should grab her, use her as a hostage, bluff his way free. The guards were outside the suite, but she had come in without their protection. *Why?* He leaned forward, and she watched as if daring him to touch her. So he did something even more perilous than taking her captive.

He kissed her.

For one astonishing instant, her lips softened. Then she gasped as if jolted back to reality. She gave him a hearty shove and sent him stumbling back into the balcony wall.

Drummer stared at her, his heart beating hard. He couldn't believe he had been such a fool to take that liberty. Ah, but what a liberty. Eyes blazing, Vizarana Jade stepped up to him, and she was truly an unparalleled sight.

Then she slapped him.

Her palm hit his cheek before he recovered his wits enough to block her strike, and his head jerked to the side. He stared at her, his hand over his smarting cheek.

"Either you have a suicide wish," Jade said, "or your brain is addled."

Drummer knew he should stop. This wasn't some prank that would get him a few nights in jail. But by the saints, what a woman. He coaxed a ripple of notes from his glittar, as erotic as they were sweet. "That's for you."

Jade's cheeks turned red. "I shall be relieved when I can send you back to your poor, put-upon family." She spun around and stalked away like a wildcat, graceful even in her annoyance.

Drummer sagged against the wall. He felt as if he had just stepped out of a whirlwind. Taka Mal's queen was a force of nature that left him spinning.

Jade sat on a polished stone bench. Trellises looped with vines and royal-buds surrounded her. Weeping fronds hung from puff-top trees and brushed the paths that curved through her private garden. Sculptures of cats peeked out of the bushes. It was lush for a desert garden, kept that way by water piped in from underground and fed to the little waterfall.

Today the serenity of the gardens did nothing to calm her.

She had a lot to do. Her meeting with the Zanterian caravan masters was in an hour. She had to study a design for aqueducts with the city planners this evening. And she needed more strategy sessions about Jazid. She had no time to brood over ill-mannered minstrels. She ought to have him clapped in chains and locked in a cell.

Either that, or in her bed.

"Bah!" Jade ripped a royal-bud off the nearest vine and hurled it into the waterfall. Mist wafted across her face, but it couldn't cool her mood. Bed, indeed. She wouldn't touch that scoundrel if the House of Dawnfield offered her a thousand urns of gold hexa-coins to take him off their hands.

Leaves rustled. As she looked up, Baz appeared around a stand of trees barely taller than himself. He wore his field outfit today rather than the dress uniform encrusted with medals.

"Light of the morning," her cousin said.

"It's afternoon," Jade grumbled.

His grin flashed. "Glad to see you, too." He sat on the bench and motioned at the ring she wore, with its large topaz. "Your secretary is looking for you. Some scrolls need your seal."

"Yes. I've work to do." She was talking to herself more than to him. "I've been thinking about Ozi."

He spoke dryly. "By whom, I take it, you mean His Magnificence, the Atajazid D'az Ozar of the House of Onyx."

Jade waved her hand. "Yes. Him. Ozi."

Baz leaned back on his hands. "Jade, my dear, I hardly think that calling our moody neighbor 'Ozi' will predispose him to ally with us against Cobalt Escar."

Jade gave him an innocent look. "Why, Baz, whatever makes you think I wish to fight Cobalt Escar?"

"Maybe that glint in your eyes, like you want to pulverize someone."

"Pulverize indeed," she muttered, thinking of Drummer. "I would like to invite Ozi here as soon as possible. Tonight, in fact. The Zanterians can take the letter with their caravan."

"Firaz and Slate have expressed concerns about your plans."

Jade frowned at him. Whenever her generals discussed things without her, she got jumpy. "Such as?"

"Such as, Taka Mal should present a stable appearance to potential allies."

She could see where this was going. They wanted her to marry Baz and "consolidate" the power of the throne and the military. "I am glad, my beloved cousin, that you all agree you should present a united support of your queen."

His gaze darkened. "They're afraid you're going to die without an heir."

"But I have an heir." Jade lifted her hand and curled it into a claw as if she were going to attack him. "You."

"It is my honor." He sounded more annoyed than honored.

"Then be satisfied with that honor."

He didn't miss her meaning. "I wish for you a long and satisfied life, Jade. I've no desire to take your throne."

"I'm glad." She believed his first sentence far more than his second. "I find myself with a certain antipathy to those who feel otherwise."

"Long and healthy. For you. For me." He regarded her steadily. "For our children."

This seemed to be the day for the men in her life to take liberties. She couldn't let her advisors push her around. If she showed any sign of self-doubt, Firaz and Slate would exploit it. Spearcaster would probably stand behind her, but she took nothing for granted.

"You presume much," Jade said.

"I would do you honor," he said, taking her hand. "For the rest of our lives."

Jade pulled away her hand. "It is gratifying to know my kin wish to support me for all our lives." Softly she added, "I mean it, Baz. I am glad."

With no warning, he took her shoulders and kissed her, his lips full against hers. For the second time in the last hour, a man had caught her off guard in a most personal manner. But unlike with Drummer, where the kiss had sent the heat of the Dragon-Sun through her body, this was like having her brother kiss her. Mortified, she thumped him on the arm and pulled away.

"Baz, what are you thinking?" Her cheeks flamed. "Stop it."

Anger flashed on his face. For a moment she thought he would claim he didn't need her permission. If he set himself against her, the political upheaval could disrupt her government and destabilize their attempts to form an alliance with Jazid.

Then her cousin exhaled. "If I offended you, I offer apology."

Relief surged over her. "Accepted."

He spoke with reserve, avoiding what had just happened. "Shall we go meet the Zanterians?"

"Yes. Of course."

As they walked to the palace, Jade's thoughts roiled. He had shaken her this time, truly shaken her, and she didn't think his patience would last much longer.

Mel found Cobalt about a fifteen minutes' walk from the palace. He was sitting by an abandoned quarry that the sunlight turned gold. She had sought his mood, but she had felt only a vague sense of his disquiet. He was guarding himself too well for her to understand any more. She hadn't expected her spell to reach this far; her efforts for Stonebreaker had strained her power. But each time she overextended herself, she recovered faster than before.

A forest had grown to the edge of the quarry, and trees hung precariously over its rim. The scent of box-blossoms saturated the air. Cobalt was gazing into the quarry, but Mel didn't think he was looking at anything. He seemed to have aged a decade in one night. Neither of them had slept. The Bishop of Spheres had presided over the laying out of the king in his most regal robes, his hair brushed back from his high forehead, his body ready for cremation. They would hold the final ceremonies today, and at sunset they would invest Cobalt with the Sapphire Throne.

She paused a short distance away, reluctant to disturb him. He was nominally alone; this was part of the King's Fields, and neither she nor Cobalt had brought their bodyguards. But sentries patrolled the area, and she glimpsed men in Chamberlight colors pacing through the woods and along the edge of the quarry. If Cobalt noticed, he gave no sign. He had withdrawn until she wondered if he no longer wanted her in his life.

"You don't have to stand there," he said, still staring at the quarry.

Startled, Mel walked over and settled next to his side. "I was worried about you."

He turned to her with a gaze bleaker even than when he had told her how, in his childhood, he would have done any-thing, *anything* for a crumb of love from his grandfather. He had set out to conquer a world to prove he wasn't worth-less, but nothing had appeased the jealous king, and noth-ing Cobalt could do now would ever change that. Mel had hoped the king's death would free Cobalt from the weight of his grandfather's contempt, but it had made matters worse.

"Tonight you become queen of the Misted Cliffs," he said.

A shudder went through her. He had once tempted her with dark promises of power and sworn to lay an empire at her feet. She didn't want an empire, but telling him that was like trying to hold on to goose down in a windstorm. Yet now when he had come a huge step closer to his goal, he looked strangely defeated.

Mel spoke in a low voice. "What did he say to you?"

"Nothing. A simple farewell."

"He never did anything simply." Not when it came to Cobalt.

He looked out over the quarry again. "It isn't important."

"Don't let it get to you! That's what he wanted. Don't let him win." She put her hand on his shoulder and turned him to look at her. "Whatever he said to you, it was malice. Don't believe his lies."

Cobalt spoke softly. "The problem, Mel, is that his lies usually have just enough truth to make you wonder."

"What did he say?"

He gaze had a distant quality. "All my life, I've felt as if I were a fraud. A false prince."

A chill went through Mel. "If he told you that, he lied."

He spoke softly. "Go back to the palace, Mel." He took her hand and kissed the knuckles. "Go on. I will see you at the memorial."

She hated to leave him like this. But forcing her company on him would only make it worse. "I'll be there."

Cobalt barely nodded, this man who by day's end would rule an empire. He sat alone, staring into whatever personal hell Stonebreaker had bequeathed him from his deathbed.

Mel ran to the stables. Ignoring the stares of the grooms, hay-sweeps, and light-bringers, she went to Admiral's stall, and the great stallion neighed in greeting. He would let no one but Cobalt ride him alone, but he accepted Mel's presence.

The man she sought, however, wasn't tending Admiral, as he often did at this time of day. Mel left the stables, walking now, at a loss. She had checked the carriage house and training ring. She didn't know where else to look.

A light-bringer came up to her, a youth about her age. He

was holding a pole with the lamp dangling from the hooked end, which he would use to aid stable hands and grooms who had to work at night. On a sunny day, when no one needed their services, light-bringers mucked out stalls or did other jobs the stable hands found for them. This fellow had been cleaning the lamp and replacing its oil.

"Your Majesty." He bowed to Mel as he had always done to Stonebreaker, and it troubled her to be treated in the same manner as someone she had so resented. It felt odd, too, that someone her own age treated her with the respect she associated with those much older.

"Are you searching for Master Matthew?" he asked.

"Yes, I am," she said, startled. "How did you know?"

"I have seen you come to Admiral's stall before, seeking him."

She did often ask Matthew for advice, not so much in caring for her horse, which she already knew how to do, but in trying to understand her husband, a far more difficult proposition.

"Do you know where he is?" Mel asked.

He motioned at a glinting white wall around the yard where stable hands were walking the horses. A gilded tower rose beyond it, topped by a spire. "He is at the cathedral."

"Ah." Mel inclined her head to the light-bringer. "Thank you." Then she smiled.

At her expression, the youth turned red, his ragged hair falling into his eyes. "You are most welcome, Your Majesty."

Mel wasn't sure why she unsettled people when she smiled, but it didn't seem to have a negative effect, so she didn't worry about it. As she crossed the yard, she wondered how it would be to live as a light-bringer. She had grown up on an orchard, and her mother had insisted she learn its workings. So Mel had cleaned stalls and fertilized crops, weeded and hoed and planted, and kept books. She had also trained as a junior officer in her father's army and discovered she was better suited to swordplay and archery than to the balls, embroidery, and fashions expected of royal women in other countries.

Had Varqelle never invaded Aronsdale and lost his throne, Mel would never have been the daughter of a king. Her parents would have lived on a farming estate in Aronsdale, and she might even have married a farm boy. Instead she had wed a dark and driven warlord. And saints help her, she had fallen in love with him.

A groom opened a door in the wall for Mel, and she went into the plaza beyond. The cathedral stood in its center, an architectural wonder of arched windows, delicate gold and silver arabesques on its walls, and stained-glass windows. The spire that topped its tower cut a sharp line against a sky streaked with high clouds.

Inside, quiet filled the vaulted, airy spaces of the cathedral. Sunlight shone through stained-glass windows that portrayed many of the saints revered in the Misted Cliffs: Sky-Rose, who added blush to the sunrise or a girl's face; Fire Opal, who brought flame from the mountains; Citrine, who dreamed the sun into the sky; Verdant, who gave life to meadows and forests; Aquamarine, who lifted the ocean into swells; Azure, who glazed the sky; Lapis Lazuli, who rode the wind on her great steed; Amethyst, who set lovers to yearning; Granite, who cracked the earth to create his thunder; and Alabaster, the celestial musician who strummed stars into the night.

Some legends claimed the saints were ancestors of the people, ancients so far in the past no histories remained of their family lines. Others named the saints as spirits of rainbows and the earth. In Aronsdale, they believed the saints had been the first mages, most of them born from the prismatic hierarchy of spells. The saints formed the court of the Dawn Star Goddess, namesake of the House of Dawnfield. Taka Mal had much the same mythology, though they called Sky-Rose the Sunrise. Instead of a Dawn Star Goddess, they revered the Dragon-Sun. Jazidians worshipped the Shadow Dragon and believed he and the Dragon-Sun fought an endless, daily battle for dominion of the skies.

Sunlight slanted through the windows and left pools of color on the cool stone floors. Dust motes drifted in shafts of colored light. The man Mel sought was kneeling at a railing. His head was bent, and his gray hair had fallen forward to hide his face, but she recognized the breadth of his shoulders, the length of his legs, his gray tunic and blue trousers, well made and well-worn. She went to him, her slippered feet muted in the cathedral.

Mel knelt on the cushioned strip of wood. "Matthew."

He raised his head, his eyes dark with exhaustion. "You honor me with your presence, Your Majesty."

"Ah, Matthew, it doesn't feel that way." Even her low voice

seemed too loud in this place. "Have you spoken with Cobalt since this morning?"

He shook his head. "The Bishop of Spheres kept him busy. I went to see him afterward, but he had disappeared."

"He went to the quarry."

Matthew was studying her face. "What troubles you?"

"Stonebreaker told him something before he died." The words were dust in her mouth. "Cobalt won't speak of it. He says only that he has always felt like a false prince."

Matthew's shoulders hunched. "Did he say why?"

"Nothing. Stonebreaker may have lied to him, out of malice." Quietly she added, "Or maybe he knew something."

Matthew regarded her with a haunted expression. "Varqelle."

Mel nodded. She had always suspected Stonebreaker gave Cobalt an army to free Varqelle because he had lost control over his grandson and hoped Varqelle would help him regain it. Instead Varqelle and Cobalt had formed a bond that shut out the late king. "I think he hated that Cobalt found acceptance with his father. He wanted to leave Cobalt a legacy of doubt, and he knew how much it meant to him to have his father's love."

Matthew looked as if his heart was breaking. "He has always had his father's love."

She laid her hand on his arm. "And that has made all the difference."

"What Stonebreaker said—it changes nothing." Matthew's posture had the tension of a fighter ready to engage. "Tonight Cobalt will become the king of the Misted Cliffs.

Nothing can stop it. Whatever Stonebreaker said to him—
it doesn't matter."

Mel knew it should be true. But she also knew her husband. It mattered to him.

Matthew had been a stable hand at Castle Escar when
Varqelle brought home his child bride, Dancer. And when
Dancer fled a year later, Matthew went with her. Tales of
Varqelle's cruelty had proliferated. Mel had no fondness for
the king who had led an army against her people, and yes,
Varqelle was a hard man who considered kindness a fault
in a king, a warrior, and a husband. But he was better than
Stonebreaker.

After Dancer left Varqelle, Stonebreaker wouldn't let her
go. No matter where she fled, he sent his army for her. He
didn't care if she stayed with her husband; he had no use for
Varqelle beyond the title he brought into the Chamberlight
line. Dancer had given him what he wanted, an heir who
could claim both the Sapphire and Harsdown thrones. And
if he turned that heir's days into a living hell, so be it.

Cobalt had never understood how Dancer could love him
as much as she obviously did and yet let Stonebreaker raise
him. She had never told him why, except to say she protected
him. Mel knew she would never say more. Neither Dancer
nor Matthew would take away his heredity by telling him
the name of his true father.

Matthew was kneeling in the slanting light from a win-
dow above them with panels of blue and frosted glass.
"I came here when I heard of the king's death," he told
Mel. "I should pray for the late king, but instead I think

of the man who will take the throne tonight. I pray the saints will help him—and us all."

On the third night of summer, when heat lay across the land and weighted the air with moisture, people filled the Hall of Sapphires in the Diamond Palace, all the elite of the Misted Cliffs, their finery and hair glistening with jewels. Their garments shone like a mage's spectrum: rose and violet and every color between.

Except blue.

Mel hadn't seen Cobalt again until they met at this hall and walked with their honor guard down the ranks of gathered nobles. She hardly recognized the man at her side. Gone were his rough riding clothes and armor. The snowy tunic he wore had the blue Chamberlight sphere emblazoned on its chest. His cutaway sleeves showed darker blue cloth beneath, and his trousers pulled over blue knee-boots. Sapphires and diamonds studded his belt. Seamstresses had sewn Mel's white velvet gown in only hours, with sapphires on the neckline, bodice, and train. Gems encrusted the two chairs on the dais where she stood now with Cobalt, as if they were in the icy center of a glittering, soulless gem.

The Bishop of Spheres raised his staff and spoke the formal words that invested Cobalt with the power of the Sapphire Throne. When it was done, the royal couple knelt before him, and he named them king and queen of the Misted Cliffs. Then they stood and looked out over the hall. The elite of the Misted Cliffs went down on their knees and bowed their heads to their sovereign—the same nobles who had stood by in Cobalt's childhood while Stonebreaker battered their future king.

Cobalt watched with no emotion. Mel cupped the sapphire sphere that hung around her neck and created a spell that glowed with blue light. She didn't care who saw; let them spread tales of the sorceress queen. What happened within Cobalt mattered more. But she couldn't heal his emotions. His pain went so deep, she questioned if his spirit could ever recover. He dwelled in darkness. She had already heard the whispers: the Midnight King would subjugate all the settled lands.

6

The Draped Room

The Atajazid D'az Ozar was in his study, standing by the bookshelf, when the tap came at his door. He looked to see Shade, his Master of Scrolls, in the entrance. Ozar's bodyguards flanked the archway, but when Ozar nodded they let the elderly man pass. Hunched and gaunt, Shade wore long robes patterned with diamonds of white and black. He was past the age when most scroll masters retired to an easy life in the royal court or a country estate. Shade had never expressed a desire to leave, and Ozar valued his services, for his loyalty and for his expertise in keeping Ozar's correspondence, both current and in the royal archives.

Even bent over, Shade was a tall man. Yet he came only to Ozar's shoulders. Aronsdale kings married for mage power; Taka Mal for beauty; Blueshire for love; and the

Misted Cliffs for political expediency. In Jazid, they selected for physical power. Ozar descended from a long line of sovereigns who chose queens for strength and height so they might pass those traits to their sons. They desired intelligent women, too, for the most successful warriors were also strategists. Ozar's two wives had served him well in that regard, bearing him three strong, quick sons, and also five daughters.

In matters of pleasure, Ozar preferred his concubines. He had recently bought a young one from a merchant who sold only to royalty: himself, Stonebreaker Chamberlight, and, many years ago, Varqelle Escar. Varqelle was dead now, and Stonebreaker far away, so Ozar had his pick of the best girls. He would have been with his newest right now if he hadn't had so much work.

Shade knelt with effort, his robes crinkling.

"Rise, friend," Ozar said. He was tired enough that he would have been tempted to sanction anyone who interrupted him this late at night. But he trusted Shade. If the scroll master disturbed him at this hour, he had good reason.

The older man stood as laboriously as he had knelt. "You honor me with your presence, Magnificence."

"What news do you bring?" Ozar asked.

Shade offered him a scroll. The Chamberlight sphere glinted on the parchment. "This just arrived."

Frowning, Ozar took the scroll. "Who was the carrier?" He knew of none that would disturb a Master of Scrolls this late at night rather than waiting for a proper audience the next day.

"One of your officers who lives as a fisherman on the coast of the Blue Ocean," Shade said. "He rode from the Misted Cliffs in less than a month."

Ozar raised his eyebrows. What could send his spy hurtling from the western ocean to Jazid at such great speed? He pulled off the blue cord and unrolled the scroll. It was a message sent to him only, from his officer. He read it—and read it again.

"Thunder and wind," Ozar muttered.

"Bad news?" Shade asked.

"It would seem so."

Shade waited.

"Chamberlight died," Ozar said. "His grandson sits on the throne." Cobalt Escar. The Midnight Prince was now a king.

Shade seemed to sag, and Ozar suspected that if the scroll master hadn't been in the presence of the king, he would have sat down. Ozar knew how he felt. He wanted to sit, too, after receiving this unwelcome news. Neither of them did, of course; it would have shown weakness, like a woman.

Ozar paced his study, thinking. "Do you still have the letter from Queen Vizarana in Taka Mal?"

"Yes, Your Magnificence," Shade said.

"Good." Ozar swung around. "I believe it is time I respond to her gracious request that I visit Taka Mal."

Shade said nothing. They both knew Ozar had deliberately waited to respond. Let the brazen wench stew. He could guess what she wanted: to pool resources. If they worked together, they could push Misted Cliffs merchants out of their export territory; if they combined armies, they could stand against Cobalt the Dark. The latter purpose had suddenly taken on more significance. They would be less tempting to Cobalt if they presented a united front.

So far, Cobalt hadn't given signs he intended to invade either country. Ozar had sent four hundred spearmen to Shazire during the war. Cobalt could have executed those who survived, but instead he accepted the men willing to swear him allegiance. Although he imprisoned those who refused, their captivity consisted of living on an island, and he allowed their families to join them. Nor had he executed the former royal family. He sent Zerod here, offered a truce, and apparently planned to let Zerod's wife and son join him in the Summer Isles, where the deposed prince now lived. All in all, Cobalt's actions didn't indicate a man intent on hostilities.

However, he hadn't allowed the spearmen to return home, which would have offered a better assurance. Nor had he signed any agreements beyond the truce, which had expired several months ago. Now Cobalt had ascended to the Sapphire throne. By itself, the Misted Cliffs was the most powerful country in the settled lands. Add the realms Cobalt had conquered, and it begged the question of whether he was a king or an emperor.

Ozar didn't like it. Cobalt had earned his dark reputation. He was honor-bound not to attack Aronsdale, but his thoughts were surely turning to the rich desert lands—Jazid and Taka Mal.

"It is time Vizarana and I talk," Ozar said. "I must do something about her. She sits on the Topaz Throne acting like a man, which she so very obviously isn't." Vizarana Jade was like a warrior's sex fantasy. She was also a vexation. Having to deal with her as an equal was maddening. Only by combining forces, however, could they stand up to Cobalt. The Chamberlight king might have more men and resources, but his disparate forces had never trained together as a whole and were unfamiliar with the terrain in Taka Mal or Jazid.

"She is a handful." Shade licked his lips. "You cannot deal with her as commander of the Taka Mal army. That takes the word 'unseemly' to heights beyond patience."

"Yes, well, being conquered by Cobalt Escar would be even more unseemly." He crossed his arms. "Is that cousin of Vizarana's still in charge of her army?"

"Baz Quaazera. Yes."

"Why the hell hasn't he married the woman and locked her up?"

"Apparently she refuses."

"He should do it anyway."

"She has powerful backing from her army. At the moment, more backing than her cousin."

"But not more than I do, eh?"

Alarm flashed across Shade's face. "You would force her into marriage? Surely that would start hostilities between Jazid and Taka Mal."

"Who said force?" Ozar rolled up the scroll from the Misted Cliffs. "She needs my army. I will offer it—on a condition."

Shade's eyes glinted. "She will make a beautiful bride, Your Magnificence."

"So she will," Ozar murmured. "So she will."

* * *

The messenger knelt to Mel, and a chill went through her. No longer was this someone else's darkly seductive custom; she would live this way for the rest of her life. Stonebreaker haunted her thoughts. It would be too easy to let this title corrupt her.

The man wore her father's livery, white and purple, a welcome sight. Mel recognized him as an officer from her father's army. She dearly missed her home, that place of light and laughter so different from this chilly world.

"Please rise," Mel said with warmth.

The messenger stood, his dusty travel clothes out of place in the Reception Hall, almost as out of place as Mel felt in her gown.

He spoke formally. "My honor at your presence, Your Majesty."

"You are welcome in my home," Mel said. He was young, hardly older than her. Although he was trying to appear confident, he was obviously exhausted.

"You must rest," Mel said. As much as she wanted to know what drove him here with such urgency, courtesy required she see to his comfort first. "Would you like food and drink? A place to relax and change?"

"Thank you. I—thank you." He seemed barely able to stay on his feet. "If I could just sit for a moment?"

"Yes. Of course." She indicated a sofa with cushions of white brocade with gold flowers. "Please join me."

He hesitated, looking from the pristine furniture to his dust-covered body.

"It's all right." Mel smiled. "I used to annoy my father no end by tramping around in my riding clothes and sprawling on the sofa with my boots on the table."

He chuckled, his face relaxing. "I recall him grumbling about it." He suddenly seemed to remember himself. His face reddened. "I mean no offense, Your Majesty."

"I know." She started toward the sofa, then glanced back at him. Softly she said, "None was taken."

He came after her, and they sat at a table tiled with blue circles. The shapes nudged her mage power. Without her intent, a green spell formed, and she *felt* his response to her, his appreciation for her hair, of all things.

Embarrassed, Mel cut off the spell. She touched her hair, which her sphere-maids had piled on her head and woven with sapphires. They seemed fascinated by its yellow color, so unusual in the Misted Cliffs. To cover her self-conscious response, she opened a gilded cage on the table. The sunbird inside trilled as she gently took it out. When she opened her palm, it perched there, its head cocked. Then it fluttered into the air and flew away, through an archway across the room.

The youth watched with bewilderment. "It's a summons," Mel said. "The bird flies to the Welcome Chamber. Then the staff knows to prepare a meal for this room."

"Thank you, ma'am." He looked confused, and when she smiled, his cheeks turned red.

"I will have someone show you to a suite where you can change," Mel said.

He was beginning to relax. "This is fine, ma'am."

"Your name is Lieutenant Kindler, isn't it?" When he nodded, she asked, "Did my parents send you?"

"With much urgency," he said. "They wanted to tell you—" He stopped as his gaze shifted past her shoulder. His face paled and he jumped to his feet.

Puzzled, Mel turned around. The welcoming staff shouldn't cause such a strong—

Oh. Her husband loomed in the archway, his dark hair wild, his eyes intense, his face fierce as he glared at Kindler.

"Your Majesty!" The messenger dropped to one knee, bumping the table, and bowed his head.

Mel stood up. "Greetings, my husband." Cobalt couldn't help the way he looked, but it wasn't helping her put Kindler at ease.

Cobalt stalked to the divan and looked down at Kindler's bowed head. "You can get up, Messenger."

Kindler rose to his feet. "I am honored by your presence." His voice shook, though whether from fatigue or fear, Mel couldn't tell.

Mel feared Cobalt would answer, *No you're not.* Instead, he said, "Why does my father-in-law send you with such urgency?"

Mel almost groaned. It didn't take a protocol expert to see the discourtesy in demanding information from an exhausted man, even one who had been about to volunteer it, which she had thought Kindler was going to do.

Kindler cleared his throat. "King Muller bids you welcome, Your Majesty. He sends his condolences for the death of your grandfather."

"He already did that," Cobalt said.

For flaming sake. Mel scowled at him. It was true her father had sent condolences and salutations to honor Cobalt's ascension. He showed courtesy by opening his message this way. Mel wished Cobalt wouldn't be so oblivious.

"Will you join us?" she asked her husband. Perhaps they could salvage this awkward moment.

"I'm not hungry," he said.

Mel was growing exasperated. *Oblivious* was kind. *Aggravatingly dense* was more accurate.

Suddenly Cobalt grinned, his flash of teeth lighting his usually somber face. "You have that look."

"What look?" She was painfully aware of Kindler listening.

"Like you want to send me to bed without dinner."

Her face flamed. Saints only knew how Kindler would take *that*. Tartly, Mel said, "We were going to talk, Husband."

"Oh. Well, in that case." He sat in a wing chair by the couch.

Relieved, Mel made an effort to relax. As she and Kindler resumed their seats, two maids bustled in, followed by a sunboy, a youth of about ten with hair falling in his eyes. The maids carried platters of meats, cheeses, and nuts, and a decanter of wine, which they set on the table. They bowed deeply to Cobalt and Mel without disturbing a single mote of the food. The sunboy returned the sunbird to its cage and clipped a treat to one of the bars. They all avoided looking at Cobalt.

Mel poured a goblet of wine for Kindler, her unspoken

apology for Cobalt's behavior. After the maids poured for Mel and Cobalt, they and the sunboy withdrew. Cobalt drained his goblet and thunked it on a table at his side. Mel sipped hers, and Kindler sat back, still wary in his manner.

"So." Cobalt considered the messenger. "You come from Applecroft?"

Kindler spoke in the formal cadences of Harsdown. "I do, Your Majesty. I bring you a message from King Muller and Queen Chime."

Mel waited for Cobalt to respond. She didn't think he was being deliberately rude. In his youth, he had avoided the royal court here, and though he had probably learned its ways, he was far more at ease with his soldiers than in the palace.

When Cobalt said nothing, Mel inclined her head to Kindler. "We thank you for carrying the message. What news do you bring?"

Lines of strain showed on his face. "It is your uncle Drummer." He set down his goblet. "Queen Vizarana has taken him hostage."

Mel stared at him. "What? No, that can't be."

Cobalt barely moved, just leaned forward a small amount, but his contained energy was so intense the air seemed to vibrate. Mel would never have thought the color black could be described as burning, but right now his eyes flamed with anger.

"Are you telling me," he asked, "that Taka Mal has attacked my wife's family?"

"Their emissaries claim Goodman Drummer is unharmed," Kindler said. "And that he will remain so as long as no Chamberlight or Dawnfield army marches against Taka Mal."

"Neither my father nor my cousin Jarid has ever coveted Taka Mal," Mel said. But she knew taking hostages to ensure the behavior of a rival sovereign had a long history in the settled lands. Taka Mal sought protection against Cobalt. He and her parents and Vizarana would all debate until they settled on a compromise. She hoped. She didn't want to think what might happen to Drummer if they couldn't reach an agreement.

"Surely we can help my uncle," Mel said.

Cobalt turned his fierce gaze on her. "Drummer is your mother's younger brother?"

"That's right. He's a minstrel." Mel smiled. "He likes to sing and play pranks. He's harmless."

"And well loved by your mother," Cobalt said.

Softly Mel said, "By all of us."

"That makes him dangerous," Cobalt said. "When a man is loved, those who care for him will do anything to make sure he comes to no harm."

Mel shivered. Cobalt had met Drummer only a few times, hardly enough to develop any affection for him. "We must help him."

"Taka Mal is wrong if they think they can control me by attacking my kin."

Kin. So he did think of Drummer as family. "Then you will send emissaries to Taka Mal?"

His expression darkened. "I will send no emissaries."

Mel felt as if she had lost her moorings. "No one?"

"Not for an insult this grave." His voice chilled. "I will send my army."

Drummer spent the morning playing his glittar. He did scales, practiced old songs, and composed new ones. By midday, he was restless. Bored. He resented the captivity.

After he finished his midday meal, he cleared out the parlor and laid down Kazlatarian rugs, plush and vibrant with sunrise hues. He practiced acrobatics, first warm-ups and then more intricate routines. He was standing on his head, doing splits in that inverted position when Jade entered the room. For a moment he enjoyed the upside-down sight of her gaping at him. She had on amazing clothes, emerald-green and silky. Gold jewelry glistened against her skin, and topazes sparkled in her upswept hair.

"What in a thousand journeys on the cinnamon road are you *doing*?" she asked.

"The what road?" Drummer somersaulted in the air and landed on his feet. He didn't even stumble, which usually happened on that maneuver. He felt as if he could fly. "Greetings of the afternoon, Your Highness."

"Light of the afternoon," Jade said. "It is what we say here."

"And you are." Drummer went over to her. "I have never seen you so captivating. Every day I wait for a glimpse of you."

She looked unimpressed. "Does this flattery of yours actually work on Aronsdale farm girls?"

He was challenging her, especially with words like *capti-*

vating, but it was true, too, that he savored their daily meetings. And for all that she insisted he vexed and provoked her, she always found an excuse to see him. She rebuffed his advances, yet never demanded he stop, which only made him try harder. Hot one moment and cold the next: She was tying him in knots.

Drummer came to within a step of her, closer than he had been since her first visit to his suite. "Aronsdale women can't compare to you."

Her lips quirked upward. "I fear you will write me more bad poetry."

"Bad? Never." He feared he was about to do something much worse. It would undoubtedly involve Jade and her lips and evoke more of her threats to throw him in a dungeon for offenses against the throne. The dungeon, however, had yet to materialize.

He rubbed his knuckles down her cheek. "You deserve only the best verses."

"And you have a death wish." But she neither moved nor pushed him away. Her eyes smoldered as her lips parted, and he thought he could die happy right there. Almost. He wanted even more to do alive, vital things with her. He touched her lips, and she closed them to kiss his finger. She stroked her hand along his arm—

Jade inhaled sharply and stepped back. "I am having a banquet tonight. You will attend. A bid-boy will be in later to dress you. You may keep the clothes as a gift."

Ai! She might as well have doused him in cold water. "What, you want me to dine with your court?"

"You are the brother of the Harsdown queen. It is fitting." She moved a wayward curl out of her eyes. "I also don't want rumors to spread that we are treating you poorly."

"And here I thought you wanted my company." He meant it as a joke, but it sounded angry. "What the blazes is a bid-boy?"

"Aronsdale men call them valets."

"Oh." At Castle Suncroft, they always offered him valets, but Drummer had never liked having someone else dress him. "He can just leave the clothes."

"Hmm." Jade made that one sound a commentary on his ability to make himself presentable. "We will see."

She swept out the door, leaving him alone, and he wanted to pound the wall with frustration.

"You mustn't!" The force of her own words startled Mel. She never raised her voice to Cobalt.

He stood by the heavy drapes that covered the windows. His white tunic bore the Chamberlight sphere, and slits in its sides showed blue-and-gold cloth underneath. A gold medallion hung around his neck. Sapphires glinted on his boots. It hadn't taken Mel long to realize he hated the clothes, for they made him look like Stonebreaker. In the privacy of their rooms he let down his guard enough for her to see hints of the emotions he hid from everyone else. It terrified her.

"You cannot storm Taka Mal!" She swept her hand out to accent her words. "Yes, Vizarana Jade wronged my family. But in her eyes, we have wronged Shazire and Blueshire. *We* started this. Not Taka Mal."

His face had gone thunderous. No one ever shouted at Cobalt the Dark. He walked slowly to her, tensed with banked physical power. When he looked down at her face, her heart beat hard. She saw the rage he controlled, anger at Taka Mal, yes, but also at the wife who defied him. His grandfather's death had done so much damage. The Cobalt she had loved this past year was gone, and she feared the late king's legacy of brutality would play out all over again in his tormented grandson.

Mel held her breath and her ground. She stood taller than most women, but her head didn't even reach his chin. He gripped her shoulders, and his palms covered them completely. She waited, staring up at him, hiding her fear, and hoped she wasn't misguided to trust he wouldn't shake her or raise his massive fists.

Cobalt's face contorted as if he were wrestling a demon within himself. Then he groaned and pulled her into an embrace. For a moment, she was too stunned to react. Then she put her arms around his waist and laid her head against his chest.

He spoke in a low voice. "I need to fight. I need to ride and fight until all the fury in me burns out."

She spoke with pain. "You could raze every village in Taka Mal and it wouldn't be enough. Don't make all the settled lands suffer the vengeance you cannot exact on Stonebreaker."

"His father gave him the wrong name," he said roughly. "It should have been Soulbreaker."

"But your soul survived." She drew back, against the iron

pull of his arms, so she could look up at him. "If you unleash your fury against those who have done you no wrong, Stonebreaker wins, for he has turned the good within you to evil."

"Queen Vizarana has wronged your family. And you are my wife. So she has wronged me."

"Her methods have precedent. Saints, Cobalt, you kept Prince Zerod's wife and son as hostages."

"I would never hurt them."

"As I hope she would never hurt Drummer." She had to make him see. "In taking Shazire, you gave her cause to believe drastic measures are necessary."

Cobalt frowned at her. "Shazire and Blueshire were part of the Misted Cliffs. We lost them because Taka Mal attacked us."

"Yes. Two *centuries* ago."

"What would you have me do? Negotiate when this desert queen has harmed your family?"

"We don't know she has harmed him." Mel couldn't bear to think of the possibility. "You've never met Drummer. He's a charmer. Women love him. He probably has Queen Vizarana eating out of his hand."

Cobalt gave her a dark look. "From what I have heard of this queen, it is more likely she would feed him to her tigers."

Mel winced. "Don't say that."

"Yet you would bargain with this barbarian queen?"

"I like it no more than you. But you know the history of the settled lands." He had studied it all his life and often talked to her about ancient military campaigns. "Even if what we really intend is to sneak him out of Taka Mal, shouldn't we at least appear to negotiate?"

"Historically, this abduction wouldn't justify a war," he admitted. "Not if we haven't tried negotiation. To attack now would look like an invasion, with Drummer as a weak excuse. It would give the Atajazid D'az Ozar motivation to ally with Queen Vizarana."

"I fear she is more likely to hurt Drummer if we attack."

Cobalt considered her for a moment. Then he went to the drapes and pulled them aside. Sunlight slanted into the room, limning his body. He stood looking at her, and she had a feeling he meant it as a message.

"What is it?" she asked.

"You." He motioned around at the room. "This is me."

Mel went over to him. "I don't understand."

"I am the room. You are the sun." He touched her cheek with a gentleness incongruous with his capacity for violent power. "I married you to stop a war. I never knew that war was within me."

"Ah, love." He saw himself as a sparsely furnished room, but to her he was a flame. For now, his fire was banked. But even if she had calmed the blaze within him, it still simmered—ready to erupt.

7

Chamber of the Candle

Drummer knew he was in trouble when his guards escorted him into the Topaz Hall. The size, the opulence, the incense—it was too much. This place had little in common with the reserved elegance of Castle Suncroft in Aronsdale, named for a simple croft, albeit for the sun. Here columns plated with gold supported a colonnade of arches that bordered the room. Ivory and gold tiles patterned the floor. Mosaics gleamed on the walls and pillars, accented with diamonds, topazes, and rubies. He wondered how any gems could remain elsewhere in the settled lands, for surely Taka Mal had them all here. The Topaz Hall glowed like the interior of a jewel, a vibrant explosion of wealth.

Guests filled the room, all in sumptuous dress, their silks glowing like the sunset, brocades adorned with jewels, scarves bright against the women's glossy hair. His guards wore dress uniforms with long, curved swords on their belts. Drummer had needed his valet after all; his new attire had far too many buttons and fastenings, especially the gold trousers. The white shirt was silk, and the brocade vest shimmered. He couldn't believe Jade had given him these clothes. They were worth a fortune. Real gold accented the garments and boots, also topazes and rubies. And jade. As far as he could see, he was the only one who wore the green stone. He didn't miss the implication; he belonged to the bearer of its name.

As Javelin, Havej, and Kaj discreetly ushered him across the room, people turned to look. Drummer was acutely aware he was the only person without black hair. He was like one of the sparkling ornaments, here to please the queen. The guards technically were keeping others away from him, but it didn't take a genius to see they were preventing him from going anywhere.

Musicians played in one corner and couples danced. Other guests conversed, sipping gold wine from goblets or enjoying delicacies provided by servers who circulated in the hall. No one offered Drummer food. No one attempted to breach the invisible wall his guards created. Women cast him intrigued glances and their men watched him with wary regard. None seemed hostile. Drummer would have liked to think it was because he was a guest, but he suspected it had more to do with how harmless he appeared compared to the darkly powerful nobles and warriors gathered here. Not that he wanted to harm anyone; he just felt outclassed.

His guards guided him past tables draped with snowy cloths, place settings of gold and crystal bowls full of citrus fruit. They ended their walk by a dais at the end of the hall with one table and no people. They waited at the bottom of its stairs.

A man with a tray of garnished lamb-curls hurried by. Drummer's mouth watered. He had been too keyed up earlier, even nauseous, and he hadn't wanted to eat, but now he was starving.

"Delicious," a woman's husky voice said behind him.

Drummer spun around and found himself face-to-face with the goddess who had turned his world upside down. For once in his life, his voice fled. He could do nothing but stare. Jade wore a crimson silk gown that wrapped her body and left her shoulders, arms and the upper curve of her breasts bare. The body-hugging drape had no adornment, but topazes, gold, and rubies glittered around her neck, in her hair and on her wrists. Drummer wanted nothing more than to peel that dress off her. He would make love to the queen while her creamy, dark skin sparkled with gems and her body moved, warm and sensual under his hands.

"Goodness," Jade murmured. "You do look hungry."

Mortified, he stepped back. He couldn't go far, though, with his guards around him. His face heated until he thought it must be the same color as her dress.

"I didn't have any lunch." He barely got the words out without stuttering.

She raised her hand to the dais. "Please join me."

He hesitated, confused. At Castle Suncroft, if he sat with

the queen, he would be considered her escort. That never happened, of course; she sat with King Jarid. At Applecroft, the "royal court" consisted of his sister's family and their guests eating around a big table in their dining room. He didn't know the customs here well, but he couldn't imagine it would be appropriate for him to act as Jade's escort. For all he knew, it might inspire her officers to slice him up with their weirdly curved swords.

His hesitation, however, didn't go over well with his guards, either. Kaj grasped his upper arm and pushed him toward the steps.

"All right," Drummer muttered, and went up the dais. His guards took him to a round table even more lavishly set than those below and had him stand by a chair. Jade hadn't come with them, and Drummer was even more visible up here. At least Javelin, who stood at his right, partially blocked him from view.

Although Drummer heard no announcement, guests were taking seats at the tables below. Maybe his being escorted here was a signal or part of a process where people were discreetly invited to sit down. Jade was walking with two men. The husky one wore the flashy red-and-gold dress uniform of a Taka Mal general. Ribbons and medals festooned his chest. Drummer recognized him; he had been the armored warrior in the throne room where Drummer had first met Jade. At the time, Drummer had thought he looked barbaric. He still thought so, but he realized now that the man had the classic features of Taka Mal nobility. In fact, he looked a lot like Jade.

The other man disquieted Drummer even more. Tall and leanly muscled, he gave the impression he controlled immense destructive forces he could unleash at any time. Gold ribbing accented his dark clothes. The sword at his side was straight instead of curved and heavier than those worn by Javelin, Kaj, and Havej. Drummer didn't like to think what it meant that Jade's guest came armed to her banquet. An older man walked at his side, gaunt in a white-and-black Scribe's robe that hung on his skeletal frame. He seemed thick with shadows.

With a sinking feeling, Drummer realized they were coming toward the dais, along with a handful of other military types, some in the gold and red of Jade's officers, some in gray and black. Sweat dampened his palms, but he didn't want to wipe them on his trousers or otherwise reveal his fear to these large and intimidating people.

Jade and the man with the sword were talking as they came up onto the dais. The general's face went cold when he saw Drummer. Had they been alone, Drummer thought the general might have struck him. For the life of him, Drummer couldn't think why. He was close enough to the table to use its circular shape in making a spell. He concentrated—and the general's mood hit him so hard he staggered. It also came with a picture from the fellow's thoughts, something that happened only rarely with Drummer's spells. He could have done without the image: The man wanted to heave him into a brick-lined pit and chain him to the wall.

The blood drained from Drummer's face. He didn't know what he had done to this man, but he prayed to Azure, the most powerful saint he knew, that he never faced the general without protection.

Jade glanced at him, but he couldn't read her as well. In part, it was because her reaction to him was neither as intense nor as vivid as with the general. But even accounting for that, he had trouble deciphering her mood. It made him wonder if she wasn't certain herself what she felt. More likely, he was foolish to think he could do real spells. He had never shown any consistent or significant ability. Not that he knew how to judge consistency or talent. He just played games with shapes.

Havej pulled out a chair, and Jade stood in front of it, facing the table and the Topaz Hall. If she was at midnight on a clock face, Drummer was at nine. The general stood at eleven o'clock, and the armed man at one, with his shadowed companion at two. The other officers took the other numbers. The guests below were also standing in front of their chairs, twelve to a table.

Jade looked around at them and inclined her head, a study in regal carriage. Then she settled into an ornately carved chair. The armed man sat next, then the general, then the others. In the hall below, the guests were also sitting. Something was missing, but Drummer wasn't certain what. As he took his seat, the other guests at the table glanced at him with curiosity. None seemed overly interested except the armed man, who studied him intently. Drummer wanted to ask why, but he held back. For all that he felt at sea with customs here, he knew enough to keep his mouth shut.

The armed man spoke courteously to Jade. "You have many guests tonight."

Jade tilted her head as if acknowledging a question. She lifted her hand and turned it palm up with her fingers pointed toward Drummer. "Gentlemen, may I present Drummer Creek Headwind, brother to Queen Chime of Harsdown."

They nodded as if he were one of them, which would have amused Drummer if he hadn't been so nervous. He returned their nods, aware of their curious glances at his guards. He felt like an insect under an enlarging lens in a laboratory.

Jade moved her hand to indicate the man with the sword. To Drummer, she said, "His Magnificence, Atajazid D'az Ozar of the House of Onyx, King of Jazid."

Drummer felt as if he fell twenty stories without moving a finger span. Onyx. Royalty. It seemed he was going to meet every ruler in the settled lands. He wanted only to wander and play his harp, not sit at tables with sovereigns who waged politics and kidnapping and war and looked as if they could eat him alive.

As a server poured wine, Ozar spoke pleasantly to Drummer, or at least as pleasantly as he could sound with a voice like gravel. "Have you been visiting Taka Mal for long, Your Highness?"

Highness, indeed. Jade hadn't said Drummer was a prisoner, but it had to be obvious. Onyx was mining for information.

"Over a month, Your Majesty," Drummer said.

Jade turned to Onyx as if to offer a response, which no doubt would be as smooth and as double-edged as his question. Before she could start, though, the Taka Mal general spoke roughly. "He is no Highness. He's a commoner."

Drummer froze, aware of everyone staring, not at him, but at the general. Most people knew the Harsdown queen was the daughter of an orchard keeper. Dawnfield kings and princes often married commoners. Mage gifts could occur anywhere. Personally, Drummer thought it was why the Dawnfield line remained strong and hale, unlike many other royal houses. No inbreeding.

Jade frowned at her general, and Drummer was again struck by their resemblance to each other. She was curved and feminine where he was husky and square jawed, but they had similar features, the same arrogant cheekbones, and the same wildness lurking under their civilized exterior. The warrior within Jade was manifest in her commander, who probably headed her army, given his favored position at the table. Drummer would have thought he and Jade were siblings, except Jade had no brothers. If her parents had also had a boy, he would be sitting on the throne.

"Baz, love, Drummer is our guest." Although her words were as smooth as Zanterian honey, Drummer felt their edge. But she called him *love*. Who was this Baz? Lover or relative? Maybe both. It often worked that way among the royal houses. If so, and the general knew of the liberties Drummer kept trying with Jade, it was no wonder Baz wanted to dump him in a pit.

Drummer couldn't block their moods. His spell continued from before, and emotions inundated him. Onyx had guessed his status and viewed him as a disposable tool. Jade appeared confident, but underneath she was aware of her vulnerability and striving to shield herself. She was also worried for Drummer. *Worried.* She hadn't brought him here to show him off. She was protecting him. The more people who knew he was her guest, the harder it would be for anyone to get away with hurting or disposing of him.

The rush of emotions intensified until his head reeled. Baz confused Drummer. The general loved Jade, but he had no sexual interest in her. As much as his love scraped like sandpaper, it wasn't violent. Onyx was another story. He had nothing resembling gentle feelings, only lust and brutality and an intense desire to subjugate the queen. Jade desired someone, too. Drummer felt her mood, but that didn't tell him which man inspired it. He hoped it wasn't Onyx, and he prayed it wasn't him, for these people would roast him alive if they knew he coveted their Topaz Queen.

Jade and Onyx were conversing, something about caravans, but Drummer couldn't concentrate. He had never experienced spells this powerfully before, and he didn't understand why it was happening now. The round table, the round plates, the round bases of the goblets, the cubes dangling from Jade's ears—so many *shapes*. He couldn't stop the spell, and he couldn't handle the deluge.

Drummer had an epiphany then. He had always assumed his talent was marginal. It had never occurred to him that his struggles might arise because he had too much ability, not too little. He had never learned to control it. Mages typically came into their powers in adolescence, but as far as he knew, it didn't have to happen that way. Hints of his talent had shown in his youth. Tonight, with so many people around him, his spells were surging and he didn't know how to stop them. Panic swept over him. If he couldn't contain this flood, it would drive him insane.

Jade had stopped talking to Ozar and was watching Drummer. On the surface, the atajazid didn't seem to notice; he was sipping his wine and listening to the shadowed man on his left. But Drummer knew Ozar was aware of his every move.

Drummer finally realized what was missing. Women. At the high table in Aronsdale, the king and queen sat with their family and honored guests. Here, the queen and her honored guests apparently sat with her highest-ranked officers. Onyx wouldn't bring his wives; no one ever saw the Jazid queens. Jade was isolated, afloat in an unwelcoming sea where the sharks felt she had no business swimming and vied for the right to tear her apart. No wonder she had never married; it would be like leaking blood into the water. Either she would have to get out then, or suffer the consequences. After a month of dealing with her every day, though, he had no doubt anyone who thought he could control her was deluded.

Vertigo surged within Drummer. He put down his fork and tried to quell his nausea. Jade motioned to someone, he couldn't see who. Then Captain Javelin leaned close and spoke in a low voice. "Are you all right, Goodman Headwind?"

"I'm…dizzy." Drummer doubted they would take him seriously if he said his spells were out of control.

"Would you care to retire?" Javelin asked.

Drummer could have closed his eyes with relief. He didn't, though, not when everyone could see. He just said, "Yes, that would be good."

Javelin must have communicated with Jade, for she nodded. No one else was paying much attention except Baz, and Drummer doubted the general would regret seeing him leave. As Drummer stood up, the other guests turned curious gazes his way. He bowed to Jade and Onyx. He had no idea if that was proper, as at Castle Suncroft, but they would attribute anomalies in his manners to his coming from Aronsdale. Jade inclined her head and smiled, though he felt her underlying worry. Onyx asked her a question, and she turned back to him. With relief Drummer left the explanations to the queen.

Mercifully, his guards didn't take him past the other guests. Instead, they went to a wall behind the dais. Havej pulled aside the heavy drapes to reveal a door shaped like the lock for a skeleton key. After they left the Topaz Hall, the voices and music receded, and Drummer no longer *felt* as much. He was aware of his guards' moods, but there were only three of them and they didn't have strong emotions now, just boredom and some concern for him.

They took him to an antechamber deep within the palace. Oil lamps glowed within glass flowers set into the ivory walls. The scrolled moldings around the ceiling and floor pleased the eye, as did the goldwood furniture. The chamber contained a chair, a bed, and nothing with a pure shape except for a little round table. The last remnants of his spell faded.

Grateful, he lay on the bed. He felt as if he had been tossed in a flood and washed up on a beach. Not only was he no longer hungry, he doubted he could keep anything down. He didn't intend to sleep, but as soon as he closed his eyes, lethargy settled over him....

"Come on," the dusky voice coaxed. "You don't want to stay all night in these stiff, scratchy clothes, do you?"

What he didn't want to do was wake up. However, the voice kept at him, and after a while he comprehended that it was Jade.

Drummer opened his eyes. He had sprawled across the bed on his stomach. Only a candle on the table lit the room. His guards were gone and the door closed, probably locked. Jade was sitting next to him, her hip against his elbow. She still wore her red silk dress, and in the candlelight, her creamy skin glowed.

"Greetings," he murmured, unsure if he was awake. This sensual vision of Jade had to be a dream. He rolled onto his side and reached up to trace his fingertips along her cheek. So soft. She took his hand and set it back on the bed—but she didn't release his fingers. So he lay there, gazing at the queen in the candlelight, and held her hand.

He wondered if she had any hint how lovely she looked in the dim golden light. "How long have I been here?"

"Most of the night. It is two hours beyond midnight."

"I'm sorry I was such a poor dinner guest. I don't know what happened." He couldn't tell her about the spells. People in Taka Mal believed magecraft was quackery or else thought mages perpetrated only evil. Jade would probably think he was crazy.

She touched his arm. "You look better now."

"Much better." Drummer stroked her fingers. So long and elegant. He wanted to kiss them. "Where are my guards?"

"I sent them outside." She hesitated. "For a Topaz Pact."

"Pact?" He looked up at her face and her full lips.

"A pact with Topaz. It means an agreement with a person who stands in representation of the throne. In the Misted Cliffs, they call it a Sapphire pact. In Harsdown, the pact is with the Jaguar. Here it is with Topaz. Me. If you agree."

Drummer had never heard of such a thing. Not that he had ever listened much. During his visits with Chime and Muller, he usually fell asleep or slipped away when they talked of politics.

"What do I have to do if I agree to this pact?" he asked.

Amusement flickered over her face. "Nothing, beautiful singer. Just stay put."

"Beautiful, eh?" He wouldn't argue with that. "I like your Topaz Pact."

Her smile softened her face. "I'm glad. Then I won't ask the guards to come back in."

So. She wanted to be alone with him. A slow smile came to him. "You're a lot better company."

She was silent for a moment. Then she spoke in a neutral tone. "Ozi has offered me a pact."

"Who?"

"Ozi. The atajazid."

He couldn't imagine anyone daring to call the Jazid king

"Ozi." Then again, Jade wasn't just anyone. "What did he propose?" As soon as the words came out, he winced. "Sorry. I didn't mean it to sound like that."

"Like what?"

"A marriage proposal."

"It was."

His drowsy contentment fled. He sat up abruptly, taking her other hand as well. "You told him no, didn't you?"

She went very still. "I have given him no answer yet."

He was suddenly aware of how close they were. He didn't stop to think; he just bent his head and kissed her. She stiffened—but this time she didn't push him away.

Drummer held her hands and took his time kissing her, savoring the warmth of her response. Finally he lifted his head the barest amount. "Think about that when you make your decision."

"You mustn't touch me," she murmured. But she showed no inclination to slap him this time. Even so, he knew he was insane to take such a liberty. Baz would flay him alive for touching her, and saints only know how Ozar would react. But he couldn't think straight around Jade. What rationality he had to start with, which many declared was little indeed, fled.

Drummer pulled her close and filled his embrace with her voluptuous body. She tensed as if to pull away. But something had changed. Maybe it was the wine, or the jeweled night, or just the right time, but she relaxed against him, her body pliant. He held his breath, afraid if he moved, it would startle her into a retreat. As much as he had pursued her these weeks, deep inside he had believed that she, a queen, would always reject him. Yet desire had simmered within her at the banquet, and now she was in his arms.

He laid his cheek against her head. Her hair slid against his skin, soft and perfumed. Bending his head, he searched until his lips brushed hers. Then he froze, sure she would object. When she parted her lips instead, he groaned and deepened the kiss, urgent rather than tender. He slid his hands onto her shoulders, gauging how much she would accept. Waiting for her protest. She put her arms around his neck and kissed him more.

The night felt like a spell, unreal, an enchantment within a filmy soap bubble that would pop if he thought about it too much. He peeled her dress all the way down to her waist, and still she didn't protest. With her body pressed against his, he felt her heartbeat speed up. He held her breasts, and his control slipped for the second time that day, but this had nothing to do with mages, except that ageless spell woman had woven over man since the first humans walked the settled lands.

They stretched out on the bed, side by side. He tugged at her dress, and her hands wandered his body, fumbling with his clothes. It took a while to take his off and much less time to unwrap her silk. Finally they lay with bare skin on bare skin. He wanted to caress her tenderly, and he wanted to shove her down and impale her body. He rolled her onto her back and eased between her thighs. Then he buried himself in her warmth, and she pressed against him with her hips. He knew he could be signing his death warrant if Baz or Ozar found out what he had done. But he couldn't have stopped even if the palace were collapsing around them.

With the candle guttering in the dim light, a minstrel from Aronsdale loved the queen of Taka Mal. No dalliance this; Vizarana Jade had taken his heart.

Topaz Mage

Clouds churned in the vast sky above Harsdown. It wasn't raining enough to soak anyone whose garments were slicked with wax. The wind and moisture exhilarated Mel as she raced Smoke through the rare summer storm. She felt more at ease in her riding breeches and thick shirt than in all those lovely gowns she wore at the Diamond Palace. She let Smoke gallop for the sheer joy of it, and her hair streamed in the gusting air. Cobalt came alongside her on Admiral, riding with her in the wild day, and Mel felt closer to him than she had since they had learned of Stonebreaker's illness.

Eventually the horses spent their pent-up energy and slowed down. Cobalt also seemed calmer, as if he, too, had needed the release. The rest of their party caught up:

Matthew and General Cragland; Kindler, the messenger
from Harsdown; and thirty warriors in an honor guard. Most
of the guard had kept pace with Cobalt and Mel, but far
enough away to give them privacy. Now, as everyone slowed
down, they gathered into a tighter group.

It was late afternoon on their fifth day in Harsdown.
The sun behind them stretched their shadows in long silhouettes. They were heading toward the Boxer-Mage
Mountains that separated Harsdown from Aronsdale.
What they sought lay at the base of those mountains in
a fertile dale, and with every step closer, Mel's spirits
lifted.

"Look!" She pointed down the long slope ahead of them.
In the distance, endless rows of pear trees spread out, rich
with the verdant foliage of early summer.

"Come on!" Mel urged Smoke into a gallop, and he took
off with renewed energy. Cobalt raced with her down the
slope. When they plunged into the familiar rows of trees,
Mel didn't know whether to laugh or cry. She reined in
Smoke, and the horses walked through the misty orchard
while the storm rumbled above them.

It took over an hour for them to come out of the trees.
They rode into a grassy field in front of a farmhouse with
many wings, arched eaves, and round windows with glass
pictures of apples and pears. The house was built from sunbask wood, warm and golden, so vivid it seemed to glow in
the wet, overcast day. Mel didn't know how she looked, but
Cobalt's face gentled as he watched her.

"Welcome home," he said.

* * *

Mel's parents met her in front of the house, her mother crying as they hugged, her father putting his arms around them as tears wet his cheeks. The bustle of people soon filled Applecroft. They couldn't all fit inside, so the Chamberlight honor guard set up camp in the fields, and Mel, Cobalt, Matthew, and Cragland stayed at the house. Mel's father also had a company of his own army stationed around the orchards. It was the trade-off they made for living in a farmhouse instead of a castle; they had to have men guarding the house and lands. The Fortress of Bones was only a few minutes' ride from the house, however, and protected the village of Granite. If necessary, the royal family and the villagers could retreat within the stone walls of that keep.

Mel's reunion with her parents was bittersweet, filled with the joy of seeing them but also with the knowledge of the crisis that brought them together. Her mother and father looked alike with their yellow hair and blue eyes, but more gray showed at her father's temples than Mel remembered. He was forty-seven, nine years older than her mother.

Mel had never known a man who enjoyed fine clothes as much as her father. He was impeccable in his tailored trousers of gold suede, his amber-suede knee-boots, elegant white shirt, and the gold vest with fastenings imported from Jazid. Her mother wore blue leggings under a tunic with fluttering layers of silk. Her parents were beautiful, she supposed, but that didn't really matter to her. She knew many exquisite people who were cold inside. The Misted Cliffs were full of them. She loved her parents for the warmth of their hearts and their unconditional love.

Before dinner, Mel went in search of Fog. She found her cat curled up on her parents' bed, obviously in command of the room and probably the house as well. Mel scooped him up in her arms. He gave a mew of protest and squirmed until she set him back on the bed. Then he sniffed at her hand and rubbed against her fingers, purring as he welcomed her into *his* house.

That evening, they dined at the big table. Afterward, they withdrew to the study: Muller, Chime, Mel, Cobalt, General Cragland, and Sphere-General Fieldson of Harsdown. Mel thought it strange to see the two generals in the same meeting. Had she and Cobalt never married, Cragland would have fought Fieldson when Varqelle invaded Harsdown to regain his throne. Yet now they sat as allies. Neither looked comfortable with the situation, but they kept their reservations to themselves. They were cut from the same cloth: rugged and intelligent, with a natural ability to lead.

Cobalt asked Matthew to sit in on the meeting. As stable master at the Castle of Clouds and a horseman for decades, Matthew had a natural instinct for strategy that involved horses, and he understood cavalry with an expertise few could claim, including most career officers. Mel suspected Matthew was also the only person in the meeting Cobalt fully trusted.

They sat in wing chairs or couches drawn into a circle, with sunbask tables between their seats and glasses of mulled wine. Candles on the mantel and tables shed golden light. Night had fallen, the time to retire, but this meeting was too important to delay until morning.

Mel could see her parents' fatigue. In the past year, her father's role as commander of the Harsdown forces had demanded more and more time, as he and his cousin Jarid trained their armies together. They called their efforts exercises, but everyone knew they were building a military capable of standing against Cobalt. Muller also had his other duties as king of Harsdown. Chime carried some of those responsibilities and ran the orchard, but it was a demanding life even in peacetime. With Drummer's abduction added to the mix, it was no wonder they were exhausted.

No one wanted the houses of Dawnfield and Chamberlight to go to war, but the tension in the study tonight gave mute witness to the lack of trust between their leaders. Mel sometimes felt as if she were a cord stretched between the two, one constantly pulled, twisted and strained until she felt as if she would snap.

"We must negotiate with the House of Quaazera," Chime was saying. "Otherwise they might hurt him."

"We all wish to see your brother free and well," General Cragland said. "But we cannot buckle to the demands of those who seek to control us."

Mel noticed how he addressed Chime with respect even though she had been his enemy during the war, nineteen years ago. People tended to like her mother. Chime had been wild in her youth, full of mischief, or so Mel had heard from her grandmother. Since then, Chime had matured into the leader who had spent the last two decades developing programs to help impoverished farmers and bee tenders in Harsdown learn techniques that would increase their output and better their lives.

"How much military training does Drummer have?" Matthew asked. "If we can get him out of there, can he ride a horse?"

"A bit, I believe," Fieldson said. "No military experience."

"He's impulsive," Chime said. Wryly she added, "He doesn't always show the best judgment."

Mel spoke the fear that had gnawed at her since they received the news. "They won't torture or execute him." She made it a statement, but they all knew the question in her words.

Fieldson shifted in his seat and Cragland averted his gaze. Even Matthew wouldn't look at her.

"We'll have him back soon," Muller said. His gentle tone hurt, for Mel knew what it meant. He couldn't give the answer she wanted to hear.

"If they harm Drummer," Cobalt said flatly, "we harm them."

Matthew scowled at him. "Wage war against Taka Mal, and we make Jazid our enemy as well."

"I have seven thousand men," Cobalt said. "Taka Mal and Jazid combined have little more than six."

"More than numbers matter," Fieldson said. "Your forces combine two disparate militaries, Shazire and the Misted Cliffs. The armies of Jazid and Taka Mal are more used to working together. They also know how to fight in the desert. Yours don't."

Mel thought of her sword practices with Cobalt's officers. She noticed differences in her training and theirs, and the training in Shazire differed even more. "We need to consider weapons, too. Shazire is less well equipped than most armies, with older swords and bows, less durable than our more modern weapons."

Cragland nodded, his face thoughtful. "That won't be true of Taka Mal or Jazid, though. They consider fighting an art."

Cobalt settled his gaze on Muller. Mel knew what he was about to say, and she wanted to shout her protest.

"If Harsdown and Aronsdale join forces with us," Cobalt said, "we would have an army unlike any ever seen in the settled lands. Twelve thousand strong. Discrepancies in training and equipment would become trivial."

Muller considered him. Mel knew that, decades ago, people had questioned her father's ability to command an army, not because he lacked training or intelligence, but because they saw his graceful, almost pretty appearance as weakness. But Mel knew him as a seasoned leader who inspired confidence, and she saw it in his unwavering gaze as he regarded Cobalt. Generals Cragland and Fieldson were taking each other's measure, and Mel could almost feel them wondering what would happen if they combined their armies. She felt the heady power in that idea. No one would stand against such a force!

No. *No.* Cobalt seduced her with his thirst for conquest. How many would die for his unquenchable need? It would never end. If the armies of Dawnfield and Chamberlight defeated the armies of Quaazera and Onyx, who would rule the new empire? Not so long ago, Dawnfield and Chamberlight had bitterly opposed each other. Mel's marriage had given them a truce, and Drummer's abduction pushed them together as wary allies, but she could never imagine either giving way to the rule of the other.

Muller finally spoke. "I will not ride against Taka Mal."

"And if Queen Vizarana executes Drummer?" Cobalt asked.

Chime rose to her feet and faced him, slender and pale in the candlelight, a wraith compared to his might. "As far as we know, Drummer is alive. We must negotiate. We must do everything we can to bring him home." Her voice shook. "Alive."

"We won't let them hurt him," Cobalt said.

"But if they do, despite our best efforts—" She took a deep breath. "I will personally argue your case for combining your armies with ours."

He went very still. "You would support such an alliance?"

Her normally melodic voice hardened. "If they kill my brother, then you destroy them."

"Mother, how could you do it?" Mel kept her voice down, even out here in the stable, away from the others. "Do you have any idea what you could unleash by saying that to him?"

Chime regarded her with a bleak stare. A lamp hanging on the wall flickered in the otherwise dark stable. Horses stamped in their stalls, and the smell of hay saturated the air.

"They took Drummer because he was the easiest to grab," Chime said. "He's my brother, and that made him a target. It's my fault."

Mel couldn't believe her *mother* had evoked Cobalt's darkness. Of all the people she thought posed a danger to the unstable peace their countries managed, she would never have included Chime.

"It's not your fault that they took Drummer," Mel said. "You can't blame yourself for their misdeeds." She went over to Chime. With a start, she realized she was taller than her mother. Before she had left, they had been the same height. Mel knew most Headwind women didn't finish growing until her age, but it still unsettled her to be taller than her mother, as if the proper order of things were reversed.

"He never grew up," Chime said.

Mel knew she meant Drummer. "He's happy. And harmless."

"He's a beautiful singer." Chime wiped away her tears before they had a chance to fall. "Sometimes I want to tell him to shape up. Then he looks at me with those big blue eyes and I just can't."

As a child, Mel had loved Drummer's pranks, tickled by his irreverence. As an adult she could see his lack of judgment. Saints only know what trouble it could bring him now. She prayed he used more wisdom in his dealings with his abductors than he had done with his life in Aronsdale.

In their meeting tonight, they had discussed many options. Cragland wanted to send spies to free Drummer. Fieldson thought they knew too little about the Topaz Palace. He proposed sending an envoy to hear out Vizarana Jade. They could scout the palace and give any rescue attempt a better chance of success. Cragland thought it would tip their hand and the queen would guess their intent. Muller wanted to at least appear to negotiate, lest the House of Quaazera become impatient and take drastic measures.

They had finally decided Fieldson would take a company of thirty Chamberlight and Dawnfield men to Taka Mal, supposedly to negotiate. Cragland would choose fifteen of Cobalt's honor guard, and in return Muller would send fifteen Dawnfield men back to the Misted Cliffs with Cobalt, as an act of good faith.

Chime wanted to go to Taka Mal. Mel wanted to go. Muller wanted to go. Cobalt wanted to take his entire army. Mel knew those weren't the best choices, but it ate away at her that she could do so little.

"He'll be all right," Mel said, as much to reassure herself as her mother. "He could soften up even Taka Mal's iron queen."

"That's what I fear," Chime said. "Then what, after he trespasses against the House of Quaazera?"

It was a good question. Mel didn't have an answer.

Be wise, Uncle, she thought. *Be wise.*

Drummer awoke alone. The candle had burned down, and someone had set a glazed basin and a pitcher next to the stump. Jade was gone. He lay on his stomach, thinking about her. How could she be so tough in public and so soft in bed? Maybe that was why she put up a shield with everyone; her softness was her vulnerability. One mistake and she could lose her throne.

His contented smile faded. One mistake. Him.

Drummer groaned and rolled over, throwing his arm across his eyes. What had he been thinking? What if she told Baz or that shadow-on-shadows king of Jazid? Baz would probably want to do a lot worse now than just chain Drummer in a pit.

She won't tell. He couldn't bear to believe anything else. Surely she knew what would happen if she revealed the truth. Nor would it go poorly only for him; she would endure censure as well, from Baz, from Ozar—

No! He swore vehemently, remembering, and sat up fast. Ozar had *proposed* to Jade. She couldn't marry that sadist. Besides, he already had a wife. Two, in fact. Surely that was enough. It wasn't even legal in other settled lands.

"Not with Jade, you don't," he muttered.

He felt nauseous. Maybe he needed food. He went to the table and found the pitcher full of water. Soap carved into a dragon rested by the basin. He didn't have a razor to scrape off his stubble, but his beard had never been heavy, and it was blond, so it didn't show much yet. He washed up and dressed, trying to look civilized. Then he tried the door. To his surprise, it opened.

Outside, a hall stretched out, ivory and topaz, with arches that framed the corridor. Arched doors, all closed, appeared at intervals. Drummer hesitated in his doorway. Despite its elegant decor, it was obviously a cell. Had they forgotten to lock him in? Perhaps Jade had sent away his guards. This could be a trap.

He stepped into the hallway. No one appeared, so he headed toward the hall where they had held the feast. When he thought of all the food he had missed, his mouth watered. It was hard to believe a few spells had so overwhelmed him. Last night he had imagined he might wield exceptional mage powers, but in the light of an ordinary day, he felt foolish for harboring such thoughts. Surely someone would have noticed by now if he was a powerful mage. Not that he had ever made spells for people; they just seemed to happen, especially lately.

A memory came to him. He had been dozing in an easy chair during a visit with Muller and Chime and overheard them discussing Mel's mage talent. Apparently it had been taking a long time to mature. Nor was it only spells. At seventeen, Mel had still been growing. It was a family trait. Chime hadn't reached her full height until eighteen. Drummer had been twenty-four. With things taking so long, he had hoped he would be tall. But no, he ended up average for Aronsdale, below average in Taka Mal, without the husky build his father and older brother enjoyed.

Maybe what he lacked in bulk he had in mage power. His assumption that men couldn't be real mages was based on what he heard from other people, but none of them were mages. He wasn't even sure what qualified as a "real" mage. Those he knew best were Chime and Muller, and neither had ever said he couldn't be like them. If it had taken him so long to grow, perhaps it had also taken his mage abilities a long time.

Drummer had lived his life like a leaf floating on the

river, drifting from year to year. His abduction had jolted him in many ways; perhaps that stirred up his mage abilities. Historians claimed the powers developed as a means of survival among his people. If that was true, it would make sense that his responded when he felt his survival threatened.

The Topaz Hall was empty, its tables cleared, its floors swept and the musician stand gone. No hint of last night's festivities remained. Unfortunately, that meant no food, either. He found a pitcher of water and slaked his thirst, but that was it. Beyond the hall, he encountered two maids carrying linens and giggling with each other. They quieted as he walked past, and one smiled. He didn't understand why Jade had left him to wander. For all he knew, he could find a horse and leave. If he could manage; he hadn't paid good attention when his father had taught him about riding. He knew how, but he had wanted neither the expense nor the responsibility of owning a horse. In Aronsdale, he had either walked or bargained for rides in someone's cart.

After last night, though, it was no longer so easy to consider leaving. He didn't know what to think. Maybe it had been a dalliance for Jade, before she took the politically expedient action of marrying the Atajazid D'az Ozar. Even Drummer, who made it his business to be apolitical, could see the advantages of such a union. Although never enemies, Jazid and Taka Mal had never been strong allies, either. But they had reason to unite against Cobalt. And here Drummer was, a hostage for Cobalt's good behavior, as if the Dark Prince were capable of good behavior.

Neither are you, Drummer told himself. If he thought Jade would throw away all that power so she could have him, he was an idiot. She had used him last night, and if he was lucky, she wouldn't tell anyone. Nothing held him here.

Drummer didn't want to leave his glittar, but he couldn't risk returning to his rooms where someone might catch him. He had no idea where to find the stables. He roamed through a maze of arches, pillars and corridors until he came out into a courtyard. Five children were playing chase around the fountain that burbled in its center. When he entered, they all stopped to stare at him.

"My greetings," Drummer said cheerfully. They clustered together and watched him with wide eyes.

He slid his hand over his vest and secretly ripped a topaz off the cloth. Then he strolled over to the children. "What do you have there?" he asked the oldest boy, a fellow of about nine.

The boy tilted his head. "What did you say?"

Drummer had a hard time understanding his accent, which he suspected worked two ways. He spoke more slowly. "There." He indicated the boy's ear with his right hand, letting the children see his palm. The topaz was hidden in his shirt cuff.

"Nothing!" the boy said.

"Are you sure?" With his palm closed, Drummer let the topaz slip into his hand. He reached behind the boy's ear and touched the skin. Then he withdrew his hand and opened it. The topaz glittered in his palm. "You're sprouting gems."

"Hai!" The boy gave a whoop. "How did you do that?"

Drummer grinned. "They must grow with your hair."

One of the girls giggled. "Sparklies don't grow in hair."

The children all gathered around Drummer. A thought came to him, spurred by the circular fountain. He wasn't certain how to make spells; usually they just came to him. But it seemed to work when he thought of shapes. He held his palm open to the sky with the topaz sparkling in its center.

"Behold!" Drummer said with a flourish. He concentrated on the shape of the fountain.

Nothing.

The children waited, earnestly trying to behold something. Feeling foolish, Drummer wondered what he had done wrong. Maybe the fountain wasn't a pure shape. Looked like a circle to him, though.

"It feels good," one of the girls said.

Drummer blinked. He did feel good. Healthy, glowing, awake, refreshed. Of course. Orange spells eased pain. Since none of them were in pain, it just made them feel better. It wasn't a particularly dramatic effect, though.

He offered the topaz to one of the girls. "Can you hold this for me?"

She took it with special care. "I won't let anything happen to it, Your Highness."

Highness? They thought he was a prince. He supposed it was a logical assumption given his clothes and unusual coloring. They probably figured he was visiting from Aronsdale. Which was sort of true, though it hadn't been his idea to come here.

Drummer pulled a big ruby off his vest. It was probably worth a small fortune. Balancing it in his palm, he focused on the fountain. He thought of red things, apples and strawberries and blushed cheeks. Red spells made light—

A column of red light shot up from his hand.

"Saint Rose almighty," Drummer muttered, stepping back. The light came with him, connected to the gem in his hand. He didn't want to drop his arm for fear the light would strike the children.

"Look at that!" one of boys whooped, while the others oohed and aahed in appreciation.

Drummer stared up at the column. "Stop," he whispered, terrified. His palm was heating up. He curled his hand around the ruby and the heat intensified. With a gasp, he dropped the gem. It clattered on the ground and the light vanished.

The children scrambled for the ruby, and one scooped it up.

"Don't touch it!" Drummer cried.

"Do more!" a boy said. Another shouted, "Do that one again!"

He took a shaky breath. Apparently the gem was harmless again. He spoke carefully, so they would understand his Aronsdale accent. "I'm afraid I can't this morning. I have to go."

With undisguised disappointment, they gave him back the topaz and the ruby. A small girl looked up at him. "Will you visit again?"

"I hope so." For the first time, he wondered what it would be like to have a child like that. He looked around at them all. "I was hoping you could tell me how to find the stables."

Most of the children looked uncertain, but the oldest boy said, "I don't know how to say. But I can take you there."

Relief swept over Drummer. A child guide was the perfect solution. The boy wasn't likely to get Drummer in trouble, and if people saw an adult with a child, they were less likely to be suspicious than if he were wandering around on his own.

Drummer swept a deep bow to him. "Thank you."

"Can we come, too?" one of the girls asked.

"Not today," Drummer said, smiling and looking apologetic.

The girls giggled and ran off, but not before Drummer overheard one whisper to another, "He's handsome."

His guide rolled his eyes. "Girls."

Drummer chuckled. "Just wait a few years."

The boy took him into another wing of the palace, keeping up a stream of chatter. They were, Drummer realized, in a servants' wing. The boy's clothes were well-made, nicer than any Drummer had worn at his age, but they weren't extravagant, which suggested his parents were on the palace staff. It could explain why the boy hadn't hesitated to be his guide. He wouldn't challenge someone he believed was a prince. Discretion and accommodation protected one's livelihood; Drummer knew that principle well, after having followed it most of his life. He suspected the staff here knew a lot more of the palace goings-on than most people realized.

He didn't want his guide to get into trouble for helping him. When the boy took him outside, into a lane between this wing of the palace and a wall, Drummer drew him to a stop. They stood in the arch of the doorway.

"How much farther is it?" Drummer asked.

The boy motioned to where the lane curved around the palace. "Just after you turn the corner."

"I can find it from here." He gave the boy a conspiratorial look. "Listen, I have a secret for you."

"A secret?" His gaze widened. "What is it?"

"Princes aren't supposed to do magic tricks."

"Why not?"

Drummer tried to think of a reason. "It scares people."

"Why?"

"They don't understand it, I guess."

"That's dumb."

Drummer laughed, though he wasn't so sure it was funny. That last spell had shaken him. He could have burned himself. When his niece Mel had visited Aronsdale last year, she had confided in him that her legendary spell at the Battle of Alzire had been only light, without heat. That had been a large spell, one much more demanding of power than his pillar. Apparently on a smaller scale, he had enough power left over to make heat.

"Will you make me a promise?" Drummer asked. "You're a grown-up fellow. I can trust you."

The boy drew himself up straight. "Certainly, Your Highness."

"Don't tell anyone you saw me or that I did spells."

"I won't."

Drummer clapped him on the shoulder. "You're a fine fellow."

After his guide ran off, Drummer walked up the alley and

turned the corner. A courtyard lay ahead of him, and stables lined its outer wall. Grooms, stable boys, light-bringers, and hay-sweepers bustled with their work in the yard. A man with a rake was passing the alley. Seeing Drummer, he froze, his face startled. Then he knelt, the rake held awkwardly in his hand.

I have to get out of these clothes, Drummer thought. He was drawing too much attention. Neither Chime nor Muller expected people to kneel to them. Aronsdale was more formal, though, and people knelt to royals at the court there.

"Please rise," Drummer said, copying the tone he had heard King Jarid use.

The man stood up, his gaze averted. Drummer wasn't sure how to act, so he just said, "Please proceed."

"Thank you, sire." The man walked on, and Drummer let out a breath, hoping he hadn't made mistakes. The fellow hadn't seemed any more certain of what to do than Drummer, which made him suspect they didn't often see visiting princes here. If he went to the stables like this, people would notice. But he had no other clothes, and the longer he spent figuring out what to do, the more chance his guards would discover he was gone. They might already be searching for him.

Well, so, he might as well brazen it out. He drew himself up and strode toward the stables.

A stable boy ran out to meet him. "Can I get your horse, Your Highness?" He was a youth of about fourteen.

"No thank you," Drummer said. "I can manage."

The boy kept running alongside him. "I can help."

It occurred to Drummer that the fellow might hope to get a reward for helping him. Well, Jade had said these clothes were his, and the gems were on the clothes. It seemed he was, rather suddenly, quite rich.

"Very well," Drummer said. "I require a horse. One I might purchase to take home with me."

"To Aronsdale?" the youth asked.

"Yes, that's right," Drummer said. "How did you know?"

"Your hair."

"Ah." He needed a hat, too, if he was going to slip away unnoticed. It didn't worry him too much that the grooms or stable hands saw him, but he was concerned about the army officer talking to a sweeper by the first stable. Sweat gathered under Drummer's collar. As the boy led him over, the officer glanced up. Drummer nodded to him and went inside the stable, aware of the officer watching him. Did he suspect Drummer was a prisoner rather than a guest? Drummer's guards knew, obviously, as did Baz. Others at the banquet might have guessed. Or maybe they had just thought he was strange, given the way he had disappeared.

Inside, the air was rich with smells of hay and manure. The youth led him past many stalls, some empty, others the home to gorgeous horses, Jazidians, the most coveted breed, sleek stallions with glossy black coats. The "smaller" mares were larger than warhorses native to Harsdown and Aronsdale. It was an advantage Jazid and Taka Mal had over other armies: stronger, faster, smarter horses. Jazidians were exorbitantly expensive, though, which was why few people owned them. Drummer had seen some at Suncroft, but they hadn't filled the royal stables the way they did here.

The boy stopped at a stall. "This one, Your Highness."

Drummer stared at the horse. "Yes," he managed to say. "He will do." He hoped he could ride it, because it was the most glorious animal he had ever seen.

"His name is Vim," the boy said.

"Vim, eh?" Drummer eyed the horse. "Does that mean he's full of energy?"

"He's a steady one, Your Highness. One of our best."

Drummer grinned at the boy. "Thank you, then."

The youth led Vim out of the stable, earning annoyed glances from the grooms, who probably wanted first shot at attending Drummer. At Suncroft, the staff had an established hierarchy, and grooms were higher than stable boys. Drummer had no doubt he was breaking unwritten rules here, but he had no time to figure it out. The officer was watching him, and Drummer didn't want to give the fellow time to decide to intervene.

As the boy saddled Vim, Drummer looked up at the horse. It was big. Really big. How would he get up? Well, yes, he knew how to put his foot in the stirrup, but he had never done it with an animal this size. He wasn't dressed to ride, he had no supplies, and he was probably insane, but if he planned on escaping, he had to go before someone realized he was loose—and before Baz or Onyx figured out he had taken liberties with the queen. The worst of it was, if she asked him to stay, he would do it. He was a fool.

Drummer turned to the boy. "Well done, young man." He

knew the youth believed he was taking Vim for a trial ride and would return to discuss his purchase with the stable master. Drummer had no intention of coming back, but he didn't want to steal the horse. Although in his younger days, he had snatched fruit from the market, he had outgrown that spate of misbehavior. He had a rough idea how much a horse cost, having watched Muller haggle for animals, but a Jazidian was worth far more than workhorses.

Drummer took the topaz and ruby out of his pocket and handed both to the boy. "Give the ruby to the stable master, as payment for the horse. You may keep the topaz."

The youth stared at the gems with his mouth open, which made Drummer wonder if he had underestimated their worth. He put on a stern face. "You will see that the stable master receives that ruby."

"Yes, sire! I will." The boy held up the topaz. "Is it really for me?"

"Of course."

"But it's so much."

"Well, you could get me a tier-stool." Drummer coined the last word on the spur of the moment.

The youth squinted at him. "Sire?"

"For getting on the horse," Drummer said. "We use them in Aronsdale." He hoped the boy knew too little about Aronsdale to realize Drummer had made it up.

"Ah!" The youth beamed at him. "Of course. Right away."

Drummer blinked. Maybe he hadn't made it up after all.

The boy ran off and soon returned with a three-legged stool. Drummer used it to swing up on Vim, and the horse nickered. The stable boy had chosen well, though; Vim controlled his energy and responded to Drummer's touch on the reins. It was a good thing, because Drummer didn't doubt the horse sensed his uncertainty. He held the reins stiffly, aware of the powerful animal under him. He was so *high*. The youth was watching, as was a groom walking horses in the yard and the officer by the stable. Striving to appear nonchalant, Drummer rode toward the gate. Mercifully, Vim obeyed his directions and trotted out, headed into Quaaz.

9

Ocean and Desert

"Gone?" Baz stared at Jade, and she thought she might incinerate under the heat of his anger. "How in a flaming dragon's hell could he be *gone?*"

"He seemed sick at the banquet," Jade said. "Apparently he was healthier than we thought."

Baz stalked back and forth in her library, a cozy room with bookshelves, windows, a globe of the world in one corner, and an abacus on the table. Jade kept the table between her and her incensed cousin and wondered how she could have been so stupid as to believe Drummer would honor a Topaz Pact. He had said he would stay put and she believed him. She was a fool. He used trickery as old as the human race to get past her guard, and she had fallen for it like a lovesick idiot.

Of course she hadn't left his room guarded while she

slept with him. She couldn't risk anyone knowing she was there. She should have locked him in when she left, made it a cell instead of their love nest. But the unlocked room had a long history in the settled lands. It spoke of trust, particularly in situations such as this. That was the Topaz Pact she had offered Drummer last night: the hostage agreed to stay put and the host agreed to treat him as a guest instead of as a prisoner. Drummer had accepted. Then he threw it back in her face.

She couldn't tell Baz. He would want to know where she got the idea that Drummer would honor such an oath. If her cousin ever found out what she had done with Drummer last night, his anger would outdo even the mythical flames of the Dragon-Sun.

Maybe if she had told Drummer his family was sending an envoy to negotiate his release, he would have trusted her enough to stay. No, she couldn't make excuses. He had betrayed the pact, and even worse, he did it after making love to her. She had always hesitated to let any man close, wary he would covet her title. In her youth, she had felt crushed by the hostility of those who thought she had no right to the throne. Baz had supported her with the military, as had her father's top officers. She learned from them, learned from everyone. Over the years, she had even developed affection for her three contentious generals, Firaz, Slate, and especially Spearcaster. But always she balanced on an edge. One misstep and she could topple from power.

Drummer hadn't been one misstep—he had been an entire march of them. A misjudgment of colossal proportions.

What did he think to accomplish, riding off with no equipment, no maps, no plans? She didn't want to care what happened to him, but she couldn't help it. He was going to get himself killed.

"He has spent a lot of time in Aronsdale jails," Jade said, dredging up what her spies had discovered. "He probably learned how to pick locks and escape cells."

"Then you should have guarded him more closely."

She had no argument with that. "We'll find him."

"We had better." He strode to the door. He stopped, though, before he opened it. Facing away from her, with his hand on the knob, he said, "Have you thought on Ozar's proposal?"

Jade had no desire to marry Ozar. But they needed his army if they were to face Cobalt Escar's growing dominion. She spoke carefully. "I may not have explored every alternative."

Baz turned, his hand on the knob as if he were prepared for a quick escape. "Marrying him would be an abomination."

Jade hated the thought of Ozar touching her, especially after the sweetness of her night with Drummer. Not that she was thinking about Drummer, curse his fickle soul.

"We need Ozar's army," she said.

"We had another option with Cobalt." He growled the words. "Now our option has stolen a Jazidian stallion and ridden away."

"He didn't steal it." Drily she added, "In fact, he overpaid."

"For the sake of the winds, Jade. He tore a ruby off his clothes. It belongs to you."

"I gave him the clothes." Another weakness on her part, lavishing gifts on her deceptively beatific guest.

Baz's expression darkened as if he were a thundercloud. "Why such an expensive gift?" He was so angry, he almost spat the words. "What did he do to earn such a treasure?"

"Stop it, Baz."

"What did he do?"

"Nothing." It was true; at the time, he hadn't yet been in her bed. "We kidnapped him. Then I insisted he dress up and let us put him on display so people would know I wasn't mistreating him. The least I could do was give him the clothes we made him wear. It was a gesture of good faith."

"Such terrible hardships we've inflicted on him," Baz said, "forcing him to wear magnificent clothes and attend a sumptuous feast. What evil shall we commit next? Give him one of our most valuable horses? We are truly vile people."

"Oh, stop."

"My men have probably found him by now," he said. "And saved his irksome hide from dehydration in the Rocklands."

Jade hoped so. She dreaded having to face Drummer, but it would be far worse if the envoy from Harsdown arrived and discovered the House of Quaazera had lost their queen's brother.

The hill known as the King's Spring was green with the first days of summer. Mel rode down behind the Diamond Palace, past the spindle trees, narrow and tall, that grew only in the Misted Cliffs. She was in the King's Fields, a large tract of land where supposedly no one ventured without the king's permission. In theory, she didn't need bodyguards here, so she had tried to send them away. They came with her anyway, but at least they were discreet enough to give her the illusion of being alone.

Twenty days had passed since she and Cobalt had returned from Harsdown. She would have liked to stay with her family until they heard about Drummer, but it could take as much as two months for the delegation to reach Taka Mal, negotiate, and return. Cobalt had duties to attend, and he had asked Mel to come back with him. That he asked instead of trying to order her mattered a great deal to Mel. So she had come.

In the countryside below the hill, she gave Smoke his head, and he galloped through fields dotted by starflowers. The air smelled of honey-dust blossoms. Spindles stood by the path like sentinels, and she passed groves of heliotrope trees, heavy with blue-green foliage. Her maids had told her that soon a profusion of purple fruit would hang from the branches, helios, sweet and tart at the same time. Until Stonebreaker's illness, she had never visited this part of the country. The land was beautifully strange, so much more lush than Harsdown.

The path changed, more sand mixing with the soil. Up ahead, hills spiked with reed-grasses hunched beside the road. Mel heard a new sound, a low rumble. She reached the top of a hill—and reined to an abrupt halt. Before her, the grasses petered out into sand dunes and then into a primeval beach; beyond that, the Blue Ocean roared into the shore.

Waves reared up, crowned with froth, then curled over and crashed on the beach.

Mel stared, unable to move. She had never been this close to an ocean before. Her trance broke when Smoke whinnied with impatience. Inhaling deeply, she took in the salty scent of the ocean. She nudged Smoke forward, and he picked his way along the path. It occurred to Mel that she didn't know if horses were supposed to walk in sand. Smoke didn't seem bothered, but she slid off anyway and walked along with him. Her boot heels kept sinking into the sand, so she took them off and rolled her leggings to her knees. As they neared the water, a wave swirled up the beach and around her feet. With a snort, Smoke backed up a step.

"Sorry," Mel said. "You stay here." She offered him an apple she had stashed in a pocket of her tunic. He gave a forgiving snort and chewed contentedly. Mel knew him well enough to trust he wouldn't wander away without her.

Mel walked to the sea. She didn't know whether to be afraid or fascinated by its rhythmic power. Water splashed her ankles. She went deeper, and it surged around her knees, making her stumble, splattering foam against her body. She stopped then. The receding water dragged at her legs like a spirit trying to pull her under. Much farther out, a wave towered at the height of two men. So wild and beautiful. The ocean was an enigma, as were her mage gifts. She had come to the privacy of this wild place hoping to learn more about both riddles—the sea and her power.

She opened the pouch she carried over her shoulder and lifted out her sphere. Tadimaja Pickaxe, a palace aide in

Shazire, had personally selected the metal for her. Blacksmiths had tooled it to be as perfectly round as possible, and it shone with the iridescent sheen found on a smear of oil after the rain.

Over the past year, Mel's abilities had developed in fits and starts. If she pushed a spell too hard, her head ached, her vision swam, and her heart beat too fast. She didn't understand why it hurt. Her mother had never been that way. But each mage did spells in her own unique style. Chime was among the strongest adepts in the settled lands, a green mage who could draw on a twenty-sided ball. A few years ago, Mel had thought she would also be a green, with a faceted sphere as her highest shape. Unlike most mages, though, who had finished developing by her age, Mel continued to grow in ability. Only Cobalt knew, and he didn't understand. However, each time she pushed hard, the spells were a little less of a strain and her recovery a little faster.

Mel thought of the blue spell she had made for Cobalt. If she really was a blue-sphere adept, she would be the strongest mage alive after her father and Jarid. But her father needed flawed shapes, which created flawed spells. Historians thought that the Dawnfield mages had bred the trait into their line thousands of years ago, creating a weapon. After centuries of dormancy, it had manifested in Muller. He had no wish to harm his family or his people, so he rarely performed spells. Mel knew even less about Jarid, only rumors of his immense power.

Mel had no mages here to help her learn. If she told her parents, they might send their mage mistress, Skylark, but that would leave them without her advice at a time when a mage's input was important in training the army. And Skylark was too elderly to travel. Mel thought it better she manage on her own, though at times she felt like flotsam tossed in the tumultuous seas of her nascent abilities.

Mel stood gripping the sphere while the ocean splattered her with froth and seaweed. She focused on the colors of the water, green and blue, and imagined her power rolling in waves, surging in force but then retreating again.

A blue light glowed around the sphere. Mel concentrated, letting her spell build and recede....

Ebb and flow...

Ebb and flow...

The rhythm became part of her, hypnotic. It eased the strain, for each time her spell built, it receded. At its highest point, her head ached, but then the spell eased. She closed her eyes and the spell flowed through her. Gradually, she became accustomed to the high points. Just as she warmed up before she practiced swordplay, so now she warmed up her spells.

Ebb and flow...

Ebb and flow...

Higher...

Higher...

Mel opened her eyes—and froze.

Blue light filled the beach. She hadn't even realized she had backed out of the water. Birds cawed overhead, soaring through the spell. Smoke stood nearby, and crabs had crawled out of the sand or water to gather around her. All glowed blue. The light saturated her, not just soothing, as would an orange spell, but giving health. In the past, a spell this powerful would have exhausted her. But she felt good. Ready for more. A little more.

Except she tried a lot more.

"Indigo," Mel murmured, though it was beyond her—

Indigo light exploded around Mel. Agony shot through her head and she dropped the sphere as she fell to her knees.

"No." Mel pressed the heels of her hands against her temples. Tears gathered in her eyes. "I'm sorry," she whispered to the animals that surrounded her. "I'm sorry."

Smoke nickered and butted her shoulder. Bleary-eyed, she peered at the horse. He seemed serene. The crabs scuttled away, and the birds sailed in circles that took them farther out on each circuit. That incredible burst of power may have hurt her, but it had done no other harm she could see. Legends said indigo spells healed emotional pain. Her father never tried, for he feared his flawed spells would create despair rather than heal anyone.

The sorrow that had plagued Mel since the war last year remained. Fear for Drummer still filled her heart. But... somehow, incredibly, it had become more bearable.

"Papa," she whispered. "You gave me your power." From her mother, she had inherited the ability to make pure spells with pure shapes. Her parents had each given her the best of themselves.

More had happened with the indigo spell, though. Mel felt...extended.

Too extended.

Her head swam and her sight dimmed.

With a sigh, she collapsed onto the beach. Darkness closed around her, replacing her colors with nothing.

The Tapered Desert had a stark beauty unlike any place Drummer had ever imagined. It was a world of red and gold stone. Rock spires rose from the earth instead of trees, and the land buckled in terraces the size of hills. When he rode along the top of a ridge, he could see for leagues in every direction. The astringent quality of the air exhilarated him. He had always thought of deserts as parched, but this one was full of oases, spots of green that flourished around water holes or rivers.

He followed a caravan trail. Vim ran easily, putting the city of Quaaz behind them with gratifying speed. Drummer kept expecting to see Baz's soldiers in pursuit. He doubted they could catch Vim, but he couldn't run the horse for too long, lest he hurt the magnificent animal.

His clothes chafed and his legs ached from riding. His muscles weren't toughened up for this. He needed to stop, to buy food, water, a map if possible. He wished he could wait out the day's heat in a shaded place, but he feared every lost second. He would find somewhere to hide after sunset. He doubted he would sleep much, but neither he nor Vim could go all day and ride at night, too, without rest.

He crested a ridge and looked down at a village on the other side. Tents clustered around one of the creeks that kept this part of Taka Mal habitable. He descended the ridge, riding warily from terrace to terrace, uncertain how the people would respond to a foreign visitor, apparently wealthy but without bodyguards. Were he wandering Aronsdale as a minstrel, he could charm the locals with song. He doubted a singing prince would inspire much confidence in Taka Mal, though. Far easier to knock him over the head and steal his clothes and horse. He didn't even have a sword. Not that it would help much. He didn't know how to use one.

As he neared the town, he realized it had no permanent buildings. Just tents. Even dusty and worn, they were beautiful, designed from dyed canvases, mostly red and gold, also some blue. Their peaked roofs overhung their walls. Tassels hung off the roofs and dangled in the wind, woven with sparkling threads.

Drummer rode down a lane of tents. Families had set up campsites, but in the heat of midday, none had fires. A few people sat in the shade or stood in tent entrances, with the flaps pulled back to let in air. It looked like a nomads' village, temporary and easily moved. The men and the women wore similar clothes, billowing trousers dyed blue, red, or brown, with colorful shirts and vests. Their garments were well kept, and a gleam of jewelry showed here and there. They looked healthy, a bit thin but not starving, which he hoped meant they were less likely to attack a seemingly rich stranger. He nodded to the people he passed and they nodded back, but no one smiled or greeted him.

He soon saw why the nomads were here. They had set up a market along the riverbank and were doing thriving business. Customers probably came from leagues around to bargain and socialize. Near the market, he dismounted and led

Vim. The first thing he needed, after food and water, were clothes that wouldn't draw attention. People flowed past him and watched with veiled curiosity. Women smiled. In the past he would have flirted in the hopes of charming a kiss later, but it was no longer a game. After Jade, he had no interest in anyone else. Men rarely saw him as a threat as long as he left their womenfolk alone. His pale coloring and slender build made him look harmless compared to these weathered, toughened hulks. He had never thought much before about how anyone viewed him, but his life now could depend on his ability to put people at ease.

He strolled with Vim along a row of produce stalls, and his mouth watered. Fragrances of spice, oil, and baked goods wafted out from an open stand of yellow-white wood. As soon as the merchant saw him looking, he called out, "I've fresh bread with cinnamon from the Mazer Narrows, my lord! It will charm your lady and sweeten your dreams."

Charm his lady indeed. Drummer doubted anything so simple could beguile Jade. He went over to peer at the breads and pastries, some steaming, probably fresh out of the oven in the stall. Drummer was salivating so much, he had to swallow. He hadn't eaten since yesterday afternoon. He hadn't wanted food earlier, with his stomach so queasy, but now he felt famished.

"It looks edible," Drummer allowed.

"Edible?" The baker, a husky man with a black mustache and large belly, sounded scandalized. "You won't find any better, not even at the palace itself." He beamed at Drummer. "Seeing as you're such a fine gentleman, I'll give you two full rolls." He indicated his succulent loaves of spice-and-butter bread. "Plus a pastry, all for only two gold tinars."

Drummer almost spluttered. Two tinars could buy this entire stall. The baker probably thought he didn't know Taka Mal coinage, since he obviously came from another country. Not that it mattered; he had no coins of any type.

"That's ridiculous," Drummer said. He pretended interest in nearby stalls, as if searching for better prospects than the baker's woefully overpriced goods. He actually had another purpose in mind.

"Do you know the other merchants here?" Drummer asked.

"My lord," the baker said with dignity. "I have superb bread. Better than anything else you will find." He waved his hand dismissively at the other stalls.

"I'm not going to give you even a little piece of a tinar," Drummer said. "Not for two clumps of bread and a pastry."

The baker stared at him with dismay. "You wound me greatly." Then he added, "But I will let you have them for one tinar."

Drummer was tempted to laugh. The fellow was audacious in his extortion attempts. "I could eat better bread at home for free," he said, which was true. No one could bake like his mother. He didn't visit his parents often, though, because they were always urging him to settle down, get married, and make them grandparents. They were very specific about the order of marriage and then babies, which made Drummer think they feared he misbehaved even more than he actually did. He was no innocent, but neither had he wanted to mislead women into believing he sought a permanent tie. His dalliances rarely went farther than kisses and cuddling. Until Jade, when he had lost all his sense.

He shifted his weight, playing the bored nobleman with nothing to do. "Of course, I'm not at home right now."

"My delicacies are just out of the oven," the baker said. "So much more interesting to eat here, eh, than someplace you see all the time."

"Perhaps." Drummer stood as if considering his wares. "I'll tell you what." He pulled a gold cord off his shirt cuff. "I will give you this for a certain trade."

The baker's eyes gleamed. "What might that trade be?"

"Talk to your cohorts here." He indicated the stalls around them. "Provision me for three days on the trail, plus get me good riding clothes that won't stand out." Drummer held up the gold. "For that, this is yours." He was overpaying, if the gold was as pure as he thought, but it was worth it if the merchant would bargain while Drummer stayed out of sight.

"How do I know that's real gold?" the baker asked.

"It is." Drummer held it out on his palm so the baker could examine it. When the man tried to pick up the cord, Drummer snapped his hand closed. "After I get my provisions."

"Done!" the man said, fast enough that Drummer suspected he could see exactly how much the gold was worth and wanted to agree before the bored lordling changed his fickle mind.

"How long to put everything together?" Drummer asked.

The merchant checked his timepiece, a scuffed watch on a copper chain. "I can manage in an hour."

"Too long," Drummer said. "Fifteen minutes."

"Fifteen minutes! I can't wrangle what you need out of these thieves that fast. Forty-five."

"Thirty," Drummer said.

"Thirty. Who can do anything in thirty?" The merchant sighed, but he also looked smug. "All right. Thirty."

"Good. I'll be back then." Drummer broke off part of the cord and set it in front of the baker, between the spice-butter loaves. "For a loaf. If you have everything I need in thirty minutes, the rest is yours."

"My pleasure, sir." The baker picked up both loaves and wrapped them in a white cloth. "Take both. My compliments."

"My thanks." Drummer accepted with more gratitude than the baker would ever guess, and then he moved away, leading Vim. He couldn't slink off to hide, lest a thief slink after him and cut his throat where no one could see. But he didn't want attention, either. He stopped once to buy a battered watch, which he paid for with a little copper cube from his vest. After that, he wandered with Vim along the edge of the market, visible but out of the crowds. He kept his wits, which he had cultivated over the past ten years, and twice he outfoxed pickpockets who tried to steal jewels off his clothes. He knew the moves, having tried them himself a few times in his youth. He had spent several nights in jails as a result, but now his savvy kept him awake and aware.

The bread tasted heavenly. After half an hour, he returned to the baker's stall. True to his word, the fellow had purchased him supplies for three days' travel, also travel bags and sturdy but nondescript clothes. He accepted the rest of Drummer's gold cord with enthusiasm, gave him all the directions Drummer requested, and effused at great length, bidding Drummer a pleasant trip.

When Drummer finally escaped, he found an outcropping of rock down the river from the market and hid behind it to change his clothes. He was soon on his way, his fine garments folded in his bags, his saddle covered by a threadbare blanket, and his yellow hair tucked into a worn cap. Although he obviously had a superb horse, he had otherwise disguised his identity, the wealthy and foreign visitor. It hadn't been a real identity to start with, but that was who Baz and his men would look for.

Drummer rode west, toward the infamous Taka Mal Rocklands.

10

The
Misplaced Minstrel

"Come back," the man said. "You must come back. I cannot do this king business without you."

Mel turned over, heavy and cold. Sand scraped under her cheek. Groggy, she opened her eyes and peered toward the voice. Her husband was crouched next to her, his hand on her shoulder. Her bodyguards stood behind him, and also Smoke, his coat sweaty.

Cobalt sat down and lifted her into his arms. He unfolded his legs so he could hold her body against his chest with his arms around her in an enveloping embrace.

"Cobalt," she muttered against his vest. "Can't breathe."

"Oh." He loosened his arms. "I seem to do that a lot."

"What happened?" she asked.

"Smoke came home without you. So did two of your

bodyguards. The other two stayed here, with you, after you collapsed. I rode Smoke back."

She thought of the sweating horse. "I must tend to him."

"I'll do it."

Mel closed her eyes. Nausea was bothering her, and she had to swallow the bile in her throat.

"You must stop these spells," Cobalt said darkly. "They do terrible things to you."

"I'll be all right." Softly she added, "I don't think I've even reached my limits." Such astonishing mage discoveries. Could she really be an indigo? She was a Dawnfield, as were the only other two indigos. But it seemed too incredible.

"I don't like it," Cobalt said.

"It is a good thing." She paused. "I think."

His arms stiffened around her. "You think?"

She nodded and just that slight movement caused her nausea to surge. With a jerk, she pulled away, leaned over his leg, and lost her breakfast into the sand.

"Mel!" When she finished, he spoke in a low voice, more to himself than to her. "Must tend my wife."

Her lips twitched upward. "You make it sound like I'm a horse."

"Mel." He actually sounded relieved to hear her tease him.

He buried the evidence of her illness, then carried her a ways down the beach and laid her down. Smoke and her bodyguards stood over her while Cobalt went to the water. As Mel sat up, her guards tactfully moved back. Cobalt strode into the waves, pulled off his shirt, and dunked it in the sea. He came back in his loose undershirt, a half-dressed king with his wet trousers plastered to his well-muscled legs. Warmth pooled within Mel. Saints, but this husband of hers was pleasing to look upon.

He gave her his wet shirt, and while she cleaned herself up, he wiped down Smoke with reed grasses. By the time he finished, she was standing again and felt stronger.

Cobalt scowled at her. "No more spells."

"I cannot stop doing them."

"They hurt you."

"Truly, Cobalt. I just need sleep."

"I've never seen you be sick that way."

"I've been feeling queasy," she admitted.

"Queasy?" He froze like a stone-bird, which hid by not moving. "In the morning?"

"Morning? No, the afternoon—" She stopped, realizing his real question. "Oh. No, I'm not pregnant."

"More than one moon-cycle has gone by since your last time."

"It has?" That gave her pause. "Are you sure?"

He was watching her with the oddest expression, as if she had grown an extra arm. "You must see Velvet."

Mel wasn't ready to be pregnant. "Who's Velvet?"

"The midwife at the palace. Come! We must hurry."

She smiled at his frazzled expression. "It takes nine months, love. A few more minutes won't matter."

He was already swinging up on Smoke. "Ride behind me."

Mel glared at him. "It's my horse. You ride behind me."

"What?"

She suspected that if she went on about what she believed customs in the Misted Cliffs symbolized about the subjugation of women, Cobalt would either stare at her in bewilderment or get annoyed. So she just said, "Help me up. In front."

He helped her swing up, and she straddled the horse. Cobalt had changed the saddle to a riding blanket, probably realizing they might have to ride together. He put his arms around her as if she were breakable pottery, which she thought was exasperating and endearing, given how hard she had been training lately to develop her upper-body strength and her ability to fight on horseback.

They headed back to the palace to find out if the Sapphire Throne would soon have another heir.

Drummer saw the soldiers when he was on a ridge above the Tapered Desert. Seated on Vim, resting under an overhang, he looked across the land he had traveled earlier today. Twenty men were crossing the tawny desert in a dispersed formation that covered a wide area. If he didn't get moving, they could catch him before evening. He had left no trail on the slabs of rock, which made it harder to track him, but he would be easy to spot on these ridges. To stay hidden he would have to slip from cover to cover, which would slow him down.

He shaded his eyes from the glare. His body hurt from all this unfamiliar riding. He felt worse than yesterday, and he hadn't even reached the Rocklands yet. Sweat soaked his clothes. He had planned to hide up here and sleep during the afternoon heat, but that was no longer an option. It would take him days to reach Aronsdale, and he had no guarantee Baz's men wouldn't pursue him in his own country. They had kidnapped him from Aronsdale once before. He had to go now, as fast as he could travel.

He spent the rest of the day sneaking from outcropping to outcropping, slinking through the lengthening shadows. It wore him out, and he was covering less distance than he would have even if he had slept through the heat and then ridden in the open later in the day. His water was low and he feared he wouldn't reach the next oasis before he ran out. Supposedly it wasn't far beyond these buckled ridges, but if the baker's directions turned out to be faulty, he would have no leeway with his water.

With the sunset flaming in the west, he finally crested the last ridge and looked down the other side. The Rocklands of Taka Mal stretched out before him, sere and flat. Stark. Gray. Foreboding. But a line of green on the western horizon marked the waterway he sought, the Saint Verdant River.

When he started down the other side, he was no longer in view of the searchers, so he rode in the open and made better time. Even with that, the sunset had cooled to embers by the time Vim reached the Rocklands. The moonless night darkened the land, and Drummer had no torch. He kept going as long as he could, but as the darkness deepened, Vim began to stumble. They had to stop; otherwise, he might cripple the horse. Miserable, he guided Vim off the trail and into an eerily jagged forest of rock spires.

It didn't take long to find a hiding place in the cavities among the spires. He walked Vim into a ragged cave and did his best to rub down the horse, check his hooves, and otherwise care for him the way his father had taught him. After he gave Vim the last of his water, he hunched on the ground and pulled the saddle blanket around his shoulders. The temperature plummeted when the sun went down; he shivered even when he wore both his riding garb and the clothes Jade had given him.

In the distance, a blackwing called out its haunting, cruel song. Drummer huddled against the wall and wondered how he would make it to morning with no water, no food, and no warmth.

Cobalt had never been comfortable in the parlor outside the suite where Velvet saw patients. He didn't belong in this female room. He feared he would break the delicate furniture or porcelain vases. He had almost never come here; just a few times to keep his mother company while she visited Velvet for whatever reason. Today he sat on the edge of a flowered divan, feeling oversize and brutish. At least the midwife had admonished his bodyguards to keep anyone else from visiting until she finished with the queen. No one else waited in the parlor. Only Cobalt. The king. The nervous king.

After an eternity, the inner door opened and his wife appeared. She stood there with her yellow hair tousled to her hips, freed from its braid. He thought perhaps he would keel over from nerves. He couldn't bring himself to ask what he wanted to know, so he said, "Where is the midwife?"

"I wanted to talk to you alone." Mel came and sat by him.

"And?" He was too tense to say anything more.

Mel watched him with an expression he recognized. Affection and amusement. He never understood her views of him, only that he somehow liked them even when they seemed unflattering. Which made no sense. Nothing about loving Mel had ever made sense.

"What?" he asked. "Why are you looking at me like that?"

"I've seen you in combat," Mel said. "I've seen you fight for your life and battle murderous highwaymen. In all those times, I've never seen you look so nervous."

"Mel!"

Her face gentled. "Yes."

"Yes?" His heart beat hard. "Yes what?"

Softly she said, "Yes, you're going to be a father."

He felt as if the room were spinning. "Saints almighty."

"It startled me, too." Her smile curved, full of mischief, the look of hers that spurred him in the night. "But given how 'friendly' we've been, it isn't that much of a shock."

Cobalt couldn't smile. He couldn't do anything. In fact, he was having trouble breathing. With a lurch, he roused himself and jumped to his feet. He had to escape. He strode away, across the room, until a gilt table blocked his way and he had to stop.

Mel came over and put her hand against his back. "Cobalt?"

He would shatter. A father. His boyhood memories were

a nightmare of violence, both physical and emotional, of fear he would be beaten or locked in the closet or whipped with the same royal belt his valet had tried to put on him yesterday. The valet hadn't understood why Cobalt yanked the belt from his hand and hurled it across the room. To that valet, the new king had surely seemed violent, harsh, even crazy. He didn't know what that belt had done to a small boy cowering on a stone floor. Cobalt would never forget. Stonebreaker had forged him into a monster, and now Mel wanted to give him a child. He would die before he inflicted himself on a small, helpless human being.

Mel had her most unbearable expression, the one full of compassion. He loved it desperately, and it terrified him, for he didn't deserve it. He always feared he would lose control and hurt her, and she would leave him. To have her love was painful, for when he loved her, he became vulnerable to losing her.

She was watching his face with those eyes of hers that saw far too much. With tenderness, she said, "You will be a wonderful father."

"*No.*" He spun away and strode across the room. The door was closed. He wanted to hit it, not in anger but in *fear.* He yanked it open and strode outside.

Cobalt didn't know where he went. Walls passed in a blur. He kept going, up narrow stairs, back stairs, seeking a place to hide from himself. He finally came to a balcony that circled a watchtower. He clenched the rail and looked out to the Blue Ocean and the beach where he had found Mel earlier, lying in the sand.

Cobalt didn't know how long he stood there staring and seeing nothing. Gradually he became aware he wasn't alone. He turned and found her a few paces away, watching him, one hand on the rail, the wind tugging at her clothes and hair. His wife, the mother of his heir. He, the false king, would become a father.

Mel spoke quietly. "You aren't Stonebreaker."

"I am what he created."

"You are a good husband and you will be a good father."

He remembered the things she had said during his campaign to reclaim Shazire. "I thought you considered me a warmonger."

"I never called you that." She paused. "Not exactly."

"You certainly implied it. Quite eloquently."

Mel came over and took one of his hands. "I didn't agree with your decision to invade Shazire and Blueshire. But I do not think you are a warmonger." Lifting his hand, she pressed the back of it against her cheek. "No matter how much you insist otherwise, I think you will be a wonderful father."

He rubbed his knuckles against her soft cheek. "You would have more luck convincing me I could pull clouds from the sky."

"But look." She motioned at the beach. "The fog comes in."

The fog was indeed rolling in from the ocean. He sighed, stymied by her refusal to see the truth. "Mel, when you look at me, your vision is clouded." He drew her near, holding her hand between their chests. Then he told her something he would admit to no one else. "I am afraid."

She held his hand tightly. "I, too."

"You're really going to have a baby?"

"Really. Probably a little less than eight months."

"A boy, do you think?" He blanched. "What if it's a girl, and she is like you? I will be the most henpecked man alive."

She laughed softly. "If it's a boy, I will be surrounded by people who grunt at me."

Cobalt embraced her, his head bent over hers. He was still afraid, but the knot had loosened enough for wonder to soak into his heart. The Sapphire, Jaguar, Alzire, and Blueshire thrones—and any others that became his—would soon have an heir.

His child.

Baz came to tell her about the disaster.

It was late afternoon, and Jade was in her study with the city builders going over plans to extend the aqueducts that brought water into Quaaz. Ozar's visit had slowed their work, but now her coercive suitor was gone and she had a great deal of business that compelled her attention.

Baz, however, compelled attention even better than aqueducts. He strode into her study in the middle of the meeting, holding his helmet under his arm, his uniform dusty from riding, and his face flushed by the sun.

"Your Majesty," he said crisply.

The moment he entered, Jade went as tense as a coil. "What happened?"

He spoke bluntly. "We've sighted the Harsdown envoy. They will be here tomorrow morning."

Jade stood slowly, her hand clenched on her stylus. "And Drummer?"

Sweat beaded on Baz's temples. "My men haven't returned."

The stylus snapped in Jade's fist. She looked down with a start, then let the pieces fall on the table. If the envoy discovered Drummer wasn't here, they would have reason to assume the worst. Jade doubted they would believe he had betrayed a Topaz Pact and run off. They would assume she was trying to cover up reprehensible acts carried out against the brother of their queen.

Her aqueduct team sat still and silent, their gazes going from Baz to her. Jade spoke with an even tone that belied the tumult of her thoughts. "We will have to reconvene tomorrow. My scroll master's clerk will arrange a time and let you know."

"Certainly, Your Majesty," the head of her team said. They all rose to their feet and bowed.

When Jade and Baz were alone, she spoke without preamble. "We must get Drummer back."

"I never expected him to last this long." Baz shifted his helmet restlessly from hand to hand. "He has no experience traveling in these lands."

"He makes his living as a wandering entertainer. He'll be fine." She spoke more to convince herself than him.

"Aronsdale is not the Rocklands." His scowl darkened his face. "When we get him back, I swear, I will personally see—"

"Baz," she warned. "We want our guest alive and well."

The thought of Drummer traveling alone in the Rocklands shook her deeply. That journey had killed far more seasoned travelers.

"And if we don't get him back?" Baz said.

"If he reaches Aronsdale, we lose our negotiating tool."

"We will look foolish if he outwits us."

"Better he outwits us," Jade said grimly, "than he dies and the envoy takes it as an act of war."

"My men have been out for three days," Baz said. "Even if they catch him tonight, they won't get back until at least a day after the envoy arrives."

"We will put off the envoy."

"And if we can't?"

They both knew the rumors, that Cobalt coveted Taka Mal and Jazid. So far he hadn't shown signs of attacking, perhaps because he wasn't the relentless conqueror of his reputation—or perhaps because he wasn't ready. He knew he would have a hard-fought war if Taka Mal and Jazid joined forces.

Jade grimaced. "I may have to marry Ozi."

"Only in a flaming hell!" Baz clunked his helmet on the table. "Ozar knows our countries can't stand against Cobalt if we don't unite. You think he will refuse the alliance if you refuse marriage? You are a lovely woman, cousin, but I doubt he considers you worth losing his throne."

"No, he doesn't. He wants mine." Her anger flashed. "Ozar is gambling with me. He wants to see how high I will push the stakes. If we do it his way, combining forces, we may dissuade Cobalt from war regardless of what happens with Drummer."

Baz was looking at her oddly. "Is that the only reason you would join with him?"

She frowned at him. "What other reason would I have?"

"If you marry Ozar and your armies vanquish Cobalt Escar, you could become the queen of Taka Mal, Jazid, Shazire, Blueshire, and the Misted Cliffs."

Jade stared at him. It was a heady thought—and dangerous. She could envision such an empire, but she also knew Ozar would never stop trying to break her spirit. She longed for something far simpler than those grandiose dreams— something much farther beyond her reach. Happiness.

She couldn't imagine achieving that goal.

Marry Ozar, go to war, lose her throne, lose Drummer. She loathed her choices but she saw no others.

The Tawny Barrens

Drummer slept fitfully through the night. Knowing he had no water, he couldn't stop thinking about his thirst. At first he felt chilled, but then he felt as if he were burning up. As soon as the sky lightened, he was up and about, preparing to leave. His body ached. Muscles hurt that he hadn't known he possessed. His thighs were chafed raw, and he couldn't walk with his legs completely straight. The last thing he wanted was to get back on Vim. But he needed water and food, and he wasn't going to find them if he didn't escape this eerie landscape of jagged stone.

As he saddled Vim, the horse stamped and snorted angrily. Drummer spoke soothingly. "I'll get you food and water soon. I promise." He walked Vim to a shelf of rock and stepped up on the flat area. It took a while to settle the horse, but finally Vim let him mount. Drummer groaned as pain stabbed his muscles. Then he rode out into the predawn murk.

When Drummer reached the caravan trail, he headed west. A dark line rimmed the horizon, the greenery he had seen yesterday. A river should be there and settlements where he could purchase supplies. He hadn't expected it to be so far. In Aronsdale, with its swells and dips, he never saw a distant horizon, just the next ridge or valley. Things were closer. Here, the open sky and endless, barren land bewildered him. He obsessed over the distant greenery and its promise of water. Water and food. Water and rest. Water and…water.

He mentally shook himself. He needed to think. It wouldn't be long before Baz's men came over the ridges Drummer had crossed yesterday. From the top, they could easily see these flatlands. He had nowhere to hide. He would have to be so far ahead they couldn't catch him before he reached cover. Normally Vim could probably outrun most any horse. But nothing was normal this morning. Without food, water or enough sleep, neither he nor Vim could last long. And he felt as if he were burning with fever.

Drummer leaned over Vim's neck. "I'm asking a lot, I know. But I need for you to give me everything you have."

Vim snorted, but he did speed up. They galloped through the cool morning. As the sun rose behind him, the day heated up. He wished his spells could conjure water, but he couldn't create something out of nothing. A red spell could only provide light or heat, which he needed right now about as much as a mallet to the head. Orange and yellow soothed pain, but they didn't fix anything. Green spells were useless here. In fact, he saw little use in them at all. Knowing how people felt just got him in trouble. Were he powerful enough to make a blue spell, he could heal his injuries. In his current condition, he would be lucky to manage even orange. He had to try, though.

He needed a shape. Weary, he rummaged in his bags until he found the clothes Jade had given him. The faceted gems were flat compared to true shapes, but a little cube dangled off the vest. A larger cube would give more power. If he remembered correctly, though, the shape determined the strength of the spell more than the size. Chime claimed that invoking three-dimensional shapes was as far beyond most mages as scaling a mountain in one jump. He didn't see what mountains had to do with it; that sounded like one of his sister's daft ideas from their childhood. He knew she was greatly respected by her people, but he remembered the tomboy he had chased through the orchards.

"It can't be that difficult," he told Vim. He had used cubes in the past, after all, to enhance his interaction with his audience.

He considered the small cube in his palm. "Red."

Nothing happened.

Drummer imagined red light—and the cube glowed.

"Ha! Chime was wrong." He wasn't certain, though. Chime was usually right about mage matters. But if that were true, then he was a more powerful mage than he had ever imagined.

Drummer tilted his head, considering. Gold was a shade of orange, the color of soothing. He imagined gold light. Nothing visible happened—but the ache in his legs receded. Although he knew it was there, it no longer bothered him as much.

"Think I can do blue?" he asked Vim. Chime said that was even beyond her. He had managed the cube, though, so maybe he could also manage blue. If he could heal himself, it would be a gift from Saint Azure.

Blue sky. He imagined it flowing into the cube—

Hai! Fire lanced Drummer's temples and he cried out. Sagging forward, he bent his head and squeezed his eyes shut while pain surged over him in waves.

After a few moments, the pain subsided. Drummer blew out a gust of air. So much for a healing spell. He opened his eyes and slowly straightened up. They were still traveling toward the line of green, which looked no closer than it had yesterday when he had come down off the ridge.

With no warning, a spell flared through him, unexpected and indistinct. A green spell. Belatedly, he realized he still held the cube. He didn't seem to have much control over his spells. But he definitely felt someone's mood. Triumph.

"Where is that?" Drummer muttered. He looked around the barren lands but saw no one.

Then it hit him. He reined in Vim and stepped the horse around to face the way he had come. Silhouetted against the sky, three riders sat on horses atop the now distant ridge. The distinctive sunrise plumes on their helmets rippled in the wind.

Baz's men.

"No!" He wheeled around and prodded Vim forward. "Come on, Vim! Run!"

The horse took off with a fluid gait that devoured the land. Drummer bent low over his neck so he would drag less against the hot streaming wind. He didn't know how long Vim could keep this pace in his depleted condition, and he didn't want to injure the Jazidian. But he had felt what Baz wanted to do to him the night before last—and that had been before Drummer slept with Jade.

A thought came to him. Was that why she had let Drummer go? She realized Baz would kill her lover. He didn't want to believe she would tell the general what she did with their hostage, but he didn't doubt Baz had riddled the palace with spies. Frantic, Drummer looked over his shoulder, nearly losing his balance on Vim in the process.

The soldiers were sweeping down the ridge after him.

"Cobalt can't be gone," Matthew said. "I overheard his secretary talking to a scribe when I delivered the stable reports to his office. Cobalt is expected to meet with the Historian of the Realm today. Then with the High Judge."

Mel walked with him past the stables, where she had hoped to find her husband. "You haven't seen him at all?"

"Not today. He has much to occupy his time." The lines on Matthew's craggy face had deepened since Cobalt assumed the thrones of Blueshire and Shazire, and now the Misted Cliffs. Although Matthew had spent the last year in Applecroft with Dancer, he often visited Alzire. He saw how

Cobalt was spreading himself too thin. So had Mel. Her husband had to learn to delegate his growing authority before he drowned in the deluge of responsibilities. He was a warrior king, not a statesman: He needed to bring people into his government who had the expertise he lacked. She thought he should appoint Baker Lightstone, the former king of Blueshire, as its governor. She had liked and trusted Lightstone all her life, and he had been more like a governor than a king, anyway. His country was so small a person could cross it on horseback in less than two days. But she had made no headway with Cobalt on the idea. He had met Lightstone only twice, first when the king surrendered to him and the next day when Cobalt had sent him into exile with his family.

She stopped by a well with a peaked roof. The liquid inside rippled with a reflection of the roof, the sky, and the filigreed edge of the palace, as if it were a dream place reachable only through the water. It was a bittersweet fancy, for in dreaming of enchanted places, she could imagine a simple life without the crushing mix of power, duty, aggression, and love she dealt with in Cobalt. And she did love him, despite everything.

The stables at the Diamond Palace housed more horses than anywhere else Mel knew, including Applecroft, the Castle of Clouds, and Alzire. Many riders walked their animals in and out of the courtyard; grooms tended Jazidians, cooling or exercising them; stable hands ran in with water; and hay-sweeps cleaned. The place bustled with life, yet a buffer existed around Mel and Matthew, as if a glass sphere isolated them. It had been this way since Mel had become a queen, in Shazire after Cobalt assumed its throne and even more here. She missed the days when people treated her like a normal person.

"What time does Cobalt meet with the Historian?" she asked.

"I'm not sure," Matthew said. "He doesn't talk to me much anymore."

"He's grieving."

"For his lost childhood. Not for Stonebreaker."

"For both," Mel murmured, gazing into the dark well. "I wish I knew what Stonebreaker told him that night."

"He hated knowing his grandson could be a better king." Matthew scowled. "He wanted to undermine Cobalt's confidence. He probably told him he would fail as a king."

She considered him. "Or about you."

"Cobalt has given me no reason to think so."

"You've hardly seen him."

He paused a moment before answering. "I would like to think he would seek me out, if he suspected our relationship might be more than king and stable master."

Mel leaned against the well, facing the courtyard. "Cobalt needs your guidance. He will listen to me in some things, but he needs a man he trusts."

"I'm a horseman," he said gruffly. "Not a king's advisor."

"You're far more to him than a horseman."

Longing came over his face. "When he was a child…" Then he stopped himself. "No. It is not my place to play the role of Varqelle."

"No, you cannot be Varqelle. Be *Matthew*—who comforted a terrified child, who hid him from the king even knowing you could be executed if Stonebreaker found out, who taught Cobalt the good in himself." More quietly she said, "You were more a father to him than anyone else alive. You and Dancer are the reason Cobalt isn't a tyrant. Perhaps me, also. But he doesn't want to talk to his mother or his wife. He needs you."

"I will talk to him. But remember this. When he is done building his empire—do not look a denial at me, Mel. We both know what he is doing. When he has run out of places to conquer, he will have to rule. It is not I who will rule with him, nor Dancer. It is you. You believe he needs to talk to me, and maybe you're right. But it is you who sit on the throne at his side."

She folded her arms, feeling cold. "I just wish he would be satisfied. He has Shazire, Blueshire, and the Misted Cliffs."

Matthew looked east to the distant cliffs. Beyond them lay Harsdown, Aronsdale, the Barrens, Jazid, and Taka Mal. His spoke with sadness. "I don't think he knows how to stop."

He was dying.

The Rocklands were killing Drummer. His lips were swollen and cracked. He was burning up. Vim plodded across the dry land. At first, Drummer had looked back often, to see if his pursuers were gaining on him. At first, Vim had outdistanced them.

At first.

Drummer knew now that he couldn't outrun his pursuers. Vim had slowed down, and the flatlands had no place to hide. He would die of thirst before he reached that distant green line, if it even existed and wasn't a mirage. Vim might die as well, because Drummer had known too little about the Rocklands to provide for his horse.

"Ah, Vim, I'm sorry." He scratched the horse's neck, as if that would achieve something. Then, wearily, he reined Vim to a stop and brought him around to face their pursuers.

The soldiers weren't far behind, five of them leading extra horses, warriors with desert robes over their clothes and scarves to protect them from the sun. They weren't pushing their mounts. They knew they had him. They wouldn't risk injuring the animals just to catch him a little sooner. Perhaps Baz would kill him when they got back and perhaps he wouldn't, but if he stayed out here, he would die for certain.

With a sense of futility, he sat watching as the soldiers approached. The capture was over in moments. One soldier came alongside Vim and took the reins. He spoke with an accent Drummer barely understood. It sounded like, "Horse something no weight."

Drummer just looked at him, too worn-out to react.

The man spoke more slowly. "Your horse must rest. And have water. You have to get off."

"Oh." Drummer wearily slid to the ground. He lost his balance and sagged against the horse, too sick to move. Vim waited, his head hanging, his sides going in and out as he breathed heavily.

The soldier dismounted and grasped Drummer's arm, holding him up. Another came over and led Vim away.

"Take care of him," Drummer rasped. "He's a good horse."

"We will," the man at his side said. He sounded respectful, which confused Drummer, who had expected hostility. He was having trouble thinking. His mind hazed and his vision blurred. When the soldier gave him a water bag, he fumbled with it, desperate to drink, and dropped the bag. The man picked it up and helped him raise its narrowed end to his mouth. Drummer gulped convulsively as warm water ran down his throat, and swallowed so fast that he choked.

"Slow down," the man said gruffly. "You are valiant to brave the Rocklands, but you must go easy now or you will get sick."

Drummer knew he was already sick. He slowed down, but he drank half the contents of the bag before they took it away. Even when he tried to focus, he couldn't see more than a shimmer of heat and merciless sun.

"What are we—?" Drummer lost his thread of thought.

"We will set up a tent," the soldier said. "You rest. Your horse, too. Sleep out the heat. We start back this evening."

Drummer swayed. "Baz will…kill me?"

The man caught his elbow. "Saints, no."

Drummer didn't know whether to be relieved—or terrified of why Baz might want him alive. His legs were melting. The Taka Mal warrior caught him as he collapsed.

The envoy from Harsdown clattered through the Sentinel Gate, the largest entrance in the wall that surrounded the Topaz Palace. The powerful riders, the stamp of their horses, the plumes of their helmets waving in the hot wind—oh yes, it was an impressive sight. Jade didn't miss the intended message, the subtle threat of more to come if these negotiations failed.

She and Baz stood on a balcony in a tower far enough removed from the yard that their visitors wouldn't see them clearly. The overhang of the tower's onion bulb shaded them from the morning's heat, but the palace baked in the sun, a gruesome reminder of what Drummer faced in the Rocklands. Jade had gone beyond worrying; she felt sick. His betrayal no longer mattered. She didn't want him to die. She wanted him back. Unfortunately, what she wanted was moot. He wasn't here, and they had run out of time.

A man on a magnificent silver stallion was leading the envoy. He wore a helmet shaped like the head of a jaguar. The deadly cats weren't native to these lands; legend claimed merchants from across the sea had brought them to the Misted Cliffs thousands of years ago and sold them to an ancient Harsdown king. Now the cats stalked the warmer regions of Harsdown, hunted and hunting, the symbol of the throne. The name Escar meant jaguar in High Alatian, a language spoken long ago. Farmers and woodsmen had always hunted the jaguars, but the House of Escar limited the number they could kill and so managed to keep the cats from dying out.

Baz indicated the man she was watching. "Sphere-General Fieldson."

"So that is the infamous general," Jade said. "Why Sphere?"

"Ranks in the Dawnfield army are based on geometry."

Baz leaned on the balcony wall and studied the men below. "Shapes subdivide each rank. The more sides a shape, the higher the rank, except that all two-dimensional shapes are lower than all three-dimensional shapes. A square-lieutenant holds a higher rank than a triangle-lieutenant, but less than a triangle-captain because all captains outrank all lieutenants."

"It must take ages to progress through the ranks."

Baz shrugged. "Not really. Shape promotions don't take long. I don't think they include every possible shape, either. Just up to eight sides, and also circles and spheres."

"How strange," she said. "But logical, I suppose. The sphere is a three-dimensional shape with an infinite number of sides, yes? So sphere-general is highest rank."

He nodded. "Fieldson is the only one."

"They have such pastoral names," she mused. "Dawnfield. Harsdown. Aronsdale. You would never think they would be so imposing."

Baz narrowed his gaze at the general. "Never underestimate that one."

Jade watched the riders with foreboding. Harsdown had sent its most formidable general to discover that she, Jade, had misplaced his queen's brother.

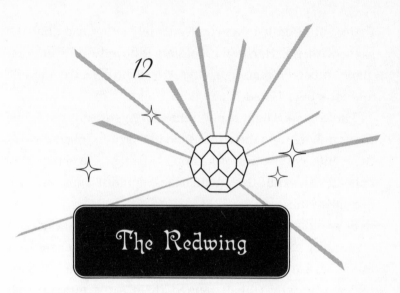

12

The Redwing

Until Mel saw the Chamberlight army gathering below the King's Spring, she hadn't fully comprehended its size. They spread across fields and trampled meadows in every direction. Soldiers were setting up camps with the help of daytenders, the men and women who came with an army to look after their needs while the warriors trained and fought.

As Mel watched the ocean of people and horses, a fierce exultation stirred within her. She fought it; she wanted peace rather than conquest. But she would defend what was hers. And she would train with the army as had mage queens of ancient times.

Cobalt's conquest of Shazire had swelled the ranks of his army. Many of the survivors had sworn allegiance to the new king. Some refused, however. Cobalt could have executed them, but he exiled them instead. Mel's father had done the same with the Harsdown soldiers who refused him allegiance nineteen years ago, after Aronsdale defeated Varqelle and took over Harsdown.

The Chamberlight army numbered eight thousand, five thousand here and three thousand in Shazire. Cobalt divided them into companies of a thousand each: Carnelian, Andalusite, Alexandrite, Aquamarine, Sapphire, Tanzanite, Iolite, Diamond.

Every company trained in many disciplines, but each had a specialty. Carnelians were superb archers. Alexandrites fought well at night and were torchbearers as well as soldiers, which was why Cobalt named them for a mineral that changed color in different light. Andalusites had many martial arts skills, just as andalusite showed many shades of orange. Historically, Aquamarines had specialized at sea warfare, but now they were foot troops. Iolites excelled as swordsmen. Tanzanites rode as cavalry, as did the Sapphires, including the king's flag bearers. Mel trained with the Sapphires. The Diamonds included all classes of soldier and guarded the palace and the Misted Cliffs. Cobalt had sent the Carnelians, Alexandrites, and Sapphires back to the Misted Cliffs after the Shazire campaign, to join the Diamonds and Aquamarines.

Mel wondered if he realized the names followed the same color scheme as mage spells, from red through violet. Cobalt had reorganized and renamed the other companies this past year. That he chose rare minerals made sense to her; they were hard, valuable, and striking, especially diamond, the hardest known substance. But the names had a certain harsh poetry she hadn't expected from Cobalt.

Today she wore the scuffed armor she donned for sword practice. Leather pants protected her legs, and she wore a leather vest. An undertunic covered her arms. Her boots came to her knees but were supple to allow for motion. Her sword hung in a tooled sheath on her belt. The quiver on her back held arrows she had brought from Harsdown, and she carried her bolt-bow.

Mel was standing on a walkway on top of the palace wall. She went to a doorway in a nearby guard tower. Inside, the watchman was sitting on a stool by an arrow-slit, gazing out the narrow opening. He glanced over as she came in and stood up to salute, knocking his fist against his rib cage. He froze in midgesture as he registered Mel's face.

The guard bowed with a jerk, his fist still against his breastbone. "Your Majesty!"

She smiled at him. "My greetings of the morning."

"My honor, ma'am." He seemed bewildered. She was growing used to such reactions; in Stonebreaker's court, women never took part in what the late king had called "affairs of import," which as far as she could tell included everything in existence except sex, child rearing, planning balls, and liaising with the domestic staff.

Mel ran down the stairs that spiraled inside the tower. At the bottom, she entered a small courtyard. Matthew was waiting on his horse, Hawkspar, an amber-hued beauty from the Goldstar breeders in the south. He handled the high-spirited horse with a confidence that calmed the animal. He had also brought Smoke.

Matthew smiled as she came over to him. "You look like an avenging angel with all that gold hair and black leather." He handed her Smoke's reins. "For someone with such an aversion to war, you outfit yourself quite well for it."

"I have an aversion to invading innocent lands." She swung into Smoke's saddle. "Not to defense."

A soldier cranked open the gate and they left the yard. Mel donned her helmet, but she left the faceplate open. Within moments, they were riding through the outskirts of the army. She wanted to get a feel for this immense force her husband was gathering, *just in case,* as he put it. She didn't believe him. One didn't bring thousands of men together "just in case."

Soldiers glanced up as she and Matthew passed and some nodded to them, but Matthew was the one they called by name. Mel doubted most even realized she was a woman rather than a youth. Not many of these soldiers knew their king's wife rode with the army.

"Cobalt told me that you counseled him to negotiate for your uncle," Matthew said.

"I did." Mel scowled. "He is amassing this army anyway."

"It seems so."

"I'm worried for Drummer." Then she admitted, "Saints know, if harm comes to him, my heart will want vengeance."

"I've never met your uncle," Matthew said. "But I know the drive to protect one's own." In a voice that reminded her of Varqelle, he said, "That fire can consume everything in its path."

"Aye." Mel thought of the child she carried, and a fiercely protective instinct came over her. She would do anything to protect the life within her.

Some fathers bequeathed their home to their children. Others might leave a farm, a dairy, a smithy. Almost all sought to provide a legacy for their family.

Mel doubted Cobalt had consciously defined that idea in his thoughts. He would tell himself that he took his army forth in case the negotiations for Drummer failed or Taka Mal decided to resume the war they started two hundred years ago. But his drive had a more ambitious edge now that pushed him even harder than before. He sought a legacy.

He would leave his child an empire.

In the Urn Parlor, Sphere-General Fieldson sat across a table from Jade. Tall vases stood in every corner, priceless works glazed in amber and yellow hues, set with turquoise, rimmed in gold. Fieldson's iron-gray hair and severe uniform made a jarring contrast to this place where Jade entertained dignitaries. He seemed primed with energy, like a jaguar ready to strike.

Her staff had set fire-lily incense on the mantel, and plumes curled up from fire-dragons enameled in sunset colors. The scent was subtle but astringent, none of the cloying fragrances favored in many noble houses. Fieldson was a warrior. She would honor him with an appropriate scent. Besides, she abhorred those sugary flower smells.

Jade knew Baz was standing behind her chair, imposing in his red-and-crimson uniform. A Dawnfield man stood behind Fieldson, sober in gray and violet. Quaazera, Dawnfield and Chamberlight officers stood around the walls of the room, their uniforms reflecting their countries: Taka Mal bright and hot, full of vigor; Dawnfield elegant and more severe; and Chamberlight, icy and gem-hard.

A bid-boy served them dark red wine in crystal goblets shaped and colored like fire-lilies. The decanter was a larger version of the fiery blossom. Fieldson waited until the boy left and then said, "So where is Goodman Headwind?"

Jade sipped from her goblet with forced calm. "His party will return from his tour tomorrow or the day after." By the Dragon-Sun, she hoped that was true! If Baz's men hadn't found Drummer, it could mean he had reached Aronsdale—or expired. Fieldson's concern over the minstrel's absence couldn't come close to what Jade felt. She didn't know whether she was angrier that Drummer had taken actions that could start a war or that he had risked his life. If he died, she would never forgive him.

"I am sorry he wasn't here when you arrived," Jade said. "We hadn't expected you so soon."

Fieldson was studying her closely. She met his gaze with the same outward confidence she presented to her own generals when they sought a weakness in her defenses. He set his goblet on the tiled table. "I will tell you something, Your Majesty. I've never been a political man. The convolutions of royal intrigue are beyond me."

Jade doubted he would have reached such a high rank if that were true. She sipped her wine. "We are in accord, then. I have never had much patience with intrigue." Which was true. It didn't make her royal court any less saturated with it, unfortunately.

"Then I will speak plainly." His gaze hardened. "Drummer should be here."

Jade gave him a look that could make even her most seasoned officers pale. It never worked on Spearcaster, but it could rattle Generals Slate and Firaz. She spoke coldly. "It is not yours to decide who should or should not be in my palace."

He didn't flick an eyelash. "It was not yours to kidnap my queen's brother."

"You misunderstand." She settled back in her chair. "He is touring my country as my esteemed guest. When he returns, you may speak to him."

He didn't smile. "I await your fulfillment of that promise." His hand tightened on the end of his chair's arms. It was a nuance Jade might have missed in her younger days, but she hadn't kept her throne by being oblivious. People said a great deal more than they realized with gestures, facial tics, and tone. Fieldson was angry. And worried. He had probably expected her to be more solicitous. But until Drummer returned, this was a gamble, and her game had better be good. First be hard, then generous. It kept people off balance. She had learned that from her parents, who kept each other unbalanced for their entire marriage. Theirs had been a union born of economics, joining the royal family with the powerful Zanterian nobility that owned the caravan guilds. It greatly benefited both Houses, but her parents had never liked each other, and they had spent their years in a constant battle of wills.

She switched smoothly into her role as host. "General, in honor of your visit, I am holding a feast tonight. My staff has prepared our best guest suites for you and your men, where you can rest and prepare."

Fieldson gave her a long, considering look. "Very well, Your Majesty."

Very well, indeed. At least he didn't keep insisting she produce Drummer. For tonight, she had a reprieve. But if Drummer didn't show up tomorrow, she would have serious trouble.

Jade was on her way to meet Baz, her escort for the feast, when her ginger-maid came running. A woman in her early forties, she had been Jade's companion for decades. Her family had named her Clovemoon because she was born under a full moon the night before they sold the cloves for their spice trade. Her blue tunic and trousers fluttered in drapes bordered by silver stars, and a blue scarf covered her dark hair.

Jade waited in the corridor while the maid caught up with her. She always felt better with Clove. In fact, Jade liked her far more than her "friends" among the nobility.

"A redwing!" Clove cried out. "At your window."

That spurred Jade into motion. She headed toward Clove. "Does it come from the army?"

"I think so." Clove hurried along the hall with her. "It flapped about the window. Then it went into the loft."

Jade tried not to hope. Any bird could fly to the recessed window in her tower, but only the trained birds knew how to enter the Message Loft, a chamber in the tower wall. To open the loft, a bird had to peck a code on the mesh that blocked the entrance. The army used redwings because they learned to tap patterns as easily as parrots learned to repeat words.

She and Clove sped into the Ginger Suite, bustled through Jade's bedroom, and entered a round chamber. The ginger-stone floor had concentric circles cut into it, and gold filigree curled on the walls, the only adornment in the otherwise empty room.

Jade crossed to the window. No birds fluttered outside, but the mesh door on one side of the recess was open. Jade could reach the loft from here using a round portal set in the wall at shoulder height and enameled with a redwing in flight. She pulled the little door open by the crystal knob in its center. In the chamber beyond, a redwing ruffled its feathers and squawked at her.

"Come, sweets," she crooned. She gently took out the bird. Its red wings contrasted with the blue under its body and its gold beak. It didn't peck at her hand, which suggested General Spearcaster's bird-adepts had trained it as a carrier.

A metal tube was attached to the bird's leg. Jade removed the tube and released the redwing, which flew up to a perch under the domed ceiling. As Jade pulled a tiny roll of parchment out of the tube, Clove watched, her face flushed. The ginger-maid was the only one Jade had confided in about her concern. Holding her breath, Jade read the parchment:

Found Drummer. Very ill. Needs doctor. Back on
Ringday. Javelin

"Hai!" Jade leaned against the wall, uncaring if it tore her
dress. Her relief that they had found him was tempered by
the rest of the letter. *Very ill.* What had happened? She would
have her physician ready. Ringday. Fifth of the week. The day
after tomorrow. At least she had a definite time to give
Sphere-General Fieldson. But she couldn't have Javelin bring
a sick Drummer into the palace. If Fieldson or his men saw,
they would think her soldiers had perpetrated nefarious
acts against the minstrel. She supposed having his honor
compromised by the queen might be construed as a nefarious act, but she didn't think it counted if they had enjoyed
the act so much.

Jade turned to Clove. The ginger-maid had anticipated her
needs, and she offered Jade a parchment, quill, and a scribe's
board with a bulb of gold ink. Jade wrote quickly:

Good work, Javelin. Doctor Quarry will be ready.
Take Drummer to guard tower, South Gate. Don't come
inside the palace. Vizarana

Jade blew on the ink until it dried, then rolled up the message and slid it into the tube. When she whistled, the redwing fluffed its plumage, squawked irately at her, and flew
down. As Jade raised her arm, the bird lighted on her wrist,
claws digging into her skin. A drop of red ran down her arm.

"Sealed in blood," she murmured. She attached the tube to the bird's leg while Clove opened the window. Jade released the redwing, and it soared away, heading for the Rocklands and—she hoped—Captain Javelin.

She would have the Master of the Guard keep close watch on the South Tower and tell Physician Quarry to be ready.

Be well, Drummer, she thought. She had to bluff two more days out of her guests and pray Drummer came back in time—

And alive.

13

The Fire Opal Court

The Chamberlight army flooded the land like a drowning sea. It swirled around forests of droop-elm and spindle trees and eddied in valleys as if they were cups filling with water. Two days later, it reached the base of the cliffs that gave their country its name and the soldiers piled against the base of the mountains in waves, the blue-and-white plumes of their helmets like froth on the breakers.

Mel mostly rode with Cobalt or Matthew. Dancer had remained at the Diamond Palace to govern in Cobalt's absence, an authority Stonebreaker would never have granted her, though after half a century as his only child she had the experience. Mel missed her company. Although Dancer had mistrusted and disliked her at first, she had gradually thawed. They would probably never be close, but Mel enjoyed Dancer's scholarly bent and dry humor.

Cooks and maids and seamstresses accompanied the army, and the wives of some soldiers, but none of them seemed comfortable with her. It wasn't only her title, but also that she was riding as an officer. Her commission was actually in her father's army, but she wore Chamberlight armor to downplay her many differences. Until recently, it had been rare for women to serve in the Harsdown army, and it was unheard-of in the Misted Cliffs.

Mel had tried to cultivate friendships among the women of the Diamond nobility, but she had little in common with them. She hadn't expected so many similarities between the Misted Cliffs and Jazid and Taka Mal. Although their countries were geographically distant, they exported and imported many goods from one another, and apparently customs came with the tangible items. As in Jazid and to a lesser extent Taka Mal, the royal court at the Diamond Palace maintained a rigid separation between men and women. Stonebreaker took it even further; in his court, women had gone veiled, a custom followed nowhere else in this modern age. Mel thought Dancer had done it as protection; the more she hid her face, the less the king could discern her thoughts. But she had always been watching, silent and unseen, navigating Stonebreaker's capricious emotional politics.

Dancer had spent the past year at Applecroft with Matthew and Mel's parents. In that place of warmth and burgeoning life, she had changed. As a historian, she was writing a treatise on the role of women in the Misted Cliffs, an aspect of history she felt was neglected. When she had returned to the Diamond Palace, just before Stonebreaker died, she no longer wore veils. The Diamond Court knew her better than they knew Mel. Perhaps in time, they would follow Dancer's more flexible ways.

The army stretched out along the cliffs that separated them from Harsdown. They took a steady but easy pace that didn't tax the horses. Oxen drew supply wagons. The horsemen passed the soldiers on foot, but when the animals rested, the troops caught up. Cobalt had left Diamond Company behind and taken the other four thousand soldiers plus about a thousand day-tenders. They would go over the cliffs in the south, where the mountains were smaller, cross southern Harsdown, and enter Shazire. At Alzire, the capital of Shazire, they would rendezvous with the rest of the army, another three thousand men.

Cobalt was riding ahead, taller in his saddle than the other warriors, with his helmet under his arm. Mel rode up alongside him. "A fine morning."

"Yes." His face was more relaxed than it had been in days.

"You seem satisfied."

"Yes."

Mel sighed. "You know, love, you are allowed to speak more than one word per sentence."

His grin flashed. "Yes."

"Oh, stop." She pretended to pull an arrow out of her quiver and knock her bow.

"What is this?" he asked. "You look lovely, trying to shoot me through the heart."

Mel lowered her lashes and contemplated him through their fringe. "Now that I know what stirs your passion..."

Cobalt rode closer. He said nothing, but his gaze told her what he wanted. Her body always heated when he looked at her that way.

"So." She cleared her throat. Then she ran out of words.

He smirked at her. "You can say more than one word, too."

Mel laughed, and they rode on together. He continually scanned the riders, troops, wagons, everything. She was one of the few people who knew that the more distant parts of the army were a blur to him. He could see fine at moderate distances, but he needed his glasses for anything far away. He disliked people knowing he wore them. It didn't really matter now; although he would never be much of an archer, he could see well enough for most everything else. But if his sight continued to worsen, someday it could interfere with his ability to command the army.

A thought came to her: Could she help his eyes? A blue mage could speed and deepen healing. But his sight wasn't injured, so she had nothing to heal. Still, she was willing to try if he didn't put too much hope in the result. Far better that than what she feared, that she would someday have to heal him after battle. She couldn't give life where it had already been lost. At night, she tossed with nightmares where he took a mortal wound and she burned out her mage powers trying to heal him while he died in her arms.

Stop it, she thought.

She couldn't help but worry, though. Supposedly Cobalt was bringing his army to establish a more permanent presence in Shazire. It didn't take a genius to see he didn't need eight thousand people for that. He intended to leave only the Andalusites in Shazire and take the other six companies and their day tenders toward Jazid, then north along the Aronsdale-Jazid border to Taka Mal.

"I've never been to Jazid," Mel mused. "When I was small, my family visited Queen Vizarana, and I met King Ozar at the Topaz Palace. But I don't know much about him. He never allows women to join discussions of state policy or governance." She gave a short laugh. "He does *not* like my parents."

Cobalt smiled. "Everyone likes your parents."

"They break Ozar's rules," Mel said. "He supposedly has said my mother would make a good concubine and my father is 'too pretty' to be a king." Mel hated the stories. She had no doubt Onyx liked her no more than her parents, and she dreaded to think how warriors in Taka Mal would treat Drummer. Her father might look innocuous, but he was a seasoned commander. Drummer had no military training. In Taka Mal, he would be a gazelle among wolves.

"Ozar and my grandfather got along well," Cobalt said.

"That figures," Mel said dourly.

His smile turned wicked. "It is a pity Ozar won't meet you. I should like to see how he reacts to my warrior wife."

"Why wouldn't he meet me? We will travel along the border of his country." She already knew what Cobalt would say, but it wouldn't do him any good. "It is customary in such situations for sovereigns to confer, lest one side assume hostilities."

Cobalt stopped smiling. "Whether or not Onyx and I meet is irrelevant. You will be in Shazire."

She met his gaze. "No."

"Yes."

"What, are we going to argue with one-word sentences?"

He scowled at her. "Someone needs to govern Shazire while I am busy." Drily he added, "You are better at it than me, anyway."

"Leo Tumbler has governed Shazire fine. He can continue."

"He is a colonel," Cobalt said, as if that explained something.

"You have to appoint a governor. You can't live in both Shazire and the Misted Cliffs." The situation had been worrying Mel. "You need one for Blueshire, too."

His face darkened. "I am not going to put Lightstone back on the Blueshire throne after I deposed him."

"What deposing?" she demanded. "You rode in with six thousand men. He had fifty. You bullied him."

"I did no such thing."

"He would make a good governor."

"No."

"If you leave me in charge in Alzire," she said, "I shall appoint Baker Lightstone as Governor of Blueshire."

"Mel!" Cobalt glowered at her. "Do not bedevil me this way."

Mel had expected he would want her to stay in Alzire. She

had also noticed he tended to defer to her in the day-to-day process of governance. She appreciated his trust, and she had no intention of endangering their child. But a mage queen rode with the army. Her own mother had ridden against Varqelle when she was pregnant. Good reason existed for kings to marry adepts. Mages brought light, literally and figuratively. Mel wouldn't help Cobalt overthrow countries, but she could minimize harm to his men, improve morale, increase health and strength, heal wounds, sway fighters not to slaughter if they were winning and calm panic if they were losing.

Cobalt claimed he had no intention of invading Taka Mal. Prior to Stonebreaker's death, she might have believed him. His fire had cooled this past year. But his grandfather had died before Cobalt could come to terms with him. In his own inarticulate way, her husband had wanted an accounting for all those years of torment. She doubted he could ever have made peace with Stonebreaker, but he might have with himself. Now she questioned if that would ever happen.

The envoy should arrive soon in Quaazera. Fieldson would send his fastest horsemen with news of the negotiations. And if they were lucky, truly lucky, the volatile mix of countries, royal houses and Cobalt's suppressed rage wouldn't explode.

When the disaster hit, Jade and Baz were taking Sphere-General Fieldson and his officers on a tour of the palace winery. They had gathered in a courtyard to watch tenders load barrels into a wagon as the Wine Master described various vintages. Jade planned to offer one of their finest bottles to Fieldson, with the hopes of appeasing his growing frustration. She sympathized. Today was Ringday, but still no word of Drummer.

"Our merlot from Kazlatar has a particularly rich flavor," the Wine Master was saying. The envoy listened politely. Baz looked bored, having heard this every time he and Jade went over the scrolls for the winery.

A commotion came from an archway across the courtyard. The two soldiers on guard were talking urgently with someone there. Then one strode toward Jade, his breastplate gleaming in the sunlight, his armor and curved sword an impressive sight. Which was the intent, of course, with Fieldson here.

The soldier stopped in front of Jade and saluted with his fist against his breastplate. "Your Majesty!"

"Is there a problem?" Jade asked.

"A day-runner is looking for you," he said. "He claims he has important news."

Jade inwardly swore. If this was about Drummer, the Master of her Watch had bungled their plans. They were supposed to let Jade know when Javelin showed up, but *only* in a manner that drew no attention, particularly in front of the sphere-general.

Maybe it wasn't Drummer. It could be another emergency. Her subjects thought she lived a glamorous life, but in truth it involved an unending stream of problems that had to be solved.

Jade turned to Fieldson with a look of apology. "I'm terribly sorry. I'm afraid I must see to this." To Baz, she said, "Please do finish the tour with our honored guests. I will return as soon as I see to whatever problem has come up."

Baz inclined his head, for once raising no objections. They had already discussed what to do when his men brought in Drummer.

Fieldson was watching them closely. "Perhaps Goodman Headwind has arrived."

"I hope so." She spread her hands out from her body to indicate her puzzlement. "We will see."

The guard escorted Jade into an adjacent courtyard. The day-runner was there, a boy of about nine with black curls that flopped over his ears. Seeing Jade, he pulled himself up as tall as his small stature would allow and pulled on his shirt, straightening his clothes. Jade couldn't help but smile at his earnest face.

"Your Magnificence!" The boy bowed. "Your Gloriousness! Your Esteemed—"

"Goodness, I'm not all that!" Laughing gently, Jade said, "What is your name?"

"Spark, ma'am." He gazed at her with a rapt face.

"Did you have a message, Goodsir Spark?" Jade asked.

"Oh! Yes." His cheeks turned red. "Captain Javelin said to run as fast as possible to let you know he had arrived. He is in the Fire Opal courtyard in the north wing of the palace. He sent for the physician, too, but Goodsir Quarry isn't here. Captain Javelin says to please bring another doctor. It's urgent."

Jade felt as if the ground dropped beneath her. *What had*

happened to Drummer? And why the blazes had Javelin brought him here? He must not have received her message. Redwings were well-trained, but even the best of them didn't always fly true. Unfortunately, Quarry was at the South tower in the city wall, waiting for Drummer. Javelin must have come through another gate.

Jade turned to the guard. "Please find Mica and take her to Captain Javelin's party." Mica was the best healer at the palace after Quarry, and also the midwife for women at the Quaazera court. "I will meet you there."

"Your Majesty," the guard said. "I should accompany you to Captain Javelin. In case there is trouble."

Trouble, indeed. It was an apt word, but no guard could protect her against the kind of trouble Drummer posed. He might have used her that night they spent together, but even if that was true, and even if for some bizarre reason he attacked her in front of Javelin, she could probably fight him off. Her parents had ensured she learned to defend herself at a young age. But Drummer wasn't going to attack anyone. He was no warrior. Why she liked him so much was beyond her, but she did, far too much.

"Thank you for your concern," Jade said. "But I'll be fine."

Although the guard hesitated, he couldn't insist. So he saluted and strode toward the palace.

"Lead on, Spark," Jade said.

"Yes, ma'am!" He set off, clearly determined to do a good job, and she smiled as he hurried her across the yard.

Spark led her through courtyards she rarely saw, those used by domestic staff at the palace. They ended up at a yard shaped like a Fire Opal blossom with scalloped sides. People filled it: soldiers from the search party, grooms and horses, more soldiers at the entrances. Smart fellow, Javelin, to post guards so no one could enter uninvited.

The captain stood across the yard, leaning over a litter on the ground. Mica was kneeling by it, talking to whoever lay there. Jade hurried through the bustle, and people bowed as she passed. She barely nodded to each, her attention on the litter. Had they carried Drummer? The possibility that he had been too ill to ride scared her more than any Harsdown envoy.

When she reached the litter, Javelin turned and bowed to her. Grime and sweat streaked his face, and she suspected neither he nor his men had rested on the journey here. His face was grim as he moved aside. Jade knelt next to Mica—and her breath caught.

Drummer lay in the litter, his eyes closed, his face pale, his breathing shallow. Jade felt as if her world stopped. She was aware of Mica and the others, but everything dimmed except this minstrel.

"Drummer?" she asked. "Can you hear me? It's Jade." Belatedly, she realized how that sounded. No visitor could use her personal name, especially not a hostage from Aronsdale. At the moment, though, she didn't care.

He slowly opened his eyes. "My greetings…" he whispered.

"You foolish man," Jade murmured, furious and terrified. "What were you doing, running off to the Rocklands?"

"Baz…?"

"We'll fix it," she said. She glanced at Mica. "How serious is his illness?"

The healer was staring at her, but she quickly found her voice. "He has the patters."

"Patters?" For saints' sake. Most people caught that as children. The name came from the way small children curled up with their parents, seeking pats of comfort during their illness. Patters came with a terribly high fever and nausea that lasted several days. With rest and liquids, the child usually recovered. It could be fatal, though, if not treated—and running around in the Rocklands sure as blazes wouldn't help.

Jade knew Aronsdale children didn't catch all the same illnesses as those in Taka Mal. Drummer's body might not have the strengths of someone from Taka Mal to fight the disease.

"Will he get better?" Jade asked.

After a pause that lasted too long, Mica said, "I think so."

Jade knew too well how to interpret that pause and response. Mica was afraid for her patient and didn't want to tell her queen.

Jade brushed the sweaty blond curls off Drummer's forehead and spoke to him in a soft voice she rarely used. "You really were sick that night at the banquet."

"I guess so," he whispered.

"Why did you run away?" Dismay welled inside of her. "You made a pact with me. A Topaz Pact. How could you break it?"

"Pact?" His breathing rasped. "I don't understand."

Didn't he know? It had never occurred to her that he might not realize the significance of their agreement. He was a queen's brother; she had assumed he would understand. "You promised not to leave the palace."

"I did?"

"That night, after you left the banquet. We talked about the pact. I said it meant you would stay put. You agreed." She hesitated, unable to remember if he had actually said yes. "At least, I thought you did."

"Jade…I thought General Quaazera would kill me."

A harsh voice came from behind them, and the scrape of metal on leather. "Why would I do that, minstrel? What have you done with my queen that would justify your execution?"

Jade jumped to her feet and whirled around. Baz stood there, his face red, his curved sword drawn and glittering in the sun. His words leaped at her like daggers. "You trusted him with a *pact?* What possible reason could he have given you to believe he would honor that trust? And why, my *untouchable* cousin, is a common-born minstrel from Aronsdale calling you by your personal name?"

Everyone around them had frozen in a tableau, staring at her and Baz—the soldiers, healer, grooms, stable hands, palace guards. Baz was breathing hard, and she knew he was one beat away from murdering their Aronsdale hostage.

"My cousin." She spoke with exquisite formality, knowing Drummer's life balanced on her words. "Goodman Headwind is unfamiliar with our customs and does not realize he may not use the queen's familiar name or the implications associated with that familiarity." Which was true. That those implications happened to be true was better left unsaid. "As to the pact, I misjudged his intent." With a silent apology to Drummer, she said, "I was misled by his apparent weakness and assumed he couldn't venture beyond the palace. His smooth ways led me to believe he would honor the agreement. I was wrong and am humbled by my mistake."

No one moved. A horse snuffled and went silent. Far away, a redwing cried. Every person there knew Drummer's life hung on whether or not the general of the army, possibly the future king of Taka Mal, would accept her words. No one was watching the west gate. And so no one saw another man enter the yard—until he stepped past Baz and fixed Jade with an icy stare.

"You lied to me," Sphere-General Fieldson said. "To torture and threaten the life of my queen's brother are acts of war."

14

Topaz Sphere

The blood drained from Jade's face. "Sir, you misunderstand."

"Stop it, Samuel," a hoarse voice said behind her.

Bewildered, Jade turned around—and found herself eye-to-eye with Drummer. He looked ready to crumple, but he was standing. Those rasping words were his, what the illness had done to his golden voice. Jade wanted to reach out, but if she touched him, even just to help him stay on his feet, Baz might finish what he had started when he drew his sword.

"Your Majesty." Drummer spoke with formal cadences. "I apologize deeply if my lapses in courtesy during my illness have offended you or any member of your court." He looked past her to Fieldson. "And Samuel, for the sake of the Azure Saints, I am neither tortured nor dead. Just sick, which is no one's fault."

Jade didn't know how he managed that entire speech when he was on the verge of collapse, but he said it beautifully. And who would have thought that the sphere-general had a personal name as exotic as "Samuel." She had never heard such.

"I apologize that my country gave you this illness," Jade said. It was a bit silly to apologize for a country making him sick, but it was the first thing that came to her mind.

Mica was standing next to Drummer, obviously ready to catch him if he collapsed. Jade turned to her, "Healer, please have Goodman Headwind taken to your apothecary and see that he receives the best treatment."

Mica bowed. "It would be my honor, Your Majesty."

Drummer didn't object as Mica and Javelin helped him lie on the litter and pulled its flapping sides closed to shade him from the sun. Fieldson and Baz watched with suspicion, and Jade didn't think either was fooled by the little play she and Drummer had put on. But she suspected neither knew whom to accuse of what.

Jade spoke to both generals. "Let us continue our discussion inside, where it is cooler." Including their tempers, she hoped.

A muscle twitched in Baz's cheek. Never taking his gaze off her face, he slid his sword into the curved sheath on his belt.

Jade let out a silent breath. She caught a barely visible relaxing of Fieldson's posture. The others in the yard stirred, looking after the horses or carrying Drummer's litter. Jade lifted her hand, inviting Fieldson and Baz into the palace. It appeared that, at least for today, no one would lose his life—or hers.

The atajazid paced along the Obsidian Hall. He had come to his fortress in the Jagged Teeth Mountains to think. Shade watched from the niche where he sat on a stool carved from onyx and inlaid with mother-of-pearl imported from the Misted Cliffs.

"What do you think?" Ozar asked. "She wishes to say no. But she hesitates."

"What I think," Shade said sourly, "is that if Queen Vizarana agrees to marry you, General Quaazera will skewer you with a shish-kebab stick."

Ozar smiled. "I believe the general would rather skewer his beloved queen. In more ways than one."

Shade arched an eyebrow, but he refrained from commenting on his sovereign's inelegant humor. "She won't marry him. She won't marry you. She likes power too much. She won't give it up."

"Ah, but that makes wresting it from her all the sweeter." Ozar reached the end of the hall, a wall of black stone, and stood considering it with his hands clasped behind his back. Then he turned and resumed pacing. "She hopes to negotiate with Cobalt Escar's envoy, using that Headwind boy as a bargaining point."

"Boy?" Shade waved a bony hand with skin like parchment. "I thought he was a girl."

"They are weak, these Aronsdale and Harsdown men. They let their women run them. If they were all like this

Drummer, it would be easy to defeat their armies. Unfortunately, there is Cobalt Escar." He reached the end of the corridor, another black wall, and turned to Shade. "Vizarana wishes me to ally with her. If her need is dire enough, she will accept my conditions."

"The need does not appear dire enough."

"It would if Escar attacked Taka Mal." Ozar thought of the Taka Mal queen. She was a taunt to his life and beliefs. "It is a simple exchange—I get Vizarana's throne and Taka Mal survives. With our forces joined, we can defeat Cobalt. Take his lands. Even the combined armies of Aronsdale and Harsdown won't be enough to stand against us then."

"They might ally with Cobalt if you attack him," Shade said. "His wife is a Dawnfield. And heir to the Jaguar Throne."

Ozar grimaced. The words were a sour taste. "I can't fathom this business of giving a throne to a woman. It invites problems."

Shade's voice rattled in the dry mountain air. "I have heard Cobalt's wife is like a man."

"Behaves like one, maybe." Ozar walked over to him. "I saw her when she was a child. She was unbearably beautiful. All that yellow hair. And blue eyes. Very strange. But attractive."

"Perhaps she hasn't aged well," Shade said.

Ozar slowly smiled. "Perhaps we should find out." He continued down the hall. "Chime Headwind is an offense against nature. Such a woman should be in a man's bed, not his office. But at least her husband rules Harsdown. The

same won't be true when their daughter takes the throne."
He stopped at the wall and tapped a code on the polished
surface.

A clink came from within the stone. When he tapped
more of the pattern, more clinks reverberated, stone pins hitting stone pins. He pushed the wall, and a lopsided section
slid inward. When he leaned his weight into it, the section
moved forward. He was making a tunnel. A scratching came
from behind him, the noise of Shade struggling to his feet,
followed by the rustle of footsteps.

The slab Ozar was pushing swung ponderously aside. It
opened into a chamber over a thousand years old, built by
one of his ancestors. The chamber had been modernized, but
it retained its original function as a place to question prisoners. Manacles and chains hung on the walls. The spiked
objects on the tables had only a thin layer of dust, and the
whips remained supple. The cell was in excellent condition,
ready for use.

Shade came to Ozar's side. "You have a plan."

"You asked what would provoke Cobalt Escar to attack
Taka Mal," Ozar replied. "The House of Quaazera has already kidnapped his wife's uncle. Perhaps they will take his
wife as well."

"Ah." Shade's eyes glinted. "And when Escar finds out
they have mistreated her?"

"I imagine he won't like it," Ozar said mildly, studying a
rack across the room.

"This plan of yours has a problem."

Ozar spoke wryly. "It has many."

"If she is here," Shade said, "why would he think Quaazera took her?"

"How would he know?" Ozar walked to a table and picked up a metal rod with serrated edges. "Especially if he's told that the House of Quaazera abducted her, just like her uncle."

"And when his wife reveals the truth?"

"She will say nothing." Ozar tapped the rod against his palm, lightly, so the serrations didn't rip his skin. "Sadly, I'm afraid she won't survive her treatment at their hands."

Shade didn't look surprised. "Quaazera will deny it."

Ozar turned to him, suddenly angry. "The Quaazeras condemned themselves when they took her uncle. My spies say he ran off and almost died in the Rocklands. Escar is far more likely to believe Taka Mal committed this atrocity." His voice hardened. "Especially when he sees her body."

Shade's gaze darkened, an expression that had given Ozar nightmares in his youth. "And when Escar descends in fury on Taka Mal, you will come to the aid of the nubile Vizarana. With conditions."

"If it works, I get everything—Cobalt Escar's realms and Vizarana's throne." Ozar struck the table with the rod, gashing its scarred wood. "The plan, however, has a flaw."

Shade's frown deepened the web of wrinkles on his ancient face. "Getting Cobalt's wife." He didn't make it a question.

"It won't be easy," Ozar said. Even so. He had contacts he had been cultivating for years in many countries. Ozar spoke in a shadowed voice. "Nothing is impossible."

* * *

Jade knew she should stay away from Drummer. He had lain in bed for three days, delirious or unconscious, fighting a fever that raged. She wanted to sit at his side every moment. If she did, though, everyone would see the truth. Baz didn't believe nothing had happened between her and Drummer, but he had so far had enough sense not to kill Drummer and start a war. Fieldson didn't trust her, and the guards she had posted at Drummer's suite made the general more suspicious. If she neglected her duties to attend their hostage like a love-addled girl, it would only inflame the situation. It surely violated some law of the spheres that Drummer mattered so much to her. But he did. She felt starved for him.

Jade spent the morning with her planners going over the upkeep of roads, bridges, footpaths, caravans, fire league, city jails, and the temples, where the people worshipped the Dragon-Sun and the spirits of the sky and sunset. Personally, Jade would have rather honored the sunrise, a more optimistic proposition, she thought. But the pantheon was what it was regardless of her preferences.

She met with Fieldson over a meal of spiced pastries and shrimp imported from the Misted Cliffs. The sumptuous food did nothing to pacify the taciturn sphere-general, who waited with impatience for Drummer to recover.

Finally Jade could take no more. After her midday meal, she slipped over to the Sunset Wing. Captain Javelin and grumpy Kaj were on guard at Drummer's suite. Going inside, she recalled the time she had found Drummer here, standing on his head with his legs scissored in the air as if that feat of athleticism were the most natural thing in the world. Beautiful, limber, dulcet-voiced Drummer, who sang like ambrosia. Now he was dying. If only he had stayed put. Javelin had told her of Drummer's resourceful trip across Taka Mal and his courage. Her minstrel had depths she doubted even he knew, and if he died, it would be a crime.

Jade found Mica in the parlor, at a table tiled with gold-wing mosaics. The healer was intent on a scroll that listed medicines they were using in Drummer's treatment.

"How is he?" Jade asked, standing next to her.

Mica looked up, her face drawn, and started to stand, until Jade lay a hand on her shoulder, implicit permission to dispense with formalities.

Mica settled wearily back into her chair. "We've given him malo herbs and cold compresses for the fever. Nothing helps."

Jade's heart felt as if it stuttered. "Is he eating?"

"We've roused him enough to take liquids. Water. Broth."

The room pressed in on Jade. She did her best to hide her intense reaction, for Drummer's sake. For his life. As she thanked Mica and headed to the bedroom, it was all she could do to keep from running.

Inside Drummer's room, Doctor Quarry was sitting by the bed, blocking her view of Drummer. Quarry was an older man, heavier than most, with gray-streaked black hair. He dipped a cloth into a basin on the lacquered nightstand, then wrung it out and applied it to Drummer's forehead.

Jade went to stand by Quarry. Drummer lay on his back

with a gold sheet drawn across his chest. Given his fever and the heat, they had dressed him in the thinnest possible sleep clothes. The only light came from candles on the mantel above the rarely used fireplace. In their dim glow, his face was sallow, his cheeks sunken. Someone had shaved his scraggly beard, which made him look even younger and more vulnerable. His pale lashes glinted against his even paler skin.

She spoke in a low voice. "Has there been any change?"

Quarry looked up at her. "None."

Jade managed a nod. She had to restrain herself from twisting the silk sash on her tunic. "I will sit with him for a while."

Quarry looked relieved for the break. He didn't question the situation even if the queen herself offered to sit in for him. It was why Jade liked him; he accepted her as herself without questions.

The doctor left the room, his footsteps muffled on the Kazlatarian rug. As he closed the door, Jade settled stiffly in the chair. Then she thought, *Enough of this,* and sat on the bed. She laid her hand against Drummer's cheek. Saints, his skin burned! She moistened his compress again and laid it back on his forehead.

"Ah…" He sighed. "That helps."

Jade froze. Then she leaned over him, her hand braced on the other side of his body. "Drummer? You are alive?"

His lashes lifted, unveiling his blue eyes. In that moment, Jade understood perfectly the desire of Taka Mal kings to seclude their women. Maybe it was in her blood, passed down by generations of desert rulers, but her wish to protect Drummer, to hide him away from any possible harm, hit her with such intensity it hurt.

"Your Majesty…" he said.

"Ah, love, call me Jade."

"Where…?"

"You're in the Topaz Palace."

"And Baz?"

She winced. "He is in a bad mood."

"Are you all right?"

Jade couldn't believe he asked such a question. He, the man they had kidnapped, whose life she had endangered when she took advantage of his honor, the man who had nearly died in the desert and then lay here on the edge of death for three days—he asked if *she* was all right.

"I am fine," she said. "It is you we're worried about."

"Just woke up…" He reached up and cupped her cheek. "I know I'm not supposed to touch you. But, Jade…I've thought about you every moment since that night." His arm dropped back to the bed.

Something strange was happening inside of her. Desert men never revealed their moods. If she married Baz or Ozar, she would live the rest of her life with their lack of affection, their harsh worldview, and in Ozar's case, his wish to subjugate her will and body. All her life, she had assumed that her marriage would be a political and economic arrangement. She had accepted that. But with Drummer, that knowledge became a weight she loathed.

She longed for affection. Her parents had seemed to like

her, or at least they never beat her. But neither had they shown love. No one had ever spoken to her like Drummer. No one looked at her the way he did, whether he was playing his glittar or standing on his head. He wouldn't try to conquer her. He would make her laugh. He would sing. Why the bloody blazes did she have to settle for a lifetime of misery? Was it too much to want happiness? She was tired of it all, so very tired.

Jade took his hand. She knew she should stop touching him. But she couldn't. She couldn't walk away.

"Drummer?" she began. But then she stopped.

He managed a wan smile. "That's me. Not that I ever drum anything."

She went to the cliff edge—and jumped. "Marry me."

His smile vanished. "Don't mock me that way."

"I'm not." She bent her head and kissed him lightly.

Drummer stiffened. Then he groaned and pulled his other arm from under the covers so he could embrace her. His passion had a subdued quality, banked by his illness, but that only made it sweeter. Right now, Jade would have promised him the world if he asked.

After a moment, though, he laid his arms back on the bed. When she raised her head, he said, "If your cousin comes in here, or if anyone sees us and tells him—truly he will kill me."

Jade knew what she had to do. "Drummer, listen. Fieldson thinks we've committed terrible offenses against you. He's ready to declare war. Your niece's husband hulks at our borders. Both Taka Mal and Jazid covet the export trade of the Misted Cliffs. Jazid offers me a military alliance in return for marriage. Aronsdale is sitting in the middle of it all like a target. The political landscape isn't stable. Something has to give. Someone is going to launch an invasion, and I can't even guarantee it won't be me."

"I know it's a mess."

"Taka Mal needs a treaty. With Aronsdale."

"Saints almighty." He stared at her. "You meant it. About marrying me."

"I can make a case that might convince at least some of my generals. It could bring peace between the Houses of Dawnfield and Quaazera, just as the marriage between your niece and Cobalt brought peace between Dawnfield and Chamberlight."

"You're forgetting one thing." His voice was growing stronger. "My niece is heir to the Jaguar Throne. That's why it worked. I'm heir to what? Nothing. I'm just a poor relation."

It was true, however much she wanted to deny it. The treaty between Dawnfield and Chamberlight succeeded because each party brought enough into the marriage to make it worth the union. It put the Jaguar Throne back into the House of Escar and guaranteed Harsdown and Aronsdale wouldn't unite against Cobalt the Dark. In return, Cobalt swore he wouldn't seek dominion over Aronsdale nor invade Harsdown to reclaim the Jaguar Throne for himself. The next heir to the throne would be *both* Escar and Dawnfield.

It was a dangerous alliance. Taka Mal and Jazid needed to counter that threat. If Jade married Ozar, it might be a union forged in hell, but it would anneal their power. Their child would be heir to both the Topaz and Onyx Thrones. What offer could Drummer make? He had no throne, no riches, no army, nothing.

"Even so," Jade said. "You are a Dawnfield through your sister's marriage."

"No one would let us marry. Not your cousin. Not the atajazid. Not Cobalt."

Jade scowled. "What will Ozi do? Attack Taka Mal and carry me off?" Knowing Ozar, he might try it if she pushed him too far. He wouldn't like it if she chose Baz over him, but she doubted he would try to stop the union. It didn't threaten his country, and it had been expected for decades. But if she married a Dawnfield, it posed him an entirely new set of dangers.

"Jade, this is crazy."

"Perhaps not." The more she thought about it, the more angles she saw. "Such an agreement would bind Aronsdale and Taka Mal to support each other. My House would agree not to align with Ozar against Cobalt. Cobalt would agree not to attack us. Aronsdale would agree to support my army against Jazid if Ozar protests my marriage and against Cobalt if he tries to stop it. Aronsdale will no longer be isolated, Taka Mal and Jazid on one side and Harsdown and the Misted Cliffs on the other." She considered him. "It could stabilize the political landscape."

He slowly pulled himself into a sitting position. One of his curls stuck up over his ear. He didn't speak, though, and Jade felt her face grow hot with mortification. Her recitation about politics was probably about as romantic as having patters.

"I don't understand politics and military campaigns," Drummer said. "I never have."

"I didn't mean for it to sound so blunt." Jade felt foolish. He didn't seem to want her.

Then Drummer said, "If you want me to marry you, and you think it will work—" his sudden smile was as brilliant as it was sweet "—I would be honored to be your husband."

Jade felt as if a heavy carpet lifted off her shoulders. She wanted to laugh, to shout, to tumble in the silk sheets with him. But she could wait. They had their whole lives—which she hoped would be more than a few days.

"I'm glad." Her smile broke through. "Very glad."

Even with his face pale and drawn from his illness, his gaze could still dance with mischief. "But I'm too young for you."

"What, twenty-eight?" She laughed, feeling light. "Five years. Almost six. I'm ancient."

"Ah, Jade." He pulled her into his arms and laid his fevered cheek against her head. "I can't believe this is happening to me. Maybe it's a delirium dream."

"Then I'm having it, too." Holding him, she pondered how to proceed. She couldn't tell Baz until she could ensure Drummer's safety. Nor did she want her cousin harmed. She did love him, as a sister would love a quarrelsome brother.

Ozar would be a greater problem. Given a chance, he might haul her off to that fortress of his and do saints only knew what to her. Before she could announce any betrothal, she needed to ensure no one killed, abducted, or tortured anyone else. She wasn't certain who to trust. If anyone. General Slate tended to align with Baz. Firaz could go either way. Spearcaster usually supported her, but he didn't respect Aronsdale, a country he considered weak. All her advisors would object to Drummer's lack of title.

Jade drew back and considered him. Drummer chuckled, a pallid echo of his laugh, but a blessing after her fears for his life. "Why do you gaze at me as if I'm a puzzle?"

She tapped his cheek. "I have to fit the pieces together so I can marry you without getting either of us in trouble or dead."

His smile faded. "I don't see how."

"I have an idea." Jade kissed him soundly. "I have to take care of some matters." She slid off the bed. "Wish me luck."

Drummer was watching her with a strange expression, as if she were a wraith that would soon dissipate. "Do you have a shape?"

She peered at him. "Shape of what?"

"A ring, cube, anything like that."

Puzzled, she took off one of the gold hoops that hung from a smaller ring in her ear. "Will this do?"

"It's perfect." He held out his hand, palm up, and she set the earring in its center. Then he just sat. Jade shifted her weight, uncertain what this meant. He looked so drained and pale, she felt certain he should lie down again.

A sphere of gold light appeared in his hand.

Jade gaped at the sphere. "What is that?"

"For you," he said softly. "A topaz sphere." He lifted his gaze to hers. "I didn't understand about the pact. I'm sorry I betrayed your trust. But I give you my word now."

The blood drained from her face. "How did you do that?"

"It's a parlor trick," he murmured, seeming to tire. The light faded.

"I've never seen anything like it," Jade said. Quietly she added, "But I will honor your pact."

He offered her the earring. "Good luck, my Fire Opal."

Fire Opal indeed. She liked the name. Soon she would give him hers. Quaazera.

15

The
Sunwood Bargain

Cobalt leaned over the rocks and looked down at the base of the cliffs. About ten feet below him, a large warrior in leather-and-bronze armor was swinging his sword—at Mel. She blocked the strike, but the force of the blow backed her up a step. As the warrior came at her with another swing, Cobalt's hand tightened on the spur of rock he was clenching, and he barely held back his shout.

Mel parried with her blade at an unusual angle and caught her opponent's sword in a twisting motion. It was a strange move, one she had used against Cobalt, odd enough that it slowed him down. It had the same effect on her opponent below. He hesitated, and she used her advantage to drive him back. He recovered fast, though, and his next parry knocked the sword from Mel's hand. He followed up with a thrust that

Cobalt's heightened instincts comprehended could cut off Mel's head if it struck home—

Cobalt vaulted over the rocks and landed with a thud next to Mel, in front of the blade the warrior brandished at his wife. In reflex, Cobalt drew his own sword. His awareness of time jumped as it did in battle, where he felt as if he acted at normal speed and everyone around him moved in a strange, incredibly slowed time. The other man froze, his sword a hand's span from Cobalt's breastplate.

The warrior flushed and lowered his weapon. Apprehension washed across his face. With the threat to Mel past, Cobalt's time sense slowed to normal.

Mel sighed. To the warrior, she said, "Thank you."

The man bowed deeply to her. "You fight well, Your Majesty." He looked as if he feared Cobalt was about to slice him up.

"You may go," Cobalt growled at him.

"Your Majesty." The man bowed again and quickly set off toward the fields where the Chamberlight army had camped.

Mel turned a dour gaze on Cobalt. "What was all that for?"

He crossed his arms. "How do you expect me to react when a man waves a sword at my pregnant wife?"

"Ah, Cobalt." She sheathed her sword and adjusted her armor. It bewildered him that she could dress so much like a man and look so womanly. Black leather did erotic things to her body. It made him want to take her to Taka Mal with him, and he couldn't do that. He had to broach the subject again, and he would have to say many words to make his point, but if he didn't put forth his best effort, his formidably articulate wife would talk circles around him until he ended up agreeing with her. This was too important for him to let that happen.

"Mel," he began.

"Yes?" She was resting her palm on the ball that formed the end of her sword hilt. Green light glowed around her hand.

"Stop that," he growled.

"It's only a mood spell." But she released the ball, and the light faded. "Sometimes I think you make them."

"Spells of emotion?" He couldn't think of anyone less likely than himself to wield them.

"Not emotion." She hesitated. "Maybe not spells. But saints, Cobalt, when you fight, it's as if you have supernatural powers. I didn't think it was possible to move that fast."

Ah. So. He pulled himself up. "I am indeed formidable."

Her lips quirked upward. "And modest."

"What did your emotion spell tell you?"

"You fear for me."

"Yes." Knowing one-word responses wouldn't be enough, he forced himself to continue. "You must stay in Alzire. I know you feel you must ride. You have the heart of a fighter. I know you can help the army. But you must, this time, listen to me." No, that wasn't right. She always listened to him. She was always respectful. Then she went ahead and did whatever she wanted. "You carry our baby." He didn't know how he could ever be a good father, but now that he had absorbed the thought of his child, he wanted intensely for it to be born.

"The army won't go into combat," Mel said. "You're going to Taka Mal only as a warning, right?" She made the question a challenge.

"Yes," Cobalt said, aware of the sun heating the hollow where they stood. Sweat gathered on his brow. "But any time you take an army somewhere, combat is possible. We will march along the Jazid border. The Atajazid D'az Ozar will bring out his army. Just in case. Queen Vizarana will gather hers. Just in case. It is too volatile. You must not come."

She rested her hand on her abdomen in a gesture that seemed so instinctual Cobalt wondered if she realized she had done it. "I wouldn't fight."

"Even so. You could be hurt." He took her hand, awkward with the gesture. It wasn't that he didn't feel the affection it implied; sometimes he filled up with so much emotion for Mel, he didn't know where to put it all. He never knew how to express it; his attempts were foolish and clumsy. Nevertheless, he had to try. He could just forbid her to come. He could have his men hold her in the Alzire Palace. But if he trampled her spirit, she might take away the love that for some miraculous reason she gave him.

Mel was watching his face, and he suspected she was using her sphere to make mood spells even if her sword wasn't making light. Actually, he wasn't sure it *didn't* have a faint glow.

She took his hand in both of hers. "All right."

Cobalt wasn't certain he had heard properly. "What?"

"I will stay in Alzire."

"You will?" Now he *knew* his hearing had problems.

She laughed softly. "Don't look so shocked."

"You never agree that easily."

"You are more convincing than you know. It comes from your heart." She placed his palm on her stomach, which as of yet showed no sign of pregnancy. "You are right, I must think of the child."

Cobalt didn't realize how much he had tensed until his body relaxed. "It is good, is it not? Having a child."

She smiled. "It is."

"You will be a good mother." He had no doubt about that.

"I hope so."

He pulled her to him. Since they had been traveling with the army, they had less time for each other. Soon they would return to their duties, he to overseeing the Chamberlight forces and she to governing Alzire. But for a few moments on this warm afternoon, they could spend time with each other.

"Let us walk for a while," he said.

She took his hand. "I would like that."

As they strolled together, a thought came to Cobalt: He should enjoy this walk because it would be his last with her. He shook off the strange mood. They would have many such times. Of course they would. He couldn't bear to think otherwise.

He would annihilate anyone who threatened her.

Jade walked down the Sunwood Corridor. Its floor-to-ceiling windows let sunlight slant across the yellow wood. She passed mosaics depicting scenes from the history of

Quaaz. Here was one that showed her many-times-great-grandmother from a thousand years ago holding a baby, the child who grew up to be Kaazar the Mighty, also called The Wise, the Quaazera king who had built this city.

She stepped through an archway into a large hall. On her right, a small arch opened discreetly into her Sunwood study, a comfortable room with an antique surveying glass mounted on a gold stand in one corner.

Sphere-General Fieldson had already arrived, escorted by the two men she sent to request his presence—her body-guards, in fact. Leadership was about judicious governance of course, but having good bodyguards never hurt, either. They now stood posted at the door. She trusted these two, not only to protect her, but to watch that her cousin Baz or his palace spies didn't "happen" by and eavesdrop. Fieldson was across the room gazing out a floor-to-ceiling window bordered by murals of her ancestors. Sunlight slanted across his face, highlighting the lines around his eyes. His strong profile reminded Jade of statues she had seen during her visits to Castle Suncroft in Aronsdale.

She went over to him. "Light of the noon, General."

He turned with a start. As he bowed, his tension seemed to crackle. "My greetings, Your Majesty." His deep voice could have sounded threatening, except he always sounded like that. He was, she had to admit, an impressive envoy.

Jade gave him her most disarming smile. "Drummer woke up."

Fieldson remained wary. "He is recovering?"

"He is indeed." Anticipating his next question, she added,

"You can see him if you would like. But first I wish to discuss something with you."

The hint of a smile had started to show on his face, but now his defenses snapped back down. "I will engage in no negotiations, Your Majesty, until I am assured he is well."

"It isn't a negotiation, exactly. Drummer and I have come to a decision." She thought of the strange, unsettling light her intended had created. Then she put the disquieting memory out of her mind; she would have time to worry about it later. "That is why you and I need to talk."

"I'm not sure I should listen to this," Fieldson said. "But I confess, you have my curiosity. What is this decision?"

Jade felt as if she were walking down a gauntlet of words. One misstep and they could demolish her. "I can't tell you yet." She held up her hand when he scowled. "I don't mean to be coy. You and I may want similar things, but neither of us is ready to trust the other. Please hear me out."

"All right." Despite his guarded manner, he seemed intrigued, as he often did in their talks, as if she were some exotic and beautiful animal. "What do you wish to say?"

"It has to do with protection."

"For Drummer."

"Yes." She took a deep breath. "And for me."

His gaze sharpened. "Protection against who?"

Jade gazed out the window at the garden, though she hardly saw the trellises heavy with fire-lilies or the dragon fountains outside that breathed water instead of flame. She didn't know how to broach the subject of her betrothal. If she misspoke in any way that could be interpreted as a betrayal of her throne or the House of Quaazera, it could have disastrous consequences.

"Has something happened to Drummer," Fieldson asked tightly, "that you fear reprisals?"

"If only it were that simple." She turned to him. "Aronsdale is in an unstable position, some might even say untenable."

"People say many things," he answered. "Talk costs nothing."

"Oh, I don't know about that." Jade regarded him steadily. "It can cost a kingdom."

His face revealed nothing. But he had to know what she meant. He came from Aronsdale and had been a king's advisor even before he went to Harsdown to serve Muller Dawnfield.

"Go on," he said.

"Consider geography," Jade said. "On one side of Aronsdale, Taka Mal and Jazid are poised to challenge Cobalt Escar. On the other side of Aronsdale, the Misted Cliffs and Shazire are united to move against Taka Mal and Jazid."

"I will believe an alliance between Jazid and Taka Mal," Fieldson said, "when I see it."

Jade knew he was probing. "Is it any less likely," she countered, "than the devil's bargain the House of Dawnfield made with the House of Escar when Mel Dawnfield married Cobalt Escar?"

"You would know better than I," he murmured, "what devils Taka Mal is willing to endure for the price of conquest."

Devils indeed. She didn't want to dwell on her brutal suitor. "Aronsdale is ruled by the Dawnfields, and they are bound by their treaty with Cobalt. But suppose he conquers these desert lands? You don't know that he will respect the treaty when nothing is left to stop him." She took a breath. "If the atajazid and I join forces, we might defeat Cobalt. Would we then turn against Aronsdale? Should they ally with their sometimes enemy, Cobalt the Dark? No matter how you look at it, Aronsdale is caught in the middle, and if they fall, so will Harsdown."

"You paint a rather dire picture."

"Do you dispute it?"

He didn't answer. Instead he asked, "I take it you have a point in outlining this state of affairs?"

"Perhaps a solution."

Jade had the gratification of seeing his surprise. "If you have that," he told her, "you are far ahead of the rest of us."

"Aronsdale should ally with Taka Mal."

He gave a startled laugh. "Why not? While we're at it, we could move the Blue Ocean to Aronsdale and flood the desert."

She smiled slightly. "I'm not joking."

"Never, in known history, have Taka Mal and Aronsdale allied. How would you convince your advisors? Your military?" He waited a moment. "Your cousin?"

"They aren't stupid," Jade said. "We must ally with someone, or we are going to end up just like Shazire."

"Why would you choose Dawnfield over Onyx?"

"The House of Onyx offers much to my House. An alliance has merit. However, I am a realist, as are my advisors. If I marry the atajazid, I could lose my throne to him."

"You don't have to marry him to ally with him."

Jade grimaced. "Apparently I do."

Fieldson took a moment to absorb that. Then he spoke with care. "I would think that if war threatens Taka Mal and Jazid, the atajazid would form an alliance with less demanding terms."

"Perhaps. One would hope to avoid such a threat."

"How?" he demanded. "By kidnapping the queen's brother?"

"No." She mentally braced herself. "By marrying the queen's brother."

Fieldson stared at her. It was the first time she had seen him truly speechless. She waited.

Finally he said, "That is—unexpected."

He was a master of understatement. "If you find it so," she said wryly, "imagine how my generals will react." One in particular.

He stood thinking. "If the Houses of Quaazera and Dawnfield were to ally, Cobalt couldn't invade Taka Mal. It would violate the treaty he signed guaranteeing he wouldn't attack any country ruled by the House of his wife's family."

"He would also have a guarantee that Taka Mal wouldn't turn against him," Jade pointed out. "The same treaty that would forbid Cobalt from attacking Taka Mal would stop us from attacking him."

Fieldson looked incredulous. "It's brilliant. Impossible, but brilliant."

She regarded him steadily. "Nothing is impossible."

"I came here to protect Drummer, not make him the target of every assassin in Taka Mal and Jazid."

"He won't be a target if he is no longer in Taka Mal when I announce the betrothal." Jade knew she had gone too far to turn back in this discussion. "Unfortunately, the announcement may put my top military officers in the unenviable position of having to choose between their queen and their commander."

"You are their commander."

"Yes, well, as you may have noticed, not everyone here considers the throne an appropriate piece of furniture for a woman." She leaned against the window frame and folded her arms. "Some will support me, some will support Baz, and most won't know what to do. My honor guard might have to protect me against a forced marriage to their commanding officer. Who do they obey? It would be a mess."

"So you need bodyguards without that loyalty conflict."

"Even better, guards with a vested interest in keeping me betrothed to Drummer Headwind."

He exhaled. "I see."

"Sphere-General Fieldson." She lapsed into the more formal cadences she used in negotiations. "Goodman Headwind's situation has given rise to concerns for his health, even his life. I offer him into your custody so that you may escort him back to Aronsdale. In return, you will leave your honor guard here, as hostages for the negotiations we wish to continue." Hostages indeed. They would be protecting her from her own kin. "Taka Mal will provide you with officers for your return to Aronsdale."

He inclined his head. "Your Majesty, I believe we may be able to find a common ground in this."

"I am glad." Jade felt as if she were falling off a cliff. This could backfire spectacularly if her new bodyguards had to fight to protect her. She sincerely hoped her truculent suitors, Baz and Ozar, had the sanity not to kill an honor guard of high-ranking officers from the Misted Cliffs and Harsdown—for that would be tantamount to an act of war against Cobalt the Dark.

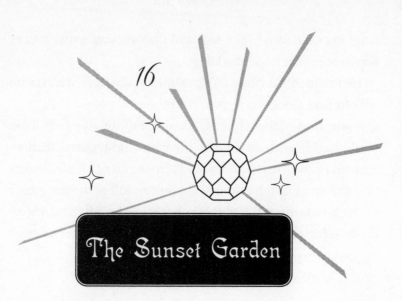

16

The Sunset Garden

Twenty-four days after Cobalt's army left the Misted Cliffs, it flowed around Alzire, the capital of Shazire, like a flood swirling around rocks. As the companies spread across meadows vibrant with summer grasses and wildflowers, the three thousand men Cobalt had left in Shazire joined them.

Alzire was one of the largest cities in the settled lands, after Quaaz and the capital of Jazid. It boasted five thousand people. But even Alzire couldn't support such a big influx of warriors tramping about its streets and carousing in its taverns. The companies set up a rotating schedule, allowing smaller groups to visit the famous city, view its exquisite arches and bridges and soaring temples, and drink its ale. With the flood controlled, the army offered an economic cornucopia to the Alzire merchants, for the soldiers had wages to spend, and gold hexa-coins were worth just as much in Shazire as in the Misted Cliffs.

Mel rode into Alzire at Cobalt's side with Agate Cragland, Matthew and a retinue of officers. Cobalt sat on his huge black warhorse and wore his Chamberlight helmet. Its faceplate was open to let the sun strike his face, and its plume rippled. With his breastplate gleaming, his already broad shoulders widened even more by leather armor studded with metal, and his broadsword strapped across his back, he looked every inch the conquering warrior king.

Their horses clopped down cobblestone streets, and pedestrians jumped back. People watched from windows and roofs and alleys. Mel felt strange riding into the city this way. Her family had always maintained good relations with Prince Zerod, Shazire's former sovereign. At her urging, Cobalt had let Zerod and his family live, but he was keeping the queen and her young son under guard in their summer palace, to ensure Zerod's behavior. If nothing went wrong, he would soon let them rejoin the deposed prince in exile. Cobalt's year of truce with the atajazid had ended last spring, and all waited to see how he and Ozar would deal with each other.

Today Cobalt took Mel to the Hall of Oceans in the palace. He laid his hand on one of the two thrones inlaid with turquoise and mother-of-pearl. "It is yours."

Mel thought of Zerod. "I cannot sit there."

"You must, in spirit if not in body."

"I will govern here as best I can while you go to Taka Mal. But I won't take that throne."

Cobalt frowned. "It was yours long before Zerod's House stole it from the Misted Cliffs."

She blinked. "Mine?"

"Thousands of years ago, a Dawn Star Empress ruled these lands, including what we now call the Misted Cliffs, Harsdown, Aronsdale, Blueshire, and Shazire." Cobalt glared as if daring her to refute him. "It is the legend of your name—the field of stars left by the empress when she rose into the sky at her untimely death." He stopped, seeming disconcerted by his own words. "I would much rather my queen sit on a throne than turn into dots of light."

She smiled. "I promise not to turn into any dots."

"Good." He seemed satisfied, and she didn't think he even realized she was teasing him.

"Do you leave tomorrow morning?" she asked.

"Before dawn."

"I will miss you," she said, which was true.

He hesitated. "Most people are glad when I am gone."

She took his hand and held his knuckles against her cheek. "I would rather have you here."

He drew her in, his arm around her waist, and pressed his lips against the top of her head. "Good."

"I've been thinking," she said, musing. "What shall we name our child?"

"Name?" He sounded confused again.

She held back her smile. "Most people have them."

"I know that, Mel," he growled. "But we don't know if it is a boy or a girl."

"It has to be one or the other." It bemused her that he

could be such a brilliant military commander, yet find the simple domestic aspects of life bewildering. "Cobalt for a boy."

"Ach! No. He could do better."

"I like it."

"Well." He sounded pleased.

"Maybe Chord for a girl."

"What, like *Rope?*"

She smiled at his outraged tone. "I meant a chord in music. But I see your point."

"Not Stonebreaker." His voice darkened. "Never Stone-breaker."

Mel had no argument with that. She could still see, in her mind, the dying king on his deathbed, whispering to his grandson. "Cobalt?"

"Yes?"

"Don't let Stonebreaker follow you from his grave."

His posture stiffened. "He follows me everywhere."

"Whatever he said that night—" She paused, unsure how to continue.

For a while he was silent. Then he said, "Chamberlight raised me. Not Escar."

"That's true." She wondered what he was about.

"My grandfather hated me."

"Cobalt, no."

"Perhaps it is because I am not a true heir."

"Of course you are!" She drew back to look up at him. "Just look at any picture of Varqelle. You have the same pro-file, same cheekbones, same hair, same eyes."

He paused, his gaze intent on her face. He started to speak, then hesitated. Finally he said, "People often remark on how much I resemble him."

"Because you do." Mel shook her head. "If Stonebreaker said you weren't an Escar, he was lying. He tried to hurt you. To undermine your confidence."

"Mel—" His face showed a vulnerability he let no one else see. "It is hard to hear my own voice instead of his."

She brushed back a straggle of hair that had escaped his queue. Was this what had haunted him since Stonebreaker's death? It was no wonder he brooded, if his grandfather had claimed he was a bastard with no right to any throne. Stonebreaker couldn't really believe it; otherwise, he would never have made Cobalt his heir. She doubted he had mentioned Matthew, for she had seen no change in how Cobalt treated him, and she knew her husband too well to believe he would be so unaffected by such news. But for Stonebreaker to plant a seed of doubt that could grow and plague his successor: yes, it was a cruelty she could imagine from him.

"He has no power over you," Mel said. "He is gone."

"I try to remember that." Cobalt seemed calmer. It was good. The more settled he felt, the less likely he was to let his torments drive him into battle. She had been fortunate in how he phrased his words: *Perhaps it is because I am not a true heir.* She could assure him without hesitation that he was of the House of Escar. He hadn't posed the crucial question, the one that would have forced her to silence or false assurances.

He hadn't asked if Varqelle was his father.

* * *

Breezes stirred Jade's hair, which she wore down today. She loved these hidden gardens, accessible only through guarded doors. They attached to the most cloistered rooms in the palace, the Sunset Suite, a place of gold and rubies, and exquisite landscapes painted on the walls. Her mother had lived in seclusion here during her marriage. Jade's ginger-maids kept these rooms spotless and gleaming, but they had been empty for years, since her mother's death. Empty, that was, until she gave them to Drummer.

Today she walked with him among a profusion of sunsnap bushes sculpted to resemble goldwings. Their scent gave the air a sweet fragrance with a dash of spice. The sunlight made his curls shimmer, and his face had regained its healthy glow.

"Sooner or later," she said, "we will have to admit you are well enough to travel."

"Later, I hope." He strummed his glittar, and its notes sparkled like drops of water flying up from a waterfall. Jade wished he could stay here forever. Supposedly he was convalescing. She had to sneak in to see him, but fortunately no one else could come here. After a grueling session with the envoy negotiators, she had "reluctantly" agreed to let Harsdown and Chamberlight men guard this suite rather than her own officers. So none of her own people saw her visits. She and Fieldson were playing a dangerous game; if anyone found out he was helping her, the situation could explode with accusations of treason.

Jade knew the time had come for Drummer to leave.

These past twenty days had been idyllic, a happier interlude than she could ever remember. If he left, she feared she might never see him again, that their plans would fall apart and violence would inflame the settled lands. If she married Ozar, she might become an empress, but she would rather have Drummer, happiness and peace.

He drew her over to a bench under a trellis heavy with yellow and red lilies. A vine-draped wall behind them curved around the bench, creating a living alcove. Within it, a fountain shaped like a lily burbled with water.

"I love it here," he said as they sat on the bench.

Jade slid her fingers into his hair, which brushed his collar in an unruly mop. She hadn't been this relaxed since—well, since she didn't know when.

He caught her hand and planted a kiss in her palm. Then he settled the glittar in his lap and braced it against his chest. "I wrote you a song," he said. "But I won't sing it unless you promise not to make fun of my poetry."

"I'll try not to misbehave." In truth, she loved listening to him sing. It was almost as much fun teasing him, though.

His grin flashed. "I didn't say you had to behave." His fingers danced across the glittar strings and a trill of notes filled the air. He warmed up with a melody of nonsense syllables. He could sing both baritone and tenor, though he seemed most comfortable as a tenor. He slid into a song with a haunting, chantlike quality:

Opal stone, moonstone,
Jewel of the night,

Glowing bone, rune stone,
Cruel inner light.

That speaks of darkness,
And never of you.

Opal stone, fire stone!
Jewel of the flame,
Never lone, dear stone,
Mine heart you can claim.

I long for your kiss,
Forever with you.

On the last word, he hit a high note and held it beautifully. Then he let it fade into the burble of the fountain. Jade didn't realize they were leaning closer until he brushed his lips across hers. Closing her eyes, she molded against him and her mouth softened. He sighed as he kissed her, and he ran his fingers over the glittar. He was touching the strings, not her, but it was as erotic as if he were strumming her body.

Finally he set down the harp and pulled her close against him. Times like this with Drummer were the only instances in her life when she let herself be soft. He was the first suitor she had trusted with her vulnerability, perhaps because his was as deep as hers. He seemed defenseless compared to the other men in her life, and it made her want to protect him with a visceral fierceness. Was this what her father had felt with her mother, why he locked her away and let so few people see her? Perhaps Jade had inherited more than his throne and his wild dark eyes.

After a while, Jade laid her head on his shoulder and stared out at the gardens beyond their bower.

"I wish I didn't have to go," Drummer said.

"I also." At least when he reached Suncroft, he and Fieldson would take her proposal to King Jarid. "If we receive the response we hope for from Jarid, I can announce the betrothal."

"He better agree," Drummer said.

"Fieldson thinks he will."

He drew back, and she straightened up to look at him. "I will memorize your face," he said. "Everything about you. The way you talk. And laugh." His wicked grin sparked. "The way you growl and stalk when you don't get your way."

She glared at him. "I never growl and stalk."

"You do." He kissed her again. "I've never met anyone with such passion, Jade. I love it."

Her breath went still inside of her. "You do?"

For a moment he didn't seem to understand her reaction. Then his voice softened. "I do, beautiful queen. All of you."

She traced her fingers along his lips. "And I you."

He held her close and the day was sharp and clear. Yet it also felt like a dream that would fade just as the last note of his song had disappeared from her garden.

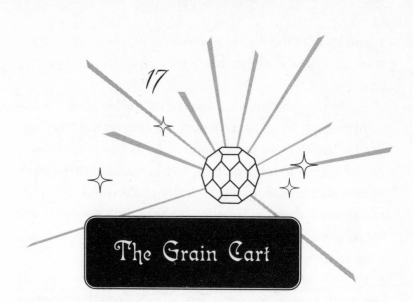

17

The Grain Cart

The Chamberlight forces were half-a-day's ride from the Jazid border when Cobalt's scout rode to him with the news: The atajazid had gathered his own army and was on the move within Jazid. It didn't surprise Cobalt. If someone brought an army to his borders, he would meet them with his forces even if both sides professed no hostile intent. The Misted Cliffs had an advantage; its borders were a wall of cliffs to the east, the Escar Mountains in the north, and the Blue Ocean to the south and west. It made the country relatively impregnable compared to his adversaries.

Potential adversaries, he reminded himself.

The land gradually became more arid. Although they passed patches of greenery around small lakes or along rivers, lush Shazire was giving way to harsher terrain. It was a land of wild beauty, of deserts and needled peaks interspersed with valleys that nurtured the increasingly rare oases.

By the time the sunset coalesced on the horizon, the forward ranks of Cobalt's army were massing on the Jazid border. He had brought six companies: Carnelian, Alexandrite, Aquamarine and Iolite on foot, and Tanzanite and Sapphire on horseback. Although the cavalry could travel faster, the horses needed rest more often, so they didn't arrive much ahead of the troops. They spent the evening gathering in a plain of rock slabs and patches of meadow.

He rode up on a spiky knoll where he could view his army spread all around. Beyond them, the shadowy lands across the border were a blur. He put on his spectacles and peered east. The distant campfires of the Jazidian army flared in the foothills of the Jagged Teeth Mountains, and the peaks above them jabbed the purple sky.

Agate Cragland rode up alongside him and indicated Ozar's army. "My scouts estimate they are four and a half thousand."

"We underestimated their numbers." Cobalt scrutinized the distant campfires, as if he could decode their secrets. "I must send an envoy to Ozar."

"A wise precaution."

"If he doesn't kill the envoy," Cobalt said.

Agate glanced sharply at him. "You have reason to believe he would commit such an act?"

In truth, Cobalt had heard of no such dishonor from the House of Onyx. But a dark history surrounded the atajazids.

They had never been known for their adherence to codes of war, nor had they ever fully shed their reputation for the barbarism that had flourished in ancient times. They no longer committed atrocities, at least none they let be known, but in recent times, no hostile conflicts had offered them the opportunity, either.

"No specific reason," Cobalt admitted. "But the House of Onyx has a brutal history."

Agate regarded him curiously. "Dancer tells me that you've studied military history for decades."

"A bit." Cobalt started to assume the nonchalance he had always adopted with Stonebreaker, who ridiculed anything Cobalt valued. Then he remembered Stonebreaker was gone. After a pause, he said, "I read it all the time, actually."

"It is good for a leader to know such chronicles."

The comment startled Cobalt. He hadn't thought Agate viewed him as much of a leader. The older man had said nothing when Cobalt became a general at the young age of thirty-three. Stonebreaker gave him the title just before Cobalt led his men to free Varqelle. The king had never made it a secret that he promoted his grandson for heredity rather than merit. Cobalt could never claim he earned his rank. No other general commented, of course, but Cobalt had assumed they felt it was unearned. His grandfather had never hidden his dissatisfaction with his heir. Cobalt had spent his life trying to prove the king wrong, but he could have conquered the world and it wouldn't have satisfied Stonebreaker. The damn old man could say nothing more on his deathbed than to swear Cobalt was a bastard who deserved no title at all, let alone the Sapphire Throne.

Cobalt raged inside at his tormentor, who blighted his life even from the grave. He could never tune out his grandfather's voice; he would hear Stonebreaker until the day he died.

He had never told his grandfather about his fascination with history. Cobalt had learned a great deal about Shazire, once a part of the Misted Cliffs. He had read widely about Taka Mal and Jazid, contrasting their campaigns to the more conservative Chamberlight approach. It had helped him envision how Shazire might have changed since Jazid ripped it free of the Misted Cliffs.

The war two centuries ago between the Misted Cliffs and Taka Mal had ended with no clear winner. Most historical accounts credited victory to Jazid and Taka Mal, which together had wrested land from the Misted Cliffs. The conflict had depleted them, though, and they couldn't hold their new acquisitions. The provinces soon became independent. The larger turned into Shazire and took many influences from Jazid. The smaller named itself Blueshire, after the meadows it shared with Aronsdale, and became like a younger sibling to that pastoral country.

Cobalt's familiarity with the complex histories of Shazire and Blueshire allowed him to see how they might react to changes. Establishing a government wasn't his forte, but Mel was good at it and she knew Shazire. If he hadn't needed her in the Misted Cliffs, he would have appointed her governor of Shazire.

Cobalt smiled. He should put Mel on the Sapphire

Throne. She could run things and he could stay with the army. She wouldn't approve of his campaigns, though, and dealing with her displeasure was more daunting than ten thousand Jazidian warriors.

In the past, Cobalt had taken for granted the constraints on the women in his life. They went veiled. Their men owned them. Many lived in seclusion. He knew women in other countries enjoyed more freedoms, but he had never thought much about it. That changed with his marriage. Even before he knew Mel, though, he had thought Stonebreaker was mistaken to deny Dancer the Sapphire Throne. Such a waste. She had far more talent for governance than her son. She would make a good Chamberlight queen.

Taka Mal had a history of queens who ruled. For all that the culture restricted women, it was a hotbed of progressive ideas compared to the Misted Cliffs. That was even truer of Harsdown. Aronsdale was in between; although women had freedom in rural areas, they had no history of power on the throne. Or maybe he should think of the "crown"; Aronsdale was the only country that gave its ruler a fancy headpiece. Cobalt didn't see the point, but the practice had a long history. He had once researched it. He traced the custom to ships that had come to the Misted Cliffs long ago from across the Blue Ocean, but he couldn't find much about them, and few visited now. In fact, he couldn't think of any in his lifetime. These days, any ship that sailed off into the Blue Ocean ended up coming back to the shore, though the sailors swore they never changed direction. Either that, or the ship vanished.

According to legend, an ancient mage had cursed the settled lands: Each century they would become more hidden from the world, until one day they would be forever cut off, with no link to other lands except for globes of the world that were centuries out of date. Cobalt found it unlikely. He was willing to admit mages existed, given that he had married one, but he had never known Mel to do harm with her spells, except to herself.

Mage queen. He didn't understand it, but his formidable wife clearly wielded some sort of power. He wished his mother had a similar focus in her life. She could have done so much given even half the chances Stonebreaker had denied her.

"Agate," Cobalt said. "You've known my mother a long time?"

The general shifted his attention from the army below to Cobalt. "Since she was born. I was eleven, then."

"What do you think she would say if I asked her to govern Shazire?"

He looked perplexed. "But she is a woman."

Cobalt smiled slightly. "Yes, I noticed."

"It seems...atypical."

"Why? She is in charge of the Misted Cliffs."

"Temporarily."

"Shazire has had queens on the throne." Cobalt suspected the people would be more willing to accept Dancer than him. "They called Zerod a prince instead of a king because he married into the royal family. He only became the ruler after the death of the previous king, his wife's brother."

"But *he* took the throne," Agate said. "Not his wife."

"Even so." The more Cobalt thought about it, the more he liked the idea. Dancer could govern both Shazire and Blueshire, which might stop Mel from this confounding idea of hers to put the deposed king of Blueshire back on his throne.

"Do you think she would do a good job?" Cobalt asked.

"I don't know." After a moment, Agate said, "I don't think Her Majesty would do a bad job."

He appreciated the respect Agate showed by using Dancer's former title, from when she was the queen of Harsdown.

"I get my interest in history from her," Cobalt said.

"She is intelligent."

"She has more patience than I do."

Agate wisely refrained from any response. Cobalt knew his temper and dark moods were often cause for comment among his men.

They remained on the knoll while the sky turned from purple to black, with the moon half-hidden behind streamers of cloud. This felt right, a place he belonged. And yet…Cobalt found himself thinking of home. He missed Mel. When she came with him, he didn't miss her, which was good. He could concentrate better. But then he worried for her safety, and now he thought a lot about the baby. This marriage business was a distraction, but such a sweet preoccupation. More and more lately, he wanted to concern himself with matters of state and fatherhood. When they reached Taka Mal, he would sign a treaty with Queen Vizarana and the Atajazid D'az Ozar. His army would be a good bargaining tool. But Mel was right: He had done enough. He had healed the two-centuries-old wound that had sundered the Misted Cliffs. His world was whole.

It was time to go home.

Across the border, in Jazid, the fires of the Jazid army burned orange, harsh in the night.

In Shazire, they celebrated the Citrine Festival with bonfires, honoring the saint who added brightness to the land. The festivities heralded the summer and their hope for a good year.

Mel hurried to her palace suite. She had been busy all day, and people had kept coming to her about the festival events, especially Tadimaja Pickaxe. He was the aide from Zerod's staff Cobalt had kept, because Mel had trusted Tadimaja all her life. He knew the palace and its workings, which today unfortunately meant he was continually reminding her of chores she hadn't realized needed to be done. Now night had fallen and she wasn't ready to appear at the ceremony in the Alzire Plaza. She was expected to wear a yellow gown and dress her hair in citrine gems. If she missed the opening or arrived in inappropriate clothes, it would be taken as an insult by the people here. She had a chance to ease their hostility toward Cobalt, and she didn't want to bungle matters.

Unrest had simmered in Shazire since the invasion, especially in the capital. In the ten days she had been here, Mel had made inroads in setting a better image for the Chamberlight presence. It had to do with diplomacy, kindness, and attention to detail, and it didn't hurt that she had a more appealing demeanor than her husband. She didn't want to hamper those efforts by appearing to scorn a celebration of such local importance.

Mel sped around the corner, into view of the royal suite—and groaned. Tadimaja was waiting outside the large double doors.

She slowed down. "Tadi, surely it can wait."

"I am terribly sorry, Your Majesty." He bowed nervously. "It's about the trainers for the horse show. We have to sign the scrolls for their payment."

"We can't. They have the scrolls. And they aren't here. They went to the plaza for the ceremony."

Tadimaja winced, his sharp features scrunching up. "Their tender is down at the stables. With the scrolls. He insists he will take their horses and leave if he doesn't receive your seal. He thinks my staff is trying to cheat him." He looked mortified. "I truly am sorry. It is my fault. I mixed up their contract with one for the fire jugglers."

Mel inwardly swore. She couldn't go to the ceremony dressed as she was now, in a flimsy tunic and harem pants. The clothes were comfortable but hardly appropriate for tonight's pageantry. "Can you get the scrolls while I'm changing? One of my maids can bring them in. I'll add the Chamberlight seal and you can take them back to Goodman Barker."

Lines of concern creased his face. "Yes, of course."

Mel recognized his expression. "Why won't that work?" She felt seconds drizzling away like sand through her fingers.

His worry lines deepened. "It's just…"

"Tadi, please. I must hurry."

"Barker doesn't trust you. If you don't come, he may leave."

The last thing she needed were rumors she had cheated Barker. She pushed back her tousled hair. "All right. Get my bodyguards and meet me here in five minutes. Let Clerk Abacus know I can't meet him on my way to the plaza."

He hesitated. "Yes. Of course."

Damn! She knew that look. "Tadi, what is it?"

"Your bodyguards went to the main entrance to meet you."

Why the blazes had they gone there? "We were supposed to meet in the Hall of Oceans."

"I'm sorry." He sounded miserable.

Mel made her decision. "It will take too long to reach the stables. If Barker leaves, we'll have to live with it."

He cleared his throat, hesitated, then said, "Of course."

Mel sighed. "But?"

"I am but a simple servant, Your Majesty."

"Tadi, just tell me."

"Barker will spread tales of deceit."

She knew he was right. But worse tales would spread if she spoiled tonight's ceremony. "I don't have time."

His face brightened. "I know hidden ways through the palace. Very fast. We will get there in no time."

"Hidden passages?"

He gave her a conspiratorial smile. "Keeping on a few of the old guards has its advantages."

"So it does." Maybe she could make it after all. And she was curious about these hidden ways. "Show me."

"Right away!"

As they hurried along the corridor, she said, "Do you remember when I came here with my parents, when I was six? I always asked you about secret tunnels. You never breathed a word." She pretended to scowl. "Shame on you."

"Now you know," he offered, smiling.

They ended up in a secluded alcove shaped like a royal-bud blossom. Tadimaja traced his fingers along a molding at waist height. Mel struggled for patience while he pressed and pushed various ridges. "Tadi, it's taking too long—"

"I've got it!" He tapped a molding, and pins clinked inside the wall. With a grunt, he pushed. A slab moved inward with the scrape of stone on stone, then swung aside to reveal a dark space.

"There!" He turned to her. "This will take us to the yard behind the stables."

"We need a light." She had no shapes to make spells.

"I know the way. Just hold my belt and follow me."

This was making her uneasy. "I don't think so."

"Your Majesty—"

"No. Please give my regrets to Goodman Barker." Mel spun around. If she ran fast enough back to her suite—

A blow slammed her head. She staggered and barely stopped her fall. Twisting around, she raised her arms in a defensive move. Tadimaja's face contorted in a snarl Mel had never seen from him before. Behind him, a lanky man with sun-weathered skin was leaving the passage: Barker, the master horse trainer. Motion blurred in her side vision, and she jerked her elbow up barely in time to block the lunge of a wiry man, another of the trainers, as he came at her from the left. Her head was spinning from the first blow, and the slippery silk of her clothes hampered her. Harem pants were made for lounging, not fighting.

Mel kicked up her leg and caught Barker in the side, knocking him into the passageway. As Tadimaja backed up, Barker yelled at him, and the wiry man struck Mel, knocking her forward. Tadimaja tried to grab her arm, but Mel turned the move against him. She caught him on her hip and rolled him over her shoulder, then brought him down hard onto his back.

Barker aimed a blow at Mel's head. As she blocked it, the wiry trainer grabbed her from behind. Tadimaja was struggling to his feet, and Barker caught her arm. Mel could hold her own against one of them, maybe two, but three? They had a great deal of strength, and the wiry one moved even faster than Mel, negating her biggest advantage over fighters who outweighed her in muscle.

Someone wrested her wrists behind her back. As he bound her, Mel shouted for help. Normally people would be in the halls: her guards, a maid or butler, a member of her staff. Tonight no one answered. Tadimaja could have arranged to have the halls cleared, but she shouted again anyway. Surely *someone* would hear.

Barker shoved a cloth in her mouth and Mel spit it out. Moving fast, she kicked him in the stomach. He gasped and doubled over, his face knotted. Tadimaja—Tadi, her lifelong friend—slapped her hard across the face. Her head snapped back against the man who had bound her wrists. Before she could recover, Tadimaja forced the wad back into her mouth and tied a gag around her head to hold it. She felt as if she would choke. She struggled, but Barker had recovered enough to grab her legs. While she fought them, Tadimaja took off her sandals and Barker tied her ankles.

"Come on," Tadimaja whispered, urgent. "We have to go."

Barker grasped Mel by the waist and heaved her over his shoulder so her torso hung down his back and her legs down his front. Then he strode into the dark passageway. Mel yelled, but it only came out as a muffled grunt. She struggled furiously, pounding her feet against Barker's front. The trainer swore and hit her across the thighs.

Her other two attackers followed Barker, and Tadimaja closed the stone door. Then they were closed into the passage—and complete darkness. "Go straight ahead," Tadimaja said. "About fifty steps. Then the path forks. Go left."

Barker moved into the darkness, gripping Mel's legs.

"She fights like a man," the other trainer said.

"I warned you," Tadimaja told him.

Barker grunted. "Sure as hell doesn't look like a man." He moved his hand between her legs. Furious, Mel twisted hard and kicked his stomach.

Barker let out a stream of profanity that would have outdone any soldier in Cobalt's army. "Listen to me, girl. Our employer wants you alive, and he'll pay more if we deliver you that way. But he can achieve his ends just as well if you're dead. You kick me one more time, and I'm going to put my hand over your nose and hold you down until you suffocate."

His employer? What maniac would pay these people to kidnap the wife of Cobalt the Dark? Surely they knew Cobalt would kill them. If this was an insurgency, she couldn't see what they hoped to accomplish. They had to know Cobalt would retaliate.

"She isn't to be touched," Tadimaja said.

"How am I supposed to carry her," Barker asked, "if I can't touch her?"

"You know what I mean," Tadimaja said.

"Why would you care?" the other trainer asked. "You're the one who betrayed her."

Tadimaja spoke with a hardness Mel had never heard him use before. "It is she who committed the betrayal. She rode in with that monster, cursed our warriors with her witch's light and took Prince Zerod's throne." Anger desiccated his voice. "She deserves whatever they do to her. But it is their decision. Not ours. They said she wasn't to be touched."

Nausea surged in Mel. She hadn't even thought Tadimaja was capable of violence. He knew her "witch's light" had stopped the Chamberlight army from massacring Shazire's warriors. He had never given any sign that he believed otherwise. He had wept with her after the battle.

"Fine," Barker muttered. "I won't touch her." Giving the lie to his words, he pushed his hand up her thigh. "But she shouldn't have kicked me."

Mel wanted to kick him again. She didn't doubt he would kill her, though, if she provoked him.

The other trainer spoke uneasily. "I hadn't realized she was so young. She can't be more than sixteen."

"Nineteen," Tadimaja said.

"It doesn't seem right. She's so, I don't know. Pretty."

Tadimaja made an incredulous noise. "That excuses their crimes, that she is young and beautiful?"

"I don't claim it does." The trainer paused. "In a way, it makes it worse. She is Cobalt Escar's greatest weapon, the lovely child-bride who never wanted to marry him. The sorceress who stopped the war. Everyone who sees her adores her. If she had gone to that festival tonight as their Citrine Queen, half of Alzire would have fallen in love with her."

"Escar uses her for his own ends." Tadimaja sounded as if he were gritting his teeth. "And she lets him."

Mel fought her fear. Before she had convinced Cobalt to keep Tadimaja at the palace, she had formed a mood spell for the aide. She had been certain his fidelity was genuine. Now she realized she had read too much into his responses, based on her knowledge of him. At one time, years ago, she had realized he was half in love with her. Had she unconsciously let that sway her into trusting him? Such a love could turn to hate with her return as the bride of a man Tadimaja saw as a despot. He had suppressed his reaction well, enough even to hide it from her spells. He knew her as well as she knew him; he had known how to evoke her trust.

She had no shapes now to form any spells. They were meant to heal, to offer light and warmth, but they could be reversed. It wasn't just out of goodness that mages swore to do no harm. Whatever they did with spells, they experienced, too, to a lesser extent, but enough to matter. If they healed others, they felt better: if they injured others, they suffered.

Even so. Better to endure pain than die. She could reverse a blue spell. What about indigo? Such spells healed emotions. Would a reversal cause insanity? She had heard tales of a power beyond indigo. Violet. The power to save a life— or take it. She had no violet and she didn't know what to do with indigo, but she could wield blue. If she had a shape.

Barker carried her through the dark. The tunnel smelled of mold. She strained to remember everything she knew about the palace. The Taka Mal architects who built it had probably put in these passages. If Tadimaja were a Taka Mal spy, that might explain how he knew about them.

They finally halted, and it sounded as if Tadimaja were going through the involved process of opening another secret door. He knew these passages well indeed, to do this all in the dark.

Barker carried her out into the night and a cramped yard behind the stables. They hurried to the smallest stable. Inside, a solitary lamp lit the darkness, so dim she could barely make out three waiting merchants. They looked like grain sellers come for the festival market. Their cart was piled with sacks of feed and hitched to a team of two horses. They would blend in all too well with the torrents of people pouring through the city tonight.

Everyone moved fast. Barker heaved her off his shoulder

and set her against the cart. He yanked the blue scarf off her head, and she gasped when he ripped out a long tendril of her hair. Then someone pulled a sack over her head and down to her feet. Before she could catch her breath, they hoisted her into the cart. The rough weave smelled of grain, and it scraped her face and stomach where her tunic pulled up. Panicked, she kicked hard, trying to get free. Someone tied the bottom of the sack, and then she was caught, lying on top of other bumpy sacks.

Something heavy landed beside her body. A second sack. A third thudded against her side. With horror, she realized they were covering her. With sacks on top of her, weighting her down, Mel screamed. Or tried. She barely make a sound. She couldn't breathe; she would die—

"Listen, Dawnfield queen." Barker's harsh voice came through the layers of grain and burlap. "Every one of these men lost someone he loved in the war. A son. A brother. A father. They all have good reason to wish your husband dead. It wouldn't take much for them to extend that to you. I suggest you be as still and as quiet as you know how. If you do, you might live."

Mel froze, breathing hard. She could survive this. She could manage. Schooling herself to calm, she repeated in her mind a nonsense chant from her childhood, over and over. Gradually her pulse slowed and her mind cleared.

Rustles came from somewhere. Then Tadimaja said, "Barker, go to the plaza. Say nothing about contracts." His voice faded as he moved away. "And you there, cut a pig for the blood. Leave her scarf and hair with the dagger."

The bags shifted as someone sat near Mel. She lay stiff and terrified as the cart creaked and rolled forward.

To where, she had no idea.

Sunrise Child

Mel didn't realize she had fallen asleep until someone dragged the bag off the cart and jolted her awake. Her muscles protested with stabs of pain. Dim light came through the sack and enough of a chill to suggest they were outside at dawn or in an overcast day.

They untied the bottom of the bag and set her on her feet, holding her up. Someone pulled off the sack. She swayed, nauseous from the miserable ride. Sunrise hadn't yet touched the horizon, and predawn light softened the barren countryside. This had to be eastern Shazire; it was the only region of the country this empty and this harsh.

Her three captors all had the brown hair, stocky builds, and medium height common to Shazire farmers. The oldest wore a beard. One of the younger men had a bent gold hoop in his ear, and the other a thick belt with metal studs. For lack of any other names, she thought of them as Beard, Hoop, and Belt. She concentrated on Hoop's earring, but the shape was too distorted for a spell.

"All right," Beard said.

Mel tensed. All right what?

The other two seemed to know what he meant. They picked her up unceremoniously and sat her on the back of the cart. Then Beard leaned down and untied her ankles. Mel could barely feel her toes or move her legs, but at least they were free.

"We're going to eat." Beard straightened up. "I'll take off the gag, but if you scream I'll put it on again and you won't get food or water. Do you understand?"

Mel nodded, relieved they didn't intend to starve her. Hoop stepped closer and untied the cloth, then pulled the wad out of her mouth. She focused on his bent earring— and a spell stirred. Then he drew back and the spell faded.

"Better?" Beard asked. They were all watching her.

Mel tried to answer, but her mouth and throat were too dry. So she nodded.

Beard spoke uncomfortably. "I want you to know something. It is true, what Barker said, that we each lost someone in the war. We have no wish to see your husband rule our country." He paused. "But it is not true that we desire to kill you. Unless you force our hand, we will deliver you alive."

"To who?" she rasped. "Where?"

"Can't say," Hoop told her.

"Taka Mal?" she asked. No one answered.

Beard indicated a campfire they had set up. "Over here."

After spending a night tied up, Mel could barely move. Hoop lifted her from the cart and helped her over to the fire, putting his arm more tightly around her body than necessary. He sat her next to Beard, who stayed put, taking advantage of his seniority while Belt and Hoop cooked food in dented tin pots. Mel shivered in the chill morning. She had nothing to warm her except her thin pants and tunic, and she hurt everywhere. She could barely sit up. Until her body recovered, she needed to guard her strength, not only for herself, but for her child. She would do anything to protect that fragile life. Anything.

Mel had never used spells for harm, but she wouldn't hesitate now. She needed a shape. She had never realized before how few perfect shapes existed in nature. Nothing in this broken landscape came close. For that matter, neither did the utensils or supplies of her captors.

Mel spoke to Beard. "Will you untie my wrists? I won't fight."

He jerked, startled from whatever thoughts preoccupied him. Then he fumbled with her wrists. It took him several moments to loosen the thongs, but finally her arms fell free. She was so relieved she didn't even care when pain shot up them.

Belt brought her a cup of water. Her arms shook, and she had to hold the cup in both hands as she drained it. Hoop gave her a bowl of meal. Just looking at food nauseated her, but she forced herself to eat. The others sat around, chewing in silence. Belt stared at her avidly while he ate. He had a scar on his chin and another on the back of his hand.

Hoop suddenly said, "You married him for a treaty."

"Do you mean Cobalt?" Mel asked.

"The king." He spoke awkwardly. "You wanted to stop him from doing to your country what he did to ours."

"Yes," she said simply. It was true, after all.

"Do you hate him?" Hoop asked.

"No," Mel said. It was none of their business.

"Pretty bride," Belt muttered.

Hoop persisted. "His Majesty's a lot older than you, eh?"

"Fifteen years." Mel wished they would stop asking personal questions. She didn't want to antagonize them, though, especially not before she found a good shape. If she incited them with a spell but couldn't hold them off, they might change their minds about killing her.

Belt's eyes gleamed. "Gets young wife. Every night."

"Shut your mouth," Beard said. "She's your queen."

Anger flashed on Belt's face. "No more." He jerked his chin at Mel. "When she wed him the Dark, her kin swore never to attack his. They all of them stood by an' watched while her husband come and took our land."

Mel had no answer. Her father had faced a grim decision when Cobalt invaded Shazire. If Muller had sent forces to defend Shazire, it would have violated his treaty with Cobalt. Then nothing would have stopped Cobalt from invading Harsdown. In the end, Muller had made a choice that haunted him. He protected his country at the price of leaving Shazire undefended.

"I don't see her attacking you," Beard said crossly.

Belt regarded him sullenly. "She's a witch."

Hoop smirked. "So how come she don't make you a pig, eh?"

"I *saw* her." Belt's face contorted. "At the Alzire fields. She walked with a sword of fire that reached into the sky and no one could touch her. If we don't put her back in that sack, she'll burn us alive."

Hoop shifted his weight. "You're crazy."

"You know what Pickaxe said." Belt was clenching his cup so hard the scar across his knuckles turned white. "Don't let her see or touch anything. It's the only way to stop her spells."

Mel shifted her weight uneasily. It was true, if she couldn't see or touch the shape, she couldn't do anything with it. She hadn't realized Tadimaja had figured that out. She had never told him.

"If I could make spells," Mel said, "I would. But I can't."

"Liar." Belt spat at the fire. "Witch."

Beard stood up, shaking out his clothes. "I don't know about hexes or witches. But we have to get moving."

Belt jumped to his feet. "Put 'er back in the sack."

"If you want her in," Beard said, "you put her there."

Belt sneered. "You're afraid of her."

"Maybe we better put her back," Hoop said.

"Please don't," Mel said, pulling herself to her feet. Her whole body protested. She didn't think she could bear an entire day in burlap. "I won't do anything."

"I have ether," Beard told her. "We were going to use it on you if we had trouble at the palace."

Her pulse stuttered. "I don't understand."

"It will knock you out," he said. "Then we won't have to cover you with the bag."

"You don't need to do that," Mel said quickly, afraid. "I won't make trouble."

A frown hardened his face. "Choose. The bag or the ether."

Mel didn't want to be unconscious. But she wanted even less to be bound and gagged and suffocating. Finally she said, "Ether."

Beard glanced at Hoop. "Go get it." Then he took Mel's arm and dragged her toward the cart. As Mel limped with him, she thought furiously, trying to see a way out of this.

At the cart, Beard put his hands on her waist to lift her up. Mel was about to push him away when his shirt shifted. She saw it then: he wore a talisman around his neck. A metal ring.

I get one chance. She could see Hoop and Belt coming back. *Make it fast.*

She regarded Beard with what she hoped was a helpless look. She didn't do helpless well, but she was scared enough to make it work. "I'm afraid."

"It shouldn't hurt you." He spoke gruffly. "I'll look after you while you sleep. No one will touch you."

She improvised frantically as she went along. "I don't have anything for good luck. I usually wear a charm around my neck." She never had in her life, but he wouldn't know that.

His gaze dropped to her chest. "You do?"

Mel wanted to sock him for staring at her breasts. "I'm afraid of bad luck."

Hoop came up to them, carrying a cloth that was soaked in some liquid. "You going to get us with bad luck?"

Beard shot him an irritated look. "Stop it."

"Sorceresses kill," he said.

"For saints' sake," Beard said. "She's not a sorceress."

"Please," Mel whispered, focusing on Beard.

"Pickaxe said not to let you see," Beard said gruffly.

"I don't need to see it," she said. That wasn't true for making a spell, but she had to say something to convince him. "I'm so scared." She added a catch to her voice. "I'll feel less afraid if I know it's there."

"You *should* be afraid of us," Belt said harshly.

Mel didn't like the way he was watching her, as if he enjoyed her terror.

"Don't got no luck charms," Hoop told her.

"I have a ring at home my mother gave me." Mel tried to sound as young as possible. "I always keep it close."

Beard made an exasperated noise. "Enough of this."

"I'm scared," Mel whispered.

"Hell and damnation." Beard yanked the cord over his head, pulling his ring out from under his shirt. "Here. This is all we got. Now be quiet." He dropped the cord around her neck and laid the ring on her chest, stroking her breasts in the process, which made her grit her teeth. Grasping the ring, she focused. A ragged spell formed—

Hoop slid his hand behind her head and plastered the wet cloth over her mouth and nose.

No! Mel tried to jerk away, but he held her head in place with the cloth over her face. Fumes saturated her…sickly sweet…her spell was dissolving…

And then her consciousness did as well.

Her Majesty's Army assembled in the Rocklands near the Saint Verdant River. The Citadel of the Dragon-Sun stood on Sharp Knife Mountain above them. Within the citadel, in the Narrow-Sun Room, Jade met at a circular table with all the commanders: her cousin, Baz Quaazera, General of the Taka Mal Army; Generals Spearcaster, Slate and Firaz of Taka Mal; Sphere-General Fieldson and Sphere-Colonel Arkandy Ravensford, formerly of Aronsdale and now from Harsdown; Penta-Major Jason Windcrier of Harsdown; and Colonel Leo Tumbler from the Misted Cliffs. And Drummer. The meeting was contentious and hot, and Jade liked none of what she heard. Her world seemed determined to implode.

"We're talking almost fourteen *thousand* men." Firaz was shouting at Fieldson. "Six thousand Chamberlight, more than four thousand Jazid, and three thousand Taka Mal. On *our* borders. Blazing hell, man, it would be insane to take an envoy of thirty men out there."

"Thirty-one," Drummer said, including himself.

Fieldson met Firaz's glare with a steely gaze, his iron-clad calm a striking contrast to his fiery Taka Mal counterpart. "Those armies hulking at your door are why we *must* leave." He motioned at Drummer. "This man is the reason we came. If I take him home, it defuses the threat."

"Then you admit Cobalt's army is a threat," Jade said

tightly. She kept asking herself the same question: *Had he known Escar was coming?* He claimed not, but she saw no reason to believe him. She should never have trusted him.

Fieldson's answer was guarded. "Cobalt has concern for his wife's uncle."

"We have dealt with you in good faith," Spearcaster said, his craggy face furrowed with anger. "Yet Cobalt brings an army."

"And you brought the Jazid Army," Leo Tumbler said.

"Ozar marches by his choice," Jade said. "Not mine." Her anger threatened to overtake her calm. What was Cobalt about, bringing his entire flaming army to meet a little envoy? If that didn't qualify as a hostile act, she didn't know what did.

General Slate practically snarled at Tumbler. "Cobalt marched up the Jazid border. If we took an army up your border, you expect me to believe you wouldn't bring yours, too?"

Baz hit the table with his palm, and the strike reverberated in the hall, which had heated with sun and tempers. "Send the boy back. Let them take their chances." He gave Drummer a scathing look. "You have been far too much trouble."

Drummer met his gaze. "I never asked to 'visit' Taka Mal."

"It's too dangerous to send him back!" Firaz said. "The envoy will be traveling with our men. Sphere-General Fieldson is the only one in that party Cobalt might consider an ally, and given the strain between Harsdown and the Misted Cliffs, even that has doubt."

"I'll go with the envoy," Tumbler said. "Cobalt trusts me."

"But I don't," Jade said flatly. The last thing she needed was a Chamberlight officer taking Drummer to Cobalt.

"The way to Aronsdale is swarming with Chamberlight men," Sphere-Colonel Ravensford said. "If Colonel Tumbler doesn't go with the envoy, you've no chance of getting through."

"It's also swarming with Jazidians," Slate countered. "If anything happens to the Headwind boy, it could infuriate Cobalt. Saints, man, it will look as if we are taunting him."

"I'm twenty-eight," Drummer said, exasperated. "Hardly a boy."

Fieldson exhaled, and Jade could guess his thoughts. If they tried to send Drummer to Aronsdale, he could be killed or captured. If they *didn't* send him, she couldn't announce the betrothal. Without the betrothal, they couldn't stop Cobalt from attacking Taka Mal. Jade didn't want Drummer to go. She didn't want to see his life endangered. She would die first. Unfortunately, she couldn't wait with the betrothal, either.

Baz turned a hard stare on Jade. "What I want to know," he said, each word slow and distinct, "is why you are having clandestine meetings with a Harsdown general."

Jade blinked. "What?"

"You heard me."

She frowned at her cousin. "I have no flaming idea what you're talking about." In her side vision, she saw Leo Tumbler turn red. She supposed in the Misted Cliffs they spoke with more restraint. Fieldson kept his face composed and slightly puzzled. Not only was he a strong commander, he was also a good actor.

Baz braced his palms on the table and leaned forward. "I heard it from your guards. You met with Fieldson in your study."

"Oh, that," Jade said, thinking fast. Damn Baz. He learned too much of what went on in this place. He couldn't know about Drummer, though, or he would never sit there even this calmly.

"Drummer had just woken up from his illness," Jade said. "I wanted the envoy to know."

"They said you talked for fifteen minutes," Baz challenged.

"Possibly. I didn't keep track." In an unfriendly voice, Jade added, "Perhaps you have better things to do with your time, cousin, than to spy on me."

Baz clenched his fist on the table. "And I would hope you had better things to do than socialize with enemy generals."

Fieldson spoke quietly. "General Quaazera, I asked after Drummer." He was doing a superb job of portraying the carefully controlled ire of someone trying his utmost to show tact in the face of absurd suspicions. "We thought he was going to die."

Baz started to answer, then mercifully thought better of it. Drummer had nearly died trying to escape, and if Baz intended to push Fieldson, he would have to answer for that.

Baz sat back and crossed his arms. "What if Drummer stays here," he said to Fieldson, "and you go to Cobalt with a contingent of officers, one third Taka Mal, one third Harsdown, and one third Misted Cliffs."

Tumbler straightened up, and Jade could see he liked the idea. As the ranking Chamberlight officer, he could vouch for the envoy's safety better than anyone else in this explosive room. It was an excellent idea. Except it wouldn't *work*. The envoy had to talk to Jarid, not Cobalt. If Cobalt intended to invade Taka Mal, the last thing he would want was an alliance between the Houses of Quaazera and Dawnfield. She could almost feel Sphere-General Fieldson searching for a plausible reason to resist the idea. He had told his Harsdown officers about the plan because they would be guarding Jade, but she doubted he had revealed anything to Tumbler.

"It just might work," General Slate said.

Jade almost groaned. Why did Slate, usually the quietest of her generals, have to choose this moment to speak? He was the one she could most rely on to keep an even temper, but at the moment that was no help.

"It's a stupid idea," Firaz stated. "What if some hothead attacks the envoy and murders Fieldson? Killing the commander of the Harsdown military is a hell of a lot worse than killing an itinerant minstrel who happens to be related to Cobalt's wife."

Drummer scowled at Firaz, and Jade wished her generals would show more tact. She could have hugged Firaz, though, for giving her an excuse to argue against sending the envoy to Cobalt.

"We have no wish for our honored guests to experience harm," Jade said. "The safety of Goodman Headwind and Sphere-General Fieldson must be our priority."

They all argued, of course. No one had a good plan. Listening to them, Jade knew what she had to do. She had hoped another possibility would present itself, but she still saw no choice. Finally she rose to her feet, and their debate trailed off. Aware of everyone watching, she went to the floor-to-ceiling window at the end of the hall. The gardens outside blazed with fire-lilies and sun-snaps that created the effect of a sunset.

Baz spoke behind her. "Jade?"

She turned around. "We have another matter to consider." She suddenly felt tired. So tired.

"Well, out with it," Firaz said.

Jade returned to the table and stood in front of her chair. She wished she could have seen just one female face.

"I haven't had my menses this month," she said.

They stared at her blankly, all these warlords from so many places. She couldn't look at Drummer.

"Your what?" Firaz said.

"Her *menses*." Spearcaster scowled at him. "You know. When a woman bleeds."

Firaz turned red under his dark complexion. "What the hell kind of comment is that to make in the middle of a war council?"

"Firaz." Baz was staring at Jade. "Shut up, General."

"I'm never late," Jade added. This was excruciating.

They looked as if they had no idea what to say. Firaz wasn't the only one who seemed confused. But not Baz. Oh no, not Baz. His face hadn't gone red this time: It drained of color. He rose to his feet, his fists clenched. Then, incredibly, he turned to Fieldson and said, "You saints-damned bastard."

Fieldson's mouth opened. "You think *I'm* the father?"

"Father?" Firaz demanded. "*What* father?"

"For saints' *sake*," Jade said.

Everything happened too fast. Baz lunged around his chair and Fieldson leaped to his feet. When Baz swung his fist, Fieldson brought up his arms, but at twice Baz's age, he barely managed to block the blow, and its force drove him back. Arkandy Ravensford, Jason Windcrier, and Leo Tumbler surged in to defend Fieldson, and Firaz and Slate were on their way from around the table, ready to launch into the fray. Spearcaster made an exasperated noise, sat back in his seat, and crossed his arms.

"Stop it!" Jade shouted. "All of you!" Drummer was looking at her, but she couldn't meet his gaze. Not yet. Not now.

They all stopped, but no one looked at her. They were too busy glaring at one another. Fieldson's gray-eyed stare had gone so cold Jade wondered it didn't freeze her hotheaded cousin. Spearcaster was still in his chair, shaking his head.

"Sit down," Jade said sourly. "All of you."

Fieldson turned to Jade and spoke with impeccable formality. "Your Royal Majesty, I apologize for the insult given to your name, to suggest I am the father of your child. I am flattered beyond belief that anyone would imagine you would bestow your interest upon my unworthy self, and I do hope the offense of that assumption has not gone beyond hope of repair."

"I thank you for your gracious words," Jade said. "You have given no offense." She scowled a Baz. "I wish I could say the same for my relatives."

"Vizarana, you go too far," Baz told her.

"Will you all please sit the hell down?" Jade said.

Spearcaster snorted, and the visiting officers reddened. Jade suspected their war councils didn't have this much excitement. No one was paying attention to Drummer, and she avoided his eyes.

They did all sit, though. The room simmered with hostility. Fieldson caught her eye, and though he gave no outward sign, she understood his message. They were there for her protection.

Jade spoke wearily. "General Fieldson is not the father."

Spearcaster leaned one elbow on the arm of his chair. "Let me guess. You are twenty-three days late."

A chill went up her back. How could he know? Mica, the midwife, had just told her this morning.

"Where the blazes do you get that number?" Firaz demanded.

Spearcaster continued to watch Jade. "A woman gets pregnant halfway through her cycle. Fifteen days. Thirty-nine minus fifteen is twenty-three. And thirty-nine days ago, the Atajazid D'az Ozar came here and proposed to our queen."

Slate thumped the table. "No wonder he brought his army to our door. We must have the wedding immediately."

Baz's words exploded out before Slate finished. "Saints, Jade, I don't *believe* you let him touch you. Not only was it a loss of honor, you also lost your most powerful bargaining point. Now you have to give him the beetling Topaz Throne." He hit the arm of his chair. "The throne should stay with the House of Quaazera. You and me."

Jade hated discussing her private life this way, but she couldn't put Baz off. She spoke with a gentleness few people ever saw from her. "Cousin, I love you like my life. But as my kin. To marry you would be like marrying my brother. I could not."

"That may be." He looked neither stunned nor upset by her words. "But it would have been better than seeing our House bow to Onyx. To get his help now, it must be on his terms."

"Not necessarily," Slate said. "She can negotiate. She carries his heir, after all."

"Oh, stop, all of you," Jade said. "It isn't his damn heir. I never let Ozar touch me."

Everyone blinked at her, even Fieldson, who did a remarkable job of looking puzzled, and Ravensford, who managed a reasonable facade of confusion. Jason Windcrier only looked uncomfortable, but as the lowest-ranked officer, he wasn't getting much notice from the others.

Jade finally summoned the courage to look at Drummer. His expression melted her heart. He was radiant, his eyes full of warmth. One might have thought she had just given him the wealth of the eleven deserts instead of news that could bring his death in any number of violent ways.

"Hell's fire," Baz said, watching them. "Tell me that what I'm thinking is wrong."

Slate spoke dourly. "Perhaps you might tell us what you're thinking."

Jade knew she had to prepare them before she revealed her explosive news. She sat down and spoke in formal tones.

"The House of Dawnfield rules Aronsdale. They are bound by the treaty signed by Escar and Dawnfield. But if Cobalt conquers Taka Mal and Jazid, what will stop him from violating that treaty and attacking Aronsdale? Even the combined armies of Harsdown and Aronsdale couldn't stand against him if he added our forces to his own." From what her spies had told her, Jade thought only one thing could have stopped Cobalt the Dark, something forever impossible now—the words, *Well done, my grandson.*

"If the atajazid and I form a union," Jade said, "then we might defeat Cobalt. Perhaps then *we* would turn on Aronsdale."

Slate raised an eyebrow. "I wasn't aware we were planning a campaign against Aronsdale."

"If you were them," Jade said, "what would you think?"

Fieldson spoke. "It has only been nineteen years since Varqelle invaded Aronsdale and tried to kill Jarid's family. I doubt he is ready to form an alliance with Varqelle's son."

Baz was having trouble breathing. "Jade, you can't do it."

"Do what?" Firaz asked, irritated. "This is a war council of riddles."

Baz never took his gaze off Jade. "If you try this, I will have my officers drag you to the temple and marry you myself."

"I would take care," Slate said, "before you pledge your officers to committing treason."

"Hear her out first," Baz said. "Then tell me that."

Spearcaster focused intently on Jade. "You want an alliance with Aronsdale, is that it?"

Jade started to answer, but Slate cut her off. "Surely you

can't mean *Prince Aron* fathered your child. He hasn't visited here in years."

"Besides," Leo Tumbler said, "he is only eighteen."

Firaz snorted. "It's no wonder all you people in the Misted Cliffs are so constipated, if you think eighteen is too young for a man to want a woman."

"General Firaz," Jade said, exasperated. "Enough." To all of them, she said, "I wasn't referring to Jarid's son Aron." *Just say it.* But she couldn't get the words out. So she took a deep breath, stood up, and walked to Drummer's chair. He watched her with a luminous expression. She sat in the chair next to his and took his hand. Then she spoke softly. "I am sorry. I would have rather told you any way but this."

His eyes were bright and wild with a happiness she had never felt in her life. "You couldn't have given me a greater gift."

Jade was aware of Fieldson on Drummer's other side, of Ravensford beyond Fieldson, of Jason Windcrier on her left. She was surrounded by Harsdown officers. She couldn't see their hands, which made her suspect they had snuck weapons into this meeting, perhaps daggers in case her hot-blooded generals blew up. Drummer held something, too, an odd metal cube.

The room was ominously quiet. Jade shifted her gaze to Baz. His eyes smoldered, and she thought they might catch fire.

"That minstrel is your child's father?" Slate asked. He didn't even disguise his bewilderment.

"Well, hell," Firaz said. "Someone ought to just kill the boy now and get the agony over with."

Jade answered coldly. "Firaz, that isn't amusing."

"Maybe he wasn't joking." Baz's voice was deadly quiet.

"You cannot marry a commoner," Slate told her. "Especially not one like him."

"Like what?" Drummer asked. He was no longer smiling.

"You have yellow hair," Firaz pointed out, as if this explained everything.

Baz focused on Fieldson. "Our queen," he said, "appears to be surrounded by people who stand to gain should she marry a man of Aronsdale. Remarkable coincidence, that." He considered Leo Tumbler. "Except you. I would imagine your commander, Cobalt Escar, would be highly interested to learn of this development."

Tumbler kept his face neutral. "I cannot claim to know his Majesty's thoughts."

Slate pushed his hand across his graying hair. "Vizarana, this is...unprecedented."

"True," Jade said. "It's also a good idea."

"That remains to be seen," Slate said.

"What remains?" Spearcaster asked. "I see no downside."

Baz flushed an angry red. "I can't think of anyone less appropriate to be the consort of the Topaz Queen."

"And why is that?" Jade demanded. "Because he won't try to replace me on the throne?"

Baz leaned forward. "That entertainer—" he waved his hand at Drummer "—is not good enough for you."

"I may not be," Drummer said, "but I'm the one she chose."

"You bring nothing to the marriage," Slate said. "No title, lands, wealth, or power. Nothing."

"Oh, nothing much," Spearcaster said drily. "Just a possible alliance that could stop Cobalt from attacking Taka Mal."

Jade was glad one of them understood. "Yes. Exactly."

"Flaming improper, if you ask me," Firaz stated. "Besides, how do we know Dawnfield will agree? Someone has to go ask him."

Spearcaster grimaced. "Sending the envoy to Aronsdale right now could be a disaster."

"I'm willing to try," Fieldson said.

As much as Jade wanted him to go, she couldn't agree. "I thank you. But you cannot risk your life." Getting Fieldson killed would land them in battle rather than in an alliance.

Jason Windcrier suddenly spoke up. "I'll go."

They all looked at the young man. Then Fieldson said, "The risk is the same to you as to the rest of us."

"Sir, I'm only a low-ranked major. We can risk my loss. If I go alone at night, I've a chance of sneaking through." Jason took a deep breath. "If I'm caught by Cobalt's men—well, I'm native to Harsdown. His wife's country. They would probably let me live."

"Ozar's men might catch you," Jade said.

"I'm willing to risk it," Jason replied.

"The Chamberlight queen may even be here," Tumbler said. "She often travels with Cobalt's army."

Jade's interest perked up. "Then it is true what they say? She is like a man?"

"She fights like a man," Tumbler said. "Sure as blazes doesn't look like one."

Jade wanted to meet this queen who defied the strictures of the Misted Cliffs. "I shall appreciate being her kin."

"Like hell," Baz growled.

"Well and all right, let the major go," Slate said. "Let us find out what Jarid Dawnfield has to say."

Jade spoke with respect to Jason. "You have our gratitude."

He awkwardly bent his head. "I will do my best."

"It could be a while before he gets back." Firaz peered at Jade. "How soon before, ah…" He cleared his throat.

Jade held back her smile. Apparently Firaz didn't mix well with women's matters, even as a father of four. "I've a few months before I begin to show."

"Ah." He flushed. "That leaves a bit of leeway."

It wasn't much. They needed to know if Jarid was willing to make this pact. If he refused, and Cobalt attacked, she might have to accept Ozar's proposal. Bah. She would rather suffer the raging hives. Ozar might refuse her, given her condition, but she doubted it. He coveted her throne too much. He would want her child gone, though. She suppressed a shudder. He might try to force a miscarriage. If she carried to term, she could send the child to live with Drummer in Aronsdale.

If Drummer survived this mess.

"Very well," Jade said. "Let us see what King Jarid says." She met Drummer's radiant gaze and wished to the saints their prospects weren't so bleak.

19

The Onyx Chamber

Nothing lit the cell. It had to be completely enclosed, for even after her eyes adjusted to the dark, Mel could see nothing.

She couldn't move. Her hands and ankles were chained to a distorted loop of metal rammed into the floor. She had spent hours kneeling by the wall with her arms pulled behind her back, semiconscious and nauseated. She couldn't reach the ring that hung around her neck inside her tunic, couldn't touch, feel, or see it—which meant no spells.

Mel had only blurred recollections of the trip here. They had drugged her with wet cloths over her nose and mouth. She drifted in and out of awareness, sick most of the time. True to his word, though, Beard kept the others from assaulting her.

She wasn't certain how long the ride had lasted. Days, more than the five it would take to reach Jazid, maybe enough to reach Taka Mal, but not as far as Quaaz. She was either in western Jazid or else in the Rocklands of southern Taka Mal. It was certainly hot enough in this saints-forsaken place to be the desert. Sweat drenched her clothes and trickled down her face.

Mel had no idea of the time. She had awoken here, her mind fuzzed, her body aching. She was no longer gagged or blindfolded, but she could barely move and shouting had produced no results. Slumped against the wall, she prayed to Azure, the saint who brought healing, for the well-being of her child.

The scrape of stone came from nearby.

Lifting her head, she looked toward the sound. Another scrape came, louder this time, hard on the ears. It reminded her of Tadimaja opening secret doors in the Alzire Palace. A vertical line appeared in the darkness. It was only gray, but after the absolute black of the past hours, it seemed bright. The line widened until it became a tall, jagged opening.

It took Mel several moments to interpret the scene. A lop-sided slab of rock had opened like a door about ten paces away, and two figures were entering, one holding a candle. They moved forward like wraiths. The one in front wore a black-and-white Scribe's robe, but he was otherwise gray, his hair, his eyebrows, even his essence, it seemed. His skeletal face had skin stretched over bone, and his eyes were hollows of shadow. He had a stooped posture, but even with his back bent, he was taller than most men. The sleeves of his robe draped from his wrists. He carried the candle, and it lit the bottom of his face as if he were a ghoul.

A second man walked behind him, larger and taller, even more threatening in his size. Where the first man was bent and gaunt, this one stood straight, with a warrior's carriage. Shadows hid his face, but the outline of a large nose showed, hooked and prominent. He was darkness and hard glints, from his black hair to his dark clothes studded with metal.

They brought shadows. The cell turned gray, its blurred outlines half-hidden, and murk gathered in the corners. The chamber wasn't normal. The walls met at odd angles and the ceiling sloped. Every surface was unrelieved black. None had the geometric designs so popular in other places. Several tables stood nearby, and none had a symmetrical cut. The shadowed objects on them had jagged outlines. Nothing in the room offered one of the most common features of human architecture—a pure shape.

This cell had been designed to hold a mage.

Whether the intent was deliberate or the architect had been crazy, Mel had no idea. But in centuries long past, the queens of Aronsdale had ridden as war mages and used their spells in ways of violence that the histories only hinted at. If an atajazid had wanted to imprison such mages, he would need such a cell.

The gray man set his candle on a table. The other man strode forward, his boot heels thudding on the stone floor. He stopped in front of Mel, and she looked up, trying to see his face. She felt ill, and she would have thrown up, but she hadn't eaten in so long, she had nothing to lose, and damned if she would give them the satisfaction of seeing her fear.

He spoke. "So it is Chime's little girl, grown up."

Mel *knew* that voice. The gravelly rasp and low timbre were distinctive enough to recognize even after ten years.

"Ozar?" she asked.

He knelt down, coming out of the shadows. The Atajazid D'az Ozar had changed little in the past decade. His high cheekbones were more pronounced and new lines showed around his mouth, but his face had the same arrogantly chiseled look she remembered from ten years ago. They had met at the Topaz Palace when he and her family were guests during a negotiation about export rights. He had frightened her then and he terrified her now.

"Mel Dawnfield." His face showed no trace of emotion.

"Why have you brought me here?" Mel asked.

He stood again, his upper body receding into shadow. Then he turned to the other man, who waited by the table. "Put her up."

What did that mean? Mel twisted her hands in the chains, but it did no good. Her efforts only sent pain shooting up her limbs.

As the older man came forward, he took a ring of keys from within his robe, which he wore over a tunic and trousers. The ring was deformed, squashed from a circle. Ozar understood better than the grain merchants how to neutralize her spells. He needed no blindfolds or gags: just keep her away from pure shapes.

The ring that Beard had given her was inside her tunic. She couldn't see it, and she barely felt the metal against her chest. Closing her eyes, she tried to sense the shape and make a spell.

Nothing.

Think. She had to find a way to touch or see the ring. But if she did, she would have the advantage of surprise only once. Her first spell would have to defeat them. How? She could reverse a blue spell and cause injury, but that little ring wouldn't provide enough power to do serious damage. If might only antagonize them.

The robed man knelt behind her and unlocked the manacles that held her ankles and wrists. Her arms were shaking. As soon as they fell free, before she could otherwise move, the gray man grabbed her upper arm and heaved her to her feet. She gasped as fire stabbed her shoulder and through her body.

"Why are you doing this?" she rasped. Surely they knew Cobalt would crush Jazid for this. Ozar was deliberately provoking him.

They dragged her into the center of the cell. As Ozar reached for a shadowed object hanging in the air above them, the gray man pulled her arms over her head. He held her hands with the palms outward, and Ozar snapped manacles around her wrists. The metal locked with a clink that echoed.

Mel hurt so much she sagged, hanging from the manacles. As they stepped back, she strained to see their faces in the shadows. The older man turned toward the wall, she couldn't see what—

A harsh grating filled the room and Mel's arms jerked. Terrified, she looked up. All she could see was the chain hanging out of the darkness. The grinding intensified, and with a wrench, the chain hoisted her into the air.

"No!" Mel gasped from the pain. She was in some mad-man's hell. She had no dispute with Ozar. Neither did Cobalt. Why would Ozar take actions guaranteed to put him at war with them?

It was excruciating to be lifted by her arms after she had been chained for so long. She bit the inside of her cheeks to keep from screaming. When the gears stopped, she was hanging from the manacles by her wrists. Ozar came back and stood considering her, his eyes level with hers, which meant her feet were dangling more than a hand's span off the floor.

"I do regret this," he said.

Mel swallowed past the dryness of her throat. "What are you going to do?"

"I'm afraid I have to hurt you."

"*Why?*"

"It doesn't matter. Not for you." He turned to the other man. "Leave evidence. Marks. Many bloodstains on her clothes."

"Why won't it matter to me?" Mel's anger and terror surged, for herself and for her unborn child. "Ozar, answer me!"

He looked her up and down, his gaze lingering on her body. "I hardly think you are in a position to give me orders."

Mel groaned from the pain. "At least tell me *why.*"

Ozar spoke bluntly. "After we hurt you, I will enjoy you, leaving evidence of my acts. Then Shade will kill you." He shook his head. "I would have rather kept you for myself. A woman like you should be enjoyed, not executed in a war.

Nevertheless, we will have a war, and you will be its first casualty."

"Why?" The horrific death he described petrified Mel. If he intended to inflame Cobalt, his method would work beyond question, better than he probably realized. When Cobalt and his army were done, Jazid would be a wasteland.

Mel thought of her child and an ancient rage stirred within her. It had come down through the Dawnfield line, through the millennia, from the misty age when a mage's battle cry inspired terror. The fury rose from a buried place. It piled up like the giant waves in tales told by aging mariners, the tsunamis that towered in monstrous cliffs of water. She wouldn't war for power, wealth or land—but she would protect her child even if it meant laying waste to a thousand kingdoms.

Ozar was watching her uneasily. Mel had no idea how she looked, and hanging from chains she was no threat. Yet he moved back from her.

"Do it," Ozar said.

Shade stepped into the light holding a long-handled whip. Mel inhaled sharply, and that was all she had time to do before he cracked the weapon. It struck her around the torso, and she screamed from the pain.

You will die, Mel thought as he drew back his arm. He struck her again and again and again, on her arms, her torso, her hips, her legs, and she screamed and screamed. It went on forever, and she thought surely she must die, because she could bear no more. But she didn't die, and the agony continued.

When Shade finally stopped, Mel was sobbing. Shade stood watching her as if he were hungry and she was feeding him.

Ozar spoke from the shadows. "I'll need her clothes."

Shade set the bloodied whip on a table. Then he came to Mel. When he was near enough, she spit on him. She was shaking, tears running down her face, but she would spit on him a thousand times.

He slapped her across the face.

Ozar's voice rumbled in the darkness. "Just get her clothes. Hurry. I want my messenger to leave soon, and I want to be back with the army by tonight."

Shade ripped off the bloodied scraps of her tunic and pants. His gaze was avid as he touched her body, and it nauseated Mel. But when he uncovered her torso, he freed the ring around her neck. She could see it by looking down. In that instant, she formed a spell. She had no time for finesse; she just blasted him. Flame leaped from the ring, and he gasped and stumbled back. His pain reverberated in Mel, but she hurt so much already, it hardly made a difference.

"Get the ring!" Ozar shouted.

Shade looked around, confused.

As Ozar strode forward, Mel hurled another burst of flame. She hit him with it, and his overshirt caught fire, a blaze that threw the cell into sharp relief. He kept coming even with his clothes burning. Grabbing the ring around her neck, he yanked and snapped the cord. With the ring hidden in his fist, her spell flared and died, leaving only his burning clothes.

Ozar tore off his overshirt and threw it to the ground, then stamped on the flames with his boots. Shade stood to the side, stooped and bent, staring at him.

"She is a witch," Shade said. "Evil."

Ozar swung around to him. "Never let her near a perfect shape. *Never!* Do you understand?"

Shade's answer whispered in the cell. "Yes."

Ozar took a deep breath and ground his boot in the last of the embers. Then he faced Mel, and his gaze burned. He held the bloodied remains of her clothes in one fist. "Shade," he said, never taking his gaze off Mel. Malice crackled in his voice. "I'm going to take these rags to the messenger. While I'm gone, you have my leave to make her pay for her deeds in any way you wish."

Shade bowed deeply. "Thank you."

Ozar spun around and strode into the tunnel. His clothes blended into the darkness until nothing showed. His footsteps faded to silence. Shade wet his lips, watching Mel, and she wanted to scream her protest. Mage power roiled within her, but it had no outlet. They had built this cell with nothing a mage could use.

Except.

She was the child of an indigo sphere mage—one who could use only flawed shapes. He considered it an aberration, for it also distorted his spells. But his court scholars had found hints in the oldest histories of other Dawnfield mages who wielded such power—ancient, furious mages whose spells blazed.

War mages.

Shade raked Mel with his gaze, and she hated him for the lust in his hollowed eyes. He didn't pick up the whip. Instead he went to a table and selected another object. The blood drained from her face. She wouldn't survive if he used that on her the way he had wielded the whip. It was a heavy flail, a large metal ball covered by spikes. A chain connected the ball to the handle that Shade gripped in his fist. He raised the ball over his head and swung it in a circle, around and around, catching glints of candlelight, letting her see what he intended.

If he meant to terrify her, he was succeeding. But Mel saw what he didn't. A sphere. A misshapen sphere. The highest known shape, yet of no use to a mage because spikes deformed it.

But she was also her father's daughter.

Mel's fury built. Higher, higher, like a wave rushing toward the shore, the ancient power rose. Her spell grabbed the imperfect ball—and slipped. Shade swung the gruesome weapon toward her, and Mel *reached*—

Her spell caught the spikes.

Power exploded out of Mel in a burst of violet light so bright it blinded her. Unlike with perfect shapes, *this spell didn't hurt*. It blazed through her as if she were a crucible for its terrible force.

A scream cut the air, not from her, from someone else, high and terrified. A thunderous crack shook the cell, and debris pelted her body. She dropped abruptly and landed hard on her knees. Her manacled hands slammed down in front of her. Mel went rigid, terrified the collapsing cell would crush her beneath tons of stone.

The violet light faded. Mel knelt in the dark while pieces of stone clattered around her. A shard of rock bounced off her cheek. Then all was still and dark. She choked in a breath. She couldn't think about what had happened—what she had done. Not yet. Not until her baby was safe.

Feeling around, she realized she was kneeling in debris. She edged through the wreckage toward Shade. It took only moments to find his body. He had no pulse. As far as she could tell, nothing had hit him, but he was very, very dead.

Mel started to shake. Violet. *Violet*. It was a legend, the power to heal mortal wounds, to pull back the dying. To give life.

And to take it.

Tears slid down Mel's cheeks. Her body had gone numb. She no longer felt the welts and gashes. Later sensation would return, and with it the full knowledge of what she had done. Now she couldn't let herself think. She searched Shade's body and found his squashed key ring. She tried to make a spell of light, but the ring was too bent and the spell slipped off it. She pushed and pulled, straining the metal. It still wasn't a true circle, but better—

Her spell caught on the ring and light flared. With her arms trembling, she lifted them so she could see the manacles on her wrists. Maneuvering Shade's keys into the lock with her palms facing outward was impossible. She rotated her wrists, gritting her teeth as the metal scraped her skin, until she could get in a key. The first one didn't work, nor the second. She could almost feel the seconds rattling by; every moment brought her closer to discovery. This torture chamber was deep in the walls, probably so screams from inside couldn't be heard outside. That might have covered the noise of the cell's destruction, but Ozar would come back.

The fifth key unlocked the manacles, and Mel threw them on the ground. If she found a better shape than the key ring, she would try healing her injuries, but she didn't dare with one this deformed; her distorted spell might hurt her or her child.

She forced herself to take Shade's clothes. They were too big, but the trousers had a drawstring she pulled tight around her waist, and she rolled up the legs and the sleeves. She gave up on the boots. She took the spiked ball and stood over Shade, gripping the handle, the weapon hanging by its chain.

"That was for my baby," she said.

Then she left the cell and its destruction, taking the weapon, her mage power—and her rage.

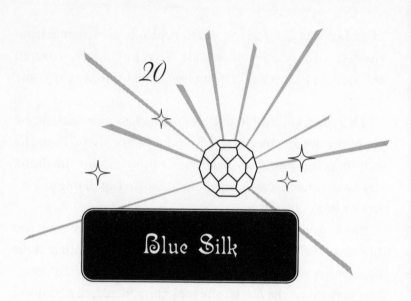

20

Blue Silk

The knock came in the evening. Jade was in the Starflower Parlor of her suite. As soon as she heard the knock, she lifted a vase out of the niche where it sat in a starflower depression. She pressed the petals of the flower in a pattern only she knew, and a narrow section of the wall swung open. Drummer stood framed in the opening, a candle in his hand and his grin audacious, as if he had personally built the secret tunnel.

Jade pulled him into her parlor. "Did you have any trouble?"

"None at all." He clunked his candle on the table and drew her into a kiss, deep and warm and hungry.

After a while, when they separated, she laughed and thumped him on the chest. "Light of the evening to you, too."

"I can't believe you told them today." His smile turned into a grimace. "Baz is going to roast me over a fire."

"He has to get you first."

He spoke intently. "Spearcaster and Fieldson came to see me. They want to talk to you. They will return later tonight. They don't think we can make it until Windcrier returns from Aronsdale."

She snorted. "So they are sneaking around to see you?"

He took a breath. "They want us to marry tonight."

"What?" This didn't sound like those two generals, who were among the most cautious of the whole group. "Why?"

Sweat gathered on his forehead. "Once we're married, your army is sworn to protect me as well as you. Assassinating the prince consort is far different than killing a minstrel who dishonored the queen. And if anything does happen to me after we're married, our child will be your legitimate heir."

It made sense, but that only made her more wary. "Why did they go to you instead of to me with this idea?"

"Baz is having our suites watched. Yours more than mine."

"They told you this?"

"Yes."

She crossed her arms. "Why should we believe them?"

"Why would they bother to lie? It's not as if I have any power here."

Jade sighed. "Because, love, everyone knows you are naive and inexperienced. They asked if you had a way to get to me, didn't they? And they wanted you to show them, yes?"

"Yes to the first. No to the second. Jade, listen. I can tell when people are lying." He folded his hand around a pendant he wore. "I'm good at reading moods."

Jade took his hand and opened it so she could see the pendant. It was the gold cube he had been holding this afternoon.

"What is this?" she asked. "A talisman?"

"For luck."

"Is it?" She looked into his face. "I too am a good judge of when people tell the truth, Drummer. To survive, I had to learn well and learn fast."

"Why would I lie about a cube?"

She remembered when he had awoken from his sickness. "You once asked me for a shape, and I gave you my earring. You held it in your hand and made light." She rolled the cube in his fingers. "Is that why you have this, too?"

He hesitated. "I can do tricks with it."

Jade studied his face. She didn't think he was lying, exactly. He was an entertainer, and it made sense he would know flashy magic tricks. But something was wrong. Or maybe not wrong, but missing.

"I have a question," she said.

"Which is?"

"You aren't telling me something." She let go of the cube and raised her hand when he started to protest. "Just tell me this. Is your secret a danger to us, our child, or Taka Mal?"

His posture relaxed. "No, insomuch as a person can answer that question. You're the queen of Taka Mal. I can't guarantee nothing I ever do, if I become your consort, will pose a danger. But to the best of my knowledge and intent, the answer is no."

Jade had to decide: Either she trusted his word or she didn't. Perhaps she was blinded by love, but she believed him. "So you think Fieldson and Spearcaster genuinely wish to see us married."

"Yes."

"What if King Jarid refuses the treaty?" Jade paced across the room. Only a few steps took her to the opposite wall. She turned to Drummer. He was watching her, his unruly hair tousled over his collar, his large blue eyes distracting. She couldn't think straight when he looked at her like that.

"If I marry you and Aronsdale turns us down," she said, "and then Cobalt attacks, we will have no ally. Cobalt will crush us."

"You have Jazid," he said.

"That alliance requires I marry Ozar."

His face twisted. "You can't marry that monster. He wants to hurt you."

She spoke quietly. "I know."

He looked as if he was going to explode. "Then how can you even consider it?"

She felt ill. "If the choice is subjugation of either myself or my country, it is no choice. I am a queen first, Drummer, and a woman second."

He came over and grasped her shoulders. "He would be crazy not to ally with you if Cobalt attacks. He knows Cobalt will go after him next. I don't believe Ozar would give up his own throne just because he can't have yours."

"You can never tell with Ozar." She regarded him uneasily. "He may have another plan we know nothing about."

"If we don't do this now, I don't believe we'll get another chance. Too much is set against us." He implored her with the unfair advantage of his eyes. "For the sake of our child. Even if Ozar has me killed so he can have you, I would die knowing my child's heritage is protected. He can't get rid of your heir."

She touched his cheek. "He would try, love."

"And if we weren't married? What then?"

"It would be much worse," she admitted. "The child would be the illegitimate offspring of a forbidden liaison rather than heir to the Topaz Throne."

He waited, watching her face. She knew what she wanted. But what was best? No matter what they did, it could bring disaster. Nothing was certain—except how she felt about Drummer.

Jade took his hands and spoke softly, letting what she felt for him warm her voice. "Then let us marry. Tonight."

Cobalt sat on Admiral, high on a ridge, and Matthew sat next to him on his gold stallion, Hawkspar. As the sun set behind them, their shadows stretched out and spilled over the edge of the ridge. A panorama spread all around them. To the southeast, the Jagged Teeth Mountains cut bleak silhouettes against the purpling sky. The starkly beautiful Rocklands of Taka Mal stretched east before him. The Pyramid Foothills of Aronsdale were behind them, mounded and rocky, but greening as one looked farther west.

Ozar's army, over four thousand strong, had massed along Jazid's northern border with Taka Mal and its western border with Aronsdale. Cobalt's army was camped across from them, just within Aronsdale, and the Taka Mal forces had gathered along the Saint Verdant River, which all three armies were using for water. It was an untenable situation, almost fourteen thousand soldiers and another three thousand tenders, all living off land that would have trouble supporting one-third that population for any sustained time.

"Maybe I should send another envoy to Taka Mal," Cobalt said.

Matthew frowned at him. "What was wrong with the one Sphere-General Fieldson took there?"

"If they could return to us, they would have done so."

Matthew didn't look convinced. "Samuel Fieldson is one of the highest-ranked generals alive. Maybe Queen Vizarana fears for his life." He indicated the massed armies. "If I were queen of Taka Mal and I had all these people hulking at my door, I wouldn't be sending an officer that valuable anywhere right now, either."

Cobalt couldn't help but smile. "If you were the queen of Taka Mal, Matthew, I do believe her suitors would be rather upset."

The stable master laughed. "I imagine so."

Cobalt's smile faded. "She might be using caution. Or she might be holding the envoy hostage." He studied the armies that stretched as far as he could see both south and east, until they became dark blurs. "I will give her one more day and then send another envoy."

"You should see this." Matthew's voice had a strange sound.

"Hmm?" Cobalt glanced at him. Matthew had twisted around in his saddle to look behind them. Cobalt maneuvered Admiral around to face west. All he saw was the same Aronsdale landscape as always. In the distance, its misty green and blue hues promised a gentler land than this harsh landscape. A haze spread across the countryside, giving it a mystical quality. It was attractive, certainly, and he saw no problem.

"What?" Cobalt asked.

Matthew gave him a strange look. "Your Majesty—"

Cobalt scowled at him. "You never call me that unless you plan on saying something I won't like."

"Maybe you should put on your glasses."

So that was it. Reluctant, Cobalt took his spectacles out of the hidden pocket in his tunic. Settling them on his nose, he peered west. The misty blue resolved into ranks of men and horses extending across the land for many leagues.

"Oh," Cobalt said. The Aronsdale army had arrived.

Matthew shifted uneasily in his saddle. "Jarid promised us safe passage."

"They haven't denied it," Cobalt said, as much to convince himself as Matthew. "They're coming to make sure we keep our battles out of their country."

The older man gave him a dour look. "What battles?"

Cobalt was barely listening. With his glasses on, he could see the beauty of Aronsdale much better. "Now that," he murmured, "is a country worth having."

"Cobalt, for saints' sake."

He pulled his attention back to his scowling stable master. "I'm not going to invade Aronsdale. If Taka Mal gives back Drummer and Jazid minds its own business, I won't attack anyone."

"And if they don't?"

"We will see." Cobalt felt the thirst within him that nothing quenched. He had promised Mel to use restraint, not in so many words but in his silences, when she looked at him and believed he could be more than he thought possible, as a king, a father, and a husband. His wife wanted a man of peace. He would never be that. But today, he would try.

Hooves pounded on the path that led up the ridge. Admiral snorted, and Hawkspar stepped nervously. A lieutenant rode around a spur, a young fellow with his hair pulled into a queue. He came forward with caution. Cobalt had noticed that many of his officers approached him in such a manner. He didn't put people at ease. Well, he was their commander. They weren't supposed to be at ease. Oddly enough, they seemed to trust him anyway and follow him with loyalty, despite Stonebreaker's years of scorn.

The youth saluted Cobalt, his fist against his rib cage. Cobalt returned the salute, curious as to what brought the lieutenant up here. "Do you have a message?" Cobalt asked.

"Not I, Your Majesty." The youth motioned down the ridge. "A man rode here from Alzire. He says he must speak with you."

Cobalt's unease stirred. Mel was in Alzire. "Bring him up."

"Yes, sir." The lieutenant wheeled his horse around and took off down the slope.

"What do you suppose it is about?" Matthew asked.

"I've no idea." Cobalt didn't want to speak. He never did when he was on edge.

The lieutenant soon returned with another rider, a man Cobalt recognized from the Alzire Palace. What was his name? Abacus. He was a clerk who kept records, also a horseman who carried messages to other towns. Cobalt couldn't imagine what brought him all the way out here, a journey of thirty days. His foreboding deepened.

Dust and dirt covered Abacus. His beard had grown out and his clothes were trail-worn. The pouch he wore strapped across his torso had frayed. He looked as if he hadn't stopped during the entire ride here from Alzire. In fact, he looked like hell.

"I am honored, Majesty," Abacus said hoarsely.

Cobalt felt like a wire pulled tight. "What is your message?"

"Sire—it is your wife."

The world suddenly went silent. Cobalt no longer heard the low thunder of seventeen thousand people. "What about my wife?"

"She—" Abacus took a shuddering breath. "She is gone. Kidnapped, we think."

Cobalt wanted to ask him to start over. He couldn't have heard properly. The one constant in his life, the one person who gave him reason to live, couldn't be gone. He had left her in Alzire for her protection.

"How long?" Cobalt's voice sounded strange. It belonged to someone else. It couldn't be his, because he was screaming inside.

"Twenty days." Abacus was shaking from fatigue.

Matthew stared at him. "You made it here in *twenty* days?"

"Yes, sir."

"Tell me what happened," Cobalt said.

"She vanished the night of the Citrine Festival," Abacus answered, trying to sit erect in his saddle, though he swayed. He reached into his bag and took out a packet of blue silk. "We found signs of a struggle in one of the stables. And this."

Cobalt took the packet. He recognized the vivid blue silk and silver embroidery. It was Mel's scarf, torn, with blood on one corner. Somehow he kept his hands steady as he inspected what the messenger had wrapped within it. Those strands of hair had to be hers; he knew no one else with hair to her waist of that bright yellow color. He had a sudden memory of the first time he had touched her hair, in his coach the night after their wedding. He had feared he would hurt her. He had seen the pretty young woman and hadn't known the strength behind that angelic face.

The scarf held one other object: a dagger with blood on its tip. *Whose blood?* Its curved blade and the hilt enameled in sunrise colors were both distinctive. In his too-quiet voice, Cobalt said, "This dagger is from Taka Mal."

Abacus spoke miserably. "Yes, Your Majesty."

"They took Mel?" Matthew asked, incredulous.

Cobalt felt as if he couldn't breathe. "They made a mistake." His calm was threatening to break open.

"We don't know anything for certain," Matthew said.

Cobalt spurred Admiral forward and took off down the slope, leaving the others behind. He had to arrange search parties, send investigators to Alzire, ride hard, scour the land, *do something.* He couldn't leave his post here, but until he knew what had happened to Mel, he would have no rest.

He swore an oath: If she had been hurt—or worse—those responsible would pay a price beyond their imagining.

21

Temple of the Dragon-Sun

The rough passage, thick with grime, had seen little use for centuries. Light from Jade's candle bounced off the coarse brick walls and the stale air smelled dusty. The tunnel twisted around the citadel and narrowed in places until its walls touched her. She kept a blanket around herself so she didn't rip or destroy her garments as she squeezed through the hidden passage.

Finally she reached a panel with an eyehole too high for her. She stepped on a brick jutting out from the wall and peered through the hole. A few candles lit the room beyond. It resembled the parlor in her own suite, except here the walls were red by the floor and lightened into rose and then gold as they shaded upward. The ceiling was blue with a few gray clouds. The citadel builders called it the Sunset Room, but Jade silently beseeched the Dragon-Sun to make it a sunrise tonight instead of an ending.

This door bore a carved starflower. She pressed its petals in a different pattern than the one she had used in her suite. Her father had taught her the secrets of this citadel, just as he had in the Topaz Palace. She carried the knowledge alone; he had told no one else but her mother. Not even Baz. Especially not Baz. Her father had known the challenges Jade would face. He had given her every tool within his power to help her hold the throne.

Jade rested her hand on her abdomen. Someday, saints willing, she would bequeath those secrets to her child. Determined, she pushed the wooden panel. It opened with a creak, and she stepped into the Sunset Room. Her candle chased away shadows in the corners, but she blew it out. She went to a small table enameled with a fire dragon and blew out the candle there. That left only the one on the mantel across the parlor, and it only lit that side of the room. Satisfied, Jade hid in the corner farthest from the mantel, behind a cabinet that displayed porcelain fire-dragons.

Then she waited.

It wasn't long before the others arrived: Drummer, Fieldson, Spearcaster, and Arkandy Ravensford.

"She's not here," Fieldson said.

Drummer looked around with obvious unease. "She'll come."

Spearcaster picked up the doused candle on the table. "Do you have a flint?"

"Somewhere." Drummer sounded distracted. "Maybe she went to one of the other rooms."

"She said she would meet us here," Spearcaster said.

Drummer wandered restlessly around the room. He was a captivating sight. His elegant gold trousers had a row of topaz buttons up their outer seams. His suede belt fit low on his hips and glinted with rubies and gold. His white shirt was Zanterian silk, and his vest had sunrise designs worked into it with gems and blue thread. Gold edged his shirt cuffs and the seams of his amber-suede boots. Someone had dressed the groom well indeed.

The officers also wore their finest. General Spearcaster was resplendent in his dress uniform, dark gold and red, with gold braid up the trousers, and his sword in a jeweled sheath. Fieldson and Ravensford wore uniforms of white and violet, with knee-boots and those oddly straight swords that seemed less deadly to Jade, less efficient in gouging the guts of an opponent. If they were lucky, there would be no eviscerating tonight.

Jade never paid much attention to her own clothes. Usually she let Clove pick them out. She couldn't tonight, though, lest the ginger-maid wonder what was going on. So Jade had chosen a sunset silk, mainly because everything in the citadel had that theme. The floor-length silk wrapped her body and had a slit up the side revealing far too much leg. The sleeveless gown shaded from crimson up through sunrise colors and into pale blue across her breasts. With her hair up and threaded with gems, her head felt heavy. She wore the Dragon-Sun jewels, a necklace of topazes, rubies, and sapphires, with earrings that dangled down her neck and bracelets on her wrists. She felt overdressed, but maybe Drummer would like the effect.

Before she married anyone, though, she wanted to hear more of what these crafty generals had to say to her charming but naive groom. He had a great deal of savvy when it came to earning his living at the market or in taverns, and she didn't doubt he knew how to charm his way out of trouble, but in her opulently cutthroat royal court, he was an innocent. She hoped he stayed this way. It was one reason she liked him so much. Even...loved him. It was true, though she had trouble saying it. She couldn't imagine life without him, and she was glad they were to marry, but given how many people wanted to stop them, she wasn't about to trust anyone.

Ravensford braced his hand against the mantel and gazed into the empty hearth. He was a burly man, probably in his forties, with a wide face and a shock of golden-brown hair that gave him a stoic appearance. Jade knew little about him except that he was a close friend of the Harsdown king and had distinguished himself during the war nineteen years ago.

"Do you ever use these fireplaces?" Ravensford asked.

Spearcaster was opening a drawer of the table. "Not often. It's usually too hot." He searched through the drawer, probably for a flint to light the candles.

Fieldson was leaning against the panel Jade had used to enter the room. "Why is it," he grumbled, "that women take so much longer than men to put on their clothes?"

Spearcaster glanced up and smiled. "The result is usually worth the wait."

"Maybe someone got to her." Drummer was pacing, his forehead creased with worry, which made Jade feel guilty. Not enough to reveal her presence, though. For all she knew, they were the ones about to "get" to her, using Drummer as their foil.

"Baz looked ready to melt the sky today," Spearcaster said. "He's letting emotions blind his logic. Any fool can see how many problems this marriage will solve."

"If Jarid agrees to the treaty," Ravensford added.

"I've known Jarid for years," Fieldson said. "I think he'll agree."

Drummer spoke darkly. "Baz and Slate and Firaz are probably somewhere right now plotting how to steal Jade away."

Spearcaster closed the drawer. "They're down with the army, discussing strategy." Drily, he added, "But then, so am I."

Drummer raised his eyebrow at the lanky general.

"Firaz is there," Spearcaster allowed. "Baz, I doubt it."

"And Slate?" Drummer asked.

Spearcaster considered the question. "He's probably with the army. He's always had a soft spot where Vizarana is concerned. If she wants to marry you, I don't think he would try to stop her even if he disagreed with the decision."

"What about the atajazid?" Fieldson asked. "He has as much stake in this as Baz Quaazera."

"But no idea of Her Majesty's condition," Spearcaster said. "My guess is that Ozar is out there with his army."

"That close?" Drummer stiffened. "You mean, Baz could get him? *Tonight?*"

"Possibly," Spearcaster said. "But I don't think he would."

It didn't sound to Jade as if they were conning Drummer. In fact, their assessment of the situation matched hers. She could wait until they left the room to look for her, and then she could come out. That would be more diplomatic than just stepping out of her hiding pace, which would reveal she had been spying on them. But waiting for them to leave the room would take too long. She wanted this wedding done as soon as possible, a finished act no one could stop.

So much for diplomacy. Jade stood up and stepped out from behind the cabinet. "Light of the morning, gentlemen."

They all spun around, the officers drawing their swords fast, Spearcaster's glinting and curved, Ravensford's and Fieldson's straight and heavy. Drummer stared as if she had risen out of the ocean on a plume of froth. The candlelight gilded his face, and his eyes seemed lit with an inner glow.

"Why the weapons?" Jade asked, cool outside, jumpy inside.

Spearcaster exhaled, a long breath, and sheathed his blade. Fieldson and Ravensford followed suit.

"My apologies, Your Majesty," Spearcaster said. "We are on edge tonight." He was staring, too. They were all looking at her that way, as if she were something scrumptious to eat, like a clam or a mussel or some other delicacy from the Blue Ocean.

Drummer came forward and took her hands. "Saints, Jade."

Self-conscious, she answered in a low voice only for him. "Is something wrong with me?"

"Believe me, no." He raised her hand and kissed her knuckles. "You are devastating, love. If you were to walk among all those armies right now, their warriors would be so helplessly smitten, they would fall to the ground and swear allegiance to you forever."

"I would hope not," Spearcaster muttered, going behind the cabinet where Jade had been hiding. "The ones who aren't ours would be violating their oaths of fealty."

Jade slanted an annoyed look at the general. "He was being poetic. It's allowed with grooms, you know."

Spearcaster tapped on the wall. "How did you get out of here? It doesn't sound hollow."

"Hmm," Jade said.

"If you know a secret way out of this citadel," Fieldson said, "we need to know. Your cousin has all the entrances guarded."

She took Drummer's hand. "In another room of this suite."

In the main room, Jade went to a niche similar to the one in her parlor. Within moments, she was opening another secret door. They filed into the tunnel beyond and closed the door. Ravensford carried a candle. It cast their shadows ahead of them in a rough passageway of large, old bricks.

"I had no idea this was here," Spearcaster said.

Jade detested having to show them. Now he would search for other passages, and knowing him, he would find them.

"You are sworn to tell no one," Jade said. "All of you."

They each gave their word. She trusted Drummer.
Spearcaster maybe. He had been the closest she had to a father since the death of the king. Actually, he had been more
like a father to her than her own father. She had great affection for him, but she had long ago learned that what he
considered her own best interest didn't necessarily coincide
with her own thoughts on the matter. If he decided to map
these hidden passageways for the army's use, she might have
a hard time convincing him to keep the secret from even his
top people. No matter what he decided, though, she knew
he would make that choice to protect his queen and her
country.

Fieldson and Ravensford were another story. She had no
reason to trust them, and as impressed as she had been with
both of them, especially Fieldson, she knew they would act
first in support of their sovereign, King Muller. As she led
them through a maze, she chose as confusing a route as possible.

Finally Jade reached the wall panel she wanted. She
turned to the others. "This opens into an alley in Sun's
Breadth, the town around the citadel."

Spearcaster stood with his arms crossed, frowning. "If
this passage lets us sneak into town, that means it could let
someone in town sneak into the citadel."

"That's why no one knows about it," she said. "And why
you are sworn to secrecy." She knew Spearcaster would set
up a guard system now that Fieldson and Ravensford knew
about the entrance.

Jade pressed a pattern into the starflower on the door and

cracked the portal open. Spearcaster leaned past her and set his palm against the wood panel. "You are sure Baz doesn't know about this exit?"

"As far as I know," Jade said.

He stepped past her, then edged open the door and peered out. After a moment he beckoned to them. They followed him into an alley with high walls on either side. Dust drifted around them, and the air smelled of night-blooming desert weed. A small animal ran past Jade's sandaled foot. She grimaced and stepped back, but she didn't cry out or even jerk.

With Drummer at her side, Jade led the way along narrow lanes hidden between buildings. She knew the route well, having often come here as a child. She had played in the alleys, accompanied by her taciturn bodyguards. Apparently it had never occurred to her parents to provide their child with friends her own age.

The Temple of the Dragon-Sun stood in a secluded area amid gardens and terraces with water flowing over the stone. The layered design of its roof matched the gardens. Pots hung from every level, lush with vines: fire-lilies, red pyramid-blossoms that opened at dawn, snap-lions, sun-orbs, and scalloped fire opal blossoms with petals as bright as flames.

As temples went, this one was small. The interior was one room, with a stone table at the far end and benches arrayed before it in curving rows. The cool spaces, all stone and air, soothed Jade's nerves. Candles shed gold light around the table but left the rest of the temple in shadow. People prayed here to the dragon spirit who put the sun in the sky, the flames in the sunset, and the fire in the souls of men and women.

The dragon priestess stood by the table, one hand resting on a scroll tied with red and gold cords. She was an older woman, slender and frail, dressed in a sunset-hued robe. Jade recognized her; she had served at Jade's fifteenth birthday celebration, when the Topaz Heir officially became an adult. Back then, the woman's hair had been mostly black, her posture straighter, her face less lined. But her otherworldly quality and her serenity were the same.

The priestess beckoned to them. "Come out of the shadows." Her voice was rich, though thinned a bit with age. "Let me look at you. I don't see so well—" She stopped as Spearcaster came up to her. "Oh, my. You?"

The craggy general knelt and bowed his head. She rapped him on the head. "Stand up, young man. Goodness, Ravi. Aren't you married yet?"

Drummer hung back in the shadows with Jade. "Ravi?" Amusement washed across his face.

"His personal name is Ravel," Jade murmured. She was glad Spearcaster was here. She wished things could have been different with Baz, too, that he would have also stood at her side. And Firaz and Slate. They meant a great deal to her despite how they always argued with her, or maybe even partly because of that.

"Doesn't the priestess know who she's going to marry?" Drummer asked.

Jade shook her head. "It was a precaution. Ravensford

dressed in old clothes and went to talk to her. He didn't say anything more than a 'young man and woman.'"

The priestess surveyed Spearcaster as he stood up, looming over her. "I've never seen you so glossed up," she said with approval. "You look quite the groom. But I would have thought a man in your position would want a formal wedding in Quaaz with all the pomp and the big temple."

His face creased with an affectionate smile. "I'm not the groom, Blessed One."

"No?" She raised her eyebrows. "These young folks must be quite something, to have you attend their wedding, especially at such an hour." She peered into the shadows. "Well, well, I can't see anything. Come forward, all of you."

Jade glanced at Drummer. "This is your last chance to escape marrying me."

He smiled at her. "I'm not so easy to get rid of, Dragon Princess." He used her dynastic title, from the ancient tales that named a queen of Taka Mal as a princess of the Dragon-Sun.

As they walked forward, holding hands, the priestess squinted. "Goodness! What a beautiful couple. Here, here, let me see bet—" She broke off as they came into the light. "Saints above," she murmured. With a grace that belied her age, she went down on one knee before Jade.

"I am honored, Blessed One," Jade said. She touched the priestess's head far more gently than the elderly woman had conked Spearcaster. "Please stand."

The priestess rose and looked over their party, including Fieldson and Ravensford in their white and violet uniforms.

She spoke quietly. "Are these the witnesses, Your Majesty? For a royal wedding, at least one other besides myself must be a citizen of Taka Mal."

"I stand as her second witness," General Spearcaster said.

The priestess nodded. "We are honored."

"Have you prepared the scroll?" Spearcaster asked.

She indicated the parchment on the table. "Everything is here, as requested."

"Shall we proceed, then?" Jade asked. Incredibly it looked as if this wild plot would succeed.

"Do you wish any extra readings?" the priestess asked.

"Nothing." Jade spoke with gentle urgency. "The faster you can marry us, the better."

"I see." The priestess paled, and Jade didn't doubt she understood the significance of a royal wedding done in secret, in the depths of the night, while three armies faced each other across a narrow strip of land that defined the border.

With Jade and Drummer standing before her, the priestess sang the Dragon-Sun chant in High Alatian, a ceremonial language with stricter rhythms than modern speech. It was a prayer to the spirits of the sky and the wind and the flames of life, wishing love and good fortune for the wedding couple.

When the priestess finished the chant, she lifted a string of fire-opal blossoms off the table. They glowed as vibrantly as Jade's silk dress. She touched Drummer's forehead with the petals. Softly she said, "What is your name, son? I need the formal version."

"Drummer Creek Headwind," he said. "Son of Appleton by blood and kin to Dawnfield by marriage."

The priestess's hand jerked, scraping the petals across his forehead, but to her credit she showed no other shock to the news that she was about to wed a Dawnfield to a Quaazera.

"Drummer Creek Headwind," she said. "Her Majesty, Vizarana Jade, Queen of Taka Mal, would take you as the Topaz Consort, her husband and the father of her heir. Do you accept?"

"Oh, yes." Drummer's face had a glow Jade had seen only twice before—yesterday when she revealed her pregnancy and tonight in the Sunset Room. He exuded a joy she would never deserve, not if they lived a century. As her consort, he would see grief and war and death, politics and deceit, treachery and violence. He had lost forever the days when he could wander the dales of his home with no concerns except to feed and clothe himself. She could offer him a throne and her kingdom and shower him with gems and gold, but she could never give him back that freedom. Perhaps if she loved him well enough and long enough, someday she would earn this joy that he gave so freely, without condition.

The priestess anointed Jade on the forehead with the fire opal. "Vizarana Jade Quaazera, do you accept this man as the Topaz Consort?"

"Yes." Jade wanted to tell the stars. "I accept."

"No!" The shout came from behind them.

Jade whirled around. Warriors were pouring into the temple, armored men with swords and snarling dragon-sun helmets. They strode up the aisle, weapons clanking, boots thudding on the stone floor—led by their commander, her cousin, Baz Quaazera.

"You're too late," Jade said. "The ceremony is done."

Baz had his gaze fixed on Drummer. He unsheathed his sword, and it glittered in the candlelight.

"Baz, no!" Jade was aware of Spearcaster, Fieldson, and Ravensford drawing their weapons. Her voice echoed in the spaces of the temple. "Think well before you wield arms against your queen and her consort, for you would be committing treason."

The warriors stopped around the table, cutting off escape but coming no closer. Except Baz. He strode into the candlelight. With dismay, Jade realized she may have underestimated how far he would go to stop this marriage. Seeing the desperate rage on his face, she knew he was capable of killing Drummer.

"Baz, no." She started forward, but Drummer and Spearcaster both grabbed her by the arm, one on either side of her, and pulled her back. Every man in the temple had drawn his blade, and she knew they were going to fight. Someone would die here, and whoever survived would face execution for murdering a queen's officer—or for assassinating her consort.

Then Drummer pulled his cube out from a pocket of his vest. He extended his arm forward at chest height with the cube resting in his open palm. With his gaze on Baz, he said, simply, "Stop."

"You cannot fight me with a little block of metal," Baz said.

With no warning, gold light flared around Drummer's hand. Baz took a fast step backward.

"It is the Dragon-Sun," Drummer said, his minstrel's voice full and resonant. "The sunset has blessed this marriage."

The light around his hand intensified and filled the temple. It turned fiery orange, then red, and finally the deep crimson at the end of the sunset as day passed into night. It lit them all with its ruddy glow.

"The Dragon breathes to protect the queen," Drummer said, and flames erupted from his hand. Jade felt their heat, yet they had no effect on him. He stood bathed in their light and stared at Baz as if challenging him to defy the dragon in its own temple. Baz didn't move.

Gradually the flames faded, leaving only candlelight. Drummer lowered his arm. Everyone stared at him; no one moved or spoke. Even Jade, who had seen his "parlor games," was frozen. This was no trick. Either her husband truly did have the blessing of the Dragon-Sun or else she had just married one of the notorious Dawnfield mages. Apprehension swept over Jade, for she didn't believe Drummer had miraculously communed with the Dragon-Sun. By the saints, what had she done? Her new husband was a sorcerer.

Baz let out a long breath. He slid his sword into its curved sheath, and at his action, the other warriors sheathed theirs. He came forward then, and Jade knew her cousin truly was a man of great courage, for she doubted any of his warriors would approach Drummer right now.

Baz spoke to Jade. "The marriage is done?"

She answered in her throaty voice. "It is done."

"Then I will mourn." His sense of betrayal was written on his face. "And tomorrow Taka Mal will fall to Cobalt the Cruel."

"We are not at war," Jade said.

"You don't think so?" Baz beckoned to someone among the warriors in the dimly lit temple.

Jade had been wrong that no other would come forward, for one of the men approached, tall and broad shouldered in his black leather and iron-gray breastplate. A massive sword hung on his belt, and a black plume topped his shadow-dragon helmet. Then he removed his helmet, and she knew this was no ordinary warrior who dared the wrath of the Dragon-Sun. The Atajazid D'az Ozar had come to her wedding.

He spoke in a shadowed voice. "When Cobalt descends on your country and your life, Vizarana, you will fight him alone."

"If Taka Mal falls," Jade said, "you are next."

"Escar will come," Ozar said, "for as people must breathe, so he must conquer. He will ride across Taka Mal like the Dragon-Sun's fire, burning all in his path. He will make Taka Mal pay for this alliance you committed tonight, until he has burned Quaaz to the ground and cut your head from your body."

Jade met his hard stare. "You words cannot terrorize me."

"He will massacre your people."

"You can't have me, Ozar, even if you threaten Taka Mal with annihilation." Her gaze never wavered. "Abandon Taka Mal now and you will lose your throne as well. If you think otherwise, you know nothing of Cobalt, and all of Jazid will suffer for it."

"You know my terms."

Her fist clenched, small and delicate compared to the warriors around them. "I have given my vows to another."

"Then fix it." Ozar's face hardened as he turned to the man at her side. "If your consort has to die so that you can fulfill your obligations, so be it."

With that, the Shadow Dragon Prince spun around and strode away, his boots ringing on the stone floor. He swept out of the temple and left his threat hanging in the air like a blade poised above Drummer's head.

22

The Violet Storm

Dawn was seeping through cracks in the walls as Mel dragged herself awake. She couldn't remember why she was lying on the floor of a rough shack.

Her memory stirred painfully. She had escaped Ozar's fortress and run, her bare feet slapping on stone. The cell had finished its collapse, and the thunder of its destruction had followed her as she raced down a corridor with its walls toppling behind her. She sped down the spiral staircase of a tower while the stairs above her fell in a traveling wave of wreckage. Just before the tower crashed down into rubble, she had run out into a courtyard beneath an overcast sky.

Mel remembered shivering in an underground storage bin with daggers and maces. She had hidden in an armory on the other side of the courtyard while Ozar and his men investigated the ruins. She couldn't even remember now what supplies she had taken from the armory. When night came, she had slipped past the wreckage of the fortress and run through the barren terrain, run and run, clenching the handle of the spiked metal ball in one hand and her stolen gear in the other.

With a groan, Mel rolled onto her side. Black leather armor was piled up nearby, with a Jazid breastplate and a Shadow Dragon helmet. She wondered dully at her priorities. She had taken a sword, belt, and dagger, but no food or water. Filled with her mind-slamming rage, she had thought only of fighting.

Of killing.

In the past, Mel had never believed the accounts of those ancient war mages. The histories were thousands of years old. Surely time had distorted and magnified the tales. Now she knew otherwise: The years had softened the truth. She had never desired the power to destroy, but she would bring down every fortress in the settled lands if that was what it took to protect her child.

She didn't understand how she had survived the collapse of her cell. Huge chunks of rock had fallen, yet miraculously none hit her. Perhaps the spell protected its maker. It made a grim sort of sense. Those mages whose spells kept them alive were more likely to have children who would carry on the trait.

Mel had found no wounds on Shade's body. She would never truly know how he died, for the destruction had buried him. Ozar probably thought she had died as well. She didn't think any stone had hit Shade, but that left only her spell. It made her sick to think she could wreak violence with gifts meant to heal.

Violet. The power of life and death. Mages felt the spells they made, not as intensely as those they created it for, but enough to matter. She knew warmth from her red spells and health from the blue. She should have felt Shade die. But she remembered nothing of his passing. Did flawed spells distort away from their wielder? It was a horrific prospect, for it suggested she suffered the least for using the worst of her abilities. The power had surely been bred into her ancestors to counter those kings who sought to contain the war mages. In the centuries since, the marriages of Dawnfield kings to the strongest mages they could find had concentrated the mage abilities. For centuries this particular trait had slept within the Dawnfield line, gathering strength.

Now it had awakened—with a vengeance.

She pushed into a sitting position. Her wounds hurt miserably, and her legs ached from her long run. She had scrambled in the dark, afraid to fall into a crack or crevice, even more afraid to make light lest someone see. The half-moon had appeared and disappeared behind streaks of cloud, her only guide.

She slowly limbered up, working through the aches and pain. Then she put on the armor. Her supplies were spotty; she had no water, but she had grabbed two pairs of leggings when she only needed one. At least she had chosen better with the armor. The leather was old and supple and fit her well. She pulled the pants over her leggings, then tugged on a vest and fastened the breastplate over it, leaving her arms bare except for the wrist guards and armbands. Metal studs riveted the belt together. The leather boots were scuffed and pitted. The armor was designed for a man of her height, but with broader shoulders and chest, which was fine; she needed the extra space in the breastplate for its namesakes.

Mel hung the dagger sheath from her belt and strapped the helmet to her back. She hefted the sword, as she had done during those long hours while she sweated in her hiding place. The blade felt well balanced and suited to her upper-body strength, which was less than that of many warriors. She compensated for that lack with her fast reflexes, but she needed a weapon light enough to utilize her advantage.

The spiked ball lay on the floor, glinting where a trickle of sunlight hit one of the sharpened points. Mel picked it up by the metal handle and swung it over her head. The chain clinked as the ball whipped in a circle. Although it was heavy, she had no problem wielding it as a flail. But for her, its greatest value lay in another aspect; its shape could unleash her mortal spells.

She wrapped the ball with the extra leggings so it wouldn't gouge her thigh, and then she fastened it to her belt. A search of the shack turned up a strip of smoked meat, a water bag, and the snares of a trapper. The bag was empty. With an apology to whoever used the shack, Mel hung the bag from her belt. She had seen oval-leaf bushes outside last night, which meant there had to be water nearby. She would fill the bag and break her fast with the meat and whatever game or edible plants she could find.

Finally, Mel peeled a strip of bark off the wall and sat down to whittle it with her dagger. She needed an exact shape, and she had trouble cutting one. Her disks and polygons came out crooked. The square was better, and it caught her spell, glowing with blue light. The weak spell barely lit up her hands, but it was better than nothing.

Mel sat with her back to the wall and cradled the square in her palms. Running her fingers along the shape, she imagined blue sky. Blue water. Blue silk. Blue eyes. Like Drummer's. The glow around her hands deepened. With no formal training, she didn't know if she could direct her spell to specific injuries. She thought of her wounds—and the light flowed into her body like a river filling a vessel. With a sigh, she leaned against the wall and closed her eyes.

She struggled to maintain the spell, however. To use such a high color, even with a low-level shape, wore her out. Finally she released the spell and opened her eyes. The last of the blue light faded from her hands. But…her aches had also receded. When she stood up, her muscles didn't protest as much. The whip had cut deep gashes yesterday, and dried blood hadn't even finished flaking off her arms, yet the wounds looked as if they had been healing for several days.

Mel let out a long breath, steadying herself. It was time to leave, to face her precarious future. Sword in hand, she opened the door. A rocky clearing fronted the hut, and several oval-leaf bushes jutted out of the ground. Beyond the clearing, the mountains cut downward in a panorama of angular slopes. To her left, peaks sheered upward; on the right, they dropped down in ridge after knife-edged ridge. She could see for leagues, and everywhere the land stuttered in the jagged-teeth formations that gave the range its name. It was beautiful in its harsh grandeur, and it took Mel's breath.

A waterfall cascaded down the peaks behind the shack. After she drank deeply and filled the bag, she ate some bitter oval-berries. She saw no wildlife; the world seemed deserted. Wind keened among the peaks and through the deep gullies between them. The sky had shed its clouds and stretched above, parched and blue.

Her best hope of survival was to find the Chamberlight army. If they were where she expected, she had more than a day's journey on foot, and to reach them, she would have to go through the Jazid forces. As long as she hid her yellow hair, she might blend in with the other soldiers. Her face didn't look masculine, but with the helmet on she could probably pass for a youth.

Mel set off, heading north.

Seventeen thousand strong, four armies gathered in a great confluence of men and horses. Cobalt rode Admiral up and down the lines as his companies trained, but he spoke to no one. He barely contained his agitation. Mel was out there. Her kidnappers had slithered past the armies, probably east into Jazid and then north into Taka Mal. His search parties had found nothing, and it would be days before his men returned from Alzire with news. His wife could be anywhere, and it was killing him.

As of yet, he had given no order to strike Taka Mal. Rumors abounded: Queen Vizarana had killed Drummer, she had brought him to the Sun-Dragon citadel, she had left him in Quaaz, she had sent him home. Cobalt hadn't intended to attack if Taka Mal negotiated in good faith. Now he no longer cared. Even if Drummer walked up to him, it wouldn't matter. Taka Mal had gone too far when they took his pregnant wife and left behind her blood.

Matthew galloped across the camp and came alongside of Cobalt. "You must prepare! We've spotted an envoy headed here from the Dragon-Sun citadel."

Cobalt gazed past the solitary peak with the citadel to the much more distant eastern mountains. Quaaz lay beyond that barrier. Was Mel there?

"Listen to me!" Matthew grabbed Admiral's reins and pulled the horse to a stop. Admiral neighed in protest, but he knew Matthew well enough that he didn't rear or bolt.

Cobalt spoke in a hard voice. "Let go of my horse."

Matthew gave him back the reins. "You don't know that Taka Mal had any part in Mel's disappearance."

Cobalt realized he was gritting his teeth. He forced his jaw to relax. "Have Agate Cragland bring the Taka Mal envoy to me."

"You must treat them as emissaries," Matthew said. "Not prisoners of war."

Cobalt wanted to pull his sword and fight, not Matthew, but someone. Anyone. It took a concentrated effort to keep his voice even. "I will treat them as appropriate."

Matthew didn't look reassured. His gaze went beyond Cobalt. "That was fast."

Cobalt brought Admiral around to face the way Matthew

was looking. Agate and several Chamberlight officers were approaching him. An unfamiliar soldier rode in their midst, a man in the gold and red of a Taka Mal lieutenant. Cobalt rode forward, aware of Matthew at his side, and they all gathered in a group, their horses stamping and snorting.

Cobalt looked from the lieutenant to Agate. "Only one man?"

"He isn't the envoy," Agate said. "He came from the south."

Cobalt narrowed his gaze at the man. "Why are you here?"

The lieutenant spoke with the drawn-out Taka Mal accent, exotic in its unusual rhythms, different from the cool, clipped tones of the Misted Cliffs. "Your Majesty, please accept my humblest pleas for your mercy. I set my life before you and beg your beneficent compassion for myself, your lowly servant."

Cobalt had never mastered the flowery, convoluted language of court intrigue. Beneficent compassion, indeed. What the blazes did that mean? If this fellow had done something wrong, he should just say so.

"Why do you need mercy?" Cobalt asked.

"I have done no evil!" The man paused. "No, that is false. I have committed a great crime. I deserted my post to come here."

Either the fellow was a consummate actor or he genuinely felt agonized. "Why did you desert?" Cobalt asked.

"I couldn't stand by while—while such atrocities—" He took a ragged breath. "I had to choose between my conscience and my post. I chose my conscience."

Cobalt frowned. "How do I know you aren't a spy sent by Queen Vizarana to infiltrate my camp?"

"Ask the envoy," the man said. "It will be here soon."

"I will," Cobalt said. "Now tell me why you came."

He blanched as if Cobalt had asked him to impale himself on his own sword. "Please know, I am only a messenger—"

"If you don't tell me soon," Cobalt said darkly, "my beneficent compassion will be all used up."

The man reached for his saddle bags, but stopped when the Chamberlight men drew their swords.

"Let him get whatever it is," Cobalt said.

His men lowered their swords, and the lieutenant exhaled. Cobalt didn't think he was pretending to be afraid. The man opened one of his bags and pulled out a bundle of brown-and-yellow cloth. With shaking arms, he held it out to Cobalt.

"I am sorry," he said.

"About what?" Bewildered, Cobalt took the bundle. It was rags, some yellow, some an ugly brown—

With a horrific sense of falling, Cobalt realized two things. The brown stains were blood. A lot of blood. And the rags were the remains of a pair of harem pants and a tunic.

Mel's clothes.

A roaring began in Cobalt's ears. He couldn't see clearly, only brown stains on yellow silk. He raised his gaze to the man from Taka Mal. Cobalt didn't know how he looked, but it wasn't only the deserter who recoiled; all of the men, even Agate, went pale.

Cobalt spoke slowly and heard his voice rumble like a distant storm. "Where is the woman who wore these clothes?"

The lieutenant swallowed, tried to speak and failed.

"Answer me," Cobalt said.

The man spoke in a burst. "She is dead, Your Majesty. She—she didn't survive—what they did to her."

"And who," Cobalt said, enunciating each word, "did it?"

"The man I was expected to serve, but cannot," the lieutenant said grimly. "General Baz Quaazera, at command of the queen."

Thunder exploded inside of Cobalt. The roaring in his ears stopped as suddenly as it began and left him in a deadly calm. He had thought Stonebreaker injured him with his cruelty, but those decades of torment were nothing compared to this moment.

Someone was speaking. Agate Cragland. "What proof do you have that General Quaazera did this?"

"I saw it," the lieutenant said.

"And who are you," Agate asked, "to see such an act?"

"Lieutenant Feldspar Kaj, of Her Majesty's personal guard."

"Well, Kaj," Agate said. "You are also a deserter. How do we know you don't bring this story out of spite?"

Kaj indicated the silk Cobalt held. "She was wearing that when they brought her in. I watched them whip her to death. I was assigned to guard her uncle, the man called Drummer, and I have also watched them torture him. Call me what you will, but I could not stay there after what I witnessed."

Cobalt found his voice. "General Cragland, where is the envoy from the citadel?"

"I told the men to take them to your tent," Agate said.

Cobalt jabbed Admiral's flanks with his heels. Despite the unusual behavior, the horse took off with a practiced gait. They had been together a long time, he and this horse, and Admiral knew what he wanted. He raced through the camp. The other men came with Cobalt, but he ignored them, for if he spoke, his control would shatter. People stared as he galloped past: cooks looked up from steaming pots, grooms stopped tending their horses and watched him with the reins hanging in their hands, archers sharpening arrows rose to their feet.

Warriors crowded the area around Cobalt's tent. His soldiers were guarding eight men in the fiery red-and-gold uniforms of Taka Mal. It took a concentrated effort for Cobalt to keep from drawing his sword. He reined in Admiral, and the black warhorse stamped up swirls of dust. As Cobalt dismounted, a groom ran up. Cobalt handed him the reins, never taking his gaze off the envoy. He strode forward, and Matthew and Agate joined him. Cobalt was aware of his men bringing Kaj, but he kept his attention on the emissaries. With a start, he realized one was General Spearcaster, a Queen's Advisor.

Spearcaster bowed. "My honor at your presence, Your Majesty."

"Is it?" Cobalt stretched out his arm and pointed at Kaj, who stood a few paces away with his Chamberlight escort. "Who is that man?"

Spearcaster frowned at the lieutenant. "Kaj? What are you doing here?"

Kaj lifted his chin. "I cannot serve commanders who commit what I have seen."

Spearcaster visibly tensed. "What are you talking about?"

Kaj looked frightened. "I can't countenance what is going on. Drummer Headwind—"

"That will be enough," Spearcaster said sharply.

"It's wrong," Kaj said.

Cobalt turned to Spearcaster, and the explosion inside him swelled. "What is it that he thinks is wrong?"

Spearcaster spoke carefully. "It isn't my place to speculate on what he may or may not have said to you."

"What was his position?" Cobalt asked. "The one he deserted?"

"He was a guard for Drummer Headwind," Spearcaster said. "But if he claims Goodman Headwind has been harmed, he lies."

"Then why did this lieutenant desert his post?"

"I cannot speak of such matters."

"Why *not?*" Cobalt demanded. "Where is my wife?"

Spearcaster blinked. "Your wife?"

"Where have you taken her?"

"Your Majesty, I know nothing of your wife." Spearcaster narrowed his gaze at Kaj. "This man in no way represents Queen Vizarana, and if he claims we have news of your wife, he lies. I have come to discuss Drummer Headwind and to request safe passage for Sphere-General Fieldson, so he may join us as your envoy."

Cobalt spoke tightly. "Take your queen a message." He whirled around and strode to where the groom was holding

Admiral's reins. Cobalt swung onto his horse. To Spearcaster, he said, "She has until sunrise tomorrow to return my wife and Drummer. If they are not in this camp when the first rays of the sun touch the earth, then I will break your army, loot your country and burn Quaaz to the ground."

He wheeled Admiral around and galloped away then, riding hard through his camp, knowing that if he paused, even for one moment, he would incinerate in the flames of his rage.

Cobalt didn't know how far he went. He left his army behind and pounded south, with the Dawnfield army to the west and his own to the east. Finally he stopped, threw back his head, and shouted at the merciless sky. His anguish rolled across the land. But the shout couldn't quench the storm within him or lessen his agony over Mel's disappearance and the gruesome tales of her death.

Hooves rustled the grass behind him. Bringing around Admiral, he saw Matthew on Hawkspar, waiting a few paces back as if Cobalt were a wild beast that might attack. Cobalt said nothing.

Matthew rode over to him, slow and cautious. "You have no proof they did what Kaj claims."

Cobalt was clenching the reins so hard his fingernails cut his skin. "Spearcaster was hiding something."

"Yes, I had that impression. But torture and murder? It didn't seem so."

"They have one day to bring Mel and Drummer."

"And if they don't have them?"

"I attack."

"It is a tricky proposition," Matthew said. "Even if Kaj is lying, even if Mel and Drummer are fine, why would the queen give up her hostages? If you attack, they lose their value. She may have them killed."

"I will see my *wife*." The explosion was building again within Cobalt. He wheeled Admiral around and took off. But no matter how hard or how far he rode, it wouldn't purge the demons of fear that haunted him.

Jade paced the long balcony. She and Drummer were staying in this citadel tower, guarded by the Harsdown envoy and Spearcaster's men. She was meeting here with all her generals for the first time since before the wedding. Baz stood by the glass doors with his arms crossed and ignored his guards. They were loyal men who had refused his orders when he sought to stop the marriage. He was the only obvious prisoner on the balcony, but several soldiers were discreetly keeping watch on Slate and Firaz, who stood with Fieldson to her right. Only Spearcaster, who stood by the railing, had no guard. And Drummer. Her new husband leaned against the wall to the left and watched her pace.

"I will not be threatened," Jade said. "Harsdown sent an envoy to speak with us." She motioned angrily at Fieldson. "We have spoken to him. We agreed to negotiate according to terms he proposed. Is Cobalt so hungry to fight that he refuses the envoy he *sent*? No! I will not be coerced by this tyrant."

"You would go to war instead?" Baz demanded.

"What choice do we have? He will never rest. Not until he conquers every country from the Blue Ocean to the Endless Desert."

Baz stalked over to her, ignoring his guards. One of them reached to stop the general, but Jade shook her head.

"You had to marry your pretty minstrel," Baz growled. "Now Ozar refuses us the support we need."

Drummer stiffened, but he shook his head slightly at Jade. She wanted to lash out at Baz, but she said only, "Ozar will not stand by while Taka Mal falls."

"Don't know about that," Firaz said. "He wanted your throne. Now that he can't have the blasted chair, maybe he doesn't care what happens to it."

"You would have had me marry him?" Jade demanded.

"Hell, no," Firaz said.

Startled, she said, "No?"

"The Topaz Throne belongs in the House of Quaazera," he said. "Besides, this treaty business with Aronsdale is a good idea."

"If it is so brilliant," Slate said sourly, "why are we facing a war with no allies?"

"Have we any news of Jason Windcrier?" Fieldson asked.

"Nothing," Jade said, disheartened. She went to the railing and looked out at her army, which was camped in the Rocklands below the Sharp Knife Mountain where this citadel stood. The Chamberlight forces were beyond hers, an ocean of warriors churning at her doorstep. The Aronsdale forces were a gray cloud on the horizon. An enigma. They might have come to ensure Escar left Aronsdale alone. Or they might be ready to support Taka Mal. She just didn't *know*.

"We haven't managed to get a single spy out," she said. "We think either Cobalt's or Ozar's men are catching them."

Drummer spoke. "I should go to meet Cobalt."

Firaz scowled at him. "You're the blasted Topaz Consort. After all that excitement getting you married to Vizarana, we hardly want you dead two days later. Defeats the whole purpose of the thing."

Jade would die before she put Drummer in danger. If she told him, though, he would insist on protecting her and her country. So instead she said the other truth she knew. "If we give in to Cobalt, we are showing weakness. He will see it. He also wants the Topaz Throne, and apparently he is willing to take it by force."

"Mel won't let him," Drummer said. "She's the water that cools his fire."

"Yes, well, what is this manure about us returning her?" Firaz growled. "Can't the man find his own wife?"

"Kaj has lied to him," Spearcaster said.

"Why would he do this thing?" Jade asked.

"We investigated him," Baz said. "It seems he had gambling debts." He gave a snort. "Someone has mysteriously paid them."

"Treason for money?" Jade said. "I cannot believe it."

Slate spoke in as gentle a manner as his gruff voice would allow. "Men have betrayed their sovereign for less."

Jade clenched her fist. "We must find out who paid him."

"We will," Spearcaster said. "But whatever troubles the

king goes beyond Kaj's lies. Cobalt doesn't strike me as a man who is easily tricked."

"He isn't," Fieldson said. "But when it comes to his wife, he has no shades of gray. He would level the Jagged Teeth Mountains if that was what it took to find her." Strain deepened the lines on his face. "As would any of the rest of us who watched her grow up from a child of sunlight to a woman."

Jade wondered who was this Mel Dawnfield that she inspired such intense emotions. "I offer my hopes that she will be found, well and alive."

"Thank you, Your Majesty." Fieldson's voice crackled with tension. "Cobalt needs to know that."

Jade looked around at her advisors. "We will send an envoy at dawn to tell him and swear we know nothing of his wife. General Fieldson, half the men in your envoy are from the Dawnfield armies. If we can get Cobalt to talk we should say we're ready to commence negotiations with him *and* King Jarid." Who just happened, conveniently, to be available.

"We'll try to arrange the meeting here," Slate said. "In the citadel."

"A good idea." Jade turned to Drummer. "If we do, you'll attend the negotiations, yes? It will put to rest Cobalt's suspicions that we harmed you."

His blue eyes, which had filled with such passion when he held her last night, were like ice this morning. "I wouldn't miss them for anything."

Fieldson came forward. "I should go with Spearcaster. I

was one of the people in the Harsdown meeting when we decided to send an envoy here. I can remind Cobalt of our discussions. And he may be more willing to believe me about his wife."

Jade regarded the gray-haired warrior from Harsdown. He was older than her generals, even Spearcaster. As fit and hale as he seemed, she feared for his safety as she would for a grandfather. She liked him even if he was the enemy. He was restrained compared to her fiery Taka Mal commanders, but just as formidable.

"King Cobalt didn't grant you safe passage," she told him.

"I don't think I'll be in danger," Fieldson said.

"Send Drummer," Baz muttered.

Jade scowled at her cousin. "Stop it."

Drummer joined them. "He's right, much as I hate to admit it." When Baz turned the full force of his irate gaze on the minstrel, Drummer raised his hands, palms outward. He didn't look too concerned, though. Jade suspected he had plenty of experience pacifying irate authorities.

"You can't go into the Chamberlight camp," Firaz said. "Let Fieldson and Spearcaster set it up. I will go with them."

Jade almost groaned. Firaz was a brilliant commander, but he had never been known for diplomacy. More than likely he would end up inflaming Cobalt.

"I thank you for your wise and magnanimous offer," she told him. "But I am greatly in need of your invaluable services here."

Firaz gave a curmudgeonly laugh. "You insult me so nicely. All right. I won't go muck up your negotiations."

Although Jade managed a smile, she felt anything but light. Maybe Cobalt had never intended to negotiate. The envoy could have been meant as no more than a distraction. Tomorrow he might seek to end her reign—but she would die before she surrendered her throne.

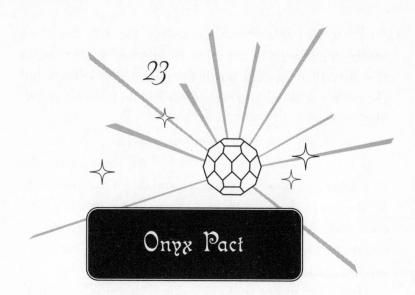

23

Onyx Pact

Drummer slipped into Vim's night-dark stall, his feet rustling in the hay, and the Jazidian neighed.

"Didn't know if you would want to see me again," Drummer said in a low voice. He offered Vim a piece of apple, and the horse munched away.

It took a while to saddle the horse, but he managed. He pulled up the hood of his jacket, then walked Vim across the yard outside the stable, their way lit by pale moonlight. A few workers were around, and a light-bringer came forward with a lamp swinging on his pole. Drummer held up his hand, declining the assistance.

Within moments, he was cantering through the town of Sun's Breadth that surrounded the citadel. He shared the cobbled lanes with scattered pedestrians on night business, even with a few other riders. Enough people were about that his passing elicited little notice. He approached the gate in the city wall amidst the bustle of arguing shop owners and their helpers, and the tower guards let him through as part of that group.

Outside, the merchants went about setting up a market near the city walls, for tomorrow. With the army in the Rocklands, and soldiers going up and down the mountain, businesses in the town were thriving. The merchants kept their impromptu market close to the wall, however, so they could quickly retreat into the protected town if hostilities erupted among the armies.

Alone, Drummer took Vim down the mountain. The well-worn path would come out in the Rocklands along the Saint Verdant River, the line of green he had struggled to reach during his first escape attempt. Tonight, he would succeed. This time he would ride right past the Taka Mal army. He knew many details about them. In fact, he had heard nothing else for the past few days. He could evade most of their sentries and posts. For those he couldn't, he knew the passwords and expected behavior, and he even had the same type of horse used by Taka Mal officers. He didn't expect anyone to stop him. But beyond that? Ozar's men were patrolling the border; to reach Cobalt's army, Drummer had to get past them.

He understood why Jade and her advisors didn't want him going with the envoy at dawn. Their plans were logical. Knowing Cobalt through Mel, however, Drummer understood him in a different light. Cobalt needed to see Drummer to believe he was all right. More importantly, he needed to see *Mel*, or have tangible proof of her situation. If Drummer could verify Jade had no connection to Mel's disappearance, he felt certain Cobalt would listen. But that was a leap of faith neither Jade nor her commanders were willing to make, especially given how few times Drummer had actually met the Midnight King. He understood that. But they were wrong. If he could reach Cobalt, he had a chance to stop this madness.

Unfortunately, he had to get through the Jazid lines first. Ozar's men might capture him. He had a plan for that, too. A good plan—if it worked. If he didn't lose his nerve. If he could convince Jade to go along with him at the necessary time. *If, if if.*

Cobalt or Ozar: Either way, Drummer would soon face one of the most formidable warlords among the settled lands.

The atajazid had yet to sleep, though midnight had come and passed. Ozar paced in his tent. He still heard the words of the messenger from Taka Mal who had come today: *Cobalt threatens to attack at sunrise.* The business with Kaj had not gone as well as Ozar hoped, for Cobalt had given Vizarana time to produce his wife. It would have worked better had Kaj delivered the queen's body, but she lay buried under tons of rubble. Although it would take time to dig out the remains of the people killed in that collapse, Ozar would have it done when this was all settled, not for the Chamberlight queen, but to honor Shade, who had been Ozar's confidant, loyal servant, and friend.

Regardless, Vizarana had trouble. Unless she convinced Cobalt that she had nothing to do with his wife's death, he would invade Taka Mal. It would be a crime for him to take the Topaz Throne. Ozar faced a difficult choice: Join with Vizarana or face Cobalt on his own.

The Jazid army was nearly five thousand strong and he could add another thousand in a year's time. They were well trained. Fighting in the desert and the Jagged Teeth Mountains would be easy for them and new to the Chamberlight army. They could, conceivably, defeat Cobalt. But if Cobalt took Taka Mal, he would gain what remained of their forces. Chances were he would massacre them, if he believed they had tortured his wife to death, but no certainties existed in that. Although Ozar had a chance to defeat the Chamberlight king, Cobalt could end up with the Onyx Throne, and that would truly be a perversion of nature.

Ozar knew if he supported Vizarana, they had a good chance of defeating Cobalt. Jazid could reabsorb Shazire, perhaps even the Misted Cliffs. It was a worthy goal, and he would take satisfaction in vanquishing this conqueror. And who knew, maybe Drummer Headwind would do everyone a favor and die in the fighting. Then Ozar wouldn't have to have him assassinated.

Damn Vizarana. He couldn't fathom why she had married that boy. Drummer was no match for her. She would walk all over him. She had been a fool, and she deserved to pay a price for her betrayal.

A rustle came from the entrance of his tent. "Sire?"

Ozar recognized the voice: General Dusk, his top advisor

since Shade's death. But no one could replace Shade. The late scribe had looked after Ozar in the atajazid's childhood, a confidant when Ozar's parents gave him no outlet for his dreams or nightmares. Shade had followed him with loyalty, always at his side. Now he was dead. Ozar didn't know why the tower had collapsed. The queen had died, too, but it was paltry revenge, for she had to die anyway. He had no one to exact vengeance on except her husband.

"Sire, shall I return later?" Dusk asked.

"No." Ozar mentally shook himself. Then he went to the entrance and pulled aside the flap. "What is it?"

Dusk stood outside in his rough-hewn sleep clothes. "My apologies for the disturbance. You have a visitor."

"So late?" Ozar frowned at him. "Who is it?"

Dusk cleared his throat. "Drummer Headwind Quaaz-era."

Ozar stared at him for a good five seconds. Then he murmured, "Well, well. Bring him in."

Dusk bowed with the deference of a general for his commander rather than the subservience expected from the lesser officers. It was appropriate for his station, but it felt strange to Ozar. Shade's reverence had always had a pointed quality that kept Ozar alert. He had been the only one who could respond to the atajazid in that manner; Ozar would accept it from no one else.

Ozar walked across the tent to a table, his manner deceptively casual, his shirt open at the neck. The flap rustled and he heard footsteps. Ozar knew it looked as if he were presenting his back to the people coming inside, but he was preternaturally aware of them and able to judge whether or not they posed him a risk, at least in the physical sense. He turned to see Dusk standing by the entrance, his hand on the hilt of his sword. The other man wasn't as tall. He wore a jacket lined with rich Kazlatarian fur, with the hood pulled up to hide his face. Ozar knew him anyway.

"You may wait outside," Ozar told Dusk.

The general bowed. "Yes, Sire."

As Dusk withdrew, Drummer pulled down his hood. He looked like an expensive item Vizarana had bought, with that exotic hair and his rich clothes, which she had undoubtedly given him. No common entertainer could afford such lavish garments, not only the jacket, but also the suede trousers and boots. That she might dally with such a toy, Ozar understood. He didn't approve of women having that freedom, but Vizarana was no child and she had ruled Taka Mal for nearly a decade. But why the flaming sun had she married him? Ozar didn't believe for one moment Drummer had the blessing of the Dragon-Sun. This whole business stunk to the mountains.

Drummer spoke wryly. "Judging from your expression, I take it you find me offensive."

"Oh, you're fine." Ozar waved his hand in dismissal. "It's your new title I find offensive." He went to a table and poured wine from a copper flask into a pair of tin cups. He didn't believe in taking luxury items to the battlefield, whether they be goldware, crystal flasks, or expensive consorts.

He offered Drummer a cup. "Care to drink?" He smiled darkly. "Pity I didn't poison it. I could be rid of you then."

His visitor didn't laugh. Ozar wasn't even certain it was a joke. Although Drummer came forward, he didn't take the cup.

Ozar set the second cup back on the table. "What do you want, Headwind?"

"Cobalt is going to invade Taka Mal tomorrow." He put his hands in the pockets of his jacket. "He says his wife is gone. Without Mel he is—a difficult man."

"My sympathies. It looks as if your status as consort will last a total of three days. Pity." With malice, he added, "Unless Escar likes boys. You're certainly pretty enough."

"What is it with you all here?" Drummer seemed more puzzled than offended. "You think having darker hair and more height makes you more masculine?"

"No." Ozar had to admit the fellow had courage. "I think being a man makes me masculine." He sipped his wine. "So why are you here?"

"To offer a bargain."

"And what sort of bargain might that be?"

"Support Vizarana tomorrow and I will annul the marriage."

Ozar narrowed his gaze. "How?"

"I married her under false pretenses. I'm a commoner." Bitterly he added, "Apparently in Taka Mal, that is enough to dissolve the union."

"What false pretenses? She knew what you were."

"Not if I claim otherwise." Drummer's face clenched. "I will swear it under oath."

"I suppose it might work," Ozar mused. "Everyone would know you were lying. But if you 'confessed' in a tribunal, they would have to annul your marriage."

"I have one condition."

"Do you now?"

Drummer dug his hands deeper into his pockets. Although Ozar had thought the jacket was gold-hued, he realized now it had a green tinge around the pockets. Odd that.

"My condition is this," Drummer said. "You do nothing to harm our child. If Vizarana agrees, give me the child to raise."

It was an intelligent solution. Perhaps the fellow had some brains after all under that yellow hair. Annul the marriage and Vizarana's baby was no longer heir to the throne, which meant her first male child with Ozar would carry the title. And he knew she was fertile. If Drummer took the baby to Aronsdale, Ozar wouldn't be plagued with that reminder of Vizarana's lover.

"If I agree to this bargain," Ozar said, "what guarantee do I have that you will uphold your part of it?"

"My word is good."

Ozar laughed shortly. "Your word." His voice hardened. "You will return to the citadel with a contingent of my men and tell Vizarana you have offered me this bargain, so she sees it is your idea and not coerced by me. Then my men will bring you back here, where you will be a hostage. When your part of the bargain is fulfilled, you will return to Aronsdale."

Drummer didn't look impressed. "How do I know you won't kill me?"

Ozar set his goblet on the table. "You don't."

"Then why should I agree?"

"Because if you don't," Ozar said, "you and your beautiful wife are going to die tomorrow."

Drummer's face tightened. "Cobalt will come for you next."

Ozar shrugged. "It won't matter to you. You'll be dead."

"Have your men guard me in the Citadel of the Dragon-Sun."

"So Vizarana's bad-tempered cousin can kill them and let her renege on the bargain?" Ozar snorted. "I don't think so."

Drummer shifted his hands in his pockets. "Then let her send some of her royal guards back with me."

Ozar had to admit, the boy knew how to bargain. It was a livable compromise. He had no desire to kill when it didn't suit his purposes, and if he let Headwind live, Drummer would take the child. He regarded the young man with curiosity. "Why not go to Cobalt and give yourself up to him? That is why he came, after all. To negotiate for you."

Drummer spoke quietly. "I would have laid my life at his feet to stop this war. But I couldn't get through. Your men caught me."

Ozar went over to him. "So you were already my prisoner."

"If you want to see it that way."

"I like it that way. It solves so many problems." He spoke briskly. "Very well. You will get your child. I will have Vizarana." He held his hand out, palm to the ceiling, in the classic offer of a bargain. "Sealed?"

Drummer pulled his hand out of his pocket and set it palm down on Ozar's. As they clasped, Ozar felt a tingle, like a residue of power. Then it vanished, and he suspected he had imagined it. No matter. It wouldn't be long before he had far more than a residue of power. Soon he would rule an empire, for even Cobalt Escar couldn't stand against his army and Vizarana's combined.

Cobalt sat with Matthew on a log behind his tent, in the dark, with a flask in his hand and a bundle between his feet that included both Mel's bloodied clothes and the packet with the dagger and her hair. Unfortunately, the ale was having no effect on the agitation that had gripped him since he saw Mel's silks.

"Did they think taking my wife hostage would incline me to negotiate with them?" he asked, incredulous. "First Drummer, then Mel, then blood and torture and death." He laughed harshly. "And they call *me* 'The Dark.'"

"I believe the idea was to extract from you a promise not to invade Taka Mal," Matthew said, for at least the fourth time.

"By killing my wife?" Cobalt took another swallow of ale. "This vile brew doesn't help." He stared into the night. With the moon out, it wasn't really dark, but he wanted no fire, no light, nothing that would bring his pain into sharper focus.

"She was pregnant," he said.

"You mean *Mel?*" Matthew asked.

"That's right." Cobalt glanced at him. "You could be like a grandfather to the baby, eh?"

Matthew's voice caught. "I would have liked that."

"Will like. *Will*." He downed the rest of his ale. Then he wiped his arm across his mouth. "Ah, saints, Matthew, if she is dead, I will die as well." He dropped the bag onto the ground. "After I destroy Taka Mal."

"What if they claim they never had her?"

"Lies."

Matthew pushed his hand through the gray mane of hair that fell to his shoulders. "How can we know? Maybe Kaj lied."

"Look at this." Cobalt picked up the bundle of silk and showed Matthew the dagger. "Taka Mal."

"It looks Zanterian."

"The famous Zanterian caravans. They will travel no more." He rummaged through the bundle for answers, but all he found was a ring on a broken cord.

"Is that Mel's?" Matthew asked. "I've never seen it."

Cobalt handed him the ring. "Neither have I."

Matthew ran his finger over the metal. "It has an inscription inside." He peered in the dark. "I can't read it."

"Come on." Cobalt stood unsteadily and walked toward his tent. Or staggered. He had a hard time keeping to a straight line. Perhaps he was drunker than he had realized.

Inside, Matthew lit a torch and held it up. Cobalt squinted at the ring. "It says…'Remember Brazi, love Flutter.'"

"What?" Matthew scowled at him. "You're drinking too much." He pulled the ring away and held it close to his face. "Always remember Baraza, love Flower."

"Flower, Flutter," Cobalt grumbled. "It's some woman's name—" He stopped abruptly. "Not Melody. *Flower.*"

Hope flared in Matthew's face. "Those silks belonged to someone else."

He wished it could be true. "Only if they took them from Mel. I had them tailored and embroidered especially for her."

"Then who is Flower?"

"Hell if I know." Cobalt studied the ring. "Baraza is a lake in Jazid. It's beautiful. This sounds like something a woman would give a man in memory of an, uh, pleasant time."

"Then why would Mel have it?" Matthew asked, perplexed. "I doubt she ran off with a woman named Flower."

"For the shape. She took it from someone." He stared at Matthew. "Someone in Jazid."

Matthew sat heavily on the trunk that served as a table. "You think a Jazidian kidnapped her?"

Cobalt felt ready to lunge, to attack, to *move,* but he couldn't, because he had even less idea than before where to find Mel. "If they took her, the atajazid may be part of this."

"You've seen his army. It's big. If he and Vizarana join forces, they may defeat us."

"More evidence points to Taka Mal than to Jazid." Cobalt began to pace, though he couldn't keep a straight line. "Is Kaj lying? Blast! If Mel were here, she could make one of those green spell things to find out if he is telling the truth." He stumbled on the edge of a carpet. "If Mel was here," he muttered, "it wouldn't matter what Kaj had to say." He stopped, breathing hard, and felt a damnable wetness in his eyes. He angrily wiped it away. He wouldn't humiliate himself by crying.

Matthew came up next to him. "Go to bed. Sleep. You have several hours until dawn."

"Can't sleep." If he stopped moving, he would have to think. If he thought, it would be about his wife. The wife that Kaj claimed he saw die. Cobalt wanted to shout his protest.

Matthew pushed him toward the pallet. "If you plan on invading Taka Mal tomorrow, you need rest."

Cobalt lay down on the pallet. He felt like a mammoth tree being felled. Matthew crouched at his feet and pulled off Cobalt's boots. Then he pulled the blanket over Cobalt. "Sleep."

"Not tired…" Cobalt mumbled.

"I know," Matthew said softly. "Good night, son."

Cobalt drifted with the heavy sensation that came before he dropped off at night. Then he slipped into the oblivion of sleep.

"No!" Jade whirled on Drummer, her night robe shimmering in the candlelight in the Narrow-Sun Hall. She couldn't believe what she was hearing. He couldn't have done this. "I won't allow it!"

"Jade—" Drummer started toward her, but his Jazidian guards brought down their ornate staffs, blocking his way.

The doors at the end of the hall slammed open and Firaz strode into the room, his robe flying out behind him, his sleep clothes wrinkled, his hair disarrayed. "What the beetling hell is going on?" he bellowed. "Vizarana, these guards of yours dragged me out of—" He broke off when he saw eight Jazidian warriors in full battle armor surrounding Drummer.

"Ah, hell," Firaz said.

Baz ran into the room, also in sleep clothes but with his sword gripped in his hand. He jolted to a stop as he took in the scene. Spearcaster and Slate entered behind him, Spearcaster with his sword belt buckled around his sleep trousers, and Slate, who seemed disoriented as he pulled a robe on over his rumpled clothes.

"He made a pact!" Jade wanted to shout her anger at the sky. She stalked to Drummer and glared at the Jazidians when they blocked her way. "Let him go. He's not going back with you. I don't care what deal he made with Ozar."

"For flaming sakes." Baz strode over to them. "You went to see Ozar?"

"I tried to see Cobalt," Drummer said. "I never made it. The atajazid's men caught me."

"See Cobalt for what?" Slate asked. His gray hair was mussed and he looked tired, older, worn down. "We were dealing with this."

"You should have flaming stayed put," Firaz said.

"For what?" Drummer demanded, with an intensity Jade had never seen him show before. "So I could watch Taka Mal fall to Cobalt because of my marriage?" His eyes blazed. "Ozar and I made a bargain. If he supports Taka Mal, I will annul the marriage."

"Annul it?" Spearcaster asked. "On what grounds?"

"We *have* no grounds," Jade told him.

"False pretenses," Drummer said. "I'm a commoner."

"Oh, this is delicious," Baz said. Jade wanted to slap him.

"What pretenses?" Firaz demanded. "We all knew."

"He'll swear it under oath," Jade said.

Drummer focused intently on her, and Jade was certain he was trying to tell her something, but he didn't want his Jazidian guards to hear. He wanted her to go along with this for reasons he couldn't say aloud.

"Jade, listen." Baz took her arm. "I must talk to you."

Spearcaster stepped forward. "Your Majesty?"

"It's all right," she said.

Baz scowled at Spearcaster. Officially Baz was his superior officer, but Spearcaster was thirty years his senior and Jade's most experienced commander. It didn't surprise her that Baz didn't challenge him. Besides, Baz was supposed to be under house arrest. Given that he would lead her army tomorrow, though, the arrest didn't carry much weight.

Baz drew her to the tall windows. Outside, stars glinted in the arid desert sky. He addressed her with atypical calm. "I have done a great deal of thinking." When she started to speak, he glared. "Do not say, 'What a change!'"

She smiled wryly. "I was only going to ask about what."

"About you." He spoke as if his words were daggers. "All my life I have assumed you and I would marry."

"Baz—"

"Hear me out." When she said no more, he continued. "Commanding the army suits me. And I won't deny it—

sitting on the throne, as your consort or as king, would have suited me."

Would have. Past tense. "But?" she asked.

"It was true what you said the other day."

"I said a lot of things."

He didn't answer directly. Instead, he said, "I could have pushed harder for marriage. I could have demanded it long ago. Slate and Firaz would have supported my claim, maybe even Spearcaster if he were convinced you would remain on the throne."

"Perhaps." Jade had always wondered what they would have done. She had expected one day she would find out. Yet here she and Baz were, both in their mid-thirties, and it had never happened.

"Why did you wait?" she asked.

"I have a great love for you, Jade. I always will." He spoke softly. "But as a sister. Not a wife."

Jade suddenly felt lighter. "I, too, cousin. For you."

He grinned. "I would make a terrible wife. Or sister."

"Baz!"

His expression sobered. "As the commander of your army, I must advise you to consider this bargain Drummer offers. We need Ozar. We have had no word from Jarid Dawnfield, no hint he will support us if—no, when—Cobalt attacks."

"And as my cousin? What do you say?"

He spoke as if his words gouged his heart. "I have never seen you so happy as these past few days."

Tears welled in her eyes. Angry at herself, she brushed them away. "I have never been this happy."

"It is Drummer." He didn't make it a question.

"I love him." She had been frantic when Clove had awoken her tonight to tell her Drummer was in the Narrow-Sun Hall—under Jazidian guard. "How can I give up my husband and my child?" Miserable, she said, "If I thought it would help, I would go to Cobalt myself and beg that he leave us alone."

Baz grasped her upper arms and looked intently into her eyes. "Never beg, Jade. *Never.*"

"The Quaazera pride." She laughed bitterly. "Don't worry, I will not destroy it, though it may end our House. But begging Cobalt will achieve nothing if he believes we killed his wife."

"You couldn't get to Cobalt anyway." Baz released her arms. "Ozar has too many patrols. They would catch you, too, just like Drummer. The only way to get through is with a full envoy of armed warriors, and even that may not be enough."

She looked to where Drummer stood watching from across the room, his forehead furrowed, too far away to hear them. "I have no proof Ozar would honor his part in this hateful bargain."

"Until your husband swears in a tribunal that he married you falsely," Baz said, "Ozar must keep him alive and well. If you assign your soldiers to Drummer, they can escort him to safety after the tribunal. That way, you are better assured of his reaching Aronsdale."

Jade averted her eyes, unable to look at Drummer while they discussed the end of the miracle he had brought into her life. "Ozar swears to spare my child if Drummer takes it."

"The child will be much safer in Aronsdale."

"I cannot give up my child!"

"And if the alternative is its death?"

A betraying tear ran down her face. "I hate this."

"Maybe Cobalt won't attack." He spoke with difficulty. "I will go with the envoy at dawn and talk to this subjugator of lands. See if I can convince him to negotiate. If he agrees, Drummer's bargain with Ozar becomes meaningless."

Jade knew how much it cost him to make such an offer on behalf of her consort. Sending the head of her army into the camp of her enemy was a risk if Cobalt chose not to honor the codes of war that protected conferences between opposing commanders. So far Cobalt had struck her as harsh, driven, and relentless, even obsessive, but he hadn't acted without honor. And sending a royal son of Quaazera would show him respect.

She spoke quietly. "Thank you. It is a courageous offer."

"Don't thank me yet. Cobalt hasn't agreed. And we would be wise to ensure Drummer is well guarded before telling Ozar of any agreement to negotiate." He regarded her steadily. "But if you don't send Drummer back tonight, we will lose Ozar's support completely. It will be the final insult after you answered his proposal by marrying another man."

Jade knew what she had to do, however much she hated it. She forced out the words. "I will send him with my best warriors."

"And I will do my best with the envoy."

"I am indebted to you."

He reddened. "Just have a healthy, hearty baby, eh?"

She managed a smile. "I will."

Slate came over to them, limping, which worried Jade. "I'm sorry to interrupt," he said. "But the atajazid's men want to take Drummer back."

Jade laid her hand on his arm. "Are you all right, Aqui?" She rarely called him by his personal name, though she had known him almost as long as she had known Spearcaster. But tonight everything was tangled up. For all that Slate debated with her about everything from politics to the best spices in food, she felt great affection for him, as she would for a stern but good-hearted uncle. It worried her to see him so drained.

"Just tired," he said, more gruffly than usual. "I don't move as easily these days as you young people."

"You'll outlive us all," Baz told him. Jade could see he shared her concern. Slate and Spearcaster were both getting older, but the years weighed more heavily on Slate.

"Stop worrying so," Slate told her. "Come. Let us deal with your husband."

In the hushed hours before dawn, they arranged for Drummer's return to Ozar's camp. Although Drummer seemed relieved she hadn't refused, she sensed his fear. She felt as if she were dying.

Soon the sun would rise.

24

The Dragon's Dawn

Mel scrabbled to the top of the ridge. It was no thicker than a fortress wall, as if some monstrous deity had pushed up giant sheets of rock in row after row. She looked down the way she had climbed, and the drop made her stomach roil. If she lost her grip, she would fall a long way before she struck the bottom of the ravine between this ridge and the previous. She was clinging to a wall of the sky. All around her, more walls reached for the heartless roof of blue that capped the world. Behind her, the sky was lightening to herald the sun that would soon edge above the Jagged Teeth.

With one last heave, Mel sprawled across the top of the ridge. It extended barely more than the length of her body before it plunged down on the other side.

She looked west.

The ridges continued in rows stretching north and south, each lower than the last. It was an incredible and untamed vista. But the panorama wasn't what made her breath catch. She had seen such vistas endlessly for the past day. What made her sit up and stare—what caused her swell of emotion—was that in front of her, to the west, she could finally see beyond the ridges. The foothills of the Jagged Teeth lay before her and an army stretched along them. Beyond that, in the misty reaches of Aronsdale, another army had gathered, one even larger than the Jazid forces. Chamberlight.

"Thank you," Mel whispered to Azure, to Lapis Lazuli who rode the wind and turned diamonds into waterfalls, and to Verdant, who tended the edible plants that had kept Mel alive. Today she could reach Cobalt—if Ozar didn't find and kill her first.

In the dimness that preceded dawn, Cobalt stood in his tent. He had lit no candles or lamps. The still morning cooled his feverish mood. Despite his few hours of sleep, he had awoken early. He broke his fast on battle rations and dressed in armor. He held his helmet under his arm, and his sword hung at his side. Soon he would know what Taka Mal had to say. He feared their words, but he feared even more to hear nothing at all, to have Mel disappear with no trace except a bloody rag.

The flap of his tent rustled, and Matthew spoke. "Cobalt? Are you awake?"

"Come in," Cobalt said.

Matthew pulled aside the flap, and predawn light poured

through the opening. He was wearing the scuffed leather armor of a cavalry man. He glanced around the dark interior, then fastened up the flap to keep the light flowing inside.

"Why are you standing in the dark?" Matthew came over to him. "Have you eaten?"

"Yes." Cobalt answered only the second question. He couldn't say he sought the calm darkness because otherwise he felt as if he would explode.

Matthew spoke quietly. "An envoy approaches from the Citadel of the Dragon-Sun."

Cobalt's pulse jumped. "Is Mel with them?"

"I don't know." Matthew started to reach out, but when Cobalt stiffened, he dropped his hand. "Cobalt, you have to be realistic. She could be in Jazid. Even if Taka Mal has her, they won't send their hostages to negotiate for the release of their hostages. And they may truly have no idea what happened to her."

"I will not negotiate for Mel," Cobalt said. Yet if they gave him evidence she lived, he would do anything to get her back. He had questions about the Jazid ring, troubled questions, but he had more evidence against the House of Quaazera than against Onyx.

Matthew was watching him with that strange expression, as if his heart were breaking. "Shall we go outside?"

"All right."

Matthew stood aside to let Cobalt go first. Cobalt didn't care about protocols. Matthew had been his childhood protector, the man who dared the king's wrath. Matthew was his confidant. His mentor. Matthew and

Agate Cragland had stood up for Cobalt at his wedding. Mel had once asked him if Matthew was his friend. Had it only been a year and a few months since then? He had known so little about friendship, he hadn't understood what she asked. He had said, *He is my stable hand.* It was what Matthew called himself until Mel gave him the title of stable master, which Cobalt acknowledged was a better description of Matthew's job. Even that seemed paltry, though. How did he define their link? Matthew was one of the few people Cobalt trusted. The only others were Mel and his mother.

He is my stable hand. That had been so very wrong.

Cobalt glanced at Matthew as they walked through the muted predawn. "Thank you."

Matthew blinked at him. "For what?"

Cobalt wanted to say: *For granting me more than three decades of the love that Varqelle, my father, could never give me.*

"For making sure I was awake," Cobalt said.

Matthew harrumphed. "After all that ale you drank last night, I thought I'd find you snoring on your stomach."

On another morning Cobalt might have laughed or growled good-naturedly. Not today. He had nothing in him but this horrible waiting sensation. Waiting to know if his wife had died.

A man approached them in the predawn dimness. Agate Cragland. The general wore armor and carried his helmet.

"My men met the envoy outside of camp," Agate said. "They are waiting for you."

Cobalt felt his pulse hammering. "Who came with them?"

Agate spoke with difficulty. "Neither your wife nor Drummer."

The morning crashed around Cobalt, in silence. "I see."

"That doesn't mean they aren't alive," Agate said.

Cobalt started walking, and Matthew and Agate joined him. The army was awakening around them, the foot soldiers and cavalry and tenders, breaking their fast, donning gear, seeing to their mounts, sharpening weapons.

Preparing to fight.

A dry wind blew across Cobalt's bare chin. He had shaved this morning in case he would see Mel. Now he wondered what his razor would do to the person who had tortured his wife. He tried to shut the images out of his mind, but his imagination didn't fail him, however much he wanted that to happen. He saw Mel screaming, and he couldn't escape that agony.

They walked on, and soldiers rose to salute him. After he passed, they settled down to their meals or tasks. They were well trained. Ready to fight. In his mind, he was already giving the order to move against Taka Mal. Or Jazid. Ozar and Vizarana were probably working together. *Someone* had taken his wife, and the maggot was out there in the Rocklands or the Jagged Teeth.

They hadn't brought Mel. Nothing they said would change that. If he invaded Taka Mal, he would start a war of far greater proportions than the one in Shazire. Jazid would probably fight with Taka Mal. The Aronsdale army remained a cipher. They might stay put, they might ally with him, or they might go against him. He didn't know. He had sent envoys to Ozar and Jarid, and they had sent envoys to him, and no one was committing to anything.

In his mind, Mel screamed as the whip struck her.

"No," he whispered. He remembered vividly why he had spent so much of his life locking his emotions in a mental fortress. If he kept everyone out, he was safe. Then Mel had shattered the walls of his inner citadel and taught him to love. Now he was paying the price, because he couldn't wall away his anguish.

The campsites became few and far between, and still he walked with Matthew and Agate. Up ahead, a cluster of riders were dismounting. Some of the men and horses bore the red and gold colors of Taka Mal; others the blue and white of the Misted Cliffs. He thought he also saw the Dawnfield violet and white. His unease grew. Had Jarid allied with Taka Mal?

As Cobalt approached, they turned to him—and he gave a start. The man in Dawnfield colors was Samuel Fieldson. Cobalt didn't know him well; they had spoken only a handful of times. But those interactions had impressed Cobalt. He trusted the Dawnfield commander more than any of these Taka Mal officers.

General Spearcaster had returned, but today he deferred to a man in bronze armor and a red-plumed Dragon-Sun helmet. The diagonal line of six enameled disks across the stranger's chest marked him as a Taka Mal general. Cobalt had never seen so many disks, even more than Spearcaster's five. The hilt of the man's sheathed sword glittered. The Chamberlight army had spent this past season training to counter those strange curved blades.

The man pulled off his helmet. He had dark hair, a strong chin, a hooked nose and the large build classic for a Taka Mal warrior. He held himself with the ease of someone confident in his authority, and he nodded to Cobalt as royalty would to royalty. His voice, rough in its nuances, rumbled with the Taka Mal drawl.

"I am Baz Goldstone Quaazera," he said. "General of the Queen's Army."

Saints almighty. They had sent the Quaazera prince himself. Cobalt didn't miss the implied honor. But Lieutenant Kaj claimed this man had whipped Mel to death.

"What have you come to tell me?" Cobalt's words scraped with the strain of controlling his emotions. "That you will negotiate for my wife? I will not bargain. Release her." His voice nearly cracked, but he kept it steady. "Or my army will march against Taka Mal."

Baz's forehead furrowed. "Your Majesty, we know nothing of your wife. I swear this to you on the honor of my House."

Anyone who tortured a pregnant woman had no honor. Cobalt pulled out the bundle he had stuffed in his helmet. Yellow silk. He spoke with difficulty. "Twenty-three days ago, my wife was taken from Alzire. Yesterday, Lieutenant Kaj deserted your army to bring me *this*." He shoved the silk at Quaazera. "Perhaps you recognize it."

The general took the cloth. As he examined it, his face paled. "It is soaked with blood."

"Those are my wife's clothes." Cobalt didn't know how he kept his voice steady. "Kaj says you tortured her to death and are doing similar to her uncle."

"He lies! We did not kidnap your wife. No one has tortured Drummer. Vizarana is a civilized and decent human being."

"And you are a good actor."

Baz flushed an angry red. "You believe a deserter before the commander of the Queen's Army?"

"He gave me evidence." Cobalt took the silk from Baz and clenched it in his raised fist. "Give me evidence that he lies! Bring my wife."

"When I last saw your future wife," Baz said, "she was nine years old. I have no idea where she is."

Agate spoke. "Then bring Drummer Headwind here."

Spearcaster and even Fieldson paled. Baz said, "We don't bring hostages to negotiate their own release."

"We need only see him," Agate said. "To know he is well."

Baz nodded his acceptance of the compromise. "He will be at the negotiations."

Cobalt didn't want to compromise. "Bring him now," he grated.

"We will not be coerced!" Baz said.

"You are not such a good actor after all," Cobalt said. "Your lies are obvious."

"Wait," Fieldson said. He looked from Baz to Spearcaster and back to Baz again. The Quaazera prince scowled at him. Then Baz spoke to Cobalt with a formality that indicated respect, though it sounded strained. "I would like to confer with Sphere-General Fieldson, your envoy."

"Why?" Cobalt demanded. "So you can plan more lies?"

"Your Majesty." Fieldson addressed him with similar formality, albeit more polished. "As your envoy, I wish to speak with you in private. But I must present it to the rest of this Taka Mal envoy. I cannot act unilaterally."

It fell within accepted protocols. Cobalt wanted to refuse anyway. Had it been Baz asking, he would have, but he knew Fieldson's reputation for veracity.

"Very well," Cobalt said coldly. "Five minutes."

Fieldson bowed, followed by Spearcaster, and after a minuscule but detectable pause, Baz did, too. The men withdrew a short distance away and spoke together. The rest of the envoy and the Chamberlight guards had stepped back, holding the horses, which left Cobalt standing between Matthew and Agate.

"They're hiding something," Matthew said.

"Yes." Cobalt spoke to Agate. "You lead the foot troops. I will go with the cavalry."

Agate didn't have to ask what he meant. "You cannot fight with your men. We can't risk your death."

Cobalt clenched the silk rags. "I must go."

"Your father told me the same thing when we went into battle in Shazire." Agate's gaze never wavered. "And he died."

Cobalt just shook his head. He couldn't sit by while his men went to war. Especially not when it involved Mel.

The three generals were coming back. They looked grim, but they seemed to have reached a consensus. Perhaps they had simply ensured their lies were consistent.

Fieldson nodded to Cobalt. "May we speak privately?"

Cobalt indicated an outcropping of rocks that jutted up like giant teeth. The sky had turned a vivid carnelian hue that painted the air and land around them red, as if they were already bathed in blood.

He and Fieldson walked away from the others, to the outcropping. Fieldson spoke without preamble. "It is true, what they told you. They know nothing about your wife."

"Why won't they show me her uncle?" Cobalt asked.

"He is no longer their hostage."

"What?" Cobalt stiffened. "Why not?"

"He is the atajazid's hostage now, by his choice." The lines on Fieldson's face were deeper than when he had left Harsdown. "Ozar refuses to ally with Queen Vizarana unless she marries him. If you attack, and Vizarana has no help from Jazid, she fears her country will fall to you. So she has agreed to marry Ozar."

It all made sense, but it also made absolutely no sense at all. "This has nothing to do with Drummer."

"It has everything to do with him. He is the reason you are here. The negotiations are to free him. Ozar knows Vizarana has no wish to marry him. He believes she seeks to trick him, and he wants assurance that any negotiation with you includes him as well as Vizarana and King Jarid. So he is keeping Drummer. It was his condition for promising to support Taka Mal if you attack."

"It's all convolutions," Cobalt said. He didn't believe Fieldson, though he couldn't pinpoint why. "What does Jarid have to do with this?"

Fieldson gave him an odd look. "Half my envoy consisted of Dawnfield officers. Jarid Dawnfield is here. We assumed he would participate in the negotiations."

Cobalt had assumed no such thing. He saw the logic, but he trusted none of this. "It is all smoke screens. I don't see my wife. Only bloody clothes."

Fieldson raked his hand through his silvered hair. "Saints know, I want to find Mel, too. I've known her since her birth, and I would lay down my life for her. But attacking Taka Mal won't tell you what happened to her."

Cobalt couldn't bear the words. "Drummer isn't here, either."

"I saw him last night. He was fine."

"Why should I believe you?"

"Let us meet at the citadel to negotiate," Fieldson said. "Yourself, Vizarana, Ozar, Jarid, and any associated officers you want to include. We will bring Drummer."

"Bring him now."

"Sire." Fieldson spoke with respect, but his voice was strained. He looked exhausted. "He is a hostage for a reason. We came to negotiate for him. I entreat you, let us negotiate as we had planned."

Cobalt wanted to hit something. He needed to release the anger and fear building inside of him, and all this talk rang false. "My condition was this—bring Drummer and my wife at sunrise or I will invade. They are not here."

"Saints, man, *look*." Fieldson waved his hand at the massed armies in every direction. "If you do this, thousands will die."

Cobalt's voice hardened. "I'm not the one who kidnapped a queen. And her uncle."

"No, you didn't. You invaded Shazire and Blueshire with no provocation."

"Taka Mal invaded the Misted Cliffs—with no provocation—and tore it apart." Cobalt felt as if he would explode. "I put it back together."

"That was two *centuries* ago."

"Two days. Two centuries. The offense remains the same."

"I implore you," Fieldson said. "Talk first."

Cobalt looked at the lightening sky in the east. He waited, and soon the edge of the sun appeared above the Pyramid Foothills like a rim of molten bronze.

"Sunrise," Cobalt said. "Your time is up."

With that, the Midnight King spun around and strode back to his army.

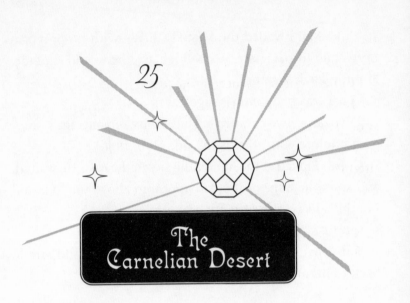

25

The Carnelian Desert

Jade raced down the corridor, her tunic rippling in the wind of her passing, her soft-soled boots pounding the ground. She reached the courtyard as the envoy entered, their horses kicking up gravel. Men shouted, armor clanked, and stable hands ran to meet them. Baz wheeled around his horse, calling to his groom while he dragged off his helmet. The moment Jade saw the grim set of his chin and his battle-ready posture, she knew the envoy had failed.

"Saints, no," she said, though no one could hear her.

Baz swung off his horse, followed by Spearcaster and Fieldson. Jade stood in the archway of the citadel with the wind clutching at her clothes while the generals strode across the yard. When they reached her, Spearcaster and

Fieldson bowed and Baz nodded, but she cared nothing now about formalities.

"Cobalt refused to meet?" she asked.

"He walked away," Baz said harshly. He turned to Fieldson. "Tell her."

"I couldn't get through to him." Fieldson looked more tired than Jade had ever seen him. "He heard what I said, but nothing would bend him from his course."

"Kaj had his wife's clothes." Baz clenched his fist as if he held the garments. "Shredded and soaked in blood. He told Cobalt we tortured her to death and are doing the same to Drummer."

"What?" Jade stared at him. "Ozar has agreed to let Drummer attend the negotiations. Let Cobalt know." Drummer was his own best proof of his well-being.

"It won't matter," Fieldson said. "Not if we can't produce his wife."

"This is insane," Jade said.

"Kidnapping his wife was brutally effective if someone wanted to provoke him into a war," Spearcaster said.

"That may be," Fieldson said bleakly. "But I doubt whoever planned this realized what he was unleashing. Cobalt isn't just a man, not when he fights. He's more. And he's angry, that deep, burning rage that nothing cools."

"I watched his men running maneuvers while we rode through his camp," Spearcaster said. "They're more than well trained. They're like gears in a machine he has oiled until it hums."

Jade felt as if she were sinking. "You don't think we can beat him even with Ozar's army, do you?"

Fieldson regarded her with a weariness that seemed much deeper than any sleep could help. After a long pause, he said, "Nothing is impossible."

Baz spoke bitterly to her. "Think who has the most to gain if you and Cobalt go to war."

"Even Ozar wouldn't go that far." Jade wasn't certain if she was trying to convince them or herself. "Bloody saints, Ozar has Drummer! And Kaj claims we're torturing him. What if Ozar agreed to let Drummer attend the negotiations to prove we were doing exactly that? Baz! We have to get Drummer back."

"Jade." Her cousin spoke with pain. "Cobalt is preparing to march. I must join our forces. I will go to Ozar and speak to him about Drummer, but our first priority must be the battle." Baz laid his hand on her arm. "Ozar has nothing to gain by hurting Drummer. The damage was done the moment the Chamberlight queen disappeared. And remember eight of our best men are with Drummer."

Eight wasn't enough. She needed eight thousand. Her voice hardened. "Ozar better have his own bodyguards. Because if he is behind this, I will kill him myself."

Drummer sat on a trunk covered by a Kazlatarian rug holding his glittar. The tent swayed with the early-morning winds. Four of his Taka Mal guards and four of his Jazidian guards were present. Two were sitting on stools, one polishing his weapons and another breaking his fast, and the others stood posted around the walls of the tent. The place was bursting at the seams with soldiers. At least the other eight of them were asleep in another tent.

Drummer idly strummed a tune on his glittar. He had laid his jacket on the trunk, and now he reached into its pocket. The cube felt solid in his hand. He took it out and set it on the rug. Then he went back to playing.

"What is that?" the guard eating breakfast asked.

Drummer regarded him innocently. "A glittar."

"Not the harp," he said, with disdain. "*That.*" He pointed to the cube.

"Oh. That." Drummer shrugged. "A good luck talisman."

The guard grunted and went back to eating his mush.

Drummer let his music wander into a rhythmic melody he played for parents who wanted their children to sleep. He concentrated on the cube. The music focused his abilities and the spell came so easily, he would have laughed had he been alone. He wove a yellow spell, hypnotic, soothing, soothing, soothing. It spread throughout the tent, invisible. That was one reason he had assumed his spells were minor. Mel's showed as colored light, and she was the strongest mage he knew. But the talent apparently manifested differently in different people. For him, colors appeared more rarely than for his niece, unless he was deliberately making a spell of light.

He played a song of sleep and dreams, and one by one, his guards drifted off. The heads of the two on stools sagged to their chests, and the men posted around the walls sat on the ground. Several lay down and the others nodded off while sitting up. He played a bit longer to make sure they were out. Then he picked up his cube, eased off the trunk, and slipped out of the tent. So far, his plans had worked as he expected. He had feared Jade would resist his coming back here even more than she had, but she seemed willing to trust him.

The morning was young and clear and hot, though the sun was barely above the mountains. It didn't reassure Drummer that so few people were about this early. The army must have moved out, a prospect that chilled him despite the day's heat, for it could mean they had gone to fight.

He slipped across the camp, staying in shadows. This was the most dangerous part of his plan, for he was clearly recognizable right now. He made a spell to shunt light around his body; unless someone looked closely, he would be invisible—he hoped.

Drummer soon reached a tent used to supply the warriors with weapons and armor. At first he thought he was in luck; no one was inside. He soon discovered that neither was the equipment; they had taken it all. His search turned up only some old leather leg guards and boots. He found a breastplate that would be too small for most Jazidian warriors, with their muscle-bound physiques. It fit him fine, though he suspected he would look like a boy to the other soldiers. The helmet had a broken faceplate, but it hid his yellow hair. His blue eyes would be visible, though; he would have to hope no one came close enough to tell.

They had taken the swords, bows, axes, and other instruments of mayhem. It didn't much matter, since he had little experience with weapons, except for a dagger. He would have liked to carry his glitter and play more spells, but he could imagine how it would look, a warrior strumming a harp. He stuffed it in a saddlebag. His search turned up nothing else useful, so he went back outside, for all appearances a Jazidian warrior. The armor felt strange and uncomfortable, but at least it protected him.

Getting a horse turned out to be more difficult, not because none were left in camp, but because several stable hands had remained behind as well. Although he found the gear he needed in a tent, he couldn't reach the horses without anyone seeing him. Finally he gave up slinking around and strode boldly into a pen with a gray stallion. It nickered while he saddled it. Two stable boys of about twelve were sitting on the fence across the pen, watching. They looked confused, uncertain whether to protest or to help him. He finished outfitting the horse and swung into the saddle, and they still hadn't figured out what to do. So he blithely rode past them, out of the pen, headed west, toward the army.

Drummer had known he might fail to reach Cobalt when he set out last night. Since he hadn't been able to sneak through the Jazid lines, he was doing the next best thing: He became part of those lines. He had used mood spells to gauge Ozar's response and determine, to the best of his ability, that the Jazid king wasn't planning to kill him. He had tried turning the spell around to influence Ozar, but the reversal had hurt, somehow. Whether or not it worked, he couldn't say, but when Ozar had agreed to the bargain, he hadn't been lying. Now Drummer would ride through the Jazid army from *within* it and achieve his goal—to see Cobalt—before the king lost his head and attacked Taka Mal.

On the morning of the fifth day in the second month of summer, the Chamberlight army marched across the western border of Taka Mal, six thousand men. The Onyx and Quaazera forces joined, over seven thousand men altogether. The armies met in the Rocklands. Each had a distinctive commander: One fought as his cousin's protector; one fought for greed; and one was driven past all reason, just as the mythical dragons of Taka Mal were driven into the mountains to mate—and then die.

They met with volleys of arrows, with the inexorable push of cavalry and foot troops, and with a crash of swords. War cries split the desert calm. So began the Battle of the Dragon-Sun, the largest war in one thousand years.

Mel pulled herself up to an outcropping and struggled to her feet. Sagging against the rocks, she closed her eyes, breathing hard. The morning had blurred into a haze as she crossed the mountains, searching desperately for paths through the sheer walls and deep ravines.

She was fortunate Ozar's fortress hadn't been higher. Had she been farther up, where no trees grew, it could have taken her weeks, even months, to come down, if she hadn't died from a fall, or starvation and thirst, or a mountain cat that had too little prey in the hollowed spaces of the Jagged Teeth.

When the fire in her overtaxed muscles eased, she walked

around the outcropping of rock and found—another outcropping. She climbed over it. On the other side, a rocky
slope dropped down from her feet, but it wasn't steep like
the inclines higher in the mountains. With wind blowing the
hair that had escaped her braid, she looked across the jum-
bled foothills to the flatlands beyond—and her breath
stopped.

"No," Mel said. *"No!"*

They were fighting. In the Rocklands, an ocean of soldiers seethed and boiled. Ozar had carried through with his
threat.

The madman had provoked Cobalt into war.

"You can't go out there!" Matthew tried to grab Admiral's
reins as he rode up alongside Cobalt.

"You go too far." Cobalt yanked away the reins, then
wheeled Admiral around and galloped away from the camp
where he had been conferring with his commanders. It didn't
matter that he was the king of three countries. He would not
stay in safety. His fire wouldn't be denied.

Cobalt rode hard and soon outpaced Matthew. He passed
the outskirts of the fighting, his sword gripped in his fist.
His "experts" claimed the weapon was too heavy and too
long, but they were wrong. Lighter swords felt like toys.
After the experts watched him train, they said no more,
though their faces had paled.

A man in Jazidian armor rode at him, large and broad
shouldered, astride a bay horse. A shadow-dragon helmet
hid his face. He shouted his war cry and swung his mace in

an arc toward Cobalt, the power of his strike obvious in the speed of the heavy weapon as it descended.

The fire that blazed in Cobalt happened only when he fought—truly fought—for his life. It was unlike anything else he experienced. Mel said it was a spell. He knew only that it filled him with greater strength and speed, and heightened senses that surpassed even his normal intensity.

Time slowed as Cobalt leaned back from the mace. Despite the speed of the descending ball, he easily evaded the blow. Admiral dodged as well, with an innate understanding of his needs. In that instant, Cobalt brought up his sword, his gaze locked on the sliver of skin above the man's breastplate and below his helmet. He swung at his opponent's neck—and felt his blade hit. The blow threw the warrior off his horse, and the man took an endless, endless time to fall. He hit the ground in a sprawl of armor and blood.

Cobalt kept riding, burning, caught in his fury. He wielded his sword and men fell. None were worthy opponents. None had strength, speed, or skill. He shouted his war cries and Admiral surged ahead. At first warriors engaged him, but soon they were wheeling their horses to flee. Foot soldiers ran. He kept on, driven by the thought of his wife and his heir dying by torture—and he, Cobalt, had done nothing, *nothing* to stop that horror.

Now they would pay, every Taka Mal and Jazidian warrior alive. He would soak the desert red with their blood.

26

Dragon Star

Drummer knew what had happened before he saw it. The shouts, the clank of mail, the scream of men and horses—it roared in the parched morning air. He was too late, too late, Cobalt had already gone to war.

Drummer rode through jagged formations, the lowest foothills of the range that towered behind him. He came around a thicket of rock spires and reined to an abrupt stop before a nightmare. The same Rocklands that had almost killed him were host now to the deaths of hundreds. Men churned across the plains as far as he could see to the north, west, and south. They wore the armor of Quaazera, Onyx, Chamberlight, but nowhere did he see Dawnfield, which meant that either Windcrier had never reached the Aronsdale army or else King Jarid had refused the treaty.

He clenched the reins. Cobalt shouldn't be in combat, but Drummer had no doubt he was out there, wreaking havoc on anyone unfortunate enough to come within reach of his inhuman speed and strength. Drummer doubted he could reach the Aronsdale army now. He couldn't go around a battle this extended. Nor could he ride through; with neither weapons nor training, he would be slaughtered within moments. If he could have reached Cobalt last night, his plan might have prevented all this, but now it was too late.

He had to do something. *But what?* He knew the tales, that Mel had stopped the Shazire battle with her magecraft, wielding what many believed had been an ensorcelled sword of fire. He also knew the truth she had told almost no one else; she had created no more than light. Anyone could have killed her had they had dared to try. No one had gone near her, but that had been at twilight, when the battle was essentially over. This was the heat of the morning and the first blast of hostilities, and no sword of light was going to stop this insanity.

Drummer retreated into the forest of rock spires. He had an idea, but he would be vulnerable, easily killed, undefended while he concentrated. He needed a vantage point where he could see the battle but not be seen, where he could create magic unlike anything he had ever tried, probably beyond his ability, but for his child and the wife he might never see again, he had to try.

He rode deeper into the spires until he was picking his way up a shallow slope with outcroppings jutting around him. He found a cave above the fighting. He led the horse to the back of the cave and rubbed it down, then left it to nibble at grass growing out of cracks in the rock. After he removed his armor, he took his saddlebags to the mouth of the cave.

He could see the fighting from here, but he had to be careful. A sheer drop-off fell from the mouth of the cave. If he exhausted himself, he might lose his balance and slip, roll or topple over the edge. Settling cross-legged at the mouth, he gazed out across the Rocklands. From this high, the battle looked even worse, for he could see the full extent of the carnage. He felt ill and wondered how Ozar could consider killing a more noble purpose than music.

Drummer set the cube on the ground. When he tried to settle the glittar in his lap, he was so tense, he nearly snapped one of the strings. He felt foolish and ineffectual, trying to stop one of the worst battles in history with a harp. He played a few notes and focused on the cube. Almost immediately, he realized he had too little strength to create a green spell substantial enough to influence the soldiers in any significant numbers. He might convince a few men to stop fighting, but that would only get them killed. He had to work with red, orange, and yellow spells, which meant he could make light and heat, and he could soothe but not heal. The lower the color level, the greater the spell he could make.

He closed his eyes and centered his spirit, seeking whatever resources gave creativity to his spells. When he opened his eyes, a gold haze surrounded him, and he saw the combat below through a curtain of light.

He began to play.

The music came from an inner place he had never drawn on before, a well of depth and sorrow. The notes saturated the air as if they were liquid, and they wept with grief. He tried to enlarge his spell to cover the battle, but it was so hard, a strain so far beyond what he had ever done that he wondered at his audacity to believe he could do anything at all with it—except fail.

But he kept playing.

Jade stood on the balcony of the citadel and watched the battle with horror. Her army, her people, her country: All would suffer from this insanity. Baz, Spearcaster, Firaz, Slate, so many others—would this be their last day of life? Just a little longer, and her marriage might have established stability in the settled lands. All that was gone, and she would never see her husband again, not even at the tribunal, for Ozar would never allow it, afraid she might change her mind.

The Aronsdale army had marched to the border, but no farther. They gave no indication they intended to join any army. The cavalry had indeed arrived at the last minute, but they didn't intend to fight.

Jade put her hand on her abdomen, and tears wet her face.

Mel slid down the slope, bringing a miniature avalanche with her. She could see the battle raging. Her chest heaved with exertion, and her hands scraped the ground and sent pebbles cascading away from her body. The slopes she had to traverse were no longer sheer, but the broken land hampered her until she thought she would shout her frustration to the sky—or at the commanders who had started this saints-forsaken war. If she were lucky, she would reach the Rocklands before the father of her child destroyed three countries.

Jason Windcrier huddled in the tent, chained to a pole. The Jazidian soldiers who had caught him called him a spy. They had beaten and starved him, and they threatened to throw him on Ozar's mercy when they had a chance. When they were done with him.

This morning they had vanished, leaving him for the first time since they had caught him two days ago. He had struggled since then with the manacles that chained him to the post. He was a strong man, hale and hearty, but the chains held him well. Finally he managed to yank the post out of the ground and collapse the tent. He staggered to his feet and fought his way out from under the canvas. A chain hung from his wrist manacles, but he was free.

He found himself on a mass of rock the height of a tower. To the south and east, the battle raged. To the west, the Aronsdale army watched, rank upon rank of their soldiers in the polygon formations adopted by Dawnfield armies, shapes their mages could use during combat to aid the army with their spells.

Jason climbed laboriously down to the ground. He was leaving a trail, he knew, but he no longer cared. By the time his captors returned, if they survived, he would have reached his goal—or died trying.

With his wrists still manacled, Jason Windcrier ran for the Aronsdale army.

* * *

Cobalt recognized Baz Quaazera by his magnificent armor and dragon helmet, which shone gold in the harsh sunlight. The prince was surrounded by his officers as they cut a swath through the battle. The Midnight King urged his horse forward.

Cobalt fought like a man possessed, for he was crazed, overcome with hatred for the monsters who had brutalized his wife. He cut down Baz's officers quickly. He acted on instinct, swinging, striking, dodging with a rhythm so natural he was barely aware of his actions. Then he was facing Baz, and for the first time he met a foe who challenged him. They fought on horseback, Cobalt with his straight sword, Baz with his curved blade. Every time Cobalt drove him back, Baz surged forward. He came in too close for Cobalt to effectively use his long sword, and their blades clanged together. He and Baz ended up alongside each other, their horses facing in opposite directions, agitated by the proximity, Baz's sword hooked around Cobalt's weapon.

"Your wife isn't in Taka Mal!" Baz told him, furious.

"Liar." Cobalt strained to break their lock. The ring with Mel's clothes had roused his suspicion of Jazid, but it didn't matter: Taka Mal and Jazid fought together. The battle fury was on him, and he saw no differences in his foes, only enemies.

"Escar, listen!" Baz said. "Ozar set it up. Kaj lied for him because Ozar paid Kaj's gambling debts."

Cobalt finally managed to break their impasse. He shoved Baz away and brought up his sword.

But he remembered the ring in Mel's clothes.

"He wanted to force concessions from Vizarana," Baz said, his chest heaving with exertion.

Cobalt went at him with a hard swing, but Baz parried and drove him back.

"Damn it, Escar!" Baz shouted. "Ozar is the one who killed your wife. Not me." Intent on his words, he lost his momentum and his defense faltered, just for an instant—but it was all the opening Cobalt needed. He swung his sword in the perfect arc to exploit his foe's exposed neck. One blow, and Baz would die.

But—the ring.

Cobalt pulled his strike and just sat on his horse, heaving in breaths. Baz froze in mid-swing, staring at him, his eyes barely visible behind the faceplate of his helmet. Then he lowered his sword, only a bit, but enough.

"You tortured Drummer," Cobalt said. "That's why you wouldn't let me see him."

"Drummer is Ozar's hostage."

"You're hiding something."

"I'm telling you the truth," Baz said. "Drummer is a hostage to force *Vizarana's* behavior." In a voice full of pain, Baz said, "She only treated Drummer the way women have been torturing men since the beginning of time. She gave him her love."

Cobalt couldn't stop fighting; he was like a machine that once started had to finish. He was literally shaking from his efforts to contain his murderous rage. But all his talking with the Taka Mal envoys these past few days, with Fieldson, with

Matthew, with Cragland, even with Baz, it all kept pointing in the same direction, away from Taka Mal and toward Jazid.

With a jerk on the reins, Cobalt wheeled Admiral around and set off across the field—leaving Baz alive. Admiral's hooves pounded the rocky ground. The fighting was sparser here, and he encountered fewer soldiers. He struck down those who attacked him and raced past those who fled, galloping toward the Jazidian command post on a plateau above the battlefield.

Cobalt couldn't have said how long it took to cross the battlefield. The fighting went in slow motion. Aeons passed in an instant. Yet almost as soon as he started, he was reining Admiral to a stop below the command center. He rode up the trail to the plateau, and Admiral neighed in challenge as they approached the guards at the top. Cobalt shouted across the open area to the tent on the other side. "Onyx! Come out!"

Warriors blocked his way, eight men in armor and helmets, black plumes restless in the wind. A man exited the tent, an officer of high rank judging from the braid on his uniform. He took one look at Cobalt and disappeared back inside. With the Jazidian guards as his escort, Cobalt rode Admiral across the plateau. This place wasn't for battle. The ancient codes of war decreed such a post an area of truce where one commander could approach another to confer or surrender. No one could come up here to interfere, neither Cobalt's men nor any more from Ozar's army. If Cobalt violated that code, these guards could kill him with impunity. However, they were in full view of the battlefield, which meant they couldn't violate the code, either; if they did, Cobalt's men would sweep over this post.

"I will speak to Onyx." Cobalt's voice rumbled.

One of the men came forward with careful respect. "You must first relinquish your sword."

Cobalt had no intention of relinquishing anything. He kept his weapon gripped in his hand. "I come to see your atajazid."

"Do you wish to surrender?" the man asked.

"I will speak to *Onyx*," Cobalt said. "Not to you. Not to Quaazera. Not even to your damned Shadow Dragon."

The officer stiffened at the insult to the dragon, and for a moment it seemed he would challenge Cobalt. Then he spun around and strode into the tent. The others remained outside, hands on their sword hilts.

Ozar didn't come out of the tent. Instead, he rode from behind it on a magnificent charger. He sat as tall in the saddle as Cobalt, and his shoulders were almost as broad in his armor. The stones in the hilt of his monstrous sword were black.

Onyx.

Ozar spoke coldly. "You come here armed to kill."

"You kidnapped my wife," Cobalt said.

The atajazid answered with scorn. "It is not my problem if you cannot keep track of your wife."

Cobalt gritted his teeth. Stonebreaker used to talk to him that way, full of ridicule for the grandson he subjected to so much pain, physical and emotional. It had filled Cobalt with a rage that had driven him to pound his fists against the stone blocks of a tower until his shredded skin dripped with blood.

"You took my wife." The storm built within Cobalt. He had to know the truth. "You whipped her to death."

Ozar considered him. Only his eyes showed through his helmet. The distant roar of combat echoed below them, and Ozar's warriors stood back, watching.

The atajazid spoke with deliberate, calculated malice. "She did have a beautiful body. I'd never seen yellow hair in a woman's crotch. And those breasts. Although they were less attractive with blood all over them."

Cobalt had his answer.

He thought he would go insane. Maybe he did. He raised his sword, and the others moved through invisible molasses. As he closed the distance between himself and Ozar, riding Admiral, his sword descended toward the king. From horseback, Ozar countered in slow motion. The responses of his warriors on foot were even more delayed, so belabored that Cobalt could judge where every one of them would be well before the man reached that position.

A man to his left was raising his blade, and Cobalt saw it would hit Admiral before Cobalt's blow connected with Ozar's sword. In mid-swing, Cobalt changed direction, slashing at the man. He cut the warrior's arm off at the shoulder. The man screamed, a drawn out sound that went on a long time.

Cobalt raised his sword to counter Ozar's blow. Incredibly, the atajazid hadn't finished his swing. Cobalt had no idea how fast he was moving, but he remembered Mel's words:

Saints, Cobalt, when you fight, it's as if you have supernatural powers. I didn't think it was possible to move that fast.

Except Mel was dead.

His blade met Ozar's with an eerie drawn-out crash. Cobalt felt the immense power and reach behind that swing and knew the atajazid was no ordinary opponent. The warriors around Cobalt assailed him, but they moved so slowly, he could engage them between his swings with Ozar. He knew what Ozar had intended; incite him into a precipitous attack so the Jazid warriors could kill him without violating the code. Except they misjudged their opponent, and the price of that mistake would be their deaths.

As Cobalt fought, his sense of time sped up and his strikes became blurs. He cut, parried, slashed, countered, and one by one the warriors fell. Then it was only he and Ozar facing each other. Ozar's men lay on the ground, incapacitated or dead, none able to fight. Two were dragging themselves and several others clear of the area before the horses trampled them.

The sky had turned crimson from horizon to horizon, or maybe it was the fire within Cobalt. The day blazed, as if the Dragon-Sun had come to earth, but it burned *within* him and exploded outward at this man who had murdered his wife and unborn child.

He drove Ozar toward the tent, intending to entangle him in its sides, but the atajazid rallied and backed him toward the edge of the plateau. Cobalt had never fought an opponent with such power or speed, and his arm was tiring. Admiral stumbled on the mace of a fallen warrior, and for a brutal instant Cobalt thought his horse would topple off the plateau. Ozar came to this combat fresh, wereas Cobalt had been fighting for most of the morning.

Then Admiral lurched forward and regained his footing.

Ozar suddenly switched his sword to his other hand and lunged at Cobalt from the left. Disoriented, Cobalt faltered, and Ozar's blade skidded on his shoulder, scraping layers off his jerkin and cutting into his arm. With a shout, Cobalt jerked the reins and backed up Admiral. He had never seen anyone change hands during a fight with such ease. His own arm ached, and blood dripped down it to the hilt of his sword.

Ozar pressed his advantage, coming in fast. He wielded his sword in his left hand with as much speed as with his right. Cobalt blocked his strikes, and every time Ozar's blade rang against his sword, Cobalt's injured arm shook with the impact.

Admiral screamed and reared, a reaction so strange that Cobalt froze, gripping the reins as he stared at the receding ground. In the same instant, a jagged sheet of light split the red sky, followed by thunder so loud it sounded as if it could crack the world in two.

The atajazid tried to cut across Admiral's legs. Infuriated, Cobalt slashed at him as the frenzied horse came down, but Admiral side-stepped when his hooves hit the ground and it threw off Cobalt's strike. Ozar came at him from the left, and Cobalt was having trouble judging his angles of attack. Ozar wasn't purely ambidextrous; he didn't fight as well with his left hand as with his right. But combined with

Cobalt's weakening arm, it was enough to give Ozar a pronounced advantage.

They fought beneath a sky that flamed. Ozar wore away Cobalt's endurance, whittling it down. Back and forth, back and forth, until Cobalt's vision hazed. Still Ozar kept at him, his left arm strong, and Cobalt knew he was facing his death in the shape of a man with a dragon helmet and black armor.

Desperate, Cobalt let his arm sag, just enough to draw in Ozar, tempting him. It was a feint; to take advantage of Cobalt's "lapse," Ozar would have to leave his right side undefended for just an instant. Expecting the atajazid's swing, Cobalt dodged the blow and came in with his own. His sword rang on Ozar's breastplate. The blow disrupted the atajazid's defense for only a second—but that was enough. With a surge of power, Cobalt let go of the reins and threw his last strength into a swing with both of his hands gripped on the hilt of his sword. He caught Ozar in the space between his breastplate and his helmet. With the sheer power behind his swing, his blade kept going—

And sliced Ozar's head from his body.

Cobalt groaned as his arm fell to his side, his sword hanging. The atajazid's severed head rolled across the bloody ground and hit a tent pole. As Ozar's horse faltered, his body slowly toppled out of the saddle and crashed to the ground.

Cobalt stared at the atajazid's body. He barely kept one hand on the hilt of his sword. Gasping with exertion, he looked around at the plateau, at the carnage and death, and he knew that if Mel had lived, she would never have forgiven him for the horrors he had wrought today. He had truly become the Midnight King.

A scar ran down Jarid's chin, giving his face a harsh quality. He otherwise had the classic Dawnfield features, the straight nose and sculpted cheekbones. His dark hair grazed his shoulders.

"He is a Harsdown officer," Aron was saying. Eighteen years old, Aron was Jarid's heir and his joy. Jarid didn't want his son to die in the furious combat across their border. He dreaded the news brought by this Harsdown major.

"And you say this man was in Taka Mal?" Jarid said.

"Yes." Aron's face darkened. "He came here in chains. He's been beaten and starved."

"Will he live?"

"The healers say yes," Aron said. "He insists he must see you. He says his news cannot wait."

"Very well," the Aronsdale king said. "Bring in Penta-Major Windcrier."

Like the sea whipped by a hurricane, with waves of violence that crashed on the shore of humanity; like a tornado that tore apart the land; like a wildfire that would blaze until nothing remained—so the fighting raged across the land of the Dragon-Sun. Mel stood on a ridge high above the battle, and she wanted to shout her protest to the sky.

She was too late.

In one year, Cobalt had lost his father and the father's love Cobalt had so long craved; his grandfather, who had left him with a legacy of pain and fury he could never reconcile; and his wife and heir, or so he believed. He would destroy entire countries in his grief and his thirst for revenge.

Taka Mal, Jazid, and Chamberlight men fought below. Cobalt's forces had the upper hand, but the Aronsdale army was approaching, banners flying, ranks of cavalry and foot troops. If they joined the violence, this would become the largest battle in the history of the settled lands. The destruction could be incalculable.

"Stop!" Mel said. She was three stories above the plain, much too far away for her words to carry over the roar of battle. To anyone below, she would be no more than a figure on a ridge silhouetted against the sky.

The red sky. It blazed. Far across the field, on a plateau as high as this ridge, two men were fighting, dark against the carnelian sky. Above them, the air flamed, gold and red and orange. Mel knew then that she had hiked too hard and too long, that the lack of food, her injuries, and desperation were making her hear things. A haunting melody wove through the clamor. It was like the music Drummer wrote, except those tunes had been playful and lacking depth. This was full of grief and power, so mournfully beautiful that it hurt.

The colors in the sky were forming a luminous figure. Vague and insubstantial, it looked like a dragon in sunset colors. She didn't understand how she could hear music, but it filled her the way a spell filled a shape. Down below, the battle raged beneath the dragon, so much killing and so much misery.

Mel took the flail off her belt and removed the cloth that protected her from the spikes. Standing with her feet planted wide on the rocky spur, she clenched the handle and extended her arm straight up with the ball hanging by its chain.

She swung the ball.

With a strength honed by years of training against soldiers heavier and more powerful than herself, Mel whirled the ball in a circle, around and around, a three-dimensional shape tracing out a two-dimensional shape. Except the ball wasn't perfect. Spikes marred its symmetry. She delved within herself for a power that had nothing to do with light or softness. Her spell caught on the circle created by the swinging ball, and the circle deepened the effect, but it wasn't enough to focus her true power. Her spell scraped across the spiked ball and didn't catch.

Swing.

Swing.

Swing.

The spell built.

The music saturated Mel. It became part of her. In the sky, an incredible figure was forming, a dragon of fire and sun. Mel drew from the music and filled her spell with power. It scraped across the spiked ball—

And caught.

The spell formed with a power unlike anything she had ever known, bigger, more intense even than in Ozar's fortress. And this time she controlled it. She stood on the ridge, swinging the flail above her head, and the ball focused her power—

It exploded outward.

A sheet of lightning cracked in the sky, though no clouds marred the roof of the world. The lightning forked in hundreds of branches that hit all over the battlefield and thunder crashed, deafening. Warriors surged away from the strikes in waves of people. The ground where the lightning hit was burned and shattered, and cracks ran out in all directions, zigzagging across the Rocklands, fast and furious.

In that instant, the dragon roared and filled the sky with the fire of his breath. Mel knew such spells. It was light, only light, created somewhere, somehow, by a mage of great power, but paired with the very real lightning, it was terrifying.

Her fury poured through the ball. She swung it and jagged sheets of lightning hammered the land as if nature had gone mad. Mel controlled the spell, hitting rock rather than people, striking again and again while the dragon roared flames across the blazing sky. The entire world, everywhere Mel could see, had turned unbearably brilliant.

Soldiers ran for shelter, desperate waves of humanity pounding off the Rocklands, seeking cover. The spell blasted through Mel until she thought it would tear her apart. Her helmet was suffocating her; she ripped it off her head, still swinging the ball. Her hair whipped around her body in the wind created by the force of her spell.

The battle fell apart in ragged patches all across the field. Warriors took shelter in the foothills or their camps. People pointed at Mel and the dragon in the sky as they ran, and their mouths opened in shouts she couldn't hear. She scorched the field with lightning, and thunder roared across the land while the Sun-Dragon bellowed its fury.

Mel didn't know how long she stood with the ancient forces blasting through her. Aeons seemed to pass. Gradually she comprehended what had happened.

The fighting had stopped.

With a groan, Mel tried to release the spell. It dragged off the ball, trailed down the spikes, and sparked into the air. She couldn't stop swinging the flail; it would fall down her arm and tear apart her limb. So she did what it was meant to do; she swung it hard and struck her target—the ground. It shattered rock where it hit, and spikes bit deep into the ridge. Cracks spidered out from the impact in an explosive burst.

In the sudden silence that followed, Mel could hear her ragged breathing. She jerked the handle and pulled the ball free. With the spiked weapon hanging at her side by its chain, she straightened up and looked out at the shattered battlefield. Everyone who could run had left. Those who remained, and who still lived, were huddled on the ground. Nothing stirred.

Except one man.

He was racing toward her on a giant black horse, beneath the blazing dragon.

Across a splintered land, beneath a lurid sky, Cobalt rode. Whatever demon had cracked open the world could destroy him as easily as a horse flicking a gnat off its haunches. But he didn't care—for he saw the figure on the ridge, her molten hair streaming around her body, and he knew that either the Dawn Star Goddess truly had descended to earth, or else his wife had come back from the dead to create the monster of all spells.

Cobalt stopped below the ridge. He jumped to the ground and set his palm against Admiral's neck. "Wait for me."

The horse nickered, but he stayed put. No path led up the sheer, rocky walls of the ridge, so Cobalt grabbed a handhold and climbed. He didn't feel the exertion. He didn't care when footholds crumbled beneath his feet or his hands slipped. He would climb this ridge, and nothing would stop him.

Finally he reached the top. He pulled himself up and stood facing the woman.

Mel.

She stared at him, her face streaked with dirt, her hair wild, her armor battered, gripping a profoundly ugly flail—and he wanted to shout, to grab her, to crush her against him, to roar his joy to the Dragon-Sun above them. Since he had never learned how to express such emotions, he did all he could do, which was say, "You're alive."

She was watching him with a strange expression, as if she were dying and full of joy at the same time. "So are you."

He had so many words for her, he jammed up and could say nothing.

"By the Saints, Cobalt," she said. "What have you wrought?"

"Vengeance."

"For me."

"Yes." He touched the armor where it covered her abdomen. "And our child."

She put her hand over his. "Our child lives." Her voice cracked. "And so do I."

The battle madness that had gripped Cobalt since he touched her bloodied silks finally released its grip. He made a choked sound and grabbed her into his arms. Mel groaned, and he could only guess what had driven her these past days. He saw the welts on her neck and hands, and knew he would find more under her armor. Ozar may not have whipped her to death, but those silk clothes had been on her when the atajazid bloodied them. His dismay and fury poured out of him, but then another emotion replaced them, something so much more powerful that it humbled and terrified him. He didn't know how to name it, except to call it love.

Mel put her arms around his waist and laid her head against his chest. They stood that way, high on the ridge, while the dragon faded in the sky. He bent his head over hers, and for one of the only times in his adult life, Cobalt the Dark wept.

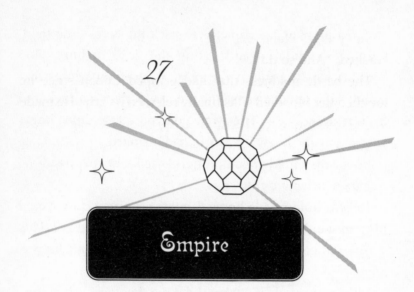

27

Empire

Wind keened across the Rocklands and past the balcony where Jade stood. She clenched her spyglass and took a shuddering breath, the first she was aware of since that moment when the Dragon-Sun had roared in a sky of fire, and lightning had torn apart the world. Never in her life could she have imagined those sheets of jagged light sweeping the land, sweeping the battlefield free of soldiers.

Until today, she had never truly believed the Dragon-Sun existed. Yet no legend spoke of a rain of lightning. She had heard music, *Drummer's* music, but so mournful. She had seen him create tricks with light, yes—but a gigantic dragon in a red sky? Even that, by itself, she might have believed. But not that plague of lightning.

The armies below had retreated, and Aronsdale had

stopped its march. People were trickling across the field, tending the injured and taking the dead to bury. Jade couldn't stop staring at the ridge where two figures had stood, silhouetted against the red sky. A dark warlock and his warrior goddess. They were gone now, Jade didn't know where, but she knew the world had changed.

Footsteps thudded behind her—she knew that tread—

Jade whirled around. "Baz!"

He was holding his helmet under his arm. Grit covered his armor and the dark stains on his hands chilled her. This wasn't the cousin she had known all her life. But he was alive.

They embraced, and tears slid down her face. When they separated, his cheeks were wet, too. He tried to smile and failed.

"We must meet," he said. "All of the leaders in this war. You, Chamberlight, Onyx, Dawnfield."

"And Drummer?" Her heart felt as if it stopped. Waiting.

"I haven't seen him."

Jade managed to nod and keep her calm, though she wanted to run wildly looking for him. Her country had to come before her consort, and until she faced Ozar and Cobalt, she wouldn't know what that meant. She set her hand on her abdomen, wondering what heritage remained for her child. "Who won?"

Baz exhaled. "I don't know. Cobalt went to fight Ozar."

"Two monsters facing each other."

"I'm not so sure." He spoke quietly. "Cobalt could have killed me. He didn't."

Jade didn't believe for a moment that the Midnight King had shown her cousin mercy. "You would have killed him."

"No." He lifted his sword hand and flexed his fingers as if they hurt. "He was inhuman. Faster and stronger than any man. I've never seen the like." Grimly he added, "I hope I never do again. He let me live, Jade, for I couldn't have bested him. No one could."

A knock came behind them. Turning, Jade saw a sergeant in the doorway, worn and battered. He had an odd look, one she couldn't read well. It wasn't fear. Sorrow? He bowed deeply. "I am sorry to disturb you, Your Majesty."

Jade heard the tension in his voice. "You have a message?"

"Downstairs," he said. "Your officers are returning."

Jade's pulse surged. She and Baz went with the sergeant down the tower stairs. He led them through the tiled halls to a side entrance of the citadel. When Jade saw who was there, she cried, "Ravi!" and broke into a run.

Spearcaster was talking with a group of men, battered but very much alive. He turned as Jade called, his face creasing with a smile. She flung herself into his arms and the aging warrior hugged her. Jade didn't care if it was inappropriate to embrace her military officers. She was too happy to see him alive.

"Well, damned and dust," a grouchy voice said. "Don't I get any of this squeezing, too?"

Jade pulled away from Spearcaster to see Firaz glaring at her. Laughing and crying at the same time, she hugged him as well. Her generals looked like hell, but they had survived.

Except…she looked around. "Is Slate with the army?"

Spearcaster exhaled and Firaz glanced away.

Baz came to her side. "I'm sorry."

"No." Jade stared at him. "Damn it, no!"

Spearcaster spoke quietly. "He died as he would have wanted, Vizarana. On horseback, defending Taka Mal."

Tears ran down her face. Moisture showed in Spearcaster's eyes, even in Firaz's. She didn't understand how people from the Misted Cliffs could be so restrained. She wanted to weep her grief to the stars. But she couldn't. Not yet.

"And Drummer?" she asked.

As soon as they all exchanged glances, her heart lurched. Spearcaster hesitated. "Vizarana—"

She felt as if her world stopped. "Tell me."

"We had word that he left Ozar's camp disguised as a Jazidian soldier. But—" He seemed to run out of words.

"But what?" She didn't want to hear, didn't think she could bear this, but it would be even worse not to know.

"I just got the report." Spearcaster laid his hand on her shoulder and spoke softly. "His body was found at the base of the cliffs. He apparently fell from a cave."

"No," Jade whispered.

His voice caught. "I'm sorry."

"No." She hugged herself, arms around her abdomen. "No!" He couldn't be gone, not her golden light. "It can't be him!"

Firaz spoke gruffly. "One of our men identified him." Miserably he added, "I so much wish I could say otherwise."

More tears ran down her face. She hated Cobalt and Ozar with a passion that filled her heart. They had taken her husband, and she wanted them to rot in a thousand hells for eternity. Now they would try to take her throne and her heir. She would kill them first, or die in the attempt, before she would let them wrest from her the legacy for her heir, the child born of the only happiness she had truly known.

"Come." She steeled herself. "We must face these kings who would destroy my country."

They met in the Narrow-Sun Hall in the Citadel of the Dragon-Sun: Escar, Onyx, Quaazera, Dawnfield. Men filled the room and guards stood posted around the walls. Few empty chairs were left at the great circular table.

Cobalt strode into the hall alone, in full armor, except for his helmet. He brought no generals. This was the man who had set out to conquer the known world and dared face a vengeful goddess. His dark eyes burned with a fire that would incinerate them all.

Jarid Dawnfield, the Aronsdale king, arrived with his son Aron, both tall and strong, though beside the Midnight King no one looked as imposing. The Aronsdale generals had strange names and geometric ranks. Jade brought Baz, Spearcaster, Firaz, and Fieldson. Dusk, the General of the Onyx Army, came with four of his generals—and without Ozar.

When they were seated around the table, Jade glanced at Baz and just barely tilted her head toward Dusk. He shook his head slightly, his face puzzled.

Jade addressed the assembly. "We cannot commence without the Atajazid D'az Ozar."

"His Majesty is injured," Dusk said. "He cannot attend."

A murmur went around the table. His news startled Jade; she hadn't expected Ozar to fight.

Cobalt's unusually deep voice rumbled. "Ozar is dead. I cut off his head."

A silence followed his words. No one seemed to know how to respond. Then Spearcaster said, "You have proof of this claim?"

Jarid Dawnfield spoke. "I saw them fight using my spyglass. What Cobalt says is true."

Jade couldn't absorb it. *Dead?* Ozar had inflicted this war on them with his brutality and his greed, but he had also been a strong leader. Such a painful irony that his death freed her from her oath to marry him. It no longer mattered.

No. *It mattered.* Her marriage remained. The child she had made with Drummer would sit on the Topaz Throne.

Jade regarded Dusk from across the table. "I would call the lack of a head more than an 'injury.'"

Dusk met her gaze, but he spoke wearily. "The injury is to all of Jazid."

"Do you represent the House of Onyx?" she asked.

"I do. The atajazid is only seven years old."

Jade hadn't realized Ozar's heir was that young. Jazid would have a child king for some years. She spoke formally. "We honor the memory of the Atajazid D'az Ozar and welcome his son to the Onyx Throne."

Jarid spoke. "The House of Dawnfield honors the memory of the Atajazid D'az Ozar and welcomes his son to the Onyx Throne."

Dusk exhaled, his tense posture easing, and relief showed on the faces of his officers. "We thank you," he said. A politician might have added more, but Dusk's answer was enough.

"No." Cobalt's voice rumbled. "The House of Onyx is defeated by the House of Chamberlight."

Jade silently swore. She had feared this. "You claim the Onyx Throne?"

He met her gaze. "And Topaz."

"You did not cut off my head," Jade said tartly. "If you try to take my throne, tomorrow we will go to battle again." She leaned forward. "You may call down the wrath of the Dragon-Sun himself, but I will never relinquish my title."

"Your men will not fight," Cobalt told her. "Not after your dragon roared in the sky."

Baz spoke sharply. "They will fight."

"If mine refuse," Jade told Cobalt, "so will yours."

"Why?" His hard gaze never left her face. "The goddess of the Dawn herself supports them."

"No!" The voice came from behind Jade.

They all looked up, and as Jade turned around, her breath caught. Mel Escar stood in the doorway like a warrior queen out of the ancient legends. She wore Jazidian armor and an iron breastplate. Welts and gashes covered her bare arms, and her yellow hair fell in wild curls around her body, down to her waist. She had the face of an avenging angel.

Mel walked into the room, never taking her gaze off her

husband, and he rose to his feet. Mel stopped in front of him. "I will not be used for a war."

Incredibly, he didn't challenge her. Jade thought he had forgotten the rest of them were in the room. He stood, taking in the sight of his wife as if she truly were the Dawnfield goddess.

His eyes flicked to her torso and back to her face.

Ah, no. Jade suspected she was the only one in the room who fully understood that look—for Drummer had often done it to her these past few days. It felt like a dagger in the grief she was barely keeping at bay. Saints help them, the Midnight King would soon have an heir.

"If you go warring tomorrow," Mel told her husband, "it will be without me."

Everyone remained frozen. Mel might be the only human being alive willing to naysay Cobalt the Dark in front of such a council. What would he do now that she refused him in this public manner? Incredibly, he didn't threaten her or raise his hand in violence. He simply inclined his head. Mel nodded, then stood by the chair at his right and faced the table. No one protested her obvious assumption that she would participate in the war council.

The Midnight King turned his burning gaze onto Jade. "If you insist on going into battle tomorrow, our men will die. Relinquish the throne and you will spare them."

Jade rose to her feet. He terrified her, but she wouldn't be cowed. "I will never relinquish my throne to you."

Dusk also stood up. Jade could guess his thoughts. Cobalt had killed Ozar. Whether or not he had a valid claim to the

Onyx Throne became a moot point if no one could stand against his army.

"Perhaps we should discuss this more," Dusk said.

Jade felt a sinking in her stomach. Without Jazid, she had no chance. She didn't know if even their combined forces could resist Cobalt's well-trained army.

Jarid Dawnfield stood up. "If you pursue the Topaz Throne, you will face my own men as well as those from Taka Mal." He met Cobalt's gaze. "My army is whole and fresh."

Relief swept over Jade, and she sent a silent thanks to the Dragon-Sun. Jason Windcrier must have made it through after all.

Cobalt stared at Jarid with an expression that at first Jade thought must be anger. Then she realized he was more puzzled than anything else. "Why would you fight for Taka Mal?" Cobalt asked, baffled. "That has *never* happened."

"We have a pact with the House of Quaazera," Jarid said.

Cobalt frowned at him. "How could you have a pact?"

"Because of me," a voice said.

Jade whirled around. A man stood in the entrance to the hall, his clothes covered with dust, his shirt ripped, his boots cracked, his hair tangled—and he was the most beautiful sight she had ever seen.

"Drummer!" Jade cried the word as her heart leaped. She ran to him, and he strode toward her, and she didn't give a flaming sun if it looked undignified. When they met, she threw her arms around him, and he held her close, his arms tight around her. She wanted to laugh, then cry, then shout. He kissed her, and Jade returned the kiss with fierce joy.

General Firaz's curmudgeonly voice came from behind them. "If you two are done, do you think we could continue?"

Jade drew her head back from Drummer, tears pouring down her face. "They told me you were dead."

He touched her cheek, his expression tender. "Just knocked out. Acrobats learn how to fall without hurting themselves."

Jade wanted to kiss him again. It was all she could do to restrain herself. Instead, she drew him to the chair next to hers. Half the people at the table were already on their feet, so she stood with Drummer facing them, defiant—and overjoyed. Even if Cobalt hadn't set a precedent here by having his consort attend the war council, Jade would have brought hers to the table.

Mel raised an eyebrow at Drummer. "It appears, Uncle, that your time here hasn't been boring."

He smiled like the sun. "My greetings, Mel."

"You do not look as if anyone was torturing you," Cobalt growled.

Baz jumped to his feet. "No one here tortured anyone!"

"Would you all sit the blazes down?" Firaz said. "I'd really rather not conduct this meeting on our feet."

Everyone blinked at him. Then a rustle came from around the table as everyone took their seats. Jade wanted to sing, and she barely held in her exuberance. She and Drummer would have time for that later. Plenty of time. Their whole lives.

General Dusk spoke to Jarid. "Quaazera had a pact with

Onyx. Queen Vizarana and her consort agreed to an annulment. The atajazid supported the Taka Mal army because the queen agreed to marry him. We have witnesses to this pact."

"You're *married?*" Mel's astounded voice rippled across the table. "Drummer, what *have* you been up to?"

He grinned at her. "I've been busy."

Jade spoke formally to Mel, unsure how to take the measure of this queen. "His Majesty became my consort three days ago."

"What majesty?" Dusk demanded. "He's a commoner."

"Not after his marriage," Baz said.

"His marriage is annulled," Dusk told him.

"My pact was with Ozar." Jade paused. "Ozar is dead."

They all looked uneasily at Cobalt. He didn't seem to talk much. Jade would have felt sorry for his wife, except she was just as alarming. Perhaps he was the brave one, to spend his nights with the reincarnation of a warrior goddess.

Cobalt spoke to Jarid. "You cannot fight my army. You have a treaty with us."

"The treaty works both ways," Jarid said. "You cannot fight us." He nodded toward Jade. "Queen Vizarana has wed a member of my House, through my cousin Muller's marriage to Chime Headwind. My oath to defend my kin supersedes my treaty to you."

"You would fight me?" Cobalt demanded.

Jarid met his gaze. "Yes. And I would call on Harsdown."

Sphere-General Fieldson spoke. "As General of the Harsdown Army, I would recommend we support Aronsdale."

"I would rather die," Mel said flatly, "than see my House go to war with itself." She glared at her husband.

Jade thought surely Cobalt would rebuke her for challenging him in front of three other sovereigns. However, he didn't seem to follow any protocols except his own. His forbidding face softened when he looked at his wife. Then he turned and spoke to Jarid. "I would not like my father-in-law go to war against me."

"It would be unfortunate," Jarid said.

"I have a solution," Jade said.

They all turned to her, guarded in their response, even her own generals. She hadn't discussed this with them. She would have preferred to, but she needed to speak before all these growling kings decided to slice up her country among themselves.

"Cobalt defeated Ozar," Jade said. "It is less clear what army triumphed in the field of battle. Cobalt has won the right to the Onyx Throne but not the Topaz Throne. Let Jazid become a realm of Escar and Taka Mal align with Aronsdale."

Dusk leaned forward, flushed with anger. "King Cobalt violated a truce of surrender—one he himself called—and murdered the atajazid."

"I called for no such truce," Cobalt said. "Why would I surrender when my army was winning?"

Anger snapped in Dusk's voice. "You came to the atajazid and called on him during battle. The codes of war apply, Escar. It was a truce. You attacked without provocation. You should be tried and executed for war crimes."

Cobalt watched him with a gaze so dark Jade prayed he never focused it on her. "Your atajazid tortured my wife. He sent a man to tell me she had been whipped to death. He gave me the bloodied clothes he ripped off her body. Off my *pregnant* wife. My queen and my heir. I consider this provocation to kill him and every general in his army, and to grind Jazid into the earth until nothing remains of its towns, its merchants, its caravans, or its so-called wonders except broken, burnt ground."

Silence followed his words. Jade had known Ozar was capable of cruelty, but she had never thought he would go so far. She believed Cobalt and his sorceress wife could do what he threatened.

And this time, Mel didn't refuse him.

In the end, they signed a treaty of unprecedented complexity. Jazid would become Cobalt's realm. He surprised Jade and spared the lives of the generals and the children of the atajazid. Harsdown, Aronsdale, and Taka Mal established a pact that bound them together. Cobalt agreed not to attack them if they didn't move against him.

No one bothered to deny the obvious. Cobalt had become the Midnight Emperor. He ruled the Misted Cliffs, Blueshire, Shazire, and Jazid. Someday his wife would rule Harsdown, and the child she carried would reign over it all. Jade expected Cobalt to call his realms after his name—Escar or Chamberlight. Instead, he named it for his wife.

So the Dawn Star Empire was born.

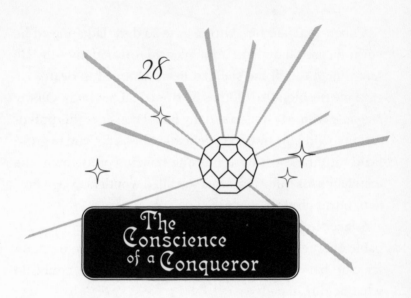

28

The Conscience of a Conqueror

Jade left her bodyguards at the entrance of the Narrow-Sun Hall and walked into the long room alone. The antiqued sunlight of late afternoon slanted through the tall windows. It was hard to believe that only yesterday, four sovereigns had made history in this room. Today, they mourned their dead. Hundreds had fallen. But it could have been far worse; had the fighting not stopped, thousands would have lost their lives. Today they began the painful journey to recovery and the complex process of establishing peace in the settled lands.

The hall wasn't empty. One soldier stood at its other end, before the tall window, looking at the Rocklands or even farther, to Aronsdale, a misty green line on the horizon. The warrior was alone, imposing in black knee-boots, black leather pants, and no breastplate, just a leather vest with nothing under it. The skimpy vest and tight pants left no doubt about the soldier's sex; her curves filled out her armor, and her gold hair, brushed now and sleek, fell down her back. Jade would never have thought armor on a female would be sensual, but even she could see why men stopped and stuttered and ran into things when Mel Dawnfield Escar walked by. She was a most unusual woman.

As Jade approached, Mel turned around. Jade joined her at the window, acutely aware of the younger woman's height. Faced with Mel's unadorned, spectacular beauty, Jade felt insubstantial, even vulnerable in her emerald silks, with bangles around her neck and wrists, kohl on her eyes and gems in her hair.

Jade inclined her head. "Light of the day, Your Majesty."

Mel returned the nod. "It is my honor to meet the Atatakamal D'or Vizarana."

Jade blinked. Jazid kings used their formal title—Atajazid D'az, or Shadow Dragon Prince—but Jade rarely went by Atatakamal D'or, or Dragon-Sun Princess. It was too hard to pronounce, for one thing, besides which, she preferred to be a queen of real humans rather than princess of a mythological dragon.

"We are kin now," she said. "Please call me Jade."

The empress nodded, accepting the honor. "I am Mel."

Jade spoke carefully. "I would wish to begin again."

Mel regarded her curiously, much as had Fieldson, as if Jade were an exotic wildflower. "Begin again?"

"We have been foes. I would like to begin again, as allies."

"Ah." Mel smiled, and it lit up her face, changing the barbarian avenger into a lovely young woman. "Yes. I also."

"I am glad to meet you," Jade said. It was true. The Escar queen fascinated her.

Mel spoke quietly. "You have made my uncle happy."

"As he has me." Jade wanted to speak of her joy, but she held back. Everything about the empress was reserved, cool, aloof. She was so unlike Drummer. Cobalt and his Dawn Star Empress frightened her.

Mel was watching her face. "Know one thing."

Jade steeled herself. "Yes?"

"As long as I live," Mel said softly, "no one will harm my uncle or anyone he loves." She paused. "Or their country."

Jade didn't know how to answer such a declaration, especially given that the empress could make it true. After a moment, when she found her voice, she said, simply, "Thank you."

Mel nodded. "Honors of the day, Your Majesty."

Jade needed a moment to interpret the phrase. It was a custom in Aronsdale and Harsdown, a way to indicate respect. Jade set her palm against her collarbone and extended her hand, palm up, the Taka Mal equivalent of the Empress's farewell. Mel smiled, and her face was transformed like sunlight warming an icy day. Then she left, striding from the hall.

"Saints above," Jade said, stunned by the empress but relieved the meeting had gone well. She gazed out the window toward Aronsdale. Soon another tread sounded in the hall. She smiled, seeing the reflection of its owner in the window. He came up behind her and put his arms around her waist.

"Light of the day, my Wife," Drummer murmured, his greeting in the custom of Taka Mal.

"My greetings, my Husband," she said, using the Aronsdale custom. She leaned her head back against him, her dragon mage, who had created a myth in the sky to dissuade his kin from conquering her lands. It would take time to understand this side of her husband. But they did, truly, have those years.

For the first time in so long, perhaps in her life, she looked toward the future with a belief that it held happiness as well as duty, that along with the hardships, she would also know joy.

Mel couldn't find Cobalt. He wasn't in the citadel or the courtyards. She walked through the town with her guards and found no trace of him. Using a glass sphere from the citadel, she formed emotion spells and focused on him, but they told her little. His moods were diffuse, distant, hard to pinpoint.

She saddled Smoke and rode down the mountain, guards riding behind and ahead of her on the steep trail. When they reached the Rocklands, they pounded across the shattered plain as fast as they could manage while avoiding the fissures and cracks, a mute testimony of the destruction Mel had wrought yesterday. Even now, heat rose from the ground, though the sun was low over the green hills of Aronsdale.

Mel focused another spell on Cobalt. His presence felt

stronger. But her mind was tired. She had used all her resources yesterday, and she needed time to recover. It would take time to come to terms with this power. Ozar had jolted to life a part of herself she had too long denied.

She found Cobalt on Admiral, high on a crag that overlooked the battlefield. Warm winds blew his hair across his face, and he brushed it out of his eyes. Her bodyguards stayed back with his guards, giving her and Cobalt as much privacy as they could ever have when they weren't within the protection of a fortress.

Admiral nickered as Smoke drew alongside of him. Cobalt smiled at Mel, an expression few people ever saw from him. It was barely discernible compared to the passionate responses that came so naturally to the people of Taka Mal, but for Cobalt it was an immense display of emotion.

"Your uncle astonishes me," Cobalt said.

She knew he meant Drummer. Who would have ever guessed her uncle was a green cube mage? He didn't seem to realize just how rare a power he held. It came far more gently to him, though, than hers did to her, especially when he played his music. "I think he will enjoy learning his abilities."

"It is good." The relaxed cast of his face tightened into a colder expression. "Unlike the situation with certain other people."

"What people?"

"Tadimaja Pickaxe."

Mel recognized his look. "You must give him and the others a proper tribunal. You cannot do to them what Ozar did to me."

"Why the blazes not?"

"Cobalt, don't." She wondered if anyone could contain this force that was her husband. "Don't make me responsible for the torture of other human beings."

"They are responsible for the crimes they committed."

"Then put them on trial and let a judge convict them." She scowled at him. "Be civilized."

"When I think of what they did to you, I do not feel civilized."

"Ozar paid with his life, his throne, and his country. They will pay with their freedom and possibly their lives." She spoke firmly. "It must end there."

He watched her with his dark look, that one that would have terrified her two years ago. She knew now just to wait.

"Very well," he finally said. "You have my word."

Mel would have closed her eyes with relief, except she didn't want to stop looking at him. "Thank you."

"My mother agrees with you about Baker, you know."

She didn't know where that came from. "About a baker?"

"Baker Lightstone. The former king of Blueshire. Or mayor, you claim."

"Your mother thinks he was a mayor?"

"No," he growled. "She agrees he should govern Blueshire."

Ah. Mel smiled. "Your mother is very wise."

"I hope so. Shazire needs wisdom."

"You will make her governor of Shazire?"

"If she agrees." He squinted at her. "If the idea is good."

"It's excellent."

"Well. So." He paused. "I will send Leo Tumbler and many troops to govern Jazid."

"Another good choice." Mel suspected the military presence in Jazid would be important for years to come.

Cobalt was silent for a while. Then he indicated a group of men searching among the crags and fissures on the plain below. "They're looking for—well, for anything that remains."

She knew he meant bodies. "You must stop this warring."

"Do you remember what you said to me about conscience?"

Mel would never forget. "You told me that if you ever went too far, I should pull you back. I said, 'Do not ask me to be the conscience of a conqueror.'"

"And yet, you are."

"You have a conscience." But she also remembered what else Cobalt had told her that morning, before he rode into Blueshire: *I cannot stop being what I am.*

"To conquer is easy," Mel said. "That challenge is to lead well. You can be a good leader. A great leader. It's time to silence Stonebreaker's voice. Don't let his legacy drive you to darkness when you're so much more than you know."

Cobalt didn't answer at first, he just looked at her as if memorizing her face. Then he said, "My eyes are getting worse. In a few years, I will need glasses all the time." He smiled drily. "I can't be a warrior with spectacles. They might get broken."

She knew that in his own oblique way, he was responding by telling her that he would no longer lead his armies out to war. And saints almighty, he was teasing her. She hadn't thought he knew how. Yet it came from a kernel of truth. She had tried to heal his eyes, but they weren't injured and didn't respond to spells. If they continued to change as he aged, in ten or fifteen years he wouldn't see well enough to effectively lead an army. He could turn over many tasks to Agate Cragland or another officer, but she knew he would feel those changes as deep losses.

Mel gentled her voice. "Spectacles make a king look wise."

He snorted, but she could tell her response pleased him. He motioned at the men below them. "I see them fine. That is Matthew in the brown trousers and green shirt."

She peered at the man. It was indeed Matthew. Yes, Cobalt could still see well enough—yet he missed the obvious.

Matthew Quietland had been born at Castle Escar, the son of a seamstress for a former Harsdown king, Cobalt's grandfather. Matthew was one year older than Varqelle, the king's only son.

His only legitimate son.

Had Matthew been born on the other side of the sheets, he would have sat on the throne instead of Varqelle, for his true father had been the Jaguar King. Varqelle had been a prince, Matthew a stable boy. Matthew had gone with Dancer to the Misted Cliffs, so he and Varqelle had lived in different countries for most of their adult lives. Varqelle died only a few months after he came into Cobalt's life, so Varqelle and Matthew hadn't been together enough for people to note the similarity. Mel had seen, aided by her mood spells, but at Matthew's request, she had sworn never to reveal the truth.

Cobalt had heard rumors of Varqelle's cruelty to Dancer, his child bride. He would never know it had driven her to seek solace in the arms of a stable boy. Varqelle's mistress discovered the queen's infidelity and threatened to reveal the truth if her rival didn't leave. In Harsdown at that time, the penalty for a queen's adultery was death—for herself, her lover, and any child of that union. Dancer had fled to the Misted Cliffs to save the lives of her son and his father.

Cobalt spoke in a low rumble. "To silence Stonebreaker's voice within me—it is not so easy, Mel."

It took her a moment to realize he was responding to her previous comment. "Stonebreaker saw the truth, that you were more than him. His jealousy consumed him."

He answered in an oddly distant voice. "Have you never wondered why he took no other wife after my grandmother died?"

"I assumed he didn't like marriage." Stonebreaker's fondness for concubines had been well known.

"He hated the Castle of Clouds," Cobalt said.

She wondered what he was trying to tell her. "Because you and Dancer went there to escape him, yes?"

"In part." He stared at the Rocklands. "My grandmother died in a fall above the castle."

"I hadn't realized it happened there."

"He never spoke of it." After a long moment, he said, "Until the night he died."

Mel went very still. "Everyone knows it was an accident."

"Of course they know," he said bitterly. "He said it was an accident. He was the king."

Mel knew of Stonebreaker's violence, had even experienced it herself. But to kill his wife? Surely he wouldn't lose control and go that far. "Your grandfather was one of the most controlled people I've ever met."

"And controlling." Cobalt shifted his haunted gaze to her. "How do you think a man like that would feel if he discovered he couldn't sire an heir?"

Her heart was beating as hard as if she were running. "But he had a child. Dancer."

Cobalt regarded her steadily. "Certainly he would never discover Dancer was actually the child of his valet, that the only reason he had a daughter was because his isolated, beaten wife had slept with another man."

Mel stared at him. Had admitting he couldn't sire an heir been even worse to Stonebreaker than acknowledging as his heir a boy who didn't carry his blood? Saints help him, had he killed his own wife to keep that secret?

"Cobalt—" What Stonebreaker had inflicted on him the night he died was even worse than she had thought. "He lied to you. To hurt you."

"It is only a story." His voice caught. "Nothing more. In the story, the queen dies and the valet disappears."

"I'm sorry," she whispered.

"Perhaps the grandson would realize such a terrible story is a blessing." Softly he said, "It would mean he doesn't carry the blood of the monster who drained his life for so many years."

Mel wiped away a tear on her cheek. "That is a gift."

"When I thought you had died—" Incredibly, his voice

shook. "I realized how little anything else meant." He took a deep, shuddering breath. "It is time to let go of Stonebreaker."

"Yes." Her voice broke on the word. "It's time."

They sat looking across the Rocklands, east to Taka Mal, west to Aronsdale and Harsdown, and the Misted Cliffs beyond. Toward the future. The daughter of a farm girl and the son of a stable hand, the grandson of a valet: Together, they had come to rule the largest empire ever established in the settled lands.

On a bright winter day in Quaaz, the people gathered in a grand plaza, below a balcony of the Topaz Palace. It was a cool day, at least for Taka Mal, enough so that some of the hundreds who crammed the plaza wore shirts under their tunics. The sun shone in the sky, and musicians played rollicking tunes. Street vendors circulated with delicacies imported from Aronsdale.

The queen appeared with her consort, that golden prince the people found so easy to love, with his quick grin, his music, and his lively charm. The queen stood tall, a dark-haired beauty in topaz silks. She cradled in her arms the baby her people had come to see, just born the day before. Vizarana Jade held up her daughter and her heir, and the people cheered.

Drummer held a cube in his hand. No one could see; indeed, it looked as if he were simply standing with his wife and child, beaming. But topaz light surrounded him and spread to his family. A luminous dragon rose into the sky, breathing golden light, and the people roared their approval. The Dragon-Sun had blessed the birth.

So the heir to the Topaz Throne came into the world, loved by her parents and celebrated by her people.

On a bright winter day in the Misted Cliffs, snow lay thick on the land, glistening and white. People gathered before their hearths while outside their homes, lakes and rivers froze. The sun shone in a crystalline blue sky, and icicles hung from eaves.

In the Diamond Palace, in the royal suite, the Empress and Emperor sat on their bed. Mel cradled her infant son, and Cobalt leaned next to her. So she offered him the baby. Uncertain and more careful than he had ever been in his life, he took the tiny boy into his huge arms and held him with wonder.

This child would be heir to the Sapphire, Jaguar, Alzire, Blueshire, and Onyx Thrones. His mother was the most powerful mage in the settled lands, a war mage as well as a healer. His father was a warrior of such ferocity, many believed him a warlock. What Mel and Cobalt bequeathed to their child, only time would tell. For now, they quietly rejoiced for the health and strength of their young son.

Finally Cobalt Escar Chamberlight put to rest the demons that had haunted his soul.

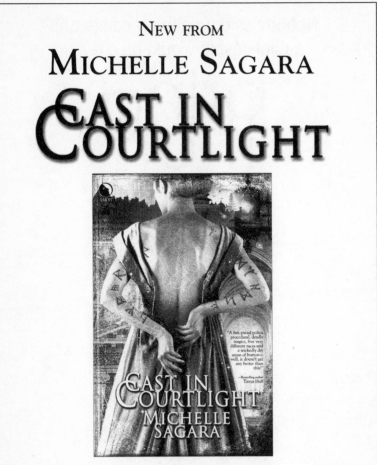

Nobody said juggling a career and
a relationship would be easy…

bring it on

On sale July 2006.

Valere's life as a retriever used to be simple, but now that she
and Sergei are in a relationship, things are getting much more
complicated. What's more, the city Valere loves is now at grave
risk. There's only one thing left for Valere to do—bring it on….

LUNA™

*Visit your
local bookseller.*